The Adventures of
Simplicius Simplicissimus

(Being a description of the life of a
strange vagabond named Melchior
Sternfels von Fuchshaim, where and how
he entered the world, what he saw, learnt,
experienced and suffered there, and
why he abandoned it again of his
own free will.)

Johann Jakob Christoffel von Grimmelshausen

Simplicissimus

Translated and with an introduction by
Mike Mitchell

Dedalus

Published in the UK by Dedalus Ltd,
24–26, St Judith's Lane, Sawtry, Cambs, PE28 5XE
email: info@dedalusbooks.com
www.dedalusbooks.com

ISBN 978 1 903517 42 0

Dedalus is distributed in the United States by SCB Distributors,
15608 South New Century Drive, Gardena, California 90248
email: info@scbdistributors.com   web site: www.scbdistributors.com

Dedalus is distributed in Australia & New Zealand by Peribo Pty Ltd,
58 Beaumont Road, Mount Kuring-gai N.S.W. 2080
email: peribo@bigpond.com

Dedalus is distributed in Canada by Disticor Direct-Book Division,
695 Westney Road South, Suite 14 Ajax, Ontario, L16 6M9
web site: www.disticordirect.com

Publishing History
First published in Germany in 1668
English translation by S. Goodrich in 1912
Dedalus editions in 1989 and 1995
New translation by Mike Mitchell in 1999
Reprinted 2005 and 2009

Translation © Mike Mitchell 1999

Printed in Finland by WS Bookwell
Typeset by RefineCatch Limited, Bungay, Suffolk

A C.I.P. listing for this book is available on request.

ABOUT THE TRANSLATOR

Mike Mitchell is one of Dedalus's editorial directors and is responsible for the Dedalus translation programme. His publications include *The Dedalus Book of Austrian Fantasy*, *Peter Hacks: Drama for a Socialist Society* and *Austria* in the World Bibliographical Series. His translation of Rosendorfer's *Letters Back to Ancient China* won the 1998 Schlegel-Tieck Translation Prize after having been shortlisted in previous years for his translations of *Stephanie* by Herbert Rosendorfer and *The Golem* by Gustav Meyrink. His translation of *Simplicissimus* was shortlisted for The Weidenfeld Translation Prize in 1999 and *The Other Side* by Alfred Kubin in 2000.

He has translated the following books for Dedalus from German: five novels by Gustav Meyrink, three novels by Johann Grimmelshausen, three novels by Herbert Rosendorfer, two novels by Herman Ungar, *The Great Bagarozy* by Helmut Krausser, *The Road to Darkness* by Paul Leppin, *The Other Side* by Alfred Kubin and *On the Run* by Martin Prinz. From French he has translated for Dedalus two novels by Mercedes Deambrosis and *Bruges-la-Morte* by Georges Rodenbach.

Dedalus features German Literature in translation in its programme of contemporary and classic European fiction and in its anthologies.

Androids from Milk – *Eugen Egner* £7.99
Undine – *Fouqué de la Motte* £6.99
The German Refugees – *Johann Wolfgang Goethe* £6.99
Simplicissimus – *J. J. C. Grimmelshausen* £12.99
The Life of Courage – *J. J. C. Grimmelshausen* £6.99
Tearaway – *J. J. C. Grimmelshausen* £6.99
The Great Bagarozy – *Helmut Krausser* £7.99
The Other Side – *Alfred Kubin* £9.99
The Road to Darkness – *Paul Leppin* £7.99
The Angel of the West Window – *Gustav Meyrink* £9.99
The Golem – *Gustav Meyrink* £6.99
The Green Face – *Gustav Meyrink* £6.99
The Opal (& other stories) – *Gustav Meyrink* £7.99
Walpurgisnacht – *Gustav Meyrink* £6.99
The White Dominican – *Gustav Meyrink* £6.99
On the Run – *Martin Prinz* £6.99
The Architect of Ruins – *Herbert Rosendorfer* £8.99
Grand Solo with Anton – *Herbert Rosendorfer* £9.99
Letters Back to Ancient China – *Herbert Rosendorfer*
    £6.99
Stefanie – *Herbert Rosendorfer* £7.99
The Maimed – *Hermann Ungar* £6.99
The Class – *Hermann Ungar* £6.99

Anthologies featuring German Literature in translation:
The Dedalus Book of Austrian Fantasy –
    editor M. Mitchell £10.99
The Dedalus Book of German Decadence –
    editor R. Furness £9.99

The Dedalus Book of Surrealism –
  editor M.Richardson £9.99
Myth of the World: Surrealism 2 –
  editor M. Richardson £9.99
The Dedalus Book of Medieval Literature –
  editor B. Murdoch £9.99

Introduction

Grimmelshausen's *Simplicissimus*, first published in 1668, is one of the great German novels and, along with *Don Quixote* and *The Pilgrim's Progress*, one of the key works of 17th-century European literature. *Simplicissimus* is itself a kind of pilgrim's progress, telling as it does the adventures of an innocent who ventures out into the world, recounting his progress from simple piety through all the vices – ambition, gluttony, greed, avarice, arrogance, hypocrisy, deception, lust – to renunciation of the world, from bare subsistence to great wealth then back to the austere life of a hermit.

But unlike Bunyan's work, *Simplicissimus* is not a symbolic journey though life. The most striking and frequently praised feature of the novel is its realism. Although the cast Grimmelshausen assembles is extremely wide-ranging, from ladies of the court and generals to dragoons, brigands and beggars, and the scene moves from Germany to France and Russia, even, briefly, to Korea, Macao and the bottom of the oceans, his main focus is on ordinary people in Germany during the savage barbarity of the Thirty Years War (1618–1648).

Grimmelshausen's stylistic range is similarly wide, from the simple piety of the hermit to satire, occasional moralising, displays of erudition, classical learning and practical knowledge, extended allegory and fantasy. But most of the book is in a plain, vigorous language which is not afraid of crude vulgarity and even the occasional awful pun. This makes the story come vividly alive and keeps it moving and is one of the reasons why it is still readable today.

Another aspect that brings the novel close to the modern reader is Grimmelshausen's humanity. The extreme horrors of the Thirty Years War are something he knew at first hand

and to which we can see parallels in the events of this century. Despite his own conversion to Catholicism, which is reflected in that of his hero, Grimmelshausen's descriptions of the sufferings of the population is suffused with a sympathy for all its victims and an abhorrence of war which goes beyond any dogmatism.

One of the purposes of the novel is to remind us of the teachings of Christ but, as is usually the case, it is the illustrations of sin which are more vivid and down-to-earth and make the livelier, if not always pleasanter, reading. The tone is set by the description of the way the troopers destroy Simplicissimus's father's farm and rape and torture the inhabitants. Many of the scenes have an almost tangible physicality, so that even today we can almost smell the shit and vomit, see the blood or feel the lice crawling over the hero's body.

There is much that is autobiographical about this story. At least, that is what is generally assumed, since there is no documentary evidence of the first twenty years of Grimmelshausen's life and much of our knowledge is derived from incidental comments in his writings. He was born in Gelnhausen (close to the Spessart where his hero comes from), in 1621 or 1622, and grew up with his grandfather. After the battle of Nördlingen in 1634, when Gelnhausen was plundered and destroyed, he fled to Hanau, where the governor was the Colonel Ramsay who appears in the novel. From then on he was involved in the wars until the Peace of Westphalia (1848) – in another book he describes himself as having been 'a snotty-nosed ten-year-old musketeer'. He fought mainly on the imperial/Catholic side, eventually becoming regimental clerk, and many of the stages in his career are mirrored in the adventures of Simplicissimus: he was captured by imperial troops and taken to Hersfeld Abbey (1635); took part in the siege of Magdeburg (1636), the battle of Wittstock (1636) and the attempt to relieve Breisach (1638). After the Peace of Westphalia he was employed as a steward and was twice an innkeeper until he eventually became mayor of a small town in the Black Forest, where Simplicissimus also ends up.

There is another aspect in which Grimmelshausen is reflected in the hero of his best-known novel. He did not enjoy the education usual for a writer at the time. He presumably learnt some Latin at the grammar school in Gelnhausen, but his education was interrupted by the wars and he never attended university. Nevertheless, as his writings show, he managed to acquire a familiarity with contemporary literature as well as classical learning and a range of current scientific knowledge while serving as a soldier or supporting his ever-increasing family (he had ten children) with his work as steward to an aristocratic estate or by running an inn. Perhaps understandably, he occasionally makes a point of showing off his erudition, but nowhere does it determine the tone of his narrative for more than a page or so.

The Thirty Years War in which Simplicissimus is caught up was a complex 'stop-go' war which was part of a longer-lasting conflict between France and Austria/Spain, between the Bourbons and Habsburgs, for hegemony in Europe. It is commonly thought of, however, as a war of religion between the Protestant territories of north Germany and Sweden and the Counter-Reformation led by the German Empire under the House of Habsburg, and that is how it appears in *Simplicissimus*. Grimmelshausen is not interested in the politics behind the warfare, but in the effects on the individual. Part of this is the way in which combatants could be tossed from side to side, fighting for one party and then for the other as necessity rather than conviction dictates.

Grimmelshausen had experienced this himself and so does his hero whose first contact is with the Protestant Hessians in Hanau. He is then captured by imperial forces and taken to Fulda, escapes and flies by magic to Magdeburg, where he fights on the imperial side; he is captured by the Swedes, with whom he goes to Westphalia, where he is taken by the imperial forces. In the imperial garrison in Soest he becomes a famous soldier, the 'Huntsman of Soest', but is eventually captured by the Swedes and kept on parole in Lippstadt, where he marries. He goes to Cologne, to recover his money, is despatched by a trick to France and on his return is taken by another section of the imperial forces, with whom he serves as a simple musketeer; he is eventually captured by the Protestant Weimar forces and serves with them until he is given leave to go and see his wife; on the way he meets his friend, Herzbruder, who is serving with the imperial forces under Count Götz (as Grimmelshausen probably did himself) and Simplicissimus once more fights for the emperor.

All this is at times confusing for the reader, but that is part of Grimmelshausen's picture of 'the world' (ie human society) where the individual is subject to forces beyond his control, the world to which Simplicissimus bids farewell (in words borrowed from Antonio de Guevara) in the final chapter.

Simplicissimus, which was originally published under a pseudonym, as were all Grimmelshausen's works, was an immediate success and a new edition published almost immediately. For this new edition he added a sixth book, the 'Continuation'. This is certainly not an organic part of the novel, consisting as it does largely of allegorical tales, fables and fantastic adventures, which do not contribute at all to the vision of the original novel. It has therefore been omitted in the present translation, which contains the five books of the first edition.

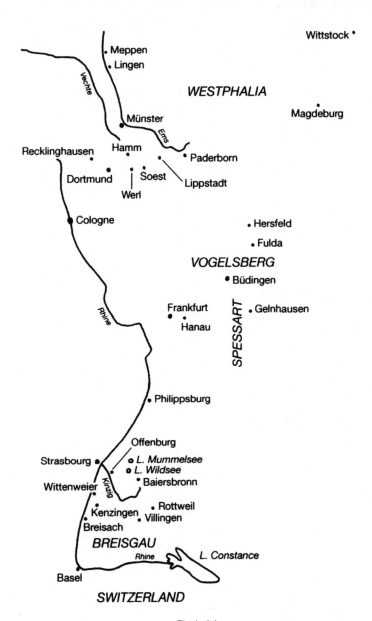

Book I

Chapter 1

Describes Simplicius's rustic origins and upbringing

In these days (which some believe to be the last days) a new sickness has appeared among ordinary people. When those who have been infected by it have scratched together enough money with their sharp practices that they can afford, besides a few coppers in their purse, to dress themselves after the latest absurd fashion with thousands of silk ribbons, or when by some lucky chance they have made a name for themselves, they immediately try to pass themselves off as knights and nobles of ancient lineage. It usually turns out that their grandparents were day-labourers, carters and porters, their cousins muleteers, their brothers tipstaffs and turnkeys, their sisters whores, their mothers bawds, if not witches; in short that their whole ancestry, right down to the thirty-second degree, is as tainted and tarnished as ever Seb Sugar's gang of thieves in Prague were. Indeed, these new-minted nobles are themselves often as black as if they had been born and bred in Guinea.

I wouldn't want to be likened to such foolish folk even though, to tell the truth, I have often fancied I must owe my existence to some great lord, or at least a gentleman, since I have a natural inclination to follow the nobleman's trade, if only I had the necessary capital and equipment.

To be serious, though, it is true that my birth and upbringing can well be compared with that of a prince, if you overlook the one great difference. How can that be? you ask. My Da (for that is the title we give to fathers in the Spessart) had a palace of his own, as good as any man's, and finer than any king could build with his own hands. Its facade was finished off with clay and its roof, instead of sterile slate, cold lead and red copper, was covered with the straw on which the noble grain grows. And to make a show of his wealth and nobility, my Da did not, as other great lords do, build the wall round his castle out of stones, such as you may find by the roadside or dig out of the ground in barren places, much less out of common brick, which can be moulded and fired in a short time. No, he took oak, that noble and useful tree from which pork sausages and fat hams grow and which takes over a hundred years before it reaches full maturity. Where is the monarch who will follow him in that?

He had his rooms and chambers blackened all over inside with smoke, since that is the most permanent colour in the world and to paint them by that method takes longer than any artist would spend on even the best of his paintings. The wall-hangings were of the most delicate weave in the world, being made by the weaver who, in olden times, dared to challenge Minerva herself to a contest. The windows were dedicated to St Notoglas for the very good reason that he knew that, counting from the hemp or flax seed, the paper with which they were covered took much more time and labour before it was finished than the finest and clearest Murano glass. It was his station in life that led him to believe that things which required much labour to produce were therefore valuable and more costly, and that costly things were best suited to the nobility.

Instead of pages, lackeys and grooms, he had sheep, goats and pigs, each neatly clad in its own livery, which often used to wait upon me in the fields, until I drove them home. His armoury was well stocked with ploughs, hoes, axes, picks, spades and forks for both manure and hay. He practised daily with these weapons; clearing the ground and digging were for him a military exercise, just as they were for the ancient Romans in times of peace. The oxen were the company he commanded, spreading manure was his fortification and ploughing his campaigning, but mucking out the stables was his noble pastime, his jousting. By these means he dominated the whole round world, as far as he could walk, and at every harvest he gathered in rich tribute from it.

All this means nothing to me and I don't give myself airs because of it, so that no one will have reason to scoff at me along with other would-be nobles from the same background. I consider myself no better than my Da was, whose house was in a merry part of the country, namely over the hills and far away in the Spessart. The fact that I have refrained from going on at great length about my Da's lineage, race and name is for the sake of brevity. This is not an application for entry to an abbey reserved to the nobility, in which case I would have to swear to my ancestry; it is sufficient for our purposes that you know that I come from the Spessart.

Since, however, it has been made clear that my Da's household was truly noble, any intelligent person will readily conclude that I enjoyed a corresponding upbringing. And anyone who believes that will not be deceived, for by the age of ten I had already grasped the principles of my Da's aforementioned noble exercises. However as far as learning was concerned I matched the famous Amphisteides, of whom Suidas reported that he could not count beyond five. The reason was perhaps that my Da, in his high-mindedness, followed the custom of the present age in which people of quality do not bother much with study, or tomfoolery as they call it, because they have other people to do their scribbling for them. But I was an excellent musician on the bagpipes, on which I could play the most beautiful dirges. In religion, however, I do not believe there was another boy of my age in the whole of Christendom who was like me, for I knew nothing of either God or man, heaven or hell, angels or the devil and could not tell the difference between good and evil. As you can well imagine, with such knowledge of theology I lived like our first parents in paradise, who in their innocence knew nothing of illness, death and dying, and even less of the resurrection. What a fine life (though you may say fool's life) where you didn't have to bother with medicine! In the same way you can judge my knowledge of law and all other arts and sciences. Indeed, so perfect and complete was my ignorance that it was impossible for me to know that I knew nothing. I repeat: what a fine life it was that I led in those far-off days. But my Da did not want me to enjoy this bliss any longer. He thought it right and proper that, being nobly born, I should live and act according to my nobility, for which reason he began to educate me for higher things and give me harder lessons.

Chapter 2

Describes Simplicius' first step up the ladder of dignity, containing also praise of shepherds and, in addition, some excellent instruction

He invested me with the most magnificent dignity that could be found, not only in his household, but in the whole world, namely with the office of herdsman. First of all he entrusted his swine to my care, then his goats, and finally his whole herd of sheep. I had to mind them, take them out to pasture and guard them from the wolf with my bagpipes (the sound of which, so Strabo writes, fattens the sheep and lambs in Arabia). I was like David, except that he had a harp instead of bagpipes, and that was no mean beginning. Indeed, it was a portent that with time, and if fortune should favour me, I would become a famous man, for from the earliest days persons of note have been shepherds, as we can read in the Bible of Abraham, Isaac, Jacob and his sons. Even Moses had to mind his father-in-law's sheep before he became leader and law-giver to six hundred thousand Israelites.

And if someone should object that these were holy and godfearing men, not Spessart peasant boys ignorant of God, I would have to agree. Yet why should the innocent that I was be blamed for that? Similar examples could be found among the ancient heathens as well as among the chosen people of God. Among the Romans there were noble families that called themselves the Bubulci, Statilii, Pomponii, Vituli, Vitellii, Annii, Caprae and so on because they had to do with those animals and perhaps even herded them. Romulus and Remus themselves were shepherds; Spartacus, who made the whole power of Rome tremble, was a shepherd. Does not Lucian record in his *Dialogo Helenae* that Paris, the son of King Priam, and Anchises, father of the Trojan prince Aeneas, were shepherds? And Endymion, renowned for his beauty that warmed even the cold heart of Selene, was he not also a shepherd? So too was the terrible Polyphemus. Even the gods, as Cornutus tells us, were not ashamed of that calling. Apollo kept the cattle of Admetus, King of Thessaly; Mercury, his son Daphnis, Pan and Proteus were all great shepherds, for which reason our foolish poets count them the guardian deities of shepherds. Mesha, King of Moab was a sheepmaster, as one can read in the second book of Kings; Cyrus, the mighty king of the Persians, was not only raised by Mithridates, a shepherd, but kept sheep himself. Gyges was first a herdsman and then became king through the power of a ring and Ismail Shah, a Persian king, also minded sheep in his youth. Philo Judaeus puts the matter very well when he says, in his Life of Moses, the office of herdsman is both a preparation for and the first step in exercising command. For just as the warlike and martial arts are first practised in the hunt, so men who are intended for government receive their first training in the gentle and amiable office of herdsman. My Da must have known this very well, and to this very hour it gives me no small hope I may yet rise to future greatness.

But to return to my own flock, you must know that I was as little acquainted with wolves as I was with my own ignorance, for which reason my father took all the more pains with my instruction. 'Kidder', he said, 'make sure the sheep divent gan too far from each other. An' keep playin' yer pipes, so the wolf won't come an' harm 'em. Yon's a fower-legged rogue and thief that'll eat up man and beast. If ye divent keep yer eye open, Aw'll gie ye a right skelpin'.' To which I answered with similar courtesy, 'Da, can ye no tell me what this wolf looks laike? Aw've nivver seen won yet.' 'Ach, ye great donkey', he replied, 'ye'll be a fule all yer laife. I divent ken what'll become ov ye. Such a big laddie and still ye divent ken what a fower-footed rogue the wolf is, ye great booby.' He gave me even more instruction, but eventually grew angry and went away

21

muttering to himself, thinking my dim wits could not take his subtle instructions.

Chapter 3

Records the sufferings of a faithful set of pipes

Then I began to play my pipes so well you could have poisoned the toads in the herb garden with it, assuming I would be safe enough from the wolf, which was always uppermost in my mind. And remembering my Ma (which is what a mother is called in the Spessart and on the Vogelsberg), who often used to say she was worried some day the hens might die of my singing, I decided to sing, to make my defence against the wolf even stronger. And I sang a song I had learnt from my Ma herself:

> O farmer, whom most men despise,
> To you of all, should go the prize.
> No one who sees what work you do
> Will stint the praise he heaps on you
>
> Where would our present fortunes stand,
> If Adam had not tilled the land?
> The sire of every noble lord,
> He dug the soil for his reward.
>
> Your power encompasses most things;
> The harvest fruitful Nature brings,
> The produce that sustains our land,
> Must first of all go through your hand.
>
> The Emperor, whom Our Lord gives
> For our protection, also lives

By your hard work. The soldier, too,
Who does much injury to you.

Meat for our table you provide,
With wine you keep us well supplied;
The earth must feel your plough's sharp blade
If corn shall grow and bread be made.

A wilderness this earth would be
But for your patient husbandry;
If there were no more farmers left
The countryside would stand bereft.

So you deserve the highest praise
Because you feed us all our days.
God's blessing falls on all you do
And even Nature smiles on you.

Who ever heard men talk about
A farmer suffering from the gout,
The torment that the wealthy dread,
That strikes so many nobles dead?

Strange in these puffed-up times to see
A man from arrogance so free.
And God, to keep you from pride's snare,
Gives you your heavy cross to bear.

Even the soldier's cruel mood
Can serve, in this, to do you good,
When he, lest you to pride incline,
Says, 'All your worldly goods are mine'.

That was as far I got with my song and no farther for in a
flash, or so it seemed, I and my herd of sheep were surrounded
by a troop of dragoons who had lost their way in the great
forest and been put back on the right track by my singing and
shepherd's cries.

Aha, I thought, these must be the rogues, these must be those four-legged rascals and thieves your Da told you about! For at first I took rider and horse to be one single beast (just as the American indians did the Spanish cavalry) and assumed it must be the wolf. So I resolved to drive these terrible centaurs away, but hardly had I inflated my pipes to do this than one of them grabbed me by the shoulder and threw me so roughly onto a spare farm horse they had stolen in the course of their depredations that I fell off over the other side and landed on my dear bagpipes, which immediately gave out heart-rending squeals, as if trying to move the whole world to pity. But it was no use, even though they spent their last breath bewailing my fall I still had to climb back onto the horse, no matter what my bagpipes sang or said. But what annoyed me most of all was that the soldiers claimed that in falling I had hurt my pipes, and that was why they had set up such a heretical wailing.

My mare took me along at a steady trot, all the way to my Da's farm. As I rode, bizarre fancies filled my mind, for I imagined that since I was riding on such a beast, the like of which I had never seen before, I too would be changed into one of these iron men. When the transformation did not happen, other foolish notions came into my head. I imagined these strange creatures had come just to help me drive my sheep home, since none of them ate any up, but hurried along together straight to my Da's farm. Therefore I kept a good look-out for my Da, to see whether he and my Ma would come to meet us and bid us welcome. But I looked in vain, for he and my Ma, together with our Ursula, who was my Da's only daughter, had slipped out of the back door without waiting for our guests.

Chapter 4

How Simplicius's home was captured, plundered and destroyed by the soldiers

I would prefer, peace-loving reader, not to take you with these troopers into my Da's house and farm, since things will be pretty bad there. However, my story demands that I set down for posterity the cruel atrocities that were committed from time to time in our German wars since, as my own example demonstrates, all such evils are visited upon us by the Almighty out of His great love towards us and for our own good. How else would I have learnt that there is a God in Heaven if the soldiers had not destroyed my Da's house, thus forcing me out into the world where I met other people from whom I learnt so many things? Until that happened I did not know, nor could I even imagine, that there was anyone else in the world apart from my Da, my Ma, myself and the servants, since I had never seen another person, nor any human habitation apart from the scene of my daily comings and goings. But soon afterwards I learnt how men come into this world, and that there will be a time when each of us must leave it again. In form I was human and by name a Christian, but in all other respects I was a brute beast. However, the Almighty took pity on my innocence, and determined to bring me to knowledge of both myself and Himself. And although He had a thousand means of achieving this, it was doubtless deliberate that the one He chose also punished my Da and my Ma, as a warning to others for the ungodly way they had brought me up.

The first thing the troopers did was to stable their horses. Then each went about his own particular task, though they all resulted in slaughter and destruction. Some set about a general butchering, boiling and roasting, so that it looked as if they were going to hold a banquet, while others went through the house from top to bottom like a devouring flame, as if the

Golden Fleece were likely to be hidden there; even our secret room was not safe from them. Another group made huge bundles of sheets, clothes and other items, as if they intended to set up a flea market somewhere; anything they were not going to take with them they destroyed. Some stabbed at the hay and straw with their swords, as if they had not had enough sheep and pigs to slaughter already, some emptied the feathers out of the mattresses and eiderdowns and filled the cases with hams and other dried meat and provisions, as if that would make them more comfortable for sleeping on; some smashed the stove and windows, as if they were sure the summer would go on for ever. The plates, cups and jugs of copper and pewter they hammered flat and packed the crumpled pieces away, bedsteads, tables, chairs and benches they burnt, even though there was a good stack of dry wood in the yard, cups and bowls they broke, either because they preferred to eat roast meat straight from the spit, or because they had no intention of having another meal there.

Shameful to report, they handed out such rough treatment to our maid in the stall that she was unable to come out. Our farmhand they gave a drink they called Swedish ale: they bound him and laid him on the ground with a stick holding open his mouth, into which they poured a milking pail full of slurry from the dung heap. By this means they forced him to lead a party to a place where they captured more men and beasts, which they brought back to our farm. Among them were my Da, my Ma and our Ursula.

Then they took the flints out of their pistols, replacing them with the peasants' thumbs, which they screwed up tight, as if they were extracting confessions from witches before burning them; they put one of the peasants into the oven and lit a fire under him even before he had confessed to any crime; they placed a rope round the neck of another and twisted it tight with a piece of wood so that the blood came spurting out of his mouth, nose and ears. In short, each one of them had his own particular method of torturing the country folk, and each of the country folk his own particular torment to suffer. It seemed to me at the time that my Da was the most fortunate of them, since he laughed out loud as he confessed, while the others cried out in pain. This honour was doubtless due to the fact that he was the householder. They put him down beside a fire, bound him hand and foot, and smeared the soles of his feet with damp salt which our old billy goat licked off, tickling him so that he almost burst his sides laughing. It looked so funny I found myself laughing too, though whether it was to keep him company or because I knew no better I could not say today. Laughing thus, he confessed his guilt and revealed to them the whereabouts of his hidden treasure, which was far richer in gold, pearls and jewels than one would have expected of a simple farmer. What they did to the women, maidservants and girls they had captured I cannot say, as the soldiers did not let me watch them. What I do know is that I heard constant pitiful cries coming from all corners of the farmhouse and I guess that my Ma and our Ursula fared no better than all the rest. While all this suffering was going on I turned the spit and in the afternoon helped water the horses, during which I came across our maid in the stable. She was so tousled and tumbled that I did not recognise her, but in a weak voice she said to me, 'Run away, lad, or the troopers will take you with them. Make sure you get away, you can see how bad . . . ' More she did not manage to say.

Chapter 5

How Simplicius ran off and was frightened by rotten tree-stumps

Now my eyes were opened to my desperate situation, and I began to think of the best way to escape. But where could I go? That question was beyond my simple mind. However, towards evening I did at least succeed in getting away to the woods. But where should I head for now? The forest and its tracks were as little known to me as the route over the frozen Arctic seas from Novaya Zemlya to China. The pitch-dark night did give me some protection, but to my mind, full of dark thoughts as it was, it was still not dark enough, and I hid in a thick bush. There I could hear both the cries of the tortured peasants and the song of the nightingales. The birds ignored the peasants and continued their sweet singing, showing no compassion for them or their misfortunes, and therefore neither did I, but curled up in my bush and fell asleep as if I hadn't a care in the world.

When the morning star appeared in the east, I could see my Da's house in flames and no one trying to put them out. I left my hiding place, hoping I might find some of my Da's servants, but was immediately spotted by five troopers, who shouted to me, 'Hey, lad, over here or we'll blast you to smithereens.' However, I just stood there, rooted to the spot and gaping at the troopers like a cat at a new barn door, because I had no idea what they were on about. They couldn't get at me because of the marsh between us, which so annoyed them that one of them fired at me with his musket. I had never seen or heard anything like the flames which suddenly shot out and the unexpected bang, which was made even more frightening by the repeated echo. I was struck with terror and immediately fell to the ground. The troopers rode on, presumably thinking I was dead, but I was so petrified with fear that I stayed there, not daring to move, for the rest of the day.

When I was once more shrouded in darkness, I got up and wandered through the forest until I saw a rotten tree-trunk glowing in the distance. This filled me with terror again, so that I turned round on the spot and set off in a different direction until I came across another rotten tree, from which I also ran away. Thus I spent the night running from one rotten tree to another until it was light and the trees lost their frightening look. But that didn't solve my problems. My heart was still full of fear and dread, my legs full of tiredness, my empty stomach full of hunger, my throat full of thirst, my brain full of foolish fancies and my eyes full of sleep. Nevertheless, I carried on walking, even though I had no idea where I was going. All the while I was getting deeper into the forest and farther from human habitation. In the things I endured in that forest I sensed, though without realising it, the effects of a lack of understanding and knowledge. A brute beast, had it been in my place, would have known better what to do for survival. Yet when I was once again overtaken by darkness, I did at least have the wit to crawl into a hollow tree and spend the night there.

Chapter 6

Is short and so full of piety that Simplicius faints

Hardly had I settled down to sleep than I heard a voice crying, 'O wondrous love for us ungrateful mortals! O my sole consolation, my hope, my wealth, my God!' and many other similar exclamations that I could neither understand nor remember.

They were words which might well have comforted and gladdened the heart of any Christian in my situation but such was my simplicity and ignorance, it was all Greek to me. And not only could I not understand what was said, I found it so strange that I was at first filled with terror. But when I heard the speaker say that his hunger would be stilled and his thirst quenched, my empty stomach suggested I should invite myself to the table too. So I summoned up my courage and crept out of the hollow tree to see where the voice was coming from. I saw a tall man with long, grey, unkempt hair falling down round his shoulders and a tangled beard that was shaped almost like a Swiss cheese. His face was yellow and gaunt, but had a kindly look, and his long gown had been mended with more than a thousand different pieces of cloth, often one sewn onto the other. Around his neck and body he had wound a heavy iron chain, like St. William of Aquitaine, and to my eyes looked so fearsome and terrifying that I started to shake like a wet dog. The crucifix, almost six foot long, that he was clasping to his chest, only served to increase my fear, so that I thought this old man must surely be the wolf my Da had told me about not long before. Quaking with fear, I took out my bagpipes, which were the only treasure I had rescued from the troopers. I inflated the sack, tuned up and made a mighty noise to drive away this abominable beast. The hermit was not a little surprised to hear a sudden and unexpected outburst of music in such a wild place, and doubtless thought some fiendish spirit had come to torment him, like St. Anthony, and to disturb his devotions. But he quickly recovered from his shock and started to mock me, calling me the tempter in the hollow tree, where I had gone back to hide. Indeed, he had so far recovered his spirits that he started to scoff at me as the enemy of mankind, saying, 'Ha, so you are come to tempt the saints without God's leave', and much more which I could not understand. His approach filled me with such terror that I fell to the ground in a faint.

Chapter 7

How Simplicius found poor lodgings where
he was kindly treated

I do not know what it was that brought me round; what I do know is that when I came to I found that the old man had placed my head on his lap and opened my jerkin. Seeing the hermit so close to me, I set up a hideous screaming, as if he were about to tear the heart out of my body. He said, 'Be still, my son, I'm not going to hurt you, just be still', but the more he caressed me and tried to comfort me, the louder I cried out, 'Oh, you're going to eat me up! You're going to eat me up! You're the wolf, you're going to eat me up!'

'Indeed I am not, my son', he said. 'Just be still, I'm not going to eat you up.'

It was a long time before I had sufficiently calmed down to accept his invitation to go into his hut with him. The wolf did not live in the hut, but the old man obviously had difficulty keeping it from the door since the cupboard was almost always bare. However, a frugal meal of vegetables and a drink of water filled my belly, and the old man's friendly manner soothed my distraught mind, so that I was soon myself again. Now I could no longer hide the fact that I was desperately in need of sleep, and the old man left me alone in the hut, since there was only room for one person to stretch out there. Around midnight I was wakened by the following hymn, which I later learnt myself:

> Come, voice of night, o nightingale
> And let your song, o'er hill and vale,
> Its soothing solace bring.
> Now other birds have gone to sleep,
> Come, come, your tuneful vigil keep,
> Your Maker's praises sing.
> And let your voice out loud rejoice.
>   Of all below
> You best can raise a hymn of praise
> To Him from whom all blessings flow.
>
> For though the light of day has flown
> And we in deepest night are thrown,
> Our voices still we raise
> To sing of God's great love and might.
> No dark can hinder us, no night,
> In our Creator's praise.
> So let your voice out loud rejoice.
>   Of all below
> You best can raise a hymn of praise
> To Him from whom all blessings flow.
>
> Now Echo's answering voice is stirred,
> Her sweet reverberant notes are heard
> Combining in your song.

She banishes our weariness
And bids us wake that we profess
God's goodness all night long.
So let your voice out loud rejoice.
Of all below
You best can raise a hymn of praise
To Him from whom all blessings flow.

The stars shine from the sky above,
Proclaiming our Creator's love
In streams of light outpoured.
The owl, although she cannot sing,
Yet with her screech shows she would bring
Her tribute to the Lord.
So let your voice out loud rejoice.
Of all below
You best can raise a hymn of praise
To Him from whom all blessings flow.

Come, nightingale, we would not be
Idle amid such minstrelsy
Nor sleep the night away.
Come, let the desert woods around
With joyous hymns of praise resound
Until the break of day.
So let your voice out loud rejoice.
Of all below
You best can raise a hymn of praise
To Him from whom all blessings flow.

All the time the hermit was singing this song, I felt as if the nightingale were joining in, as well as the owl and Echo. So sweetly melodious did it seem, that if I had ever heard the morning star and had been able to play its tune on my bag-pipes, I would have slipped out of the hut to add my notes to the hermit's. As it was, I fell asleep and did not wake until the day was well advanced when I saw him standing before me, saying, 'Up you get, my child. I'll give you something to eat, then show you the way through the woods so you can get back to where people live and reach the nearest village before dark.'

I asked him, 'What kind of things are they, 'people' and 'village'?'

He said, 'What, have you never been to a village, do you not know what people are?'

'No', I said, 'this is the only place I have been. But tell me, what are people, what is a village?'

'Lord save us!' said the hermit, 'you must be simple-minded or crafty,'

'No', I said, 'I'm not Simple Minded, nor Crafty, I'm my Ma and Da's little lad.'

The hermit was amazed at this. With much sighing and crossing of himself he said, 'Well, my dear child, I have a mind, God willing, to teach you better.'

He proceeded by question and answer, as is set out in the following chapter.

Chapter 8

*How Simplicius demonstrated his excellent
qualities through noble discourse*

Hermit: What are you called?
Simplicius: I'm called 'lad'.
Hermit: I can see you're not a girl, but what did your mother and father call you?
Simplicius: I haven't got a mother or father,
Hermit: Who gave you that shirt?
Simplicius: My Ma, of course.
Hermit: What does your Ma call you, then?
Simplicius: She called me 'lad' – also 'rascal', 'numskull' and 'gallows-bird'.

Hermit:	And who was your mother's husband?
Simplicius:	No one.
Hermit:	Well, who did she sleep with at night?
Simplicius:	With my Da.
Hermit:	What did your Da call you?
Simplicius:	He also called me 'lad'.
Hermit:	What is your Da called?
Simplicius:	He's called 'Da'.
Hermit:	What did your mother call him, then?
Simplicius:	'Da'. Sometimes also 'Master'.
Hermit:	Did she never call him by any other name?
Simplicius:	Yes, she did.
Hermit:	Well, what was it?
Simplicius:	'Lout', 'foul peasant', 'drunken sot' and other things when she was scolding him.
Hermit:	You're an ignorant creature, not knowing your parent's name, nor even your own!
Simplicius:	Huh! You don't know them either!
Hermit:	Can you pray?
Simplicius:	Can I do what, pray?
Hermit:	I mean do you know the 'Our Father'?
Simplicius:	Yes.
Hermit:	Well say it then.
Simplicius:	Our father which art heaven, hallowed be name till kingdom come, thy will do heaven and earth, give us trespasses as we give for our trespassers, lead us not in two temptations, deliver us from kingdom, the power and the glory, for ever amen.
Hermit:	God help us! Do you know nothing of the Lord God?
Simplicius:	Yes, it's at home on the shelf by the door to our chamber. My Ma brought it back from the fair and stuck it up there.
Hermit:	O gracious Lord, only now do I see how great is Your mercy in granting us knowledge of Yourself, since anyone who lacks it is not truly human. O Lord grant that I may so honour Your

	holy name and be as tireless in my thanks for this grace as You were generous in granting it to me. Listen, Simplicius (for that is the only name I can give you), when you say the Lord's prayer, this is what you must say: Our Father, which art in heaven, hallowed be thy name. Thy kingdom come. Thy will be done in earth as it is in heaven. Give us this day our daily bread. And –
Simplicius:	And some cheese to go on it, right?
Hermit:	Hold your tongue, child, and learn. You need that much more than cheese. You are a numskull, just as your Ma said. A lad like you shouldn't be interrupting an old man; instead you should hold your tongue, listen and learn. If I only knew where your parents lived, I would take you back to them and tell them how children ought to be brought up.
Simplicius:	I don't know where to go. Our house has been burnt down, my Ma ran away, then came back with our Ursula, and my Da too, and our maid was sick and lying in the stable.
Hermit:	Who burnt your house down?
Simplicius:	Some iron men came, sitting on things as big as oxen but with no horns. These men slaughtered all our sheep and cows and pigs, and then I ran away and after that our house was on fire.
Hermit:	And where was your Da?
Simplicius:	The iron men tied him up, then our billy goat came and licked his feet and made him laugh, and he gave those iron men a lot of silver pennies, big ones and small ones, and some pretty yellow ones, too, and other fine, glittering things and pretty strings of little white beads.
Hermit:	When did this happen?
Simplicius:	Why, when I was supposed to be looking after the sheep. They tried to take my bagpipes away from me as well.
Hermit:	And when were you looking after the sheep?

Simplicius:	Weren't you listening? When the iron men came. And then our Ann told me to run away, otherwise the soldiers would take me with them, by that she meant the iron men, and so I ran away and came here.
Hermit:	And where do you intend to go now?
Simplicius:	I have no idea. I'd like to stay here with you.
Hermit:	Letting you stay here would suit neither you nor me. Eat, then I'll take you to some other people.
Simplicius:	Won't you tell me then what kind of things these 'people' are?
Hermit:	People are men and women, like you and me, your Da and your Ma and your Ann. When there are many of them together we call them people.
Simplicius:	Oh.
Hermit:	Now go and eat.

That was our conversation, during which the Hermit kept looking at me and sighing deeply; whether it was because he felt such pity at my simplicity and ignorance, or because of something I only learnt several years later, I do not know.

Chapter 9

*How Simplicius was changed from a
wild beast into a Christian*

I started to eat and stopped chattering, which, however, only lasted until I had appeased my hunger and the old man told me to leave. Then I sought out whatever flattering words my rough peasant tongue could supply, all of which were aimed at getting the hermit to keep me with him. And even though he found my presence irksome and a burden, he decided to allow me to stay with him, more to instruct me in the Christian religion than to avail himself of my services, old though he was. His greatest worry was that a youth of my tender years would not put up with such a hard life for long.

My probationary year was a period of some three weeks. It was in the early spring, when gardeners have to prepare the soil and I had to show my aptitude for that profession. I came through it so well that the Hermit was particularly pleased with me, not just because of the work, which I was used to doing, but because he saw that I was as eager to hear his teaching as my heart, still soft and smooth as a wax tablet, proved quick to embrace it. For that reason he became even more zealous in leading me along the path of goodness. He began his instruction with the fall of Lucifer, then proceeded to the Garden of Eden, and when we had been cast out, along with our first parents, went through the laws of Moses and taught me, through God's ten commandments and their interpretation (which commandments he said were a true guide to recognising the will of God and leading a holy life, pleasing to God), to distinguish virtue from vice, to do good and spurn evil. Then he came to the gospels and told me about Christ's birth, suffering, death and resurrection, concluding with Judgment Day, painting a picture of heaven and hell.

All this he set out in sufficient detail without going on for too long, concerned rather to put it in a way I could best understand. He would finish one topic before starting on the next and was so skilful and patient in dealing with me and my questions that he could have found no better way of filling my mind with his knowledge and wisdom. Both his life and his conversation were a constant sermon for me which, with the help of God's grace, bore fruit in my mind, that was not as stupid and wooden as might have seemed. The result was that in the aforementioned three weeks I not only learnt everything a Christian ought to know, but conceived such love for the teaching that at night I could not get to sleep for thinking about it.

Since then I have often reflected on this and come to the conclusion that Aristotle was correct when, in Book 3 of *On the Soul,* he compares man's soul to a blank wax tablet on which all kinds of things can be noted down, and concludes that this was done by the supreme creator so that these smooth tablets should be diligently marked with impressions and exercises and thus brought to completion and perfection; Averroes, commenting on the passage in Book 2 of *On the Soul* where the philosopher says that the intellect is a potentiality which can only be activated through knowledge, i.e. that the human mind is capable of all things but that nothing can be put into it without diligent exercise, comes to the clear conclusion that this knowledge or exercise leads to the perfection of the soul which, of itself, contains nothing at all. This is confirmed by Cicero in Book 2 of his *Tusculan Disputations*, where he compares the soul of a person lacking instruction, knowledge and exercise to a field which is naturally fruitful but which, if it is not cultivated and sown, will bring forth no fruit.

All this I proved through my own example. The reason why I so quickly grasped everything the hermit told me was because he found the wax tablet of my soul quite smooth and empty, free of any previous images that would have made it difficult for something else to be impressed upon it. Despite all this, however, I still retained a pure simplicity compared with other men, so that the hermit, neither of us knowing my real name, called me Simplicius.

I also learnt to pray, and when he decided to give in to my determination to stay with him, we built a hut for me similar to his own, out of branches, brushwood and clay. It was like the tents the musketeers build for themselves when campaigning, or, to be more precise, like the clamps farmers make in some places for their turnips and so low I could hardly sit upright in it. My mattress was made of dry leaves and grass and as big as the hut itself, so that I do not know whether to call my abode a hut or a covered bed.

Chapter 10

How he learnt to read and write in the wild woods

The first time I saw the hermit reading the Bible I could not imagine whom he could be having such a secret and, as it seemed to me, earnest conversation with. I could see his lips moving, but no one talking to him, and although I knew nothing about reading and writing, I could tell from his eyes that he was occupied with something in that book. I noted which book it was, and when he put it aside I went to get it and opened it. The first thing my eye lit upon was the opening chapter of the Book of Job with a fine woodcut, beautifully coloured in, at the head. I asked the figures in it strange questions and when I received no answer I said, just as the hermit crept up behind me, 'You little wretches, have you lost your tongues? Haven't you just been chatting to my father (that was what I called the hermit) for long enough? I can see you're driving off that poor Da's sheep and have set fire to his house. Stop, stop! I'll put out the fire', and I stood up to go and fetch some water, for I thought it was needed.

The hermit, whom I didn't realise was behind me, said, 'Where are you off to, Simplicius?'

'Oh, father', I replied, 'there are soldiers who have taken some sheep and are going to drive them off. They've taken them away from that poor man you were talking to just now. His house is going up in flames as well and if I don't put them out it will burn down to the ground', pointing with my finger at what I could see as I spoke.

'Stay where you are', said the hermit, 'there's no danger.'

'Are you blind?' I answered in my rustic manner. 'You stop them driving the sheep off and I'll fetch the water.'

'But', said the hermit, 'these pictures are not alive. They have been made to show us things that happened a long time ago.'

39

'But how can they not be alive?' I replied. 'You were talking to them a moment ago.'

The hermit was forced to laugh, contrary to his habit, and said, 'My dear child, these pictures cannot speak, but I can tell what they are and what they're doing from these black lines. This is called reading, and while I was doing it you supposed I was talking to the pictures, but that was not the case.'

'If I'm a human like you', I replied, 'then I ought to be able to tell the same things as you can from the black lines. I don't follow what you're saying. Dear father, teach me how to understand this matter.'

At that he said, 'Very well, my son, I will teach you so that you will be able to talk to these pictures, only it will take time. It will take patience on my part and hard work on yours.' Then he printed the alphabet for me on pieces of birch bark and when I knew the letters I learnt to spell, then to read and eventually to write, even more clearly than the hermit himself, since I printed everything.

Chapter 11

Concerns food, household goods and other necessary things we must have in this earthly life

I spent about two years in that forest, that is up to the time the hermit died and something over half a year after that. Therefore it seems a good idea to tell the reader, who is often curious to know the least detail, about our way of life there.

For food we had all kinds of garden produce, turnips, cabbages, beans, peas and suchlike, nor did we despise beech nuts or wild apples, pears and cherries. Often we were so hungry we were happy to eat acorns. Our bread – cake might be a better word – we baked in hot ashes from maize we ground up. In the winter we caught birds with snares and gins; in the spring and summer God sent us fledglings from the nests; often we made do with snails and frogs, and we were not averse to fishing with nets and rods since not far from where we lived was a stream full of fish and crayfish, all of which made our diet of coarse vegetables more palatable. Once we caught a young wild pig, which we kept in a pen, fed on acorns and beech mast, fattened up and finally ate, since the hermit said it could be no sin to enjoy things God had created for all the human race for that very purpose. We did not need much salt, and no spices at all, for we did not want to arouse our thirst seeing that we had no cellar. The little salt we needed was given to us by a pastor who lived about fifteen miles away and of whom I shall have much to say later on.

As far as household goods were concerned, I can say that we had enough. We had a spade, a pick, an axe, a hatchet and an iron pot for cooking, which did not actually belong to us, but were borrowed from the pastor mentioned above, and each of us had a worn, blunt knife. These were our property, and that was all. We did not need bowls, plates, spoons, forks, cauldrons, frying pans, a grill, a spit, a salt cellar or other items of crockery and kitchenware, for our pot served as our bowl, and our hands were our forks and spoons. If we wanted to drink, we did it from the spring through a reed, or we dipped our mouths in, like Gideon's warriors. As for all kinds of cloth – wool, silk, cotton and linen – for bedding, table-cloths and wall-hangings, we had nothing but what we stood up in, since we believed we had enough if we could protect ourselves from rain and frost.

There was no regular order or routine to our doings, apart from on Sundays and feast days, when we set off around midnight so that we could reach the church of the above-mentioned pastor, which lay some way out of the village, early enough to avoid being seen by anyone. While we were wait-ing for the service to start we sat on the broken organ, from where we could see both the altar and the pulpit. The first time I saw the pastor climb up into the latter, I asked my hermit what he was going to do in that huge tub? After the service we slipped away just as quietly as we had come. And when we reached our home, weary in body and legs, we ate our poor meal with a good appetite. The rest of the time the hermit spent praying or instructing me in holy matters.

On workdays we did whatever needed doing most, depending on the season and the time we had at our disposal. Sometimes we would work in the garden, at others we collected the rich compost from shady spots and out of hollow trees to use instead of dung to improve our garden; we would weave baskets or fish-nets, chop up firewood, fish or do anything to banish idleness. And while we went about all these tasks, the hermit never ceased instructing me in all good things. It was a tough life, and I learnt to endure hunger, thirst, heat, cold and hard work, but above all to know God and to serve Him honestly, which was the most important lesson. And that was all my faithful hermit wanted me to learn, for he thought it was enough for a Christian to reach his goal if he worked hard and prayed hard. And that was why, although I had been well enough taught in religious matters, and understood my Christian belief – and also could speak German as beautifully as if it was the spelling book itself speaking – yet I remained a simpleton. When I left the woods I cut such a sorry figure in the world that even the dogs ignored me.

Chapter 12

*Reports on a fine way to come to a blessed end
and get oneself buried cheaply*

One day after about two years, when I was still scarcely accustomed to the hard life of a hermit, my best friend on earth took his pick, gave me the spade and, following his daily habit, led me by the hand into our garden where we used to say our prayers.

'Now Simplicius, my dear child', he said, 'the time has

come, praise be to God, for me to depart this life, to pay my debt to nature and leave you behind in the world. And since I can foresee some of the things that will befall you in your life and well know that you will not stay long in this wilderness, I have determined to give you some precepts to strengthen you on the path of virtue on which you have started out. These will be an infallible guide and will lead you, if you live your life according to them, to eternal bliss and you will be found worthy to join the elect, beholding the face of God for all eternity.'

These words flooded my eyes with tears, just as the dam the Swedes constructed flooded the town of Villingen. They were more than I could bear, but I said, 'Dearest father, are you going to leave me alone in this wild forest? Then shall –' More I could not say. My heart overflowed with love for my father and this made the torment so sharp I collapsed at his feet, as if dead. He helped me up and comforted me as well as time and the occasion allowed, at the same time reproaching me for my error, asking me if I thought I could oppose the divine order? 'Do you not know', he went on, 'that that is something neither Heaven nor Hell can do? Would you burden this weak body of mine, which is longing for rest? Do you imagine you can force me to stay longer in this vale of tears? No, my son, let me go. All your wailing and sobbing cannot compel me to stay any longer in this place of misery, especially against my will now that God's express will is calling me away. Instead of indulging in useless crying, follow my last words, which are these: the longer you live, the better you should seek to know yourself, and do not let your heart abandon this practice, even if you should live to be as old as Methuselah. The reason why most men are damned is that they never learn what they are, nor what they can and must be.'

He went on to advise me to avoid bad company, for the harm it could do was more than he could say. And he gave me an example, saying, 'If you put one drop of Malmsey into a bowl of vinegar, it will immediately turn to vinegar; if, on the other hand, you put a drop of vinegar in Malmsey, it will mingle with the wine. My dearest son', he said, 'above all be steadfast, for those who persevere to the end will find eternal bliss. If, however, contrary to my hopes it should happen that human weakness makes you fall, then quickly rise again through sincere repentance.'

That was all the advice this conscientious and pious man gave me. Not because that was all he knew, but firstly because he felt I was too young to be able to take in more on an occasion like this, and secondly because a brief word is more easily remembered than a long speech; and if it is pithy and to the point it does more good by making you think than a long sermon which is easily understood and just as easily forgotten.

The reason this pious man thought these three points – to know yourself, avoid bad company and be steadfast – were essential was doubtless because he practised them himself and found they stood him in good stead. After he had come to know himself, he shunned not only bad company, but the whole world and remained true to that resolve, on which doubtless eternal bliss depends, until the very end, the manner of which I will describe now.

After he had given me this advice, he started to dig his own grave with the mattock. I helped as best I could, doing as he told me, but with no idea what he was aiming at. Then he said, 'My dear, true and only son (for apart from you I have fathered no other creature to the glory of the Creator), when my soul has gone to its destined abode, it will be your duty to pay your last respects to my body and cover me with the soil we have dug out of this hole.' At that he took me in his arms, kissed me and pressed me to his breast, much more strongly than would have seemed possible for a man in his condition.

'Dear child', he continued, 'I commend you to God's care and die happy because I trust He will look after you.' I for my part could do nothing but weep and moan. I clung to the chains he wore round his neck, thinking I could hold on to him and stop him leaving me. But he said, 'My son, let me see if the grave is long enough.' Taking off his chains and his robe, he lay down in the grave, like someone going to bed, and said, 'O almighty God, take back the soul You gave me. Lord, into

Thy hands I commend my spirit', after which he gently closed his lips and eyes. But I stood there like a jackass, not imagining his dear soul could have left his body, since I had often seem him in such a trance. As I usually did when that happened, I remained beside the grave for several hours in prayer. When, however, my beloved hermit still did not get up, I got down into the grave and started shaking, kissing and caressing him. But there was no life left in him, since cruel, pitiless death had robbed poor Simplicius of his faithful companion. I watered or, to put it better, embalmed his lifeless corpse with my tears, and after I had spent some time running to and fro, wailing miserably, I started to heap the earth over him, more with sighs than with the spade. Scarcely had I covered his face than I jumped down into the grave to uncover it again, to see him and kiss him once more. This went on for the whole day until I had finished. These were all his funeral rites, his exequies, his funeral games, since there was no bier, coffin, shroud, candles, pall-bearers or mourners, nor any clergy to sing his requiem.

Chapter 13

Simplicius drifts along like a reed on the pond

A few days after the hermit had died I went to the pastor I mentioned before and told him of my master's death. At the same time I asked his advice about what to do at this turn of events. Yet despite the fact that he advised against staying in the forest any longer, I boldly followed in my predecessor's footsteps and spent the whole summer living the life of a devout monk. But time changes all things, and the grief I felt for my hermit gradually lessened; at the same time the sharp winter cold quenched the inner fire of my firm resolve. The more I started to waver, the lazier I became at my prayers since, instead of contemplating divine and heavenly thoughts,

I allowed myself to be overcome with the desire to see the world. As I was thus no longer capable of living a good life in the forest I decided to go back to the pastor and ask him if he still advised me to leave the forest. So I set of for his village, but when I got there I found it in flames, for a party of troopers had just plundered it, killed some of the peasants and driven off the rest, apart from the few they had taken captive, among them the pastor himself. Ah God, how full of trouble and adversity is a man's life! Scarcely has one misfortune ended than we find ourselves in the next. It does not surprise me at all that the heathen philosopher, Timon, set up many gallows in Athens for people to hang themselves and bring their wretched lives to an end by inflicting one brief moment of pain on themselves.

The troopers were ready to depart and were leading the pastor on a rope. Some of them were shouting, 'Shoot the rogue!' while others wanted money from him. He, however, raised his hands and begged them to remember the Last Judgment and spare him out of Christian compassion. But all in vain, for one of them rode him down and gave him such a blow to the head that he fell flat on the ground and commended his soul to God. The other villagers who had been captured fared no better.

Just when the soldiers seemed to be going mad with murderous cruelty, a swarm of armed peasants came pouring out of the wood. It was as if someone had disturbed a wasps' nest. They started to yell so horribly, to swing their swords and fire their guns so furiously that my hair stood on end, for never before had I seen such a brawl. The men of the Spessart and the Vogelsberg will not lie down and let themselves be trampled over on their own dung heap, no more than those of Hessen, the Sauerland and the Black Forest. This sent the troopers packing and they not only left behind the cattle they had taken, they cast off bag and baggage, throwing away all their plunder so that they themselves should not fall prey to the villagers. Even then some were captured.

This entertainment almost took away my desire to see the world. If this is what goes on in it, I thought, then the wilderness is more pleasant by far. However, I still wanted to hear what the pastor would have to say about it. From the wounds and blows he had received, he was quite weak and feeble, and he told me he could neither help nor advise me, since he himself was in a situation where he would probably have to beg for his bread. If I were to continue to stay in the forest I could expect no assistance from him since, as I could see with my own eyes, both his church and parsonage were in flames.

At that I made my way sadly back to my hut in the woods. Since my journey to the village had brought me little comfort but had turned my mind once more to pious thoughts, I decided I would never leave the wilderness again. I was already wondering if it would be possible for me to live without salt (which until now the pastor had always brought) and so do without mankind altogether?

Chapter 14

A curious comedy of five peasants

So that I could carry out my decision and become a true anchorite, I put on the hair shirt my hermit had left me and girded myself with his chain. It was not that I needed them to mortify my recalcitrant flesh. I put it on so that I would be like my predecessor both in my way of life and in my dress; also this garment provided better protection against the harsh winter cold.

On the second day after the village had been burnt and pillaged, as I was sitting in my hut praying and at the same time roasting carrots over the fire for my sustenance, I was surrounded by forty or fifty musketeers. Although astonished at my strange appearance, they ransacked my hut, looking for things that were not to be found there, for all I had was books, which they threw into a jumble since they had no use for them. At last, when they had a better look at me and could tell from my plumage what a poor fowl they had caught, they could easily work out what meagre pickings were to be had here. Then they expressed their astonishment at my hard life and greatly pitied my tender youth, especially the officer who commanded them. He bowed respectfully to me, at the same time asking me to show him and his men the way out of the forest, for they had been lost in it for some time now. I did not refuse, and led them to the nearest path to the village, since that was the only way I knew.

Before we were out of the forest, however, we saw about ten peasants, some armed with firelocks, others busy burying something. The musketeers ran at them crying, 'Stop! Stop!' to which the peasants replied with their muskets. But when they saw they were outnumbered by the soldiers, they ran off quickly so that none of the tired musketeers could catch them. They therefore decided to dig up what the peasants had just buried, which was all the easier since the peasants had left their picks and shovels behind. Hardly had they started digging, however, than they heard a voice from below crying out, 'You wanton rogues! You arch-villains! Do you think Heaven will leave your unchristian cruelty and knavery unpunished. No! There are still honest men enough alive who will take such vengeance on you for your brutality that none of your fellow men will ever lick your arses ever again.' At this the soldiers looked at each other, not knowing what to do. Some thought they were hearing a ghost, I thought I was dreaming, but their officer told them not to be afraid and keep on digging. They soon uncovered a barrel and, breaking it open, found a fellow inside who had neither ears nor nose left, but was still alive despite that.

As soon as he had recovered a little, and recognised some of the soldiers, he told them how, the previous day when men from his regiment were out foraging, the peasants had captured six of them. Only an hour ago they had made them stand one behind another and shot five of them dead. However, as he was at the back and the bullet had not reached him after going through the five bodies, they had cut off his nose and ears, though not before forcing him to lick – if the reader will forgive me for mentioning it – the arses of five of them. When he found himself thus mocked by these despicable, God-forsaken wretches, he heaped on them the foulest abuse he could think of. Even though they were going to spare his life, he told them exactly what he thought of them in the hope that one would lose patience and put an end to his suffering with a bullet. It was all in vain however. He annoyed them so much they put him in the barrel in which the musketeers had found him and buried him alive. As he was so keen to die, they said, they had decided not to grant his wish, just to spite him.

While he was bemoaning the agony he had been through, another party of foot-soldiers appeared from one side. They had met the peasants, captured five of them and killed the rest. Among the captives were four of those for whom the mutilated trooper had been forced to perform the shameful service only a short time ago. When the two parties realised, from their shouts, that they were on the same side, they came together and once more the trooper told what had happened to him and his comrades. Then you would have been astonished to see how the peasants were maltreated. Some of the soldiers were so furious they wanted to shoot them straight away, but others said, 'No. First of all we must subject them to torture, but thoroughly, to pay them back for what they did to this trooper.' While this was going on the peasants received such blows to the ribs with muskets that I was surprised they did not start to spit blood. Finally a soldier stepped forward and said, 'Gentlemen, the abominable way these five peasants treated this rascal (pointing to the trooper) brings shame on all soldiers, so it is quite right for us to wash out this blot on our honour by making these rogues lick the trooper one hundred times.' Another, however, said, 'This fellow is not worth the honour we do him. If he had not been such an idle coward, he would surely have died a thousand deaths rather than perform this shameful service, to the dishonour of all soldiers.' Finally all were agreed that each of the peasants who had been thus cleansed should perform the same service to ten soldiers; and each time they must say, 'Herewith I wash away and erase the shame the soldiers imagine they suffered when a coward licked our backsides.' They put off a decision as to what they would do with the peasants afterwards until the latter had carried out their cleansing task. But the peasants were obstinate, and neither promises to let them go free, nor torture could make them comply.

Meanwhile one of the soldiers took aside the fifth peasant, who had not had his arse licked, and said to him, 'If you will deny God and his saints, I will let you go wherever you like.' To this the peasant answered that he had never thought anything of the saints and had had little to do with God, and swore a solemn oath that he did not know God and had no desire to enter His kingdom. At that the soldier fired a bullet at his forehead, which, however, had no more effect than if he had fired at a mountain of steel. Then he drew his sword and said, 'Oho, so that's who we're dealing with, is it? I promised to let you go where you liked, so now I'm sending you down to hell, since you don't want to go to heaven', and split his head right down to the teeth. As the peasant fell, the soldier said, 'That's the way to avenge yourself, punishing these rogues in this world and the next.'

At the same time the other soldiers were dealing with the four peasants who had had their arses licked. They bound their hands and feet together round a fallen tree in such a way that their backsides (if you will forgive me again) were sticking up nicely in the air. Then they pulled down their trousers, took several yards of fuse, tied knots in it and ran it up and down in their arses to such effect that the blood came pouring out. The peasants screamed pitifully, but the soldiers were enjoying it and did not stop their sawing until they were through the skin and flesh and down to the bone.

However, they allowed me to return to my hut, since the party which had just arrived knew the way, so I never saw what they finally did to the peasants.

Chapter 15

Simplicius's hut is pillaged, which brings him strange dreams of the country folk and what happens to them in war

When I arrived home I found that my tinder-box and all my household possessions were gone, together with the meagre store of food I had grown during the summer in my garden and saved for the coming winter. What should I do now? I wondered. I quickly learnt the truth of the saying that necessity soon teaches you to pray. I gathered all my wits together to try and work out what I could do. Since, however, I was almost completely lacking in experience nothing that looked likely to succeed occurred to me. The best I could think of was to commend myself to God and put my trust in Him alone. Otherwise I would doubtless have fallen into despair and perished.

Beside that, I was so preoccupied with the things I had heard and seen that day that I thought less about food and how I was going to survive than about the enmity between soldier and peasant. But so cruelly did they persecute each other that my simple mind could come to no other conclusion than that mankind must consist not of one race, all descended from Adam, but of two, wild and tame, like other animals.

Such were my thoughts as I fell asleep, wretched and cold and with a hungry stomach. Then it seemed, as if in a dream, that all the trees around my hut changed and took on a different appearance. At the top of every tree sat a noble cavalier and the branches were covered with all kinds of men in place of leaves. Some of them had long pikes, others muskets, short swords, halberds, banners, drums and fifes. It was a brave sight, all neatly arranged, descending row upon row. The roots, however, consisted of people of little consequence, artisans, labourers, farmers and the like, who, nevertheless, gave the tree its strength, which they renewed whenever it needed it. They even replaced the fallen leaves from among their number and to their own even greater detriment. All the while they complained about those who were sitting in the tree, and not without good reason, for the whole weight of the tree was resting on them and squeezing all the money out of their purses, even though they had seven locks. And if the money did not come, the commissaries would give them a good going over with a scourge they called a military execution, forcing sighs from their hearts, tears from their eyes, blood from under their nails and the marrow from their bones. And yet there were some jokers among them who were not worried about all this. They made light of it and mocked them instead of comforting them in their distress.

Chapter 16

Of the ways of the military in the present time, and how difficult it is for a common soldier to be promoted

Thus the roots of these trees passed their days in misery and lamentation, but those on the lowest branches had to put up with even greater toil and hardship. The latter, however, were always merrier than the former, though they were also insolent, cruel, mostly godless and at all times an unbearably heavy burden on the roots. There was a rhyme about them:

> Hunger, thirst, cold and heat,
> Empty purse, weary feet,
> Ruthless killing, wanton strife
> Add up to a lanzknecht's life.

This rhyme was not in the least a fabrication, it corresponded to the facts of a soldier's life. Their whole existence consisted of eating and drinking, going hungry and thirsty, whoring and sodomising, gaming and dicing, guzzling and gorging, murdering and being murdered, killing and being killed, torturing and being tortured, terrifying and being terrified, hunting and being hunted, robbing and being robbed, pillaging and being pillaged, beating and being beaten, being feared and being afraid, causing misery and suffering miserably – in a word, injuring and destroying and in turn being injured and destroyed. And nothing could stop them, neither winter nor summer, snow nor ice, heat nor cold, rain nor wind, mountain nor valley, meadow nor marsh, not ravine, pass, sea, wall, water, fire or rampart, not father or mother, brother or sister, not danger to their own body, soul or conscience, nor the loss of Heaven or of anything else for which there are words. They went about their business until, one by one, they expired, perished, died, croaked their last in battles, sieges, attacks, campaigns, and even in their quarters (the soldiers' earthly paradise if they should chance upon a fat farmer). Only a few survived who, if they had shown no skill at robbery and extortion, in their old age provided us with our best beggars and vagabonds.

Immediately above these wretches sat old poultry thieves who had spent some years in peril of their lives on the lowest branches, but had managed to struggle through and have the good fortune to escape death so far. These looked more earnest and respectable than those on the lowest branches because they had risen to the next rank. But above them were even higher ones, who also had a higher opinion of themselves since they had command over the lower orders. These were called jerkin-beaters because of their habit of dusting the jackets – and the heads – of the pikemen with their sticks and halberds and giving the musketeers a dose of birch-oil to grease their muskets with.

Above these the tree-trunk had an interval or gap, a smooth section without branches and greased with all the lotions and soaps that malice could devise, so that no man, however good he was at climbing, could scale it, neither by courage, skill or knowledge, unless he came from the nobility. It was more smoothly polished than a marble column or a steel mirror.

Above this part sat those with the banners, some of them young, some quite well on in years. The young ones had been hauled up by their cousins, but the older ones had climbed up under their own steam, either by a silver ladder known as the Bribery Backstairs, or by some other bridge that Fortune had made for them, no one else being available. Above them were even higher ones, who had better seats but still had toil, worries and opposition. However, they enjoyed the advantage that they could lard their purses with slices of the fat which they cut – with a knife called War Levy – out of the root. Their greatest skills they showed when a commissary came with a tub full of money and poured it over the tree to refresh them. Then they caught the best of what was raining down on them and let through as good as nothing to the lowest branches. That was why more of the lower ones died of hunger than by the hand of the enemy, a danger to which those above seemed immune. Thus there was a continual scrabbling and climbing on the tree because everyone wanted to sit in the highest, happiest places.

There were some lazy good-for-nothings, however, not worth the army bread they were given. These made no effort at all to reach a higher position and just did what their duty required. The lower ones who were ambitious hoped the higher ones would fall so they could take their place. But when one out of ten thousand succeeded, their success only came at that disgruntled age when they would be better employed sitting in the ingle-nook roasting apples than facing the enemy in the field. And if there was a man who was in a good position and did his duty honestly, he was envied by the others, or lost both his rank and his life through some unforeseen, unlucky bullet. Nowhere was it harder than at that smooth part of the trunk I mentioned before, for any officer who had a good sergeant was unwilling to lose him, which would be the case if he were made an ensign. So instead of the experienced soldiers it was scribblers, footmen, overgrown pages, poor nobles, vagabonds and parasites, or someone's cousin, who became ensigns and thus stole the bread out of the mouths of those who deserved it.

Chapter 17

Although, as is right and proper, the nobles are preferred to common men in war, many from the despised classes still achieve high honours

This annoyed one sergeant so much that he began to complain loudly, but a lordling said, 'Do you not know that the high ranks in the army have always been filled with nobles, they being most suited to those offices? Grey beards alone do not defeat the enemy, otherwise one could hire a herd of billy-goats. People say,

> Choose a bull that's young and strong
> To make the herd obey.
> Despite the claims of older beasts,
> He'll see they do not stray.
> The herdsman can rely on him
> Although he's in his youth.
> That wisdom comes with age alone
> Is prejudice, not truth.

Tell me, thou old cripple, are not nobly born officers better respected by the troops than those who have been common soldiers? And how can you keep discipline in war when there is no respect? Cannot the general trust a nobleman better than a peasant lad who has run away from the plough and has no thought of doing good by his own parents? A true nobleman would rather die with honour than bring dishonour on his family through treason, desertion or behaviour of that kind. It is laid down that the nobility should be given precedence in all things and John of Platea expressly states that the nobility should have preference in filling offices and that it is proper that they should be preferred to commoners. This is usual in all legal systems and is confirmed by the Bible, for it says in Ecclesiastes 10, 17, 'Blessed art thou, O land, when thy king is the son of nobles', a magnificent testimony to the precedence due to the nobility. And even if one of your kind is a good soldier, inured to the smell of gunpowder and able to give a good account of himself in every action, yet that does not mean he is equally capable of giving orders to others. This quality, on the other hand, is innate to the nobility, or acquired in earliest youth. Seneca says, 'A heroic soul has this quality, that it is urged on towards honour; no noble spirit takes pleasure in small and worthless things.' Publio Fausto Andrelini expressed this in a distich:

> If you are low-born of rustic stock,
> Nobility of soul will never be yours.

Moreover the nobility has greater means to aid their subordinates with money and find recruits for weak companies than a peasant. As the saying has it, setting the peasant above the nobleman is a recipe for disorder. Also the peasants would become much too arrogant if they were made lords straight away, for it is said,

> You'll never find a sharper sword
> Than a peasant who's been made a lord.

If the peasants, by reason of ancient and acknowledged custom, had military and other offices in their possession, as the nobility does, they would certainly do all they could to stop a nobleman acquiring them. In addition, although people are often keen to help you soldiers of fortune (as you are called) to rise to high honours, you are generally so old by the time you have been tested out and found worthy of higher things that one must have misgivings about promoting you. By then the fire of youth has gone out and your only thought is how best to pamper and protect your sick bodies, worn out by all the hardships you have been through and of little use for warfare, caring not who fights and gains honour. A young hound is much more willing in the chase than an old lion.'

The sergeant answered, 'Who would be foolish enough to serve in the army if he had no hope of being promoted for his good conduct and thus rewarded for his loyal service? The Devil take such wars. The way things are at present, it makes no difference whether one does one's duty properly or not. I have often heard our old colonel say he wanted no one under his command who did not firmly believe he could rise to be a general through performing his duty well. The whole world must acknowledge that those nations which promote common but honest soldiers and reward their courage most often triumph in battle. One can see this in the Persians and Turks. It is said,

> A lamp gives light, but must be primed
> With oil or else its flame soon dies.
> So loyalty needs its reward,
> A soldier's courage needs its prize.'

The lordling replied, 'If an honest man has genuine qualities which come to the notice of his superiors, then he will certainly not be overlooked. Nowadays you can find many men who have abandoned the plough, the needle, the cobbler's last and the shepherd's crook for the sword, who have acquitted themselves well and through their bravery been raised high above the gentry to the rank of count and baron. What was the imperial general, Johann von Werd? A farmer. The Swede Stallhans? A tailor. The Hessian colonel, Jacob Mercier, had been a shoemaker and Daniel de St. Andree, the commandant of Lippstadt, a shepherd. There are many other examples which, to save time, I will not mention here. This is not something which is new to the present, nor will there in the future be any lack of low-born but honest men who rise to high honour through war; it even happened in the past. Tamburlaine was a swineherd who became a powerful king, the terror of the whole world; Agathocles, King of Sicily, was a potter's son; Telephas, a wheelwright, became King of Lydia; the father of Emperor Valentinian was a rope-maker; Maurice the Cappadocian, a bondslave, became emperor after the second Tiberius; John of Tzimisces was a scholar who became emperor. Flavius Vobiscus records that Emperor Bonosus was the son of a poor schoolmaster; Hyperbolus, the son of Chermidi, was first a lamp-maker then Prince of Athens; Justinus, who ruled before Justinian, was a swineherd before becoming emperor. Hugh Capet, a butcher's son, was King of France; Pizarro, likewise a swineherd, was later Governor of Peru and weighed out gold by the hundredweight.'

The sergeant answered, 'All this sounds well enough, but I can still see that the doors to some positions of dignity are kept closed to us by the nobility. Scarcely have they crawled out of the shell, than nobles are immediately given places which we cannot think of attaining, even if we have done more than many a nobleman who is now appointed colonel. And just as among the peasantry many a noble mind wastes away because a man lacks the means to study, so many a brave soldier grows old still bearing his musket who deserves command of a regiment and could have rendered his general great services.'

Chapter 18

Simplicius takes his first steps into the world and fares badly

I had had enough of listening to the old ass. Indeed, I felt he deserved the treatment he complained of because he often thrashed his soldiers like dogs. I turned again to the trees, with which the whole countryside was filled, and watched how they moved and knocked against each other. The men in them rained down by the score; a crack, and there was one on the ground already, dead in a second. In the same second one lost an arm, another a leg, a third his head. As I watched I thought that all the trees I could see were just one tree with Mars, the God of War, on the top, and covering the whole of Europe with its branches. It seemed to me that this tree could have overshadowed the whole world, but since it was blasted, as if by a cold north wind, by envy and hatred, suspicion and malice, arrogance, pride, avarice and other such fine virtues, it appeared thin and sparse, which was why someone had carved the following rhyme on its trunk:

The holm-oak, scarred and blasted by the wind's chill breath,
Breaks its own branches off, condemns itself to death.
When brother fights with brother, civil war will start,
Bring pain and grief to all and tear the land apart.

The mighty roar of the destructive wind and the crash of the falling tree woke me from my sleep. I was alone in my hut. I began to consider again what I should do. It was impossible for me to stay in the forest because everything had been taken away, leaving me with no means of survival. All that was left were a few books, scattered in a jumble on the ground. As I gathered them together, the tears streaming from my eyes, at the same time begging God to guide me and show me where I should go, I chanced upon a letter the hermit had written before his death:

'Dear Simplicius, when you find this letter, leave the forest straight away and save yourself and the pastor, who has been very good to me, from the present troubles. God, whom you should ever keep before you and pray to at all times, will bring you to a place best suited to you. But keep Him always in mind and be diligent in His service, as if I were still with you in the forest. Remember and follow my last instructions and you will come through. Farewell.'

I showered thousands of kisses on the letter and on the hermit's grave, then set out to look for people, walking in a straight line for two days and finding a hollow tree to sleep in when night overtook me; my only food was the beech nuts I picked up as I went along. On the third day, however, I came to a flat field not far from Gelnhausen where I enjoyed a true feast, for it was covered in sheaves of wheat. It was my good fortune that the peasants had been driven off after the Battle of Nördlingen and had not been able to gather them in. As it was bitterly cold, I made a shelter in one of them and filled my belly with ears of corn from which I rubbed off the husks. It had been a long time since I enjoyed such a meal.

Chapter 19

How Hanau was taken by Simplicius and Simplicius by Hanau

When day broke I ate some more wheat then went straight to Gelnhausen. There I found the gates open. They were partly burnt, but still half barricaded with piles of dung. I went in but could see no living person. On the other hand the streets were strewn with dead, some of whom had been stripped naked, others down to their undershirt or petticoat. This pitiful sight was a terrifying spectacle for me, as anyone might imagine. In my simplicity I could not conceive what calamity had overtaken the town to leave it in such a state. Not long afterwards, however, I learnt that imperial troops had surprised a company of Weimar dragoons there. I had not gone two stones' throw into the town when I had seen enough and turned back and went round it through the meadows until I came to a good road which took me to the splendid fortress of Hanau. When I came upon the first sentries I tried to pass through, but two musketeers immediately came out, seized me and took me into their guard room.

Before I go on to relate what happened to me, I must describe my strange dress, for my clothing and appearance were so outlandish, so bizarre and unkempt that the governor even had a painting done of me. Firstly my hair had not been cut at all for eighteen months, neither after the Greek, nor the German or French fashion, had not been brushed, combed or curled, but still grew in all its natural profusion with more than a year's worth of dust on it, instead of the powder fools of both sexes scatter over their wigs, and it framed my pale face so neatly that I looked for all the world like a barn owl hunting for a mouse or about to seize its prey. And since I used to go bare-headed all the time and my hair was naturally curly, I looked as if I were wearing a turban. And my dress matched this headgear, for I was wearing the hermit's coat, if I can still call it a coat: the original garment from which it had been made had completely disappeared, apart from the basic shape which could be discerned beneath a thousand patches of different coloured cloth, sewn together with all sorts of stitching. Over this threadbare and often repaired coat I wore, instead of a cloak, the hair shirt, from which I had cut off the sleeves to make me a pair of stockings. Looped round my body were iron chains, neatly crossed front and back, as Saint William is usually represented in paintings, so that the figure I made was almost like those who have been prisoners of the Turks and now go about the country begging for their comrades. My shoes were made of wood and the laces woven from the bark of the lime-tree; my feet inside them were the colour of boiled lobster, as if I were wearing stockings of Spanish red or had dyed my skin with Pernambuco wood. I do believe that if any travelling showman had taken me and presented me as a Samoyed or Greenlander he would have found many a fool willing to part with a copper to see me. Even though anyone with a modicum of intelligence could easily deduce from my lean, half-starved look and neglected dress that I was not a fugitive from some kitchen or lady's chamber, even less from the household of some great lord, I was still subjected to rigorous questioning by the guard. And just as the soldiers gaped at me, so I stared at the fantastic get-up of their officer, to whom I had to give an account of myself. I did not know whether he was a he or a she, for he wore his hair and beard in the French fashion, with long tresses hanging down each side, like horses' tails, and such havoc had been wrought on his beard that there were only a few hairs left between his nose and mouth so that you could hardly tell he had one at all. No less confusing as regards his sex were his wide breeches, which seemed to me more like a woman's skirt than a man's trousers. Is this a man? I asked myself. If so, then he ought to have a decent beard, for the fop is not as young as he would like to appear. If it's a woman then why does the old whore have so much stubble round her mouth? It must be a woman, I thought, for a real man would never show himself with such a wretched apology for a beard. Even billy-goats have a sense of shame and will not venture one single step among a strange flock if their beards have been clipped. I was so uncertain what to think that, knowing nothing of the current fashions, I eventually decided he must be a woman.

This mannish woman, or womanish man, as he seemed to me, had me thoroughly searched but found nothing apart from a notebook made out of birch-bark in which I wrote my daily prayers and where I had also placed the farewell note from the hermit that I mentioned in the last chapter. He took it away from me but since I did not want to lose it I fell down before him, clasped him by the knees and said, 'O dear hermaphrodite, please let me keep my prayer-book.'

'You foolish boy', he answered, 'who in the Devil's name told you I was called Herman?' He then ordered two soldiers to take me to the governor, and he also gave them the book to carry because, as I immediately realised, the fop could neither read nor write.

So I was led into the town and everyone ran to gape at me, as if some sea monster were on show. And as they saw me, each one formed their own idea as to what I was. Some assumed I was a spy, others a madman, yet others a wild man, and some even thought I was a spectre, a ghost or some such phenomenon. There were also those who took me for a fool, and they would have been closest to the truth had it not been for the knowledge of God I had in my heart.

Chapter 20

How he was rescued from prison and torture

When I was brought before the governor, a Scot by the name of James Ramsay, he asked me where I came from. I answered that I did not know, so he asked, 'Where are you going, then?' Again I answered, 'I don't know.' 'What the Devil do you know, then?' he said. 'What is your business?' Once more I answered that I didn't know. He then asked, 'Where is your home?' and when I again replied that I didn't know, the expression on his face changed, whether from anger or astonishment I couldn't say. Since, however, everyone tends to suspect the worst, and especially since the enemy was close at hand and had, as already reported, taken Gelnhausen the previous night and destroyed a regiment of dragoons, he came round to the view of those who through I was a traitor or spy and ordered me to be searched. He was told by the soldiers of the watch who had brought me to him that this had already been done and that nothing had been found but a notebook, which they handed to him. He read a few lines and asked me who had given it to me. I answered that it had always belonged to me, since I had made it and written in it myself. 'But why on birch-bark?' he asked.

'Because the bark of other trees is not suitable', I replied.

'Do not be impudent', he said. 'I am asking why did you not write on paper?'

'Because', I said, 'we had no more left in the forest.'

'Where? In which forest?' the governor asked, at which I took up my old refrain of 'I don't know.'

At that the governor turned to several of his officers who were in attendance and said, 'Either he is an arch-rogue or he is a fool. But he cannot be a fool since he can write so well.' As he spoke he leafed through the book, to show them my handwriting, and did it so vigorously that the hermit's letter fell out. He got one of the men to pick it up, but I went pale because I considered it my greatest treasure and holy relic. The governor noticed this and it made him even more suspicious of treachery, especially after he had opened the letter and read it, for he said, 'I know this hand. This has been written by some officer I know well, though I cannot at the moment think who it is.' He must have found the contents strange and incomprehensible too, for he said, 'Without doubt this must be some code which nobody can understand apart from the one with whom it has been agreed.' He asked me what my name was, and when I answered 'Simplicius', he said, 'A fine one we have here! Away with him, clap him in irons, hand and foot'. And so the two soldiers accompanied me to my new lodgings, namely the goal, and handed me over to the keeper who, in accordance with his orders, adorned my hands and feet with iron fetters and chains, as if I were not carrying enough already with those I had round my body.

As if this were not enough for a welcome to the world, along came the torturer and his henchman with their cruel instruments which, notwithstanding the fact that I could comfort myself with my innocence, made my wretched situation truly terrifying. 'Ah, God!' I said to myself, 'It serves you right Simplicius, for abandoning the service of God to go out into the world. Now you have received the just reward for your folly, you disgrace to the Christian faith. O unhappy Simplicius, see where your ingratitude has brought you. Scarcely has God revealed Himself to you and taken you into His service than you run away from His service and turn your back on Him. Could you not have gone on eating acorns and beans and thus served your Maker undisturbed? You knew very well, didn't you, that your teacher, the faithful hermit, had fled the world and chosen the wilderness? And you abandoned it, you blind dolt, in the hope of satisfying your shameful lust to see the world!? Look where it has brought you. You thought to feast your eyes and now you are condemned to perish in this deadly labyrinth. You unthinking simpleton, was it not clear to you that your blessed mentor would not have exchanged the pleasures of the world for the hard life he led in the wilderness if he had not been certain he could never find rest, true peace and eternal bliss in the world? Poor Simplicius, off you go now and receive the reward for your vain thoughts and foolish presumption. You cannot complain of injustice, nor comfort yourself with your innocence. Of your own accord you rushed to meet this torture and the death that will surely follow.'

Thus I accused myself, asked God for His forgiveness and commended my soul to Him. In the meantime we were approaching the Thieves' Tower but, as the proverb says, God's help is closest where need is greatest. As I was standing outside the prison, surrounded by guards, amid a large throng of people, waiting for the door to be opened so I could be taken in, the pastor whose village had recently been burnt and plundered, who was also under arrest, wanted to see what the commotion was. When he looked out of the window and saw me he shouted out in a very loud voice, 'Is that you, Simplicius?' When I heard him and saw him I couldn't stop myself from stretching out my hands towards him and crying, 'O father! O father! O father!' He asked me what I had done. I replied that I didn't know; they had presumably brought me here because I had run away from the forest. When, however, he heard from those standing around that I was thought to be a spy, he asked them not to proceed further against me until he had explained my case to the governor. This, he said, would help set both of us free and prevent the governor from harming us wrongfully, since he knew me better than any man alive.

Chapter 21

How fickle fortune smiled on Simplicius

He was allowed to go to the governor, and over half an hour later I was fetched and taken to the servants' hall, where two tailors, a cobbler with shoes, a shopkeeper with hats and stockings and another with various articles of clothing were already waiting to clothe me as quickly as possible. They took off my coat, chains and all, and my hair shirt, so that the tailors could take my measurements. After that a barber appeared with lather and fragrant soaps, but just as he was about to demonstrate his art on me there came a counter order which alarmed me very much: I was to put my clothes back on again. However, the intention was not as bad as I feared. A painter came with all his equipment, with red lead and vermilion for my eyelids, lake, indigo and vermilion for my coral lips, gamboge, ochre and yellow lead for my white teeth, which I was baring, so hungry I was, lamp-black, charcoal and raw umber for my golden hair, white lead for my terrible eyes and many other pigments for my weather-stained coat. He also brought a whole handful of brushes.

This man started to study me, to sketch in an outline, to lay a ground, to put his head on one side in order to compare his work with my figure: now he changed my eyes, now my hair, added a quick touch to my nostrils, in short corrected everything he had not got right at first, until he had a model as true to nature as Simplicius was. Only then was the barber allowed to set about me with his soap and lather. He washed my head and must have spent an hour and a half on my hair, finally trimming it after the current fashion, for I had more than enough. After that he put me in a bathtub and washed the three or four years of dirt off my starved, emaciated body. No sooner had he finished than they brought me a white shirt, shoes and stockings, together with a turn-down collar, hat and feather; the breeches were beautifully decorated and trimmed all over with gold lace. All that was missing was the jerkin, but the tailors were working on that at top speed. The cook appeared with a bowl of meaty broth, the maid with a drink. So there sat my lord Simplicius, like a young count, splendidly turned out. I tucked in heartily even though I had no idea what they intended to do with me. I had not yet heard the phrase, 'the condemned man ate a hearty supper', so that tasting this first meal seemed more sweet and pleasant to me than I can express. Indeed, I scarcely think I have ever in my life felt more intense pleasure than at that meal.

When the jerkin was ready I put it on, but in my new clothes I cut such a poor figure that it looked as if the tailors had dressed a fence post. They had been told to make the clothes too large, in the hope that I would quickly put on weight, which, with the good food, I did, visibly. My forest garments, together with the chains and other pieces, were put in the art collection with the rare objects and antiquities, and my life-size portrait placed beside them.

After supper his lordship was given a bed the like of which he had never before slept in, neither in his Da's house nor in the hermit's hut. But I could not sleep because my belly growled and grumbled the whole night through. The reason must have been either that it did not yet know what was good for it or that it was still astonished at the delightful new dishes it had been given. But it was cold, so I just lay there until the sun was shining once more, musing on the strange hardships I had been through during the last few days and on how faithfully the Lord God had come to my aid and brought me to such a good place.

Chapter 22

Who the hermit was from whose company
Simplicius had benefited

That morning the governor's steward ordered me to go to the above-mentioned pastor to hear what his lord had said to him about me. He gave me a bodyguard to take me there. The pastor led me into his study, made me sit down and said, 'My dear Simplicius, the hermit with whom you lived in the forest is not only the brother-in-law of the governor, he also helped him gain promotion in the army and was his closest friend. The governor was kind enough to tell me about him. From his earliest youth he at all times showed both the courage of a heroic soldier and the devout godliness usually only found in a monk, two virtues which are rarely seen together. His piety coupled with unhappy experiences so conspired to make him discontented with the world that he repudiated his nobility and considerable estates in Scotland, where he was born, because all worldly affairs had come to seem vain, stale and corrupt to him. In a word, he hoped to exchange his present high rank for a better glory to come. His noble spirit felt disgust at all worldly splendour and all his hopes and all his endeavours were directed towards the wretched existence in which you found him in the forest and shared with him until his death.

In my opinion', the pastor went on, 'he was led astray by reading too many popish books about the lives of old hermits. However, I will not conceal from you how he came to the Spessart and fulfilled his desire for such a wretched hermit's life, so that in future you can tell other people about it. The second night after the bloody battle of Höchst had been lost, he arrived at my parsonage, alone and unattended. It was towards morning and I and my wife and children had only just gone to sleep because the noise throughout the countryside made by both pursued and pursuers had kept us awake the whole previous night and half of this. He knocked on the door, at first gently, then furiously enough to wake myself and my sleepy servants. At his request, and after a short exchange of words, which was very cautious on both sides, I opened the door and saw the noble gentleman dismounting from his steed. His sumptuous clothing was bespattered with the enemy's blood as much as it was adorned with gold and silver and since he was still holding his naked sword in his hand, I was filled with fear and dread. But once he had sheathed it and had nothing but civil words for me, I began to wonder why such a brave lord should be asking a poor village pastor for shelter in such friendly fashion. He was so handsome a figure and so magnificently attired that I addressed him as Count Mansfeld. He replied that he was the Count's equal, if not his superior, in misfortune alone. There were three things he grieved over: the loss of his wife, who was close to her term; the loss of the battle; and the fact that he had not had the good fortune to die in it for the gospel, like other honest soldiers. I tried to comfort him, but soon saw that his noble heart needed no comfort. Then I set before him what food we had in the house and got the servants to make up a soldier's bed of fresh straw, which he insisted upon, even though he was much in need of rest.

The first thing he did in the morning was to give me his horse and to distribute his money, of which he had no small amount on him, and several valuable rings among my wife, children and servants. I did not know what to make of this since soldiers are more in the habit of taking than giving. I had some qualms about accepting such generous presents and objected that I did not deserve them nor could I do anything to earn them. I added that if people were to see me and my family with such riches, especially the valuable horse, which I could not hide, everyone would conclude that I had helped to rob or even murder him. He told me I should not let that worry me, he would give me a note in his own handwriting to protect me from that danger; when he left my parsonage, he went on, he did not even want to take his own shirt with him,

69

to say nothing of his other clothes. With that he revealed to me his resolve to become a hermit. I tried everything I could to dissuade him, especially since I felt such an intention smacked of popery, and reminded him that he could do more to help spread the gospel with his sword. However, my efforts were all in vain. He went on and on at me until I gave in and provided him with the books, pictures and utensils he had when you found him. The only thing he would take in return for everything he had given me was the woollen blanket he had slept under that night on the straw mattress which he had made into a coat. And he also insisted I exchange my waggon-chains for one of gold on which he kept the portrait of his love – those were the chains he always wore. He kept no money, nor anything of monetary value. My servant guided him to the most desolate spot in the forest and helped him build his hut there. The life he led and the way I occasionally helped him you know as well, if not better than I.

After the battle of Nördlingen was lost and I, as you are aware, was stripped of all my belongings and badly beaten, I fled here to safety because I had my best things in storage here. And when my cash was about to run out, I took three rings I had from the hermit, including his signet ring, together with the aforementioned gold chain and portrait, to a Jew, to turn them into money. But such was their value and fine work-manship that he offered them for sale to the governor, who immediately recognised the coat of arms and the portrait. He sent for me and asked where I had obtained such jewels? I told him the truth, showed him the hermit's deed of gift, in his own handwriting, and explained all that had happened, how he had lived in the forest and eventually died. The governor refused to believe me and put me under arrest until he had learnt the truth. He was about to send out a mounted patrol to visit the hut and bring you here when I saw you being led to the tower. The governor now has no reason to doubt my story. I have the evidence of the place where the hermit lived and the testimony of you and other witnesses, in particular of the sexton, who often let you into the church before daylight. In your prayer book he also found the hermit's letter, which bears witness not only to the truth, but also to the hermit's piety. So now, for the sake of his late brother-in-law, the governor would like to do something for both you and me. You can decide what you would like him to do for you. If you would like to study, he will pay your expenses; if you desire to learn some trade, he will find you an apprenticeship; if, however, you want to stay with him, he will treat you like his own child, for he said that even if a dog came to him from his late brother-in-law, he would take it in.' I answered that I did not care what the governor did with me.

Chapter 23

Simplicius becomes a page; how the hermit's wife was lost

The pastor kept me in his apartment until ten o'clock before he went with me to the governor to tell him of my decision, because that meant he could lunch with the governor, who kept open table. Hanau was blockaded then, and things were so expensive for ordinary people, especially those who had fled to the safety of the fortress, that there were some who, formerly proud, were now not ashamed to pick up off the streets the frozen turnip peelings thrown out from the houses of the rich. The pastor was so successful that he even managed to sit beside the governor at the head of the table, while I waited on them with a plate in my hand, under the instruction of the steward. I was as proficient at this as a donkey at playing chess, but the pastor's ready tongue made up for all my clumsiness. He said I had been brought up in the wilderness and had never lived among people so that I should be excused because I had no way of knowing how to behave. The loyalty I had shown towards the hermit and the harsh life I had endured with him were, in his opinion, to be admired and not only excused my clumsiness but made me preferable to the most polished young nobleman. He went on to tell them how I was the hermit's chief joy because, as the latter frequently used to say, my features were so much like those of his beloved. The hermit, he added, had often marvelled both at my steadfastness and unchanging determination to stay with him, and at many other virtues which he had praised in me. To sum up, he could not emphasize enough the fervent earnestness with which the hermit had recommended me to him shortly before his death, confessing that he loved me as much as if I had been his own son.

This tickled my ears and the pleasure more than made up for all the hard times I had been through with the hermit. The governor asked whether his brother-in-law had not known that he was commandant of Hanau. 'Certainly', answered the pastor, 'for I told him myself. And although he had a cheerful expression and a half smile on his face, yet he received the news as coolly as if he had never heard the name of Ramsay. The more I think about it, the more I have to marvel at this man's steadfastness of purpose in the way he could bring himself not only to renounce the world but also to put his best friend so completely out of his mind, even though he knew he was nearby.'

The governor was no soft-hearted woman but a brave soldier, yet there were tears in his eyes as he said, 'If I had known he was still alive and where I could find him, I would have had him brought to me, even against his will, so that I could repay all the kindnesses he had done me. Since, however, that is denied me, I will take care of his Simplicius in his place. Ah!' he went on, 'I think the honest gentleman had good reason to mourn the fate of his pregnant wife. In the pursuit she was captured by an imperial mounted patrol. That was in the Spessart, too. When I heard that, and thinking my brother-in-law had died in the battle for Höchst, I immediately sent a trumpeter to the enemy to ask after my sister and ransom her. However, all I achieved was to learn that the patrol had been scattered by some peasants and my sister lost in the skirmish. To this day I do not know what has become of her.'

This was what was said at table between the pastor and the

governor about the hermit and his beloved. The couple were all the more pitied because they had only had one year together. But I became the governor's page, and such a fine fellow that the people, especially peasants, whom I had to announce to my master were already calling me Young Master.

Chapter 24

Simplicius reproaches people and sees many false idols in the world

At that time my only worthwhile qualities were my clear conscience and devout mind, accompanied by the purest innocence and simplicity. All I knew of vices was that I had heard their names or read about them. If I saw someone actually indulging in one I found it strange and horrifying because I had been brought up always to bear the presence of God in mind and to try as hard as I could to live according to His holy will. And since I knew God's will, I used to measure people's actions and character against it, and when I did that it seemed to me I could see nothing but iniquity all around me. God! how astonished I was at first when, ever conscious of His law and the gospel and Christ's warnings, I saw what was done by those who claimed to be his disciples and followers. Instead of the plain dealing one should expect from every honest Christian, I found nothing but hypocrisy among the inhabitants of the world and such countless follies that I was unsure whether I was among Christians or not. It was clear that many were well aware of God's will, but few showed any serious intention of carrying it out.

So I had a thousand strange thoughts and fancies in my mind and was sorely tempted to break Christ's command, when He said to us, 'Judge not, that ye be not judged.' On the other hand, I remembered the words Saint Paul wrote in the fifth chapter of the Epistle to the Galatians, 'Now the works of the flesh are manifest, which are these: adultery, fornication, uncleanness, lasciviousness, idolatry, witchcraft, hatred, variance, emulations, wrath, strife, seditions, heresies, envyings, murders, drunkenness, revellings and such like; of the which I tell you before, as I have also told you in time past, that they which do such things shall not inherit the kingdom of God.' Everyone, I thought, does these things openly, so why should I not openly conclude from the words of the Apostle that not everyone will be saved?

Along with pride and greed and their worthy retinue of minor vices, gluttony and drunkenness, whoring and buggery were daily practices among those of position and wealth. What shocked me most of all, however, was the fact that some, especially soldiers, whose vices are generally not very severely punished, made a joke both of their own godlessness and of God's holy will. For example I once heard an adulterer, who even expected praise for his shameful deed, speak these godless words, 'It serves the spineless cuckold right that I've given him a pair of horns. To tell the truth, I did it less to please the woman than to spite the man and through it take my revenge on him.'

'What empty vengeance', answered one right-thinking person who was present, 'if it means sullying your own conscience and bringing on yourself the shame of the adulterer!'

'What do you mean adulterer?' he replied with a scornful laugh. 'I follow the commandment which says thou shalt not covet thy neighbour's wife. Did you not hear when I told you I did it not out of desire for her but to revenge myself on her husband? The Lord says, Thou shalt not steal. Have I stolen? No, I just borrowed the fool's wife for a while. God joined them together and it is not I but God who will put them asunder through death.' He continued with his Devil's catechism, and I sighed to myself and thought what a blasphemous sinner he was, until I could stand it no longer and said to him, even though he was an officer, 'Do you not think these godless words are a worse sin than your adultery?' He merely replied, 'Do you want a box on the ear, you insolent young puppy?' And I think he would have given me a good thrashing, too, if he had not been afraid of my master. But I held my peace, and afterwards I saw that it was not uncommon for an unmarried person to make eyes at someone who was married and vice versa.

While I was still studying the path to eternal life with the hermit I wondered why God had so strictly forbidden idolatry to His chosen people. I imagined that anyone who had come to know the true, eternal God would never honour or worship any other, and therefore in my simple mind I concluded that the commandment was unnecessary. Ah, foolishness bred of ignorance! No sooner had I entered the world than I realised that despite this commandment almost every man had his own particular idol, some even had more than the heathens, both past and present. Some kept theirs in their strong-box, in which they placed all their hope and trust; there were those who had their idol at court and put all their confidence in him, even though he was only a sycophantic courtier and often a more idle wretch that the worshipper himself, since his frail divinity was based on nothing but the April showers of a prince's favour; for others their idol was their good name, if they only had that they imagined they were demigods; yet others, namely those whom the true God had given a sound brain so that they were skilled in some of the arts and sciences, had theirs in their head; these forgot the divine Giver and concentrated on the gift, in the hope it would bring them prosperity; there were also many whose god was their own belly, to whom they daily made the kind of sacrifices the heathens of antiquity made to Bacchus and Ceres; and if their belly rebelled, or other infirmities appeared, then they would make a god of their doctor and seek their refuge in the pharmacy, which would often as not speed them on their way to death.

Many fools made for themselves goddesses out of scheming tarts whom they called by many different names, worshipping them night and day with a thousand sighs and singing hymns to them containing nothing but their praises, together with a humble request for the young lady in question to take pity on their folly and become as foolish as their suitors. On the other hand there were women who had set up their own beauty as their god which, they imagined, would find them a husband, let the true God in Heaven say what He will; instead of other sacrifices, this idol was daily anointed and kept alive with all kinds of paints and powders, creams, salves and other lotions.

I saw people who considered a well-situated house their god, for they said that as long as they lived in it they enjoyed good fortune, the money seeming to pour in through the windows. I was particularly astonished at this foolishness, for I saw the reason why the occupants prospered in this way. I knew a man who for several years could not sleep properly because of his tobacco shop, to which he had devoted his heart, mind and all his thoughts, which ought to be dedicated to God. Day and night he sighed over it a thousand times, for it brought him his prosperity. But what happened? The misguided fellow died, vanishing as completely as the smoke from his own tobacco. I thought, 'O wretched man! If only you had valued your soul's eternal bliss and the glory of the one true God as highly as you valued your idol, which appeared on your shop-sign in the form of a Brazilian Indian with a roll of tobacco under his arm and a pipe in his mouth, I would have no doubt at all that you had won yourself a crown to wear in the next world.'

I met another ass who had even more miserable gods. At a gathering where everyone was telling how he had managed to feed himself and keep alive during the terrible famine this man said, in plain German, that the snails and frogs had been his lord god, for if it had not been for them he would have starved to death. I asked him what God himself had been to him, who had provided such insects to sustain him, but the poor simpleton had no answer. What surprised me even more was that I had never heard of anyone, neither the old, idol-worshipping Egyptians, nor the modern American savages, proclaiming such vermin their god as this empty-headed prattler did.

A noble gentleman was once showing me round his art collection, which contained many fine and rare works.

Among his pictures there was none I liked better than an *Ecce Homo* because it was painted in such a way as to arouse the compassion of those who looked at it. Next to it hung a Chinese picture, done on paper, showing the Chinese idols, some of which looked like demons, sitting in majesty. The owner asked me which piece in his collection I liked best. When I pointed to the *Ecce Homo*, he said I was mistaken, for the Chinese picture was rarer and therefore more valuable. He would not be without it, even for ten like the *Ecce Homo*, he said. 'Sir', I asked, 'is what you say with your lips the same as what you feel in your heart?'

'Certainly it is', he answered.

'Why then, the god of your heart is the one whose portrait your lips confess is of greatest value.'

'What bizarre reasoning', said the owner. 'It is its rarity I value.'

'What can be rarer or more wonderful', I replied, 'than that the Son of God should suffer for our sakes, as is portrayed in this picture?'

Chapter 25

*How Simplicius found everything in the world strange,
and how the world found him strange as well*

Just as these and an even greater number of false idols were honoured, so the true divine majesty was despised. I saw none who desired to keep His word and commandments, on the contrary, I saw many who resisted Him in everything, even outdoing the publicans in evil, who were open sinners at the time when Christ walked on earth. Christ said, 'Love your enemies, bless them that curse you, do good to them that hate you, and pray for them which despitefully use you and persecute you, that ye may be the children of your Father which is in heaven. For if ye love them which love you, what reward have ye? Do not even the publicans do the same? And if ye salute your brethren only, what do ye do more than others? Do not even the publicans do so?' But not only could I find no one who desired to obey this command of Christ, everyone did exactly the opposite. There is a saying, 'The bigger the family, the more enemies you have', and nowhere was more envy to be found, more hatred, malice, strife and discord than between brothers, sisters and other relations, especially when there was an inheritance to be shared. And everywhere the craftsmen hated each other, so that I was compelled to conclude that, compared to them, the tax-gatherers, publicans and open sinners, who were hated by many for their wickedness and godlessness, must have been far better than we Christians of today in the exercise of brotherly love, since we have Christ's testimony that they loved each other. And I reflected that if we earn no reward unless we love our enemies, what severe punishment must we expect for hating our friends! Where love and loyalty should be greatest I found the worst treachery and strongest hatred. Some lords worked their loyal servants and retainers into the ground, while some servants swindled their honest lords. I saw too that there was constant squabbling between man and wife. Many a tyrant treated his faithful wife worse than a dog, while many a loose trollop made a fool and an ass of her honest husband. Many despicable lords and masters cheated their honest servants out of their rightful wages and kept them on short commons in both food and drink. On the other hand I saw many unfaithful servants who ruined their honest masters by theft or negligence. Merchants and craftsmen each charged more extortionate prices than the other and used all kinds of chicanery to deprive the farmer of the fruits of his honest toil. On the other hand there were peasants so godless that, if they were not blessed with sufficient craftiness, they would put on a show of simple-mindedness to accuse other people, even their lords.

I once saw a soldier slap another hard on the face and imagined, at that point not having seen a brawl, the latter would turn the other cheek. I was wrong. The injured party drew his weapon and struck his assailant on the head. I cried out to him at the top of my voice, 'What are you doing, friend?' 'Devil take it', he replied, 'I would be a coward and rather die if I did not have my revenge. Only a knave would let himself be bullied like that.' The noise of the dispute between the two grew louder and louder as their supporters, bystanders and others who came running set about each other. I heard men swear by God and their souls in such devil-may-care fashion that I could not believe they thought their souls were their most precious jewel. But that was mere childish chatter compared with the cursing that followed, 'A plague, a pox on it! Devil take me, and not just one! May a hundred thousand come and carry me off!' Seven blessed sacraments were not enough for them, they conjured them by the hundred thousand, by the barrel-load, the ship-load, the moat-full, making my hair stand on end with horror. Again one of Christ's commands came to mind, where he said, 'Swear not at all; neither by heaven, for it is God's throne, nor by the earth, for it is his footstool; neither by Jerusalem, for it is the city of the great king. Neither shalt thou swear by thy head, because thou canst not make one hair white or black. But let your communication be, Yea, yea; Nay, nay, for whatsoever is more than these cometh of evil.' Thinking about all this and what I had heard and seen, I came to the conclusion that these brawlers were no Christians and so I sought other company.

What I found most horrifying was to hear some braggarts boasting of their wickedness, sin, shame and vice. Every day I kept hearing such people say, 'By Christ, we had a skinful yesterday! I must have got blind drunk three times and spewed up the lot just as often. Christ, didn't we give those rascally peasants a thrashing! Christ, didn't we take some booty! Christ, didn't we have a good time with those women and girls!' Or, 'I cut him down as if he'd been struck by lightning. I shot him and you could see nothing but the whites of his eyes. I tricked him so neatly and left him for the Devil to fetch. I tripped him up so he broke his neck.'

Every day my ears were filled with this kind of unchristian talk, and even worse than that, I saw sins committed in God's name, which filled me with sorrow. It was the soldiers who most often did this, saying for example, 'In God's name let us go out on a raid and plunder, steal, shoot, cut down, assault, capture, burn', and whatever other atrocities they perpetrated. The war-profiteers dared to sell their goods, 'In God's name', so they could fleece people and bleed them white to satisfy their fiendish greed. I once saw two rogues hanged who went to burgle a house at night. They placed a ladder against the wall, but when one of them was about to climb in the window 'in God's name', the vigilant householder appeared and threw him down 'in the Devil's name' so that he broke his leg, was caught and strung up with his accomplice a few days later.

Whenever I heard or saw this kind of thing, I had to say my piece, and when, as usual, I came out with a quotation from the Bible or some other well-meant reproach, people took me for a fool. I was so often ridiculed for my good intentions that eventually I lost patience and determined to keep silent. However, such was my Christian love of mankind, that I could not. I wished everyone had been brought up by the hermit, assuming that then many would see the ways of the world as I saw them, with the eyes of Simplicius. I was not clever enough to realise that if the world were full of Simpliciuses there would not be as many vices for their eyes to see. But still it is true that a worldly man, being accustomed to all vices and follies and sharing in them, does not in the least realise what a dangerous path he and his companions are on.

Chapter 26

A strange new way of greeting each other and
wishing each other the best of luck

Thinking now there was some doubt as to whether I was
among Christians or not, I went to the pastor and told him
everything I had heard and seen and how I had concluded
that the people could not be Christians since all they did was
to mock Christ and His commandments. I asked him to clear
up this confusion so that I would know what to think of my
fellow men. 'Of course they are Christians', the pastor replied,
'and I would advise you not to call them anything else.'

'My God!' I replied, 'How can that be? Whenever I point
out to someone the sin they are committing against God I am
mocked and ridiculed.'

'That does not surprise me', answered the pastor. 'I believe
that if the first Christians, who lived at the time of Christ, if
even the Apostles themselves were to rise from the dead and
return to the world today, they would ask the same question
as you have and be thought fools by everyone, just as you
were. What you have seen so far is quite normal and mere
child's play compared with other acts of violence, both open
and secret, against God and man, there are in the world. But
you must learn to accept it. You will meet very few Christians
like Samuel, your hermit.'

While we were talking, a number of enemy prisoners were
led across the square. This interrupted our discussion because
we too went to look at the captives. As we did so I heard a
piece of nonsense I would not have dreamt possible. It was a
new fashion of greeting and welcoming each other. One of
our garrison had previously served the emperor and knew
one of the prisoners. Delighted to see him, he went over and
shook him heartily by the hand, saying, 'Pox on you, brother,
are you still alive? By the holy fuckrament, the Devil looks

81

after his own! Strike me blind, but I thought you'd been hanged long ago.' The other replied, 'I'll be damned, brother, is that you or isn't it? Devil take you, how did you get here? For the life of me I never thought I'd ever see you again. I assumed the Devil would have come to fetch you long ago.' And when they parted, instead of 'God be with you', they said, 'See you on the gallows! Perhaps we can get together tomorrow and drink ourselves stupid.'

'Is that not a fine, pious welcome?' I said to the pastor. 'Are they not most Christian good wishes? Have these men not a most godly plan for tomorrow? Who would know they were Christians? Who could listen to them without astonishment? If that is the way they talk to each other in brotherly love, what does it sound like when they quarrel? If these men belong to Christ's flock and you are their appointed shepherd, I think it is your duty to lead them to better pastures.'

'Yes, my child', answered the pastor, 'that is the way it is with soldiers, God have mercy on them. If I were to say anything it would be no better than preaching to the deaf, and all I would achieve would be to arouse the hatred of these godless fellows and put myself in danger.'

I expressed my surprise and continued talking to the pastor a little while longer before going to wait on the governor, for I had his permission to go out at certain times to look at the town and see the pastor. My master had heard of my simplicity and thought it might be cured by wandering around, seeing this and hearing that, and being taught by others – that is to have the corners rubbed off me and be knocked into shape.

Chapter 27

The secretary's office is fumigated with a strong stench

My master's favour towards me increased with every day because as time passed I came to resemble more and more not only his sister, who had married the hermit, but the governor himself. The good food and idle life quickly made me sleek. And I enjoyed the same favour in many quarters, for anyone who had business with the governor was generous to me as well. His secretary was especially well-disposed towards me. He had to teach me arithmetic and derived much amusement from my simplicity and ignorance. He had only recently left university and was therefore still full of student pranks, which sometimes made him look as if he had a screw loose. He often managed to convince me that black was white and white black, so that although I started by believing everything he said, I ended up believing nothing.

I once criticised him for his dirty inkwell but he replied that it was the best thing in his whole room for he could draw up out of it anything he wanted: fine gold ducats, fine clothes, in short all his possessions had been fished out of his inkwell one by one. I refused to believe that such magnificent things could be obtained from such a paltry container. He replied that it was the *spiritus paperi*, as he called the ink, that did it, and that an inkwell was called a well because you could draw up all sorts of things out of it. I asked how he got them out since the opening was hardly big enough to put two fingers in. He answered that he had an arm in his head that did the work and he hoped that soon it would pull out a beautiful and rich young girl for him. If luck were on his side he believed he could even obtain land and servants of his own from it; that had certainly happened in the past. I marvelled at his skill and asked if there were others who had mastered it.

'Certainly', he said. 'All officials, doctors, secretaries,

procurators, advocates, commissioners, notaries, merchants, dealers and countless others can, and if they work hard at pulling things out they usually become rich men.'

'So the farmers and other hard-working people are fools to earn their bread by the sweat of their brow instead of learning this art?' I said.

'Some do not know how useful this art is', he replied, 'and therefore have no desire to learn it. Some would like to learn it but lack the arm in their head or something else that is needed. Others have learnt the art and have the arm, but do not have the knack of using it to get rich. Yet others have learnt the art and have the skill, but live in Stony Ground and do not have the opportunity of exercising them that I have.'

While we were talking about the inkwell (which reminded me of Fortunatus's inexhaustible purse), I happened to pick up a book in which the correct modes of address were listed. In my opinion it contained more nonsense than I had yet set eyes on. I said to the secretary, 'These are all children of Adam, all of the same substance, namely dust and ashes. Where, then, do these great differences come from? Most Holy, Most Invincible, Most Serene? Are those not attributes of God? One is gracious, another worshipful. And always well-born, high-born, most nobly born? We know they were born! No man falls from the skies, appears out of the water or grows out of the earth like a cabbage. And why only your Excellency? Why not Your Wyellency or Your Zedellency?'

The secretary had to laugh at me and took the trouble to explain this or that title and especially the forms of address, but I insisted that the titles did not do justice to men. It would surely reflect greater honour on a man to be addressed as 'most friendly' than as 'most worshipful'? And the word 'well-born' was a flat lie, as any baron's mother would tell you if you asked her whether she felt 'well' while her son was being born.

I laughed so much at this that I broke wind with a violence that made both of us start. As if the terrible noise were not enough, it immediately announced its presence to our noses, filling the whole of the room. 'Get out', shouted the secretary.

'Go and join the other pigs in the pigsty. That's where you belong, not talking to decent people.' But faced with the awful stench, he was forced to beat a retreat as well. Thus I put myself in bad odour, as the saying goes, with the secretary, which meant an end to the enjoyable times I had in his office.

Chapter 28

Out of jealousy a man teaches Simplicius soothsaying and another fine art

This misfortune was not at all my fault. The unaccustomed food and medicines they gave me every day to set my shrunken stomach and shrivelled intestines to rights generated many a violent thunderstorm and strong wind in my belly which tormented me severely as they sought to force their way out. I could not imagine there was anything wrong in letting nature have its way down there, especially as it was impossible to resist such a strong internal force in the long run anyway. The hermit had never warned me about this (presumably because we were rarely visited by such uninvited guests), nor had my Da ever forbidden me to let these jokers loose on the world, so that I was in the habit of giving free passage to anything that wanted to get out until, as I have just related, I lost the good-will of the secretary.

The secretary's favour would not have been such a great loss had not a worse misfortune happened to me. I suffered the fate of every honest man who comes to court, where everyone prepares treachery against another, like Goliath against David, the Minotaur against Theseus, the Medusa against Perseus, Circe against Ulysses, Nessus against Hercules, even mothers against their own sons. There was another page besides me, a downright snake in the grass who had been with the governor for a couple of years already. Since we were the same age, I took him to my heart; I imagined myself David and he was my Jonathan. But he was jealous of me because of the great favour the governor showed towards me, which increased with every day. He was afraid I would step into his shoes, and behind my back he eyed me with resentment and looked for ways of tripping me up, hoping that my fall would prevent his own. But my eye was as innocent as my mind, and I confided all my little secrets to him, although since these consisted of nothing but simplicity and piety he could not use them against me.

Once we talked together in bed for a long time before going to sleep and the conversation came round to soothsaying, which he promised he would teach me for nothing. He told me to put my head under the cover, for that, he said, was the way he would teach me the art. I obeyed and lay there eagerly awaiting the arrival of the spirit of soothsaying. 'Strewth! It announced its arrival to my nose and so pungently I had to take my head out from under the cover.

'What's wrong', asked my instructor.

'You farted.'

'There', he said, 'you say sooth. You see, you've learnt the art already.'

I did not take that amiss, for in those days I saw no harm in anything. What I did do was to ask him how he managed to let them off so silently. My companion answered, 'That's easy. You just have to lift up your left leg, like a dog pissing against the corner of a house, and repeat under your breath, Je pète, je pète, je pète, at the same time pressing as hard as you can, and they'll slip out as quietly as if they'd just robbed a safe.'

'Good', I said. 'Then when there's a stench people will assume it's the dogs that were responsible for the foul air, especially if I lift my left leg up nice and high.' If only, I thought, I'd known the art this morning in the secretary's office!

Chapter 29

How Simplicius got two eyes out of one calf's head

The next day the governor gave a princely banquet for his officers and friends because he had received the good news that his side had taken the fortress of Braunfels without the loss of a single man. Like any other servant, it was my duty to help serve the dishes, pour out wine and wait at table with a plate in my hand. A large, fat calf's head (which people say no poor man may eat) was given to me to take up. Because it was well cooked, one of its eyes was hanging out, along with all the bits and pieces, and I found it an attractive and seductive sight, made even more enticing by the fresh smell of the juices and the ginger sprinkled over it. I felt such a craving for it that my mouth began to water. In short, the eye made eyes at my eyes, my nose and my mouth, and seemed to be begging me to stow it away in my starving stomach. I needed no second asking, but followed my desire. As I was walking along I scooped out the eye with a spoon I had been given that very day and did it so neatly, and packed it off to its destination so quickly that no one noticed until the splendid dish was on the table and gave both me and itself away. When he saw that one of the tastiest pieces was missing, the carver gave a start and my master immediately realised why. He had no intention of becoming the butt of gibes about the man whose servants dared serve up a one-eyed calf's head at his banquet. The cook was summoned to the table and interrogated, along with those who had been serving, with the result that poor Simplicius was exposed. It came out that when the calf's head had been given him to bring up, both eyes were still in. What had happened after that no one could say. With what seemed to me a terrifying expression on his face, my master asked me what I had done with the calf's eye. Quickly I whipped my spoon out of my pouch and demonstrated the answer to the

87

question, giving the calf's head the coup de grace and swallowing the second tasty morsel in the twinkling of an eye.

'Par Dieu', said my master, 'that trick tastes better than ten whole calves.' Everyone present applauded the governor's wit and described what I had done out of simplicity as an incredibly clever subterfuge, promising courage and fearless resolve for the future. Not only did I escape punishment by repeating what I had done to deserve it, I was praised by sundry buffoons, sycophants and court jesters for having acted wisely in bringing the two eyes together again so that they could support each other in the way nature intended, both in this world and the next. My master, however, warned me not to try the trick on him again.

Chapter 30

How one can get merry little by little and without realising it end up blind drunk

At this banquet (and I assume it happens at others) the guests came to table like good Christians, saying grace quietly and, to all appearances, very reverently. This reverent silence, as if they were eating in a Capuchin monastery, lasted as long as they were occupied with the soup and first courses. But hardly had each one said 'In God's name' three or four times than it all became much livelier. It is beyond my powers to describe how each man's voice gradually grew louder and louder the longer he spoke; I could perhaps compare the whole company to an orator who starts his speech softly and ends up with a voice like thunder. The servants brought dishes called appetisers, because they were well spiced and were to be eaten before the drinking began, to give the diners a good thirst. The same was true of the *entremets*, which were chosen so that they went well with the drink, to say nothing of all kinds of French *ragoûts* and Spanish *olla podridas*. These dishes were very skilfully prepared and had countless different ingredients, with the result that they were so peppered and spiced, mixed and masked (all to give a good thirst), that the original natural ingredients were completely unrecognisable. Even the Roman epicure, Gnaeus Manlius, coming from Asia as he did and bringing the best cooks with him, would not have recognised them. I wondered whether such dishes might not destroy the senses of a man who indulges in them – and the drink, to encourage which they have mostly been concocted – and change him, perhaps even transform him into a beast?

Who knows, perhaps these were the means Circe used to change Ulysses' companions into swine? I saw these guests gobble up the courses like pigs, swill the wine like cattle, behave like asses and finally spew like dogs. They poured the fine wines of Hochheim, Bacherach and Klingenberg into their bellies from glasses the size of buckets and the effects very quickly made themselves felt higher up, in their heads. Then I saw to my astonishment how they all were changed. Sensible people, who only a short while ago had been in full possession of their faculties, suddenly started acting the fool and saying the silliest things imaginable. The longer the banquet went on, the more stupid their tricks became and the bigger the toasts they drank, so that it seemed as if tricks and toasts were trying to outdo each other until the contest ended up in a wallow of obscenity.

The funniest thing about this was that I had no idea where all this giddiness came from since the effect of wine and even drunkenness itself were unknown to me. It set off all kinds of fantastic ideas in my mind as I thought about it; I could see the strange expressions on their faces but did not know what had caused them. Up to that point each one had emptied his plate with a good appetite, but once their bellies were full they were hard put to it to carry on, like a waggoner who can get along fine with his fresh team on level ground but hardly moves at all going uphill. But once their heads were full as well, this physical incapacity was compensated for by other qualities they had imbibed along with the wine: in the one case boldness, in another the sincere desire to drink a toast to his friend or in a third good old-fashioned German chivalry that will not leave a toast unacknowledged. There came a point, however, when even these noble qualities failed them. Then they started challenging each other to pledge their lords, one of their friends or their mistress by pouring the wine down their throats by the quart. Many paled at the thought and broke out in a cold sweat, but the bumper had to be downed. Eventually they started making a racket with drums, fifes and lutes as each measure was emptied, and let off their pistols at the same time, doubtless because the wine had to take their bellies by storm. I could not work out where they put it all. What I did not know was that even before the wine had had a chance to warm up inside them they very painfully brought it up out of the same orifice down which they had just poured it at great danger to their health.

The pastor was also present at this banquet and, being human like all the rest, had to leave the room. I followed and asked him, 'Pastor, why are the people behaving so strangely? What makes them reel about like that? It seems to me they have taken leave of their senses. They have eaten and drunk their fill. Devil take them, they keep on saying, if they can drink any more, and yet they still don't stop tossing it back. Are they forced to do this or do they squander the wine of their own free will and against God's?'

'My dear child', the pastor replied, 'when the wine comes in the door, a man's wits fly out of the window. This is nothing compared to what is still to come. They will probably not break up until shortly before dawn. Even though their bellies are crammed full they still have a long way to go before they are really merry.'

'But', I said, 'won't their bellies burst if they keep on stuffing so much in? And how can their souls, which are in the likeness of God, remain in such hoggish bodies, where they must feel as if they were imprisoned in the darkest of dungeons, the most verminous of jails, without the least spark of godliness? How can their noble souls allow themselves to be tormented in this way? Is it not as if their senses, which ought to be the instruments of their souls, were buried in the bowels of brute beasts?'

'You just keep quiet', said the pastor, 'unless you want to get a good thrashing. This is not the time for preaching, and if it were, I could do it much better.'

After that I looked on in silence as they wantonly wasted food and drink which could have been used to feed the poor Lazarus languishing at our gates in the form of several hundred refugees from Wetterau, whose hunger was plain for all to see, for the cupboard was bare.

Chapter 31

How the trick Simplicius learnt backfires and he is taught a song with a new beat

As I stood there with a plate in my hand, waiting at table, my mind was plagued with all kinds of strange thoughts and fancies, and my belly refused to leave me in peace either. It kept on rumbling and grumbling to let me know there were some jokers inside that wanted to get out into the fresh air. I thought I would take advantage of the great racket to help conceal the opening of the pass, at the same time using the trick my fellow page had taught me the previous night. Accordingly I lifted up my left thigh as high as I could and pressed with all my might. I was going to repeat the magic words 'Je pète' three times but when, contrary to expectation, the immense load that came ripping out of my backside did so with a resounding blast, I was so startled I did not know what I was doing. I was as terrified as if I were standing on the gallows with the hangman about to put the noose round my neck. This sudden shock was so disconcerting that my own limbs refused to obey me. At the unexpected sound my mouth also rebelled, unwilling to allow my backside the privilege of speaking for me alone. Although born to talk and shout, it was supposed to whisper the words I wanted to say, so no one would hear, but just to spite my backside it said them out loud, yelling as if someone were about to cut my throat. The more booming the blast of wind from below, the louder 'Je pète' rang out from above, as if the entry and exit to my belly were vying with each other to see which could speak with the most thunderous voice.

This brought me some relief in my bowels but also an angry look from my master. The unexpected explosion fairly sobered up his guests, but I was tied to a feeding trough and given such a beating that I can still remember it today, and all because, despite my efforts, I could not hold back my wind. Those were the first blows I received as punishment since I first drew breath because my foul discharge had made that difficult for others. Incense-burners and candles were brought and the guests took out their musk-balls and pomanders, even their snuff-boxes, but the most aromatic perfumes had little effect. As a result of this scene, which I played out better than the best actor in the world, my belly was at peace, but my back throbbed from the beating, the guests had a stench in their nostrils and the servants a great deal of difficulty making the room smell sweet once more.

Chapter 32

Once more deals with nothing but the orgy of drinking and how to get rid of any priests who are there

After all this had been sorted out I had to carry on waiting at table as before. The pastor was still there and people kept urging him to drink like all the rest. He, however, refused to keep pace with all the toasts, saying he had no intention of swilling his drink like an animal. At that one of the hard drinkers there offered to prove that it was he, the pastor, who was drinking like an animal, whilst the boozer himself and all those around were drinking like human beings.

'An animal', he said, 'only drinks as much as it needs, enough to quench its thirst, because it doesn't know what is good and doesn't like wine. We human beings, on the other hand, enjoy having a good drink and letting the noble juice of the vine slip down our throats, as our fathers did before us.'

'That may well be', replied the pastor, 'but it is my duty to avoid excess. One beaker is enough for me.'

'Let it never be said I stopped a man of honour from doing his duty', said the other and had a huge bowl filled with wine, which he then proffered to the pastor who, however, got up and walked away, leaving the man clutching his bucket of wine.

Once he was out of the way things started to get out of hand. It began to look as if this banquet was designed as an opportunity for people to have their revenge on others by getting them drunk, bringing shame on them or playing them some trick or other. Whenever one of them, no longer able to sit, stand or walk, had to be carried out, another would shout, 'That's quits. You got me liquored up like this before, now you've had a taste of your own medicine', and so on. The one that could hold his drink best boasted about it and thought himself no end of a hero.

Eventually they were all reeling around as if they had eaten henbane seeds; they were like the clowns in the carnival, and yet there was no one who thought it comic apart from me. One was singing, another crying; one was laughing, another groaning; one was cursing, another praying; one was shouting, 'Don't give up!' another was beyond speech; one was quiet and peaceful, another wanted to drive the devil out with his bare fists; one was sleeping silently, another gabbling so that no one else could get a word in; one was telling the story of an affair of the heart, another recounting the bloody deeds he had done in battle; a few were talking about the church and spiritual matters, others of politics, reasons of state and the affairs of the Empire. There were those who could not keep still and ran to and fro, others lay on the floor, incapable of moving a muscle, never mind standing up and walking; some were still eating like ploughmen, as if they had been starving for a week, while others were spewing up everything they had eaten during the day. In a word, everything they did was so comic, foolish and strange, and at the same time sinful and godless, that compared with it the stench I had let out, for which I had been so cruelly beaten, seemed nothing more than a joke.

Eventually some serious fighting started at the bottom of the table. They threw glasses, goblets, bowls and plates at each other and used not only their fists but stools, chair-legs, daggers and anything they could lay their hands on, so that the blood was running down over their ears.

Chapter 33

How the governor shot a most foul cat

My master soon put an end to the fighting, and once peace had been restored the master-drinkers took the musicians and women with them to another building, where there was a large room which was dedicated to another kind of folly. My master was not feeling well, either from anger or overeating, and stretched out on a sofa. I let him lie there where he was so that he could rest and sleep, but hardly had I reached the door than he tried to whistle for me, but nothing came out. Then he called to me, though all he managed to say was 'Simply'. I ran over to where he was and saw he was rolling his eyes like an animal being slaughtered. I stood there like a dunce, not knowing what needed to be done. The governor pointed to the sideboard and gabbled, 'Br-bra-bring tha-that, you s-so-son of a bitch, fetch the ba-ba-basin, I have to-to shoo-shoo-shoot a cat.' I rushed over and brought the wash-basin and by the time I got to him his cheeks were bulging like a trumpeter's. He quickly grabbed me by the arm and made me stand so I had to hold the basin right in front of his mouth, which suddenly burst open with painful retching, emptying a stream of such foul slimy stuff into the said basin that I almost fainted from the unbearable stench, especially since (if you will forgive my mentioning it) a few gobbets splashed up into my face. I almost followed suit, but when I saw how pale he had gone I was so afraid his soul would depart along with the vomit that my own nausea was forgotten. He broke out into a cold sweat and his face looked like that of a dying man. But he recovered almost immediately and sent me to bring fresh water so he could rinse out his wine-skin of a belly.

After that he ordered me to take the cat away. Lying there in the silver basin, it did not strike me as disgusting; it looked rather like a bowl full of appetisers for four men. I could not bring myself simply to pour it away, especially since I knew my master had not had anything bad in his stomach but exquisite, delicious vol-au-vents and all kinds of roasts – poultry, game other meats – which were all still clearly recognisable in the basin. I hurried off with it, but did not know where to take it or what to do with it. My master was the last person I could ask, so I took this splendid feast to the steward and asked him what I should do with the cat.

'Take it to the tanner, you fool', he said, 'so he can tan its hide.'

When I asked where I could find the tanner, he realised how simple I was and said, 'No, take it to the doctor so he can examine it and see what our lord's state of health is like.'

I would have gone on this April-fool's errand if the steward had not been afraid of the consequences. He told me to take the stuff to the kitchen with orders that the maids should put it on one side and season it well. This I did in all earnestness and was heartily mocked by those hussies for my pains.

Chapter 34

How Simplicius spoilt the dance

By the time I had managed to get rid of my basin my master was just going out. I followed him towards a building where I saw men and women, married and single, jumping about together in a large room so that the whole place was seething. There was such a stamping and caterwauling I thought they had all gone mad, for I could not imagine what the point of all this frantic frenzy was. I found the sight so frightening, so horrifying and terrifying that my hair stood on end. The only explanation I could find was that they had all taken leave of their senses. As we came closer I saw that it was the guests from our banquet, and they had certainly still been in their right minds that morning. 'My God', I thought, 'what do these poor people think they are doing? They must be suffering from an attack of collective insanity.' Then it occurred to me that it might be some fiendish spirits that had disguised themselves to mock the whole human race with their wild prancing and monkeyish behaviour. They would surely never act in a way so unbecoming of human beings if they had human souls and God's likeness within them.

As my master went into the house and entered the room the frenzy was just ceasing, apart from a bobbing and bowing of heads and such a scratching and scraping of feet on the floor that I thought they were trying to erase the footmarks they had made during their wild stamping. From the sweat pouring down their faces and their puffing and panting I could tell that it had been hard work. Yet the happy expressions on their faces indicated they did not find the exertion unpleasant.

I dearly wanted to know the reason for all this madness, so I asked my companion and bosom friend, the one who had recently taught me the art of soothsaying, what was the meaning of this frenzy, the purpose of this furious skipping and strutting. He told me the truth of it was that all those present had come to an agreement to demolish the floor by stamping on it.

'Why do you think', he said, 'they're in such a hurry? Can't you see they've already smashed the windows to amuse themselves? The floor's for it next.'

'Good Lord', I replied, 'then we'll all go down with it and break our necks as we fall!'

'Yes', said my companion, 'that's what they're aiming to do, and they couldn't care less. You'll see, as soon as it gets really dangerous each one will grab a pretty woman or girl. They say that couples that fall down holding each other don't get hurt at all.'

I believed this and was seized with such fear I might be killed that I did not know what to do. And when the musicians, whom I had not noticed until then, started playing and the men rushed over to the women, like soldiers dashing to their posts when the drum sounds, and each grabbed one by the hand, I could already see the floor giving way and myself and many others breaking our necks. But when they started jumping up and down, making the whole building shake, because the band had struck up a lively tune, I thought, 'This is the end'. I assumed the whole building would suddenly collapse and was so terrified I promptly clutched like a bear the arm of a lady of high rank and even higher virtue, with whom my master happened to be conversing, and clung on to her like a burr. When she, not knowing the strange ideas I had in my head, kept trying to pull her arm away, I became desperate and started to scream as if someone were murdering me. As if that were not enough, something slipped out into my trousers which gave off an awful stench, the like of which I had not smelt for a long time.

·All at once the music stopped and the dancers and their partners stood still. The noble lady, to whose arm I was clinging, was highly offended because she thought my master had ordered me to do it to make a laughing-stock of her. Therefore the governor ordered me to be beaten and then locked up somewhere, since this was not the first trick I had played on him that day. The orderlies who were to carry out the punishment not only took pity on me, they were unwilling to come too close because of the stench, so that they omitted the beating and shut me up in the goose-coop under the staircase. Since that time I have often reflected on this matter and have come to the conclusion that excrement which is emitted due to fear and terror gives off a much worse smell than the product of a strong laxative.

Book II

Chapter 1

How a goose and a gander mated

While I was penned up in my goose-coop I worked out the things I said about dancing and drunkenness in my book *Black and White: The Satirical Pilgrim,* published a few years ago, so that it is unnecessary to waste words on them here. I feel I must point out, however, that even at the time I did wonder whether the dancers would really have demolished the floor with their wild stamping or whether I had been the victim of a hoax.

Now I want to continue with my story and tell you how I got out of my goose-jail again. I had been squatting on my heels there for three whole hours, until the *praeludium veneris* (the decorous dancing, I should have said) was over, when someone crept up and started rattling the bolt. I was listening as carefully as any sow pissing into water, but the fellow at the door not only opened it, he slipped in as quickly as I would have liked to slip out. What is more, he dragged a woman in with him, leading her by the hand, just as I had seen them do when they were dancing. I had no idea what was going to happen, but by then I had had so many strange adventures that day that my simple mind had become accustomed to them and I had decided to bear everything fate would send in uncomplaining silence. Accordingly I pressed up against the door in fear and trembling, expecting the worst.

Immediately a whispering started up between the two. I could understand nothing of what was said except that one party was complaining of the awful smell in the place while the other was trying to make the first forget about it. 'Be assured, o most beautiful creature', he said, 'that it pains me to the heart that a malevolent fate has not granted us a more becoming place to enjoy the fruits of love. But despite that, I can truly say that your sweet presence makes this wretched hole more exquisite than the most delightful paradise.' After that I heard kissing and observed strange postures, but since I did not know what it all meant, I continued to remain as silent as a mouse. When, however, a funny noise started up and the coop, which only consisted of boards nailed together under the staircase, began to creak and the woman to moan as if she were in pain, I thought that these must be two of the crazy people who had been trying to demolish the floor and had come here to do the same to my prison and kill me. The moment this thought came into my head I opened the door, to escape being killed, and shot out with a fearful yell which was naturally as loud as that which brought me there in the first place. I did, however, have my wits sufficiently about me to lock the door behind me and make for the open door of the house.

That was the first wedding I had ever been present at in my life, though I had not been invited. That meant I did not have to give a present, but later on the bridegroom did present me with a whacking bill, which I paid in full.

I am not telling this story, reader, just to make you laugh, but so that my history will be complete and also that you may consider carefully what the fruits of dancing can be. It is certainly true, I believe, that during the dance many a bargain is struck which will later bring shame on a whole family.

Chapter 2

On the merits of a good bath at the right time

Although I had managed to escape from the goose-coop, I now realised the full extent of my misfortune, for I had shitted my trousers and did not know what to do about it. Everything was quiet and everyone asleep in my master's lodgings, so that I dared not approach the sentry standing by the door; they refused to let me into the main guard-house because I smelt so awful, and it was too cold for me to stay out in the street. I was at a loss what to do. It was already well past midnight when it occurred to me to seek refuge with the pastor I have mentioned so often. This seeming a good idea, I knocked at the door and kept on for so long that eventually the maid, somewhat annoyed, let me in. When she smelt the load I brought with me (her long nose immediately ferreted out my secret) she became even angrier and started to scold me, which her master, who by this time had more or less slept off the effects of the banquet, soon heard. He called the pair of us to his bedside. His nostrils twitched as he quickly got to the bottom of my problem and said that, despite the calendar, there was never a better time to have a bath than when in the state I was in at the moment. He ordered the maid to get my trousers washed before daybreak and to hang them by the stove in the sitting room. He also told her to find a bed for me, for he could see I was numb with cold.

Hardly was I warmed up than it started to get light and the pastor appeared at my bedside to find out what had happened to me. (My shirt and trousers still being wet, I could hardly get up and go to his room.) I told him everything, beginning with the fine art my fellow page had taught me and how disastrously it had turned out. Next I described how, after he had gone, the guests had taken leave of their senses and (as my comrade also explained to me) had decided to demolish the floor of the building. I told him of the dreadful fear that had seized me, the way I had tried to save myself from being killed and how I had been locked in the goose-coop for it. I also told him everything I had seen and heard of the pair who had set me free and how I had locked them in the coop in my place.

'Oh Simplicius', the pastor said, 'Your prospects are as good as nil. You had a fine situation, but I'm very much afraid you've thrown it away. Now out of that bed as quick as you can and get out of my house before they find you here, otherwise I might fall into your master's disfavour along with you.'

So I had to go off in my wet clothes, having learnt how well regarded by all and sundry a man is when he has his master's favour and how looked down upon when he has lost it. I went to my master's quarters, where everyone was still sleeping like a log apart from the cook and a couple of maids. The latter were cleaning up the room where the banquet had been held the previous evening while the former was preparing breakfast or, rather, a cold collation from the left-overs. First I came upon the maids. Parts of the room were covered in broken glass from the goblets and window-panes, others were full of what the guests had evacuated, both from above and from below, and in some places there were such large pools of spilt wine and beer that the floor was like a map on which you could have drawn various oceans, islands and continents. The stench in the whole room was far worse than in my goose-coop, so I didn't stay there long. I went to the kitchen to dry off my clothes at the fire while I was still wearing them, waiting, in fear and trembling, to find out what fate would have in store for me once my master had woken up. At the same time I reflected on the folly and senselessness of the world and went over in my mind everything that had happened to me during the previous day and night, as well as the things I had seen and heard. The result was that I came to see the hermit's life of poverty and indigence as a happy one and wished that both he and I could return to our former situation.

Chapter 3

The other page gets his due reward for his instruction and Simplicius is elected fool

After my master had got up he sent his bodyguard to fetch me from the coop, but he returned with the news that he had found the door open and a hole cut behind the bolt with a knife, by which means the prisoner had let himself out.

However, before this news reached him my master learnt from others that I had been in the kitchen for a long time. Meanwhile the servants had been sent running to and fro to invite the guests of the previous evening to breakfast. Among these was the pastor, who was summoned to appear sooner than the others because my master wanted to talk to him about me before they sat down to table. His first question was whether the pastor considered me sly or stupid; whether I was very simple-minded or very devious. He told him everything about my unseemly behaviour the previous day, and how it had been taken amiss by his guests, who thought it had been done deliberately to make fun of them. He went on to relate how he had had me locked up in the goose-coop to stop me doing anything else to bring him into disrepute, but that I had broken out and was now taking my ease in the kitchen, like a young lord who was too fine to wait on him. Never in his life had he had so many tricks played on him as I had done in the presence of all those respectable people. Since I had behaved so foolishly, the only thing he could think of was to have me soundly thrashed and send me packing.

The guests had gradually assembled whilst my master was complaining about me and when he had finished the pastor answered that if the governor would have the patience to hear him out he would tell him some things about me which would not only reveal my innocence but also correct the wrong impression those who were disgusted by my behaviour had of me.

While they were talking about me in the room above, down below in the kitchen Ensign Madcap, who was the one I had left locked up together with his lady in my stead, got me to agree, by threats and a silver coin, to keep quiet about his exploits.

The tables were set and, as the previous day, well supplied with food and diners. Yesterday's carousers were all in a devil of a state and to put their heads and stomachs back in order were now sipping wines mixed with fruits, spices and bitter herbs. All they could talk about was themselves and how they had drunk the others under the table. There was not one of them would confess he had been blind drunk, although the previous evening some had claimed the devil should take them if they could drink any more. Some did say they had been quite merry, but others maintained that no one got blind drunk any longer since it had become the fashion to be merry. However, once they had tired of recounting and listening to their own follies, it was Simplicius's turn to suffer. The governor himself reminded the pastor of his promise to recount all the comic things that had happened.

First of all he asked them to forgive him if he had to use words unbecoming his cloth. Then he explained the natural causes of the gases which plagued my guts, through which I had given such offence to the secretary in his office, and went on to describe how I had been taught, along with soothsaying, a trick to contain them, which had turned out very badly. He pointed out how strange the dancing must have appeared to me, since I had never seen it before, and recounted the explanation I had been given by my fellow page, which was what had made me grab the noble lady and got me locked up in the coop.

All this he narrated in such a prim and proper manner that the guests almost split their sides laughing. At the same time he made such humble apology for my simplicity and ignorance that I was restored to my master's favour and allowed to wait at table. But the pastor refused to say anything of what I had seen in the coop and how I had been released from it because he thought that might offend some old maids (of both sexes) among them who thought clergymen should always be strait-laced and straight-faced. My master, on the other hand, to amuse his guests asked me what I had given my fellow page in return for teaching me such fine tricks. When I answered, 'Nothing', he said, 'Then I will see he gets his due reward for his instruction' and had him tied to a feeding trough and thrashed just as I had been the previous day after I had tried out his trick and discovered that I was the one who had been tricked.

By now my master had enough proof of my simplicity and decided to play on me for his own and his guests' entertainment. He realised the musicians had no chance as long as I was to hand; with my simple ideas everyone thought me better than a whole orchestra. He asked me why I had cut a hole in the door of the goose-coop. I answered that someone else must have done it.

'Who then?' he asked.

'Perhaps the man who came in while I was there.'

'Who came in while you were there?'

I replied, 'I'm not allowed to tell anyone.'

My master, being quick-witted, saw the way to trap me into revealing the truth. All of a sudden, catching me unawares, he asked who had forbidden me to tell anyone and I immediately answered, 'Ensign Madcap.'

By the way everyone laughed I realised I must have let the cat out of the bag and Ensign Madcap, who was sitting among the guests at the table, went as red as a beetroot. I refused to say any more until I had his permission, but all it took was a nod from my master to Ensign Madcap, in place of an order, and I could tell them everything I knew. My master then asked me what Ensign Madcap had been doing in my goose-coop.

I replied, 'He brought a young lady in with him.'

'What did he do after that', my master said.

'It seemed to me that he wanted to relieve himself in the coop', I replied.

'And what did the young lady do at that?' my master asked. 'Was she not embarrassed?'

'Certainly not, sir' I said. 'She lifted up her dress in order (you will surely, esteemed reader, who so love decency, virtue and morality, forgive my vulgar pen for writing down the coarse words I used at the time) to have a shit.'

At this all present burst out into such loud laughter that my master could no longer hear me, never mind ask any more questions. And that was quite right and proper, otherwise the respectable maiden (sic) might have been publicly shamed.

Then the steward told the assembled company how I had recently come back from the ramparts saying I knew where thunder and lightning came from. I had seen, I said, huge beams, hollowed out inside, on half waggons. Into these they had stuffed onion seeds together with an iron turnip with the root cut off, then tickled the beams a little with a pronged spear and out of the front poured smoke, thunder and infernal flames. More such comic stories were brought out, so that they did nothing during the whole meal but talk and laugh about me. This resulted in a general consensus, which was to lead to my downfall, that if they continued to do their best to make a fool of me, in time I would develop into a fine jester, fit to be set before the greatest rulers and capable of bringing a smile to the lips of a dying man.

Chapter 4

Of the man who provides the money, and of the military service Simplicius performed for the Swedish crown, through which he was given the surname Simplicissimus

While they were guzzling and gorging as they had done the day before, the guard brought a note for the governor announcing the arrival of a commissioner sent by the Swedish War Council to review the garrison and inspect the fortress. He was already at the gate, which put a damper on the festivities. The joyful laughter died away like the wail from a punctured set of bagpipes and both musicians and guests vanished like tobacco smoke, leaving only their smell behind. My master set off for the gate with the adjutant, who carried the keys, a detachment of the main guard and many lanterns in order to admit the old inkslinger, as he called him, himself.

He swore he wished the devil would break the man's neck into a thousand pieces before he got into the fortress, but as soon as he had let him in and greeted him on the inner drawbridge he was almost holding his stirrup – indeed he did so! – to show he was the commissioner's humble servant. They were both so keen to demonstrate their respect for each other that when the commissioner dismounted to accompany my master to his lodgings on foot each tried to insist on walking on the left.

'Oh', I thought to myself, 'what a father of lies rules mankind, always using men to dupe each other.'

We were approaching the guardhouse and the sentry called out, 'Who goes there?' although he could see it was my master. He refused to answer, wanting to leave the honour to his guest, so the sentry repeated his challenge even louder. Finally the commissioner replied to the last 'Who goes there?' with, '*The man who gives the money!*' They passed the sentry and since I was some way behind them I heard the sentry, who was a new recruit who had formerly been a well-off young farmer's son from the Vogelsberg, mutter, 'A lying customer you are. "The man who gives the money"! A bloodsucker who takes the money, more like! You've squeezed so much money out of me that I would to God you were struck down dead before you left the town.'

From that moment I concluded that this foreign gentleman in the velvet doublet must be a holy man, for not only did the curses run off him like water off a duck's back, all those who hated him treated him with respect, love and kindness. That very same night he was served a right royal meal, made blind drunk and put to bed in a magnificent four-poster.

At the review next day everything was at sixes and sevens. Even a simpleton like me managed to deceive the clever commissioner (for they do not appoint innocent children to positions like that). It took me a mere hour to learn what was necessary, which was to count up to five and nine while beating a drum. Since I was too small to pass for a musketeer, they decked me out in a borrowed uniform (my page's knee-breeches being unsuitable for the purpose) and gave me a borrowed drum (doubtless because I myself was a borrowed child) with which I successfully came through the inspection. They did not trust my simple mind to be able to remember an assumed name, to which I would step forward and answer, so I had to remain Simplicius. The governor himself chose my surname and had me entered in the roll as Simplicius

Simplicissimus, thus making me the first of my line, like a whore's bastard, even though, by his own admission, I resembled his sister. I retained both first name and surname afterwards, until I learnt my true name. As Simplicius Simplicissimus I played my role pretty well, to my master's advantage and only minor detriment to the Swedish crown. And that was all the military service I performed for Sweden in my whole life, so that her enemies have little cause to view me with hostility.

Chapter 5

How Simplicius was dragged down into hell by four devils and treated to Spanish wine

After the commissioner had departed again, the pastor I have mentioned so often called me secretly to his lodgings and said, 'O Simplicius, I feel sorry for your youth and your future unhappiness moves me to pity. Listen, child. I know for certain that your master is determined to deprive you of all sense and turn you into a fool. For this purpose he is already having a suit of clothes made and tomorrow you must attend the school where you are to lose what sense you have. There you will doubtless be so horribly tormented that, assuming neither God nor natural means can prevent it, you must surely lose your wits. Since, however, that is an unpleasant and dangerous business, and for the sake of the pious hermit and your own innocence, I have decided out of true Christian charity to give you advice and other necessary assistance, namely this medicine. Follow my instructions and take this powder, which will so strengthen your brain and memory that you will come through it all with no damage to your reason. Here too is an ointment to rub on your temples, your spine, your neck and your nostrils. Use both of these in the evening, before you go to sleep, since you will never be certain you may not be fetched from your bed at any time. But make sure no one hears about my warning or sees the medicines I have given you, otherwise we will both be in trouble. And while you are suffering this outrageous treatment take care not to believe everything they tell you; at the same time pretend you do believe everything and say little, so that your instructors will not notice they are wasting their breath. If you don't, your torment will be changed to something I don't know about. But after you have put on your fool's coat and plumes come and see me again so that I can give you more advice. In the meantime I will pray to God that he will keep you healthy in both mind and body.' Thus having finished, he gave me the powder and ointment and I went back home with them.

And everything turned out as the pastor had predicted. I had hardly fallen asleep when four men disguised in frightening devil's masks came into my bedroom and started jumping about like acrobats and carnival clowns. One was holding a red-hot hook, one a torch. The other two set about me, dragged me out of bed, danced up and down with me for a while and forced me to put on my clothes. I, however, pretended I thought they were genuine devils and started shouting for help at the top of my voice and behaving as if I were frightened to death. They announced that I had to go with them and tied a cloth round my head so that I could neither hear, see nor shout. They took me by a roundabout route, up and down many stairs, ending up in a cellar in which a large fire was burning and where they untied the cloth and started to toast me in Spanish wine and malmsey. They believed they had persuaded me I was dead and in the depths of hell, for I deliberately behaved as if I believed all the lies they told me.

'Go on', they said, 'have a good drink, since you have to stay with us for ever. If you refuse to join in with us you'll end up in that fire.'

The poor devils were trying to disguise their voices so I wouldn't recognise them but I immediately realised they were my master's orderlies. However, I didn't show I'd recognised them and laughed up my sleeve that I had made fools of these fellows who thought they were fooling me. I drank my share of the Spanish wine, but they downed more than I did since such heavenly nectar rarely came the way of the likes of them. I swear they would have become drunk sooner than I, but when the time seemed right I began to stagger and reel, as I had seen my master's guests do recently, and refused any more drink, pretending to want only to sleep. At this they prodded me with their hooks, which they kept putting in the fire, and chased me to all four corners of the room, so that it looked as if they had taken leave of their senses themselves. They wanted to make me drink more, or at least not to sleep, and when I fell down during the chase, which I often did deliberately, they picked me up and pretended they were going to throw me on the fire.

They treated me as a falconer treats the falcon, keeping it awake so that it will respond more quickly to its training. This was what I found most difficult to bear. I could probably have outlasted them as far as drunkenness and sleepiness were concerned, but they did not stay there all the time, taking turns instead, so that I necessarily came off worst. Three days and two nights I spent in that smoky cellar, with no other light than the glow of the fire. My head started to ring and throb fit to burst so that finally I had to think up some trick to get rid of the torment along with my tormentors. Since I needed to relieve myself anyway, I took a lesson from the fox that urinates in the dogs' faces when it can no longer outrun them; at the same time I tickled my throat with my finger to make myself vomit, which I did to such effect that the cellar was filled with a foul stench that even my devils couldn't bear to be near me. So then they wrapped me up in a sheet and thrashed me so savagely that it felt as if all my internal organs were falling out, and my soul along with them. Eventually they knocked me senseless and I lay there as if dead, so that I have no idea what else they did to me.

Chapter 6

How Simplicius went to heaven and was turned into a calf

When I came to I was no longer in the gloomy cellar with the devils, but in a splendid room and in the hands of three of the foulest old women that ever walked the earth. At first, as I opened my eyes just a little, I thought they must be fiendish spirits. If, however, at that time I had already read the old heathen poets, I would have assumed they were the Eumenides, or at least one particular one I would have taken to be Tisiphone come from the underworld to rob me, like Athamas, of my wits, since I was aware that I was there to be turned into a fool.

She had eyes like two will-o'-the-wisps and between them a long, skinny hawk's nose, the tip of which reached down to her lower lip at least. I could only see two teeth in her mouth, but these were so perfectly long, round and thick that in shape they were like a ring-finger, in colour like the gold of the ring itself. In fact, there was enough ivory there for a whole mouthful of teeth, only it was poorly distributed. Her face was like Spanish leather and her white hair hung down in weird tousled knots because she had just been brought from her bed. Her long breasts I can only compare to two limply dangling cow's bladders from which two thirds of the air had leaked out; at the end of each hung a dark brown spigot half the length of my finger. Truly, a terrifying sight which would, however, have made an excellent antidote to the inordinate lust of lecherous goats. The other two were no more beautiful, except that they had snub monkey's noses and were slightly more decently dressed.

When I had recovered from the shock, I realised that one was our dish-washer, the other two orderlies' wives. I pretended I was unable to move, though I was genuinely paralysed when these honest grannies proceeded to strip me stark naked and clean me up like a baby. They were very gentle about it and showed great patience and sympathy for me, so that I almost told them the truth. But I said to myself, 'No, Simplicius, never trust an old woman. Look on it as a triumph if you, young as you are, can deceive three crafty old hags a man could use to catch the devil himself in open ground. Look on it as an experience which shows there is hope you may go on to greater things when you are older.'

Once the three had finished they put me in a magnificent bed, where I immediately fell asleep. They then left, taking with them their buckets and washing equipment as well as my clothes and all the filth they had cleaned off me. I reckon I must have slept uninterruptedly for more than twenty-four hours and when I woke up there were two pretty boys with wings standing by the bed, all decked out in white gowns, taffeta ribbons, pearls, jewels, gold chains and other eye-catching trappings. One was holding a gilded basin full of biscuits, sweets, marzipan and other confectionery, the other a goblet. These two claimed to be angels and tried to persuade me I was in heaven, having survived purgatory and escaped both the devil and his mother. I should ask, they said, for anything my heart desired; they had sufficient supplies of whatever I might want or, if not, it was in their power to procure it. I was tormented by thirst and, seeing the goblet, asked only for a drink, which they were more than willing to give me. However, it wasn't wine, but a sweet-tasting sleeping draught which I drank down in one gulp and fell back to sleep as its warmth spread through my veins.

The next day I woke up again (otherwise I would still be sleeping) to find myself no longer in the bed, nor in the splendid chamber, but imprisoned in my goose-coop once more, where it was horribly dark, as it had been in the cellar. What is more, I was wearing a suit of clothes made out of calfskin with the rough side on the outside. The trousers were tight-fitting, in the Polish or Swabian fashion, and the jacket of an even more clownish cut. A headpiece like a monk's cowl had been pulled over my head; it was adorned with a splendid pair of donkey's ears. I had to laugh at my own misfortune. I could tell from the nest and feathers I had been provided with what kind of queer bird I was supposed to be. That was the point at which I first started thinking about how I might turn it to my best advantage. I decided to play the fool as foolishly I could, at the same time waiting patiently to see what fate had in store for me.

Chapter 7

How Simplicius reconciled himself to
the state of a brute beast

I could easily have got out using the hole the mad ensign had made in the door, but since I was to be a fool, I decided not to. I not only played the fool who has not the wit to get out of his own accord, I even behaved like a hungry calf that wants its mother and my loud mooing soon attracted the attention of those who had been set to keep an ear open for me. Two soldiers came up to the coop and asked who was in it. 'You fools', I answered, 'can't you hear that there's a calf in here.' They opened up the coop and pulled me out with great expressions of surprise that a calf could talk. They were about as convincing in their roles as a novice actor with forced gestures is at representing the character he is supposed to be playing. I kept feeling they needed my help to act out their farce. They discussed among themselves what to do and decided that the best idea would be to offer me to the governor, who would give them more for me, being a calf that could speak, than they would get from the butcher. They asked me how things were and I answered, 'Pretty rotten.'

'Why?' they asked.

'Because the custom here seems to be to shut up honest calves in goose-coops', I said. 'Surely you fellows must realise that if I am to grow into a proper ox I must be reared in a manner appropriate to a decent young bullock.'

After this brief exchange they led me across the street to the governor's lodgings. A large crowd of boys followed us and since they joined me in mooing like a calf a blind man would have assumed from the noise that a herd of calves was being driven along the street. To the eye, however, it looked like a pack of fools, young and old.

So I was presented to the governor by the two soldiers as if they had just captured me while out foraging. He gave them a small reward and promised me the best of everything if I were to stay with him. 'Pull the other one!', I thought to myself, but I said, 'Certainly, sir, but I must not be shut up in that goose-coop. We calves can't stand that kind of treatment if we are to grow up into fine beasts.'

The governor promised me better quarters and thought no end of himself for having made such a splendid fool out of me. I for my part thought, 'Just you wait, sir. I have survived the ordeal and it has only served to toughen me up. Now let's see which of us can put on the best act to the other.'

Just then a farmer who had fled to the town was driving his cattle to the drinking trough. As soon as I saw them I left the governor and ran towards the cows, mooing like a calf as if I wanted to suck at their udders. But even though I was wearing their kind of skin they were more frightened of me than of a wolf and shied and scattered as quickly as if they had trodden on a hornets' nest in August. The farmer could not get the herd back together again, to the great amusement of the crowd of people which immediately gathered to watch this cavalcade of fools. My master laughed fit to burst and finally said, 'One fool makes a hundred more.' And I thought to myself, 'If the cap fits . . . '

Just as from that time on everyone called me the Calf, I had a special mocking nickname for each and every one of them. Most people, and my master in particular, found them very appropriate for I christened each according to his qualities. To put it in a nutshell, in general people considered me a simple-minded idiot and I thought everyone a clever fool. In my opinion that is the way of the world: every man is happy with his own wits and imagines he is the cleverest of all.

My prank with the farmer's cattle made a short morning even shorter, for it was around the time of the winter solstice. I waited on my master during the midday meal as before, at the same time getting up to all sorts of strange tricks. When it was my turn to eat no one could get any human food or drink down me at all, all I wanted was grass, which was not to be had at that time of the year. My master had two small calfskins brought from the butcher's and dressed up two small boys in them. He got them to sit at table beside me and for the first course gave us winter salad and told us to tuck in. He had a live calf brought in and got them to put salt on the salad to encourage it to eat it. I stared at this, as if in astonishment, but those standing around urged me to join in.

'It's nothing new', they said, seeing that the fare left me unmoved, 'for calves to eat flesh, fish, cheese, butter and other things. What? Sometimes they get themselves blind drunk too! The beasts know what's good for them nowadays. It's gone so far', they added, 'that there's only a tiny difference between them and humans, and you insist on being the only one who won't join in?'

This argument persuaded me, all the more because I was hungry and not because I had already seen for myself how humans could be more swinish than swine, more savage than lions, more lecherous than goats, more envious than dogs, more headstrong than horses, more uncouth than donkeys, more drunken than newts, more cunning than foxes, more voracious than wolves, more mischievous than monkeys and more poisonous than snakes and toads. They did not even have the innocence of a calf; the only difference between them and brute beasts was in their shape, and yet they all ate human food. So I ate my fill with my two fellow calves, and if a stranger had seen us together at table he would surely have thought Circe had come back to life to turn human beings into animals again, while in fact it was my master who practised that art. My supper was served in the same way as my midday meal and just as my table-mates, or parasites, had to eat with me to encourage me to eat, so they had to accompany me to bed, since my master would not allow me to spend the night in the cow-shed, which I would have done to fool those who imagined they had made a fool out of me.

I came to the conclusion that the Good Lord gives each person sufficient wits to survive in the station to which He has called them. Some people, whether they can put 'Dr' in front of their name or not, vainly imagine they alone know it all, but there are as many clever fish in the sea as ever came out of it.

Chapter 8

*Of some people's marvellous memory and
other people's forgetfulness*

By the time I woke up in the morning my two becalfed bedfellows had already gone, so I got up and when the adjutant came to fetch the keys for the city gates I slipped out of the house to go and see the pastor. I told him everything that had happened, how I had been through both heaven and hell. When he saw that I had qualms of conscience about deceiving so many people, especially my master, by pretending to be a fool, he said, 'You don't need to worry about that. The foolish world wants to be deceived. Seeing they have left you with your wits, use them to your own advantage, imagine yourself a phoenix that has gone through the fire, from lack of understanding to understanding, and has been born again to a new life. But do not forget that you are not out of the wood yet. That fool's cap you have on is still a danger to your reason and the times are so strange that no one can say whether you will escape from it with your life or not. A person can run down to hell quickly enough, but getting out again takes a great deal of sweat and toil. You are not yet man enough to deal with the danger you face, not by a long chalk, even though you might imagine you are. You are going to need more caution and understanding than you did when you had no idea what understanding – or the lack of it – was. Do not put too much trust in your own abilities, wait for things to change of their own accord.'

His changed manner towards me was deliberate. I imagine he could tell from my expression I thought no end of myself for having managed to survive through a combination of his advice and my masterly deceit. For my part, I suspected from the look on his face that he was sick and tired of me. And indeed, what did he get out of his acquaintance with me? So I changed my tune and thanked him for the excellent medicines he had given me to keep me in my right mind. I even made impossible promises and said I would pay him back everything I owed him. This was more to his taste and soon put him in a different mood. He praised his medicines and went on to tell me about the art of mnemonics, invented by Simonides Melicertes and perfected through the efforts of Metrodorus Scepticus, who could teach people to remember everything they had heard or read simply by repeating one word. All of which, he said, would not have been possible without the medicines to strengthen the mind that he had given me.

'Yes, my dear pastor', I thought to myself, 'I have read about Metrodorus's art of memory in the books you lent the hermit. And quite different things they said.' But I was was not so foolish as to say that. To tell the truth, it was only in becoming a fool that I found my wits and started to watch my tongue.

The pastor went on to tell me how Cyrus could call each of his 30,000 soldiers by name, Lucius Scipio all the citizens of Rome by theirs and Cineas, Pyrrhus's ambassador, could repeat the names of all the senators and nobles the day after his arrival in Rome. 'Mithridates, King of Pontus and Bithynia', he said, 'ruled over peoples speaking twenty-two different languages and could dispense justice and even speak to them all in their own language. The learned Greek, Charmides, could tell people anything they wanted to know from any book in the whole library if he had read it just once. Ravisius reports that Lucius Seneca could repeat 2,000 names in the order they had been spoken and repeat two hundred lines of poetry recited by two hundred different pupils, starting with the last and going back to the first. Esdras, as Eusebius writes, knew the Pentateuch by heart and could dictate all five books word by word to the scribes. Themistocles learnt Persian in a single year. Crassus could speak the five different dialects of Greek in Asia Minor and dispense justice to his subjects in each. Julius Caesar could read, dictate and give audience all at the same time. I will pass over Hadrian, Portius Latronus and all the other Romans and just remind you that St. Jerome knew Hebrew, Chaldaean, Greek, Persian, Median, Arabic and Latin. The hermit, Antony of Thebes, knew the Bible by heart just from hearing it read aloud. And Colerus, following Marcus Antonius Muretus, writes of a Corsican who, having heard 6,000 names, could repeat them in the correct order.

I am only telling you this', he continued, 'so that you will not think it impossible for a person's memory to be strengthened and preserved by medicine, just as there are many ways in which it can be weakened or even destroyed. Pliny the Elder writes, in book seven of his *Natural History*, that there is no faculty in man so feeble as memory; through illness, fright, fear, worry or distress it can lose much of its strength or even disappear entirely. We read of a scholar in Athens who forgot everything he had learnt, even the ABC, after a rock had fallen on his head. Another, through illness, forgot his servant's name, and Messala Valerius Corvinus, who had previously had a good memory, could not even remember his own name. Hans Scratch, in the sixtieth folio of his *Fasciculus Historiarum* (which sounds as pretentious as if it were written by Pliny himself) tells of a priest who drank the blood from his own veins, which resulted in him forgetting how to read or write, although his memory was otherwise unaffected; when, one year later, he drank the same blood at the same place and the same hour, he found he could read and write again. More credible is what Johann Weiher claims in book three of his *De praestigiis daemonum*, namely that if you eat bear's brains you will imagine you have become a bear yourself, quoting the example of a Spanish nobleman who, after he had eaten some, ran about in the wild, thinking he was a bear. My dear Simplicius, if your master had known that art you would more likely have been transformed into a bear, like Callisto, than into a bull, like Jupiter.'

The pastor told a lot more of this sort, gave me some more of his medicine and instructed me how to behave in future. With that I went back home, taking more than a hundred young boys with me who ran behind, bellowing like calves. My master, who had just got up, ran to the window and, seeing so many fools at once, was gracious enough to laugh heartily at them.

Chapter 9

Back-handed praise of a fair lady

As soon as I got back to the house I had to go to the drawing room, for some noble ladies were visiting my master and wanted to see and hear such a fine fool. I stood there like a deaf-mute so that one of them — it was the one I had grabbed at the dance — said she had been told this calf could speak, but now saw that it was not true. I replied, 'For my part I thought that monkeys couldn't speak, but from what I hear now that is not true.'

'What?' said my master. 'You think these ladies are monkeys?'

'If they are not', I replied, 'they will soon become monkeys. I didn't intend to become a calf, and yet I have.'

My master asked me how I could tell they were about to turn into monkeys and I replied, 'Our monkey has a bare backside, and these ladies bare their bosoms, which other maidens keep covered.'

'You piece of mischief', said my master, 'you are a foolish calf and you speak as you are. These ladies quite rightly show what is worth seeing, but monkeys go naked because they have no clothes. You had better make up for your offence quickly or I'll have you whipped and let the dogs chase you to the goose-coop, just as we do with recalcitrant calves. Come now, let us hear if you can praise a lady properly.'

At that I looked the lady up, from toe to top, and down, from top to toe, with an adoring gaze, as if I were about to ask for her hand in marriage. Finally I said, 'Master, I can see what's wrong. It's all that wretched tailor's fault. He's sewn the parts that should come up to her neck and cover her breasts onto the bottom of the dress. That's why it trails along so much behind. The bungling fool should have his hands chopped off if he can't do any better. Lady', I said, turning to her, 'get rid of him before he makes you a laughing stock and go to my Da's tailor. They call him Master Paul and he made beautiful pleated skirts for my Ma, our Ann and our Ursula. They were finished off nice and straight at the bottom and I'm sure they didn't drag in the mud like yours. You wouldn't believe what lovely clothes he made for the hussies.'

My master asked me whether my Da's Ann and Ursula were more beautiful than these ladies. 'Oh no, master', I replied. 'This lady has hair as yellow as baby shit and the parting is as white and and as straight as if she had been hit on the scalp with a curry-comb. And her hair is in such neat rolls it looks like hollow pipes, or as if she had a pound of candles or a dozen sausages hanging down each side. And oh, look at her lovely smooth forehead, is it not more beautifully curved than a fat buttock and whiter than a dead man's skull which has been hanging out in the wind and rain for years? But it's a pity her delicate skin has been so spoilt by powder. When people see her who don't know about it, they might think she has hereditary scabies which causes scales like that. And that would be an even greater pity for her sparkling black eyes. They glitter brighter than the soot on the door of my Da's stove which had such a terrifying gleam when our Ann stood by it with a bundle of burning straw to heat the room, as if there were enough fire in it to set the whole world ablaze. Her cheeks are nice and rosy, but not as red as the new ribbons

122

with which the Swabian carters from Ulm adorn their cod-pieces. But the deep red she has round her muzzle surpasses that colour by far and when she laughs or speaks (watch out for this, sir) you can see two rows of teeth in her mouth which look as neat and sugar-like as if they had been cut out of a piece of white turnip. Oh divine creature, I cannot believe it would hurt if you bit one with them! Her throat is as white as curdled milk and the little breasts below it are of the same colour and surely as firm to the touch as a nanny goat's udders bursting with milk. They do not hang down slackly, like those of the old women who cleaned up my bottom when I was in heaven recently. And oh, sir, look at her hands and fingers! They are so slender, so long, so supple, so lithe, so dainty! Just like those gypsy women had to pick your pocket with. What, though, is all this compared with her body itself. It is true I cannot see it naked, but is it not as delicate, slim and graceful as if she had had the running tomtits for eight whole weeks?' At this there was such loud laughter that they couldn't hear me any longer, nor could I speak, so I made myself scarce. There were limits to the amount of mockery I was willing to take.

Chapter 10

Tells of nothing but heroes and famous artists

This was followed by the midday meal at which I once again put on a lively performance. I had decided I would castigate all follies and censure all vanities, for which my current position was well suited. No guest was too great for me to reproach and upbraid him for his vices, and if one objected then either the others laughed him to scorn or my master would remind him that no wise man gets angry at a fool. Ensign Madcap, who was my worst enemy, I put on the rack straight away. However the first to reason with me, at a nod from my master, was the secretary. I called him a fabricator of titles and mocked him for all the obsequious modes of address he used, asking how he would have addressed mankind's first father, Adam.

'You talk like an unreasoning calf', he answered. 'You don't realise that since our first parents many different people have lived who so ennobled themselves and their family through rare virtues such as wisdom, heroic deeds and useful inventions that others raised them above all earthly things, even above the stars, making them into gods. If you were human, or if you had at least read the histories like a human being, you would see the differences between humans and would allow them their titles of honour. Since, however, you are a calf and incapable of achieving any human honour, you talk of this matter like a stupid calf, begrudging the human race something they delight in.'

'I have been just as much a human being as you', I replied, 'and have also read quite a lot, enough to conclude that either you do not understand this matter properly, or your own advantage stops you from saying what you think. Tell me, what are these marvellous deeds and admirable inventions which are sufficient to ennoble whole families for several hundred years after the death of the heroes or the artists themselves? Do not the heroes' strength and the artists' wisdom and understanding both die with them? If you cannot see that, and if parents do pass on their qualities to their children, then I must assume your father was a codfish and your mother a stick-in-the-mud flounder.'

'Ha!' answered the secretary, 'if this is going to be decided by insults, then I could point out that your father was a coarse Spessart peasant, but although the greatest oafs come from there, you have sunk even lower by becoming a brainless calf.'

'Exactly', I replied. 'That is just what I've been saying, namely that the parents' virtues do not pass on to the children, so that the children are not automatically worthy of their parents' titles. It is no disgrace that I have become a calf, since in that I have the honour to follow in the footsteps of the mighty King Nebuchadnezzar. Who knows whether it is not

God's will that I should become a man again like him, and a greater one than my Da? I praise those who ennoble themselves by their own virtues.'

'Assuming, for the sake of argument alone,' the secretary said, 'that children might not always inherit their parents' titles, you must admit that those who ennoble themselves by their own achievements are worthy of all the praise they get? And if that is the case, then it follows that it is right to honour their children for the parents' sake for, as they say, blood will out. If there were still some of Alexander the Great's descendants here today, who would not honour in them their forefather's bold courage in battle? He showed his desire to fight when, as a child and too young still to bear arms, he cried because he was afraid his father might win everything and leave no conquests for him. Did he not conquer the whole world before he was thirty and wished there were another for him to overcome? Did he not, when abandoned by his men in a battle against the Indians, sweat blood from sheer rage? Did he not look as if he was surrounded by flames so that even the barbarians fled from him in battle out of fear? Who would not think him higher and greater than other men? Does not his biographer, Quintus Curtius Rufus, attest that his breath smelt of balsam, his sweat of musk and his dead body of rare spices?

And here I could add the examples of Julius Caesar and Pompey. The first, above and beyond the victories he won in the civil wars, engaged in battle fifty times, defeating and killing 1,152,000 men; the other, besides the 940 ships he took from pirates, captured and subdued eight hundred and seventy-six cities and towns, from the Alps to the southernmost point of Spain. Of the fame of Marcus Sergius I will say nothing, and only dwell briefly on that of Lucius Siccius Dentatus, who was Tribune of the People when Spurius Turpeius and Aulus Eternius were consuls. He took part in a hundred and ten pitched battles, eight times defeating men who had challenged him; on his body he had forty-five scars from wounds to show, all of them in front, none in his back, and he marched through Rome in the triumphs of nine generals, which they had chiefly earned through their courage. The fate of Marcus Manlius Capitolinus would be no less, if it had not been diminished by the manner of his death, for he could show thirty-three scars, not to mention his saving the Capitol and its treasures from the Gauls. And what of Hercules and Theseus and all the rest, whose undying fame it is almost impossible to recount? Should these not be honoured in their descendants?

But now I will turn from war and weapons to the arts. They appear to be of lesser importance but the masters in them still achieve great fame. What skill do we not see in Zeuxis who, by his ingenuity and craft, deceived the birds into thinking the grapes he had painted were real; or in Apelles whose picture of Venus was so natural, so beautiful, so perfect, so exquisitely delicate in every line that the young men fell in love with her. Plutarch writes that Archimedes pulled a large ship, laden with goods, across the market square in Syracuse with one hand on one single rope, just as if he were leading a packhorse by the bridle. Twenty oxen could not have pulled it, to say nothing of two hundred calves like you. Should he not be honoured by a special title which reflects his skill. He also made a mirror with which he could set the enemy's ships on fire while they were out at sea; and Ptolemaeus devised a remarkable mirror which could show as many faces as there are hours in the day.

And who would refuse to praise the man who first invented letters? Indeed, who would not praise above all others the one who first invented the noble art of printing, which has brought such benefits to mankind? If Ceres was considered a goddess because she invented agriculture and the grinding of corn, why should it be wrong to honour others with titles which reflect their achievements? True, it is unimportant whether a brute calf like you with your unreasoning bullock's brain can take this in or not. You are like the dog which lay on the straw in the manger and would not let the ox have it, even though it could not eat it itself. You will never achieve any honour and so you begrudge it to those who are worthy of it.'

Seeing that he was trying to force me into a corner, I answered, 'The glorious deeds of heroism would indeed be praiseworthy, if they had not been accomplished with the injury and death of many others. What kind of praise would you call that which is stained with the blood of so many innocent people? And what kind of nobility is that which has been won by the annihilation of so many thousands of other people? As far as the arts are concerned, what are they but vanities and follies? They are as empty, vain and useless as the titles which they might bring a man. They serve either greed, lust or luxury, or to kill other men, like those terrible guns I saw recently on the half-waggons. We could manage quite well without writing and printing if we would only follow the example of that holy man who said that to contemplate the wonders of Creation and recognise God's omnipotence the only book he needed was the whole wide world itself.'

Chapter 11

On the tribulations and dangers of being a governor

My master also wanted to have his fun with me and said, 'I see that you despise the titles of nobility because you do not think you will ever be ennobled.'

I replied, 'Master, if I were to be offered the honour of your position here and now, I would not accept it.'

My master laughed and said, 'That I can believe; all an ox wants is his oats. But if you had nobility of spirit, which those of noble birth should have, then you would strive after high honours and dignities with all your might. For my part, I am happy that fortune has raised me above others.'

I sighed and said, 'Oh what a wearisome happiness! Master, I assure you that you are the most wretched person in the whole of Hanau.'

'How do you mean? How do you mean, Calf?' said my master. 'Tell me the reason, it's not obvious to me.'

'If you do not know, or feel', I replied, 'how many worries and cares you are burdened with as governor of Hanau, then you are blinded by your great desire for the honour you enjoy, or else you are made of wood and completely unfeeling. You give the orders, it is true, and everyone who comes before you has to obey you. But do they do it for nothing? Are you not their servant? Do you not have to take care of each and every one of them? Look, you are surrounded by the enemy and the responsibility for holding this fortress falls on you alone. You must look for ways of inflicting damage on your opponents, at the same time making sure your sallies are not detected. Does it not quite often happen that you stand on guard like a common soldier? And as well as that you have to see that there is no shortage of money, ammunition, food or men so that all the time you are extorting contributions from the whole countryside around. When you send out your soldiers to do that, the best work they do is robbing, plundering, stealing, burning and murdering. Only recently they plundered Orb, captured Braunfels and burnt Staden to the ground. They brought you the booty, true, but you have a heavy responsibility to bear in the eyes of God.

There is enjoyment as well as honour, I grant you, but do you know who will enjoy the treasures you are collecting? And even assuming you manage to keep the riches (which is uncertain), you will have to leave them behind when you depart this life. All you will take with you is the sin you incurred in amassing them. If you do have the good fortune to enjoy your booty, what will you be doing but squandering the sweat and blood of the poor who at present are living in misery, lacking the basic necessities and even dying of starvation?

Oh, and how often do I see how the heavy burden of responsibility keeps you awake, with your thoughts restlessly running hither and thither, while I and the other calves sleep peacefully, without a care in the world. But if you don't do all this it could cost you your head if you overlook something that needs to be done to safeguard the people in your charge or the fortress. I have no such cares, and since I know that I must pay my debt to nature, it doesn't worry me if someone attacks my byre or that I have a constant skirmish with work to survive. And if I die young I will at least have avoided the laborious life of a draught ox.

You, however, have people setting a thousand different traps for you so that your life is nothing but constant worry and interrupted sleep. You have to fear both friend and foe, who are doubtless trying to take either your life or your money or your reputation or your command or anything else you have, just as you would like to do to them. Your enemies attack you openly, while your supposed friends secretly envy you your good fortune, and you are not even safe from your subordinates. I will say nothing of the way you are daily tormented and driven hither and thither by your burning desire to achieve even greater fame, to rise to a higher command, to amass greater riches, to play a trick on the enemy, to surprise this or that stronghold, all things which, in short, injure others and are both harmful to your soul and displeasing to the Lord our God. And what is worst of all, you are so fawned on by your toadies that you no longer know yourself, so blinded and poisoned by their flattery that you cannot see the dangerous path you are on. They give their approval to everything you do, all your vices they call virtues. For them your cruelty is justice, and if you lay waste to the country and all who live there, they say you are a brave soldier, urging you on to harm others so that they can retain your favour, at the same time filling their purses.'

'Who taught you to preach like that, you idle good-for-nothing?' said my master.

'My lord', I replied, 'am I not right when I say you have been so corrupted by your bootlickers and backscratchers that you are already beyond help? Other people can easily see your vices and do not judge you in important matters alone, but find plenty to criticise in minor matters of little account. You can see enough examples of this in great men of the past. The Athenians grumbled about Simonides simply because he talked too loudly; the Thebans complained about Paniculus for spitting; the Spartans criticised Lycurgus for always

129

walking with his head bowed; the Romans found fault with Scipio for snoring too loudly in his sleep, thought it an ugly trait in Pompey that he scratched himself with one finger alone and mocked Julius Caesar because he did not do his belt up neatly; the people of Utica maligned Cato because in their opinion he ate too greedily, filling both sides of his mouth at once; and the Carthaginians disapproved of Hannibal for always going about bare-chested.

What do you think now, sir? Do you still think I should change places with a man who, besides a dozen or so drinking companions, toadies and parasites, has more than a hundred – probably more than ten thousand even – open and secret enemies, slanderers and jealous rivals? Besides, what happiness, what pleasure or joy can such a man have who is charged with the care and protection of so many people? Is it not your duty to watch over all of them, to look after them and listen to all their complaints and grievances? Wouldn't that be arduous enough in itself, without having so many who begrudge you your good fortune and seek to bring you down?

I can see how hard it is for you, how ill it often makes you. And what will your reward be, sir, what will you get out of all this? If you don't know, then let Demosthenes tell you who, after having loyally supported and defended the common good and the rights of the Athenians was, contrary to all law and justice, banished from the country and driven into the misery of exile, as if he had committed some dreadful crime. Socrates was paid back with poison; Hannibal was so poorly rewarded by his countrymen he was forced to wander the world, a wretched outlaw; the same happened to Marcus Furius Camillus, who had freed Rome from the Gauls, and the Greeks similarly rewarded Lycurgus and Solon, one of whom was stoned to death, the other had one eye put out before being banished as a murderer. No, you can keep your position and the rewards it brings, you'll share neither with me. For even if everything goes well for you, you will still take nothing with you but a bad conscience. If, however, you try to follow your conscience you will soon be removed from your command as incompetent, for all the world as if you had become a stupid calf like me.

Chapter 12

Concerning the understanding and skills of some unreasoning animals

Whilst I was talking, all those present stared at me, astonished that I could make such a speech which, as they confessed, would have been hard enough for a man with his full quota of wits, if he had to give it *extempore*. But I ignored them and concluded my speech as follows:

'So that, dear master, is why I would not want to change places with you. Nor do I need to, since the springs give me a healthy drink instead of your fine wines, and He who allowed me to be turned into a calf will surely also bless the herbs that grow in the ground so that they will provide both food and lodging for me, as they did for Nebuchadnezzar, while nature has provided me with a good fur coat. You, on the other hand, often feel sick at the sight of the best dishes and the wine gives you a headache and will soon bring you other illnesses as well.'

My master answered, 'I don't quite know what to make of you. You seem to have much too much sense for a calf. Perhaps under that calf's skin you have a jester's coat on?

I pretended to be angry and said, 'Do you humans think we animals are fools, then? Well you have another think coming. I tell you, if older beasts could talk as well as I can they could be of greater use to you than those to which you put them now. If you think we are stupid, just tell me who taught the wild wood pigeons, jays, blackbirds and partridges to purge themselves with bayleaves? And the doves, turtle doves and hens with dandelion? Who taught cats and dogs that they should eat the dew-soaked grass if they want to clear out their full bellies? And the tortoise to heal a bite with hemlock, or the deer, when it is wounded, to look for dictamnus or wild calamint? Who showed the weasel to use rue if it is going to fight with a bat or snake? Who taught the wild pigs to recognise ivy and the bear mandrake, and who told them they were good to use as medicine? Who suggested to the eagle that it should look for eaglestone and use it if it has difficulty laying its eggs? Who is it told the swallow to use celandine to strengthen the sight of its young? Who instructed the snake to eat fennel when it is going to shed its skin and its sight is weak? Who taught the stork to give itself an enema, the pelican to bleed itself and the bear to get the bees to act as leeches?

I might almost say that you humans have learnt your arts and sciences from us animals. You eat and drink yourself to death, which we animals never do. A lion or wolf that is starting to get too fat starves itself until it is slim, healthy and full of life again. Which shows the greater wisdom?

As well as all this, look at the birds of the air, look at the diverse construction of their dainty nests. Since no man can copy their work, you must acknowledge that they have both greater understanding and greater skill than you humans. Who tells the summer visitors when to come to us in spring to hatch out their young, and to leave in the autumn for warmer lands? Who teaches them to agree on a gathering place before the journey? Who guides them, who tells them the route? Perhaps you humans lend them a compass so they won't get lost on the way? No, good people, they know the way without you, and how long it will take and when they must set off from one place for another.

Again, look at the industrious spider, whose web is nigh on a miracle. Can you find one single knot in its whole work? Which hunter or fisherman taught it how to spread out its net and, depending on the net it has used, to sit either in the farthest corner or right in the middle to lie in wait for its prey? You humans marvel at the raven which, as Plutarch reports, kept dropping stones into a pot half full of water until the water came high enough for it to drink out of it in comfort.

What would you do if you lived among the animals and observed all the other things they did? Then you would really have to acknowledge that it is clear that all animals have something to teach you in the special natural powers they possess in all their feelings and responses, be it caution, strength, gentleness, wildness. Each knows the others, they are different from each other, they look for what is good for them, keep away from what is harmful and avoid danger, gather what they need to feed them and sometimes even deceive you humans. This was why many ancient philosophers paid serious attention to these matters and were not ashamed to discuss whether unreasoning animals did not also have understanding. That is all I have to say on this subject. Go and watch the bees making wax and honey and then tell me what you think.'

Chapter 13

Contains all sorts of things; if you want to know what they are you must read it yourself or get someone to read it to you

At this those gathered round my master's table pronounced various judgments on me. The secretary maintained I should be judged a fool since I considered myself an animal with the power of reason and people who were not all there but still thought themselves as rational as the next man were the best, most entertaining fools of all. Others said that if someone could only cure me of the delusion I was a calf, or persuade me I was human again, they would consider me rational or sane enough. My master himself said, 'I think he is a fool because he is not afraid to tell everyone the truth. On the other hand what he says is not what you would expect from a fool.' All this they said in Latin, so that I shouldn't understand it. Then my master asked me if I had done any studying while I was still human.

I replied that I had no idea what studying was. 'But, master', I went on, 'tell me what these studs are with which you go studying. Is that perhaps what you call the bowls with which you go bowling?'

At this Ensign Madcap said, 'Wha's wrang wi' the man? The de'il's in him, that's wha's wrang. He's possessed, it's the de'il aye speakin' thru him.'

Then my master asked me, seeing that I had turned into a calf, whether I still prayed like other men, as I had done before, and whether I believed I would go to heaven.

'Of course', I answered. 'I still have my immortal human soul and, as you can well imagine, it will not want to end up in hell, largely because it has had such a hard time there once already. I have been transformed, just as Nebuchadnezzar was, and I too will presumably turn back into a man when the time comes.'

'Amen to that', said my master with a deep sigh, from which I deduced he regretted having had me turned into a fool. 'But tell us', he went on, 'how you do your praying.'

At that I knelt down and raised my hands and eyes to heaven in true hermit fashion. Since my master's remorse, which I had noticed, touched my heart and comforted me, I could not hold back my tears. Thus it was to all appearances with deepest reverence that, after saying the Lord's Prayer, I prayed for the whole of Christendom, for my friends and enemies, and that God would grant that I might live in this world in such a way that I would be found worthy to praise Him in eternal bliss. This was a reverent prayer the hermit had composed and taught me. Some of the soft-hearted onlookers were almost crying because they felt such pity for me and even my master had tears in his eyes.

After the meal my master sent for the pastor. He told him everything I had said and indicated that he was concerned there were dark forces at work, perhaps the devil himself was involved seeing how I had at first appeared quite simple-minded and ignorant but now was saying astounding things.

The pastor, who was best acquainted with me, replied that they should have considered these things before they had had the presumption to turn me into a fool. Men, he reminded them, were made in the image of God and should not be played with just for sport, as if they were brute beasts, especially when they were so young. However, he could not believe that the evil spirit had been allowed to interfere since I had always commended myself to God through fervent prayer. If, however, contrary to all expectation that was the case, then they would have a serious charge to answer for before God, since there was hardly any worse sin than for one man to deprive another of his reason, thus making it impossible for him to praise and serve God, which was the principal purpose for which he had been created.

'I have', he went on, 'already assured you that he is intelligent but does not know the ways of the world. The reason for this is his simple upbringing out in the wilds with his father, a coarse peasant, and your brother-in-law. If people had been more patient with him he would, with time, have made better progress. He was just a simple-minded, God-fearing child unacquainted with the wicked world. I have no doubt that he can be brought back to his right mind if he can just be cured of the delusion that he has turned into a calf. We can read of a man who firmly believed he had turned into an earthenware jug and asked his family to put him up on a shelf so he would not be knocked over; another imagined he was a cock and and in his madness crowed both day and night. There was yet another who thought he had already died and wandered around as a ghost, refusing both medicine and food and drink until a clever doctor paid two men to pretend they were ghosts, but ones who loved to drink. They joined the other and persuaded him that modern ghosts were in the habit of eating and drinking, through which he was cured.

I myself had a sick farmer in my parish who, when I visited him, complained that he had some three or four barrels of water in his body; if he could get rid of it he believed he might get well again. He asked me either to slit him open, so that it would run out, or to hang him up in the smokehouse so that it would dry up. I talked him into believing I could get rid of the water in another way. I took a spigot they use for wine or beer barrels, tied a length of intestine to it and the other end to the bunghole of a bathtub, which I had had filled with water. Then I pretended to stick the spigot into his belly, which he had wrapped up in rags so that it wouldn't burst, and let the water run out of the bathtub. The poor fellow was so pleased that he threw off the rags and in a few days was his old self again. Another man who imagined he had swallowed all sorts of horse equipment, bridles and the like, was helped in a similar way. The doctor gave him a strong laxative and put some of those things underneath the stools he did during the night so that he thought he had excreted them. And there was another madman who believed his nose was so long it reached the floor. They stuck a sausage onto his nose and kept cutting off slices. When they got to his nose he felt the knife and shouted out that his nose was back in its old shape again. If they could be cured then I am sure our good Simplicius could be too.'

'I can well believe that', said my master, 'but what concerns me is that he was so ignorant before and now he can talk – and so perfectly – of things which you would not expect to hear from many older, more experienced and better read people. He went through all those qualities of the animals, and described my own character so precisely, as if he had spent his whole life out in the wide world! It amazes me and I wonder whether I shouldn't regard what he said as an oracle or a warning from God.'

'My lord', answered the pastor, 'there is a natural explanation for all this. I know that he is well-read, because both he and the hermit read all my books, and there were quite a lot of them. And since the lad has a good memory, but at the moment has nothing to occupy his mind and has forgotten who he is, he can regurgitate things he has previously stored in his brain. I am confident that with time he can be restored to normality again.'

Thus the pastor left the governor suspended between hope and fear. He spoke up for me in excellent fashion, securing good times for me and for himself access to the governor. Their final decision was to wait and see for a while, which the pastor proposed more for his own advantage than for mine, for by coming and going, pretending it was all for my sake, he gained the favour of the governor, who took him into his service and appointed him chaplain to the garrison, which was no small matter in those difficult times and I was glad of it for him.

Chapter 14

Tells how Simplicius led the life of a nobleman and how the arquebusiers robbed him of it by carrying him off

I can truthfully boast that from then on I enjoyed my master's grace, favour and affection to the full. My happiness was complete, apart from the fact that I had one calfskin too many and several years too few, although I didn't realise that at the time. The pastor did not want me brought back to my right mind just yet because he thought it would not be in his interest. My master, seeing that I liked music, sent me to study with an excellent lutenist. I picked up his skill pretty quickly, even surpassing my teacher in that I could sing better to the lute than he could. So I served my master well, amusing, entertaining and astonishing him.

All the officers were courteous to me, the richest citizens gave me presents and the servants and common soldiers treated me with respect because they could all see how well-disposed my master was towards me. One would give me this, another that, for they knew that jesters can often achieve more with their masters than honest behaviour. And that was the purpose behind the gifts. Some gave me presents to stop me from lampooning them, others to get me to lampoon someone else. In this way I came by quite a lot of money, most of which I handed over to the pastor as I still had no idea what to do with it. And since no one dared even to give me a dirty look, I had nothing to cause me vexation, worry or care. All I thought about was my music, or devising clever ways of pointing out this or that person's faults. I lived off the fat of the land and my body grew visibly stronger day by day. Soon you could tell I was no longer mortifying my flesh in the forest with water, acorns, beech-mast, roots and herbs, but that my hearty meals were washed down with Rhine wines and strong Hanau beer. In those wretched times that was a great mercy, for the whole of Germany was ravaged by war, pestilence and famine and Hanau itself surrounded by enemy forces, yet I did not suffer in the least.

My master's intention, after the siege was lifted, was to present me either to Cardinal Richelieu or Duke Bernard of Weimar. Not that he hoped for any great reward, but he claimed he could no longer bear to have the living image of his lost sister, whom I came to resemble more and more, parade before his eyes every day in such a ridiculous garb. The pastor advised against it. He felt the time had come for him to perform his 'miracle' and restore me to my right mind. He told the governor to get two calfskins and have two boys wrapped up in them; then he was to arrange for someone to pretend to be a doctor, prophet or magician and perform strange ceremonies as he removed the calfskins from me and the other boys, claiming to be able to turn animals into humans and vice versa. He was sure, he said, that in this way I could be changed back into my old self and easily persuaded I had been turned back into a human being along with the others.

When the governor had given his approval to this sugges-tion, the pastor told me what he had agreed with my master and easily persuaded me to go along with it. But jealous for-tune refused to let me get rid of my fool's outfit so easily or to continue to enjoy my life of luxury. While the tanner and tailor were preparing the costumes for this farce, I was playing with some other boys on the ice outside the ramparts. Some-one, I don't know who, brought along a party of arquebusiers, who surprised us and seized us all, slung us over the backs of some farm-horses they had just stolen and carried us off. At first they were in some doubt as to whether to take me along with the others or not. Finally one said, in Czech, 'Let's take the fool as well and bring him to the colonel.' To which another replied, 'Yes, by God! Put him on the horse. The colonel can understand German, he'll have some fun with him.' So I had to get on a horse too and learn how one single moment of bad luck can rob you of all well-being and take you so far away from all comfort and happiness that it haunts you for the rest of your days.

Chapter 15

*Simplicius's life as a dragoon; his experiences
with the arquebusiers*

Although the alarm was immediately raised in Hanau and a party of troopers rode out to harry the arquebusiers, they only managed to hold them up for a little while and could not win back their prisoners. The Czechs, being light dragoons and slippery customers into the bargain, escaped without difficulty and continued towards Büdingen, where they fed, handed over the sons of the rich Hanauers to the citizens to be ransomed and sold the horses and other goods they had stolen. Then they set off again straight away, before it was really dark, never mind waiting for daybreak. They rode quickly through Büdingen Forest in the direction of Fulda, carrying off whatever they could en route. Robbing and plundering did not seem to slow down their rapid progress at all, they were like the devil who, as people say, can run and shit at the same time and still not miss anything on the way. So we reached Hersfeld Abbey, where they were quartered, that same evening with a large quantity of booty. It was all divided up, but I was given to the colonel, Marcus von Corpus.

Everything about life with that gentleman seemed disagreeable to me, almost barbarous. The tasty morsels I had enjoyed in Hanau became coarse black bread and stringy beef or, at best, a hunk of stolen bacon. Wine and beer had turned into water and instead of a bed I had to make do with the straw in the stable next to the horses. Instead of playing the lute, which everyone had enjoyed, I was sometimes made to crawl under the table with other boys and howl like a dog, to be pricked with the officers' spurs, which I did not find in the least amusing. Instead of taking walks, as I had done in Hanau, I was allowed to ride out with the foragers, groom horses and muck out the stables. This foraging is dreary toil and not without danger to life and limb. All it consists of is roaming the villages, threshing, grinding, baking, stealing, taking any-thing you find, tormenting and ruining the farmers, yes, even raping their maids, wives and daughters. And if the poor farmers refused to take this lying down, or even had the audacity to rap one or other of the foragers (and there were many like that in Hessen in those days) over the knuckles when they caught them at this, then the soldiers cut them down, if they could catch them, or at least sent their houses up in flames.

My master had no wife (soldiers of that type do not have women accompanying them), no page, no manservant and no cook, but there was a motley crew of grooms and boys who looked after both him and the horses at the same time. He was not too proud to saddle his horse himself or to feed it with his own hand. He always slept on straw or the bare ground, cover-ing himself with his fur coat. The result was that lice were often seen wandering over his clothes, which did not embar-rass him in the least; on the contrary, he would laugh when someone picked one off. He had his hair cut short and wore his whiskers untrimmed in the Swiss fashion, which came in useful when he disguised himself in peasant clothes, which he often did, to go out and reconnoitre the ground. Although, as you have heard, he did not give lavish feasts, he was respected, loved and feared by his men and those who knew him. We were never at rest, always going here or there; sometimes we attacked, sometimes we were attacked. We were never for a moment idle in our attempts to weaken the strength of the

Hessians, nor did the Hessian general, Count Holzapfel, leave us in peace, but captured many of our dragoons and sent them to Kassel.

This restless life was not to my taste at all and I often vainly wished I was back in Hanau. My biggest problem was that I could not talk with the men properly, so that I kept on being pushed and shoved around by everyone, battered, bruised and beaten. The colonel's favourite amusement with me was to make me sing to him in German and blow the horn like other stable lads, at which I was boxed round the ears so hard that the blood came pouring out. I must admit that this did not happen very often but once was enough to last me for a long time. Eventually, since I was no use at foraging anyway, I started to take over the cooking and to clean my master's weapons, which he was very particular about. And I did it so well that I gained my master's favour; at least, he had a new fool's outfit made for me out of calfskins with much larger donkey's ears than I had before. And since my master was not very fastidious as far as his palate was concerned I didn't need any great skill at cookery. But I soon tired of it, as we were often short of salt, fat and spices, so that day and night I spent the time thinking of a good way to escape, especially since it was spring again. To this end I offered to clear away the entrails of sheep and cows, which were lying all over the place in our quarters, to get rid of the awful smell. The colonel thought this a good idea and I set about it. At last, when it grew dark, I didn't return, but slipped away into the nearest bit of forest.

Chapter 16

*Simplicius makes a good haul and becomes
a thieving woodlander*

It looked, however, as if the longer I lived the worse my situation was going to get, so that I even started to think I must have been born to misfortune. Only a few hours after I had escaped from the Czech arquebusiers I was captured by some robbers who doubtless thought they had made a good catch. In the darkness they could not see my fool's outfit and two of them took me away to some place in the woods. When we stopped, in the pitch darkness, one immediately demanded money from me. He put down his gauntlets and gun and started to search me, asking, 'Who are you? Have you any money?' But he got the shock of his life when he felt my hairy coat and the donkey's ears on my cap, which he thought were horns, and saw the glitter of sparks that you often get when you stroke animal skins in the dark. He started and shrank back. I immediately noticed this and, not giving him time to think or recover his wits, rubbed my coat with both hands so that it glowed as if I were full of burning sulphur, replying in a fearsome voice, 'I am the devil. I am going to wring your neck and your companion's too.' This terrified the pair of them so much that they hurtled off through brake and briar as if pursued by all the fires of hell. Even the pitch darkness didn't slow them down. They kept running into rocks and stones, trunks and branches and falling over, but they picked themselves up just as quickly again. This continued until they were out of earshot. I meanwhile was laughing out loud, which echoed through the woods, doubtless a terrifying sound to hear in that dark, lonely wilderness.

When I went to continue on my way I tripped over the musket, so I picked it up, since I had already learnt to use one during my stay with the Czech arquebusiers. A little further on my foot caught a knapsack which was made of calfskin, like my coat. I picked that up as well and found that hanging from it was an ammunition pouch containing powder, shot and the like. I slung it on my back, shouldered the rifle like a real soldier and hid in some thick bushes not far away, intending to sleep there for a while.

However, as soon as it was light the whole party returned, looking for the musket and knapsack. I pricked up my ears like a fox and kept as quiet as a mouse. When they found nothing they mocked the two who had run away from me. 'You cowardly fools', they said, 'you should be thoroughly ashamed of yourselves. Letting one man on his own frighten you, chase you away and take your musket!'

'Devil take me', one of them swore, 'if it wasn't the devil himself. I felt his horns and rough skin.'

The other put on a show of anger and said, 'I don't care whether it was the devil or his mother, I want my knapsack back.'

Another of the robbers, the one I took to be their leader, replied, 'What do you think the devil would want with your musket and knapsack? I bet my life the fellow you miserable wretches allowed to escape has got them both.' One of the others disagreed and said it could be that some peasants had been there since then, found the things and taken them. Eventually this argument won the day and they all believed they had had the devil in their hands, not least because the one who had tried to search me in the dark not only assured them of it with dreadful oaths but also gave a most vivid description of the rough, glittering skin and two horns as certain signs I was truly the devil. I suspect if I had suddenly appeared to them again the whole band would have run away.

Finally they left, having spent a long time looking and not finding anything. I opened up the knapsack to see if it contained any food I could eat for my breakfast. The first thing I pulled out was a bag with some three hundred and sixty ducats in it. I was pleased to find them, no question about it, but I assure you I was even more pleased to find the knapsack was as well supplied with food as with money. Since such yellow boys are too few and far between among the common soldiers for one to be carrying that many with him out on a raid, I concluded that he must have picked them up secretly during the course of the previous night's expedition and slipped them into his knapsack so he wouldn't have to share them with the others.

After that I had an enjoyable breakfast and soon found a spring where I refreshed myself and counted my ducats. Even if my life depended on it I couldn't say in which country or district I was then. I only ate sparingly of my provisions and I stayed in the forest as long as they lasted. When my knapsack was empty, however, hunger drove me to the farms. I crept into cellars and kitchens at night, took what food I found that I could carry and bore it off to the wildest part of the woods. There I led the life of a hermit, just as I had before, except that I stole a lot and prayed very little. Nor did I live in one place alone, but roamed here and there. The good thing was that it was the beginning of summer; however, I could also use my musket to light a fire with whenever I wanted.

Chapter 17

How Simplicius was borne off to see the witches at their dance

While I was roaming the woods I met various country people, but they always ran away from me. I don't know exactly what the reason was. Perhaps the war had made them timid, driving them away from their homes and never leaving them in peace? Or perhaps the robbers had spread the story of their encounter with me throughout the countryside and those who saw me believed, like them, that the Evil One was abroad in the area? This made me begin to worry that my provisions might run out and I would be faced with starvation unless I ate herbs and roots, which I was no longer used to.

Plagued by these thoughts, I was glad one day to hear two

woodcutters at work. I followed the sound of their axes and when I saw them I took a handful of ducats out of my satchel, showed them the gleaming gold and said, 'If you men will look after me I will give you this handful of gold.' But the moment they saw me and my gold they took to their heels, leaving their mallets and wedges behind, and their bread and cheese too. I filled my knapsack with the latter and headed back into the woods, despairing of ever enjoying human company again.

I spent a long time thinking this over and concluded, 'Who knows what will happen to you. You've got money and if you can deposit it in security with honest people you can live on it for a long time.' At that it occurred to me that I ought to sew it up. I made two armbands out of the donkey's ears that frightened people off so, filled them with the ducats I had saved in Hanau and the ones I had taken from the robbers and put them on my arms above the elbows. Now that I had my money secure, I went back to breaking into the farms, taking what I needed from whatever stores I could find there. I may have been simple-minded, but I was cunning enough never to go back to any place where I had already stolen something, however little. In this way I was very successful as a thief and was never caught at my pilfering.

One evening towards the end of May I had once again entered a farm in my usual, though unlawful quest for food. As I went into the kitchen I realised that there were still people up (by the way, I never went to houses where there were dogs). I left the door leading out into the yard wide open, so that if there was any threat of danger I could make a quick getaway, then sat, quiet as a mouse, to wait until I felt sure the people had gone to bed. While I was waiting I noticed a crack in the hatch into the living room. I crept over to it, to see if the people were anywhere near ready to go to bed, but my hopes were dashed when I saw that they had only just got dressed. Instead of a candle they had a sulphurous blue lamp on the bench by the light of which they were greasing sticks, brooms, pitchforks, stools and benches. Then, one after the other, they flew out of the window on them.

I was amazed and felt a shiver of terror. Since, however, I had become accustomed to even greater horrors and, anyway, had never read or heard of witches, I thought little of it, especially as everything had happened so quietly. After they had all left I went into the room myself, thinking about what I wanted to take and where I should start looking for it. Mulling this over in my mind, I sat down astride one of the benches. Hardly was I seated than the bench, with me on it, shot out of the window. My satchel and musket, which I had put down on the floor, I left behind, as payment for the magic grease, so to speak. Sitting down, flying off and landing all happened in a trice. At least it seemed to me that I was instantaneously transported to a large crowd of people. (Of course, it is possible I was so terrified I didn't register the time the journey took.)

They were all involved in a strange dance, the like of which I have never seen before or since. They were holding hands in several rings, one inside the other, and they all had their backs to each other, as in pictures of the Three Graces, that is with their faces turned towards the outside. The innermost ring consisted of some seven or eight people, the next probably twice that many, the third more than both of them put together and so on until the outer ring which had more than two hundred in it. One ring or circle was dancing round to the left, the next to the right, making it impossible for me to see exactly how many rings there were nor what it was in the middle that they were dancing round. The way all the heads wound in and out was funny and at the same time strangely eerie.

And the music was just as strange as the dance. It seemed to me that each dancer was singing his or her own song, which produced a bizarre harmony. The bench I came on had landed close to the musicians, who were standing outside the circles. Instead of pipes, flutes and shawms some of them were merrily blowing away on grass-snakes, adders and slow-worms. Others were holding cats, blowing up their backsides and fingering their tails, producing a sound like bagpipes. There were some fiddling away on horses' skulls as if they were the finest violins and others playing the harp on cows' skeletons such as you see lying around the knacker's yard, and there was even one holding a bitch under his arm, grinding away with her tail and playing on her dugs with his fingers. And all the time the demons were trumpeting through their noses so that the woods resounded with their din. As soon as the dance was over the whole hellish crew started bawling and bellowing, ranting and raging, screaming, stamping and storming as if they had all gone raving mad. You can imagine how terrified I was.

In the midst of all this racket a man came up to me. He was carrying a gigantic toad under his arm, easily as big as a side drum; its intestines had been pulled out through its rear end and stuffed back into its mouth, which I found so disgusting it made me want to puke. 'Come on, Simplicius', he said, 'I know you can play the lute very well. Why don't you give us a nice tune.' I almost fell over with the shock when the man addressed me by my name and was struck dumb. I imagined I must be dreaming and silently begged that I would wake up. However, the man with the toad, whom I was staring at fixedly, kept thrusting his nose out and in like a turkeycock until he was pressing down on my chest so that I was almost suffocating. Then I cried out loud to God, at which the whole crew vanished. In a trice it was pitch dark and I was so overcome with terror that I fell to the ground and must have made the sign of the cross at least a hundred times.

Chapter 18

Why no one should accuse Simplicius of drawing the long bow

Since there are some people, scholars in particular, who do not believe that witches exist, never mind fly through the air on broomsticks, I do not doubt there will be those who will accuse Simplicius of making the whole story up. It is not my intention here to argue with people who think that. Indeed, since nowadays making up tall stories is no longer an art but a trade almost everyone has mastered, I cannot deny that I would be a poor writer if I could not do it too.

As for those who deny that witches can fly, I will simply remind them of Simon Magus, who flew through the air with the aid of an evil spirit and was brought crashing to the ground by St. Peter's prayer. Nicolas Remi, a brave and sensible scholar who had a good number of witches burnt in the Duchy of Lorraine, tells the story of John of Hembach. When he was sixteen his mother, who was a witch, took him with her to their sabbath to play while they danced, as he could play the whistle. So he climbed up into a tree and whistled away, making sure he had a good view of the dance (perhaps because everything seemed so fantastic). Eventually he said, 'God help us, where does all this crazy rabble come from?' Hardly had he spoken these words than he fell down from the tree and dislocated his shoulder, but when he called out for help there was no one there. He told people about his experience, but most thought he had made it all up until shortly afterwards Catherine Prevost was arrested for witchcraft. She had attended the same sabbath and confessed to everything, even though she had not heard the rumour Hembach had spread.

Majolus gives two examples of men who attended a witches' sabbath. One was a farm labourer who rode clinging to his wife's back, the other an adulterer who took his mistress's ointment and smeared himself with it. There is another story of a servant who got up early to grease the cart but in the darkness picked up the wrong pot. The cart rose up into the air and had to be pulled back down again. Olaus Magnus tells how King Hading of Denmark, having been driven out by rebels, flew back across the sea to his kingdom on Odin's spirit that had turned itself into a horse. And it is a well-known fact that both wives and unmarried girls in Bohemia have their lovers brought to them during the night and from a long way off on the backs of goats. The story Antonio de Torquemada tells of the student you can read in his *Jardín de flores curiosas*. Grillandus writes of a respectable burgher who observed that his wife was in the habit of rubbing some ointment on herself then flying out of the house and forced her to take him with her to the sabbath. During the meal there was no salt, so he asked for and, not without difficulty, eventually got some, at which he said, 'Here comes the salt, thank God.' Immediately the lights went out and everything disappeared. When it was day again he learnt from some shepherds that he was not far from the town of Benevento in the Kingdom of Naples, that is a hundred miles from his home. Although he was a rich man he had to beg to make his way home. As soon as he did get back he denounced his wife to the authorities as a witch and she was burnt at the stake.

How Doctor Faust and others, who were no magicians, still travelled through the air from one place to another is well enough known. I myself was acquainted with a maid who had a similar experience. (The maid and her mistress are both now dead, although the maid's father is still alive.) She was greasing her mistress's boots by the fire. When she had done one she put it down, to do the other, and it flew straight out of the chimney. This story, however, was hushed up. I am only telling it now to convince people that witches and warlocks do sometimes fly to their gatherings and not to get you to accept that I did so myself. I leave that up to you, but if you don't believe it, you will have to think up some other way in which I went in such a short time from Hersfeld or Fulda (I still don't know where I was, wandering round in the forest) to the vicinity of Magdeburg.

Chapter 19

Simplicius becomes a fool again, as he was before

To get back to my story, I can assure you that I stayed lying on my belly until it was completely light. I did not have the courage to get up; at the same time I was still in doubt as to whether I had dreamt the whole thing or not. Although I was fairly frightened, I was not too frightened to stop myself going to sleep. I presumed I could not be in any worse place than the wild woods, which I was used to since that was where I had spent most of the time since I had been separated from my Da.

It wasn't until some foragers woke me at about nine the next morning that I saw I was lying in the middle of open fields. They took me with them to some windmills and then, after they had ground their grain, to the camp outside Magdeburg. There I was handed over to the colonel of a foot-regiment who asked me where I came from and what master I had served before. I told him everything, just as it had happened. Since I did not know what to call the Czech arque-busiers, I described their uniforms and imitated their language and told the colonel I had run away from them. I said nothing of my ducats and what I told them about flying through the air and seeing the witches dance they took to be invention and fool's talk, principally because I got rather carried away when I reached that part of my story.

By this time a large crowd had gathered round (one fool makes a thousand). Among them was a man who had been a prisoner in Hanau the previous year where he had served in the Protestant army before rejoining the Imperial forces. He recognised me and immediately said, 'Hey, that's the commandant of Hanau's calf!' The colonel questioned him about me, but all the soldier could tell him was that I could play the lute well, that the arquebusiers from Colonel Corpus's regiment had captured me outside Hanau and that the commandant had been sorry to lose me because I was an amusing fool. At this the colonel's wife sent to another, who played the lute and always had one with her, to ask to borrow her instrument. When it arrived I was handed it and told to play a tune. I said, however, that they should bring me something to eat first since an empty belly, such as I had, would not harmonise very well with a fat belly such as the lute had. They did this, and once I had eaten my fill and washed it down with some good Zerbst beer I let them hear what I could do, both playing and singing. At the same time I talked gibberish, saying the first thing that came into my head, to make people think I was as big a fool as my outfit suggested. The colonel asked me where I was heading for, and when I answered that I didn't care we soon agreed I should stay with him and be his page. He wanted to know what had happened to my donkey's ears. 'Aha', I said, 'if you knew where they were you would find they would suit you pretty well.' But I was careful to say no more about them, since all my money was hidden in them.

I soon became a familiar figure to most of the officers in the camps of both the Saxon and the Imperial regiments and I was especially popular with the women, who decorated my cap, sleeves and severed ears with silk ribbons of all sorts of colours. I think some of the fops must have copied the current fashion from me. The money the officers gave me I charitably put back into circulation down to the very last copper by getting drunk on Hamburg and Zerbst beer, which I found very much to my taste, with a group of like-minded companions. Beside that, there were plenty of chances of a free drink wherever I went.

But when my colonel bought me a lute of my own – he presumed he would have me with him for good – he appointed a kind of tutor to keep an eye on me and whom I was to obey, which meant that I could not roam round the camps at will any longer. This tutor was a man after my own heart, quiet, intelligent, learned, a good but not excessive conversationalist, and, what was most important, God-fearing, well-read and knowledgeable in all kinds of sciences and arts. I had to sleep in his tent with him at night and during the day I was not allowed out of his sight. He had been councillor and minister to a prince. He had also been very rich, but had been completely ruined by the Swedes; his wife was dead and his son so poor that he had to leave the university and join the army of the Elector of Saxony as a company clerk. My tutor had taken service with the colonel as equerry, waiting for the fortunes of war along the Elbe to change so that he could be restored to his former glory.

Chapter 20

*Is rather long and deals with playing with dice
and things connected with that*

Since my tutor was getting on in years, he could not sleep right through the night, and this led to him discovering my secret within the first few weeks and hearing from my own lips that I wasn't the fool I pretended to be. He already had his suspicions, since he was familiar with the science of physiognomy and had formed his own conclusion from his study of my face. The proof, however, came one night when I awoke at midnight. I got up and reflected on my life and strange adventures, thanking God out loud for all His blessings and all the dangers He had rescued me from. Then I went back to bed, sighing deeply, and slept until morning.

He heard everything, but pretended to be fast asleep. This happened for several nights running, until he was absolutely certain my wits were sharper than those of many an older man who thought much of himself. He said nothing of this to me in the tent because the walls were too thin and he had reason not to let anyone else in on the secret before he was convinced of my innocence. One day I went for a walk outside the camp and he allowed me to go because it gave him the chance to come to look for me and talk to me alone. He found me, as he wanted, in a lonely place, rehearsing my thoughts, and said, 'My dear friend, I only want what is best for you, and for that reason I am glad to have the chance to speak to your here alone. I know you're not the fool you pretend to be and would rather not have to continue in that wretched and despised situation. I am an honest man and if you will trust me and tell me how this came about, I will give you all the help and advice I can to try and get you out of that fool's costume.'

I was so overjoyed at this that I embraced him as if he were a magician come to free me from my fool's cap. We sat down on the ground and I told him the story of my life. He read my palm and expressed his astonishment at the strange things which had happened to me and at those which were still to come. However, he advised me not to lay aside my fool's outfit too soon for, he said, by chiromancy he could see the threat of prison hanging over me, bringing danger to life and limb. I thanked him for his kindness towards me and his good advice, asking God to reward him for his honesty and him to be a true friend and father to me, since I was alone in the world.

Then we set off and came to the gaming yard where they joust with dice and every oath has blood, thunder or a pox on it. The yard was about as big as the Old Market in Cologne and was covered with tables or cloaks spread on the ground, all surrounded by gamblers. Each group had three of these rectangular devil's bones to which they entrusted their fortune, for they had to share out their money, giving some to one, taking some from another. At every coat or table there was an umpire whose job it was to keep an eye on the game and see that no one was cheated. I almost wrote 'vampire', for these umpires hired out the cloaks, tables and dice and were so adept at taking their percentage from the winnings that they usually ended up with most of the money. However, they got very little out of it since they usually gambled it away again, or if they did spend it, it went on drink, or on the surgeon's services as there were always a lot of cuts and bruises to be mended.

It was astonishing to see these foolish people, all of whom thought they were going to win, which was impossible unless they picked their stakes out of someone else's pocket. Although they all hoped their luck would be in, some hit and others missed, some won and others lost, so that some roared and others cursed, some cheated and others were duped, the winners laughed and the losers gnashed their teeth. Some sold their clothes and any articles of value they had, and others won that money off them as well. Some demanded honest dice, while some wanted loaded ones and secretly slipped them into the game, but others threw them away, broke them, chewed them and tore the cloak on which the game was being played.

Among the doctored dice were so-called Netherlands dice which you had to roll along the ground, because the faces with the five and six on were as sharply pointed as the sawing horses they put soldiers on as punishment. Then there were the 'Oberland dice' which you had to cast with a high 'Bavarian toss'. Some were of horn and made so that they were light on top, heavy at the bottom, being loaded with quicksilver or lead, with chopped-up hair, sponges, chaff or coal; some had sharp corners, on others they had been completely worn away; some were long, like clubs, others broad, like tortoises. However, all these different types had but one purpose, cheating, and they rolled the way they had been made to roll, no matter how you threw them, whether you flipped them up into the air or let them trickle gently onto the cloak. There was nothing you could do about these loaded dice, not to mention those that had two fives or sixes or, at the other end, two ones or twos. With these devil's bones they cheated, tricked and stole the money off each other, which they had perhaps originally acquired by robbery, or at least at danger to life and limb or through hard work.

While I was standing there observing the gaming-yard together with the gamblers and their stupidity, my tutor asked me what I thought of it. 'I don't like the way they keep on blaspheming', I answered, 'but otherwise I have no opinion on it since I don't know the game and don't understand what is going on.'

'This', he replied, 'is the worst, most abominable place in the whole camp. They are all trying to take the others' money and losing their own in the process. A man just has to set foot in here with the intention of gambling to break the tenth commandment, which says *Thou shalt not covet any thing which is thy neighbour's*. If you gamble and win, especially by cheating with loaded dice, you break the seventh and eighth commandments. It can even make you into a murderer if the man whose money you have won has lost so much that he is plunged into poverty, misery and despair or falls into some other foul vice. It is no use trying to excuse yourself by saying, 'I risked my own money and won honestly', for you came to the gaming-yard with the express intention of getting rich through another man's loss. And even if you then lose and gamble your own money away, that is not sufficient penance. Like the rich man, you will have to answer to God for squandering what He gave you to support yourself and your family. Any man who goes to the gaming-yard with the intention of gambling is in danger of losing not only his money, but life and limb and, what is worse by far, his own soul. I am telling you this, Simplicius, since you say you know nothing of gambling, in the hope that you will never become better acquainted with it.'

'But if gambling is such a terrible and dangerous thing', I replied, 'why do the authorities permit it?'

'I won't say it is because some of the officers gamble themselves', my tutor answered, 'but the soldiers themselves refuse to give it up. Indeed, they are unable to give it up. Anyone who has taken up gambling, who has been bitten by the gambling bug, as they say, will eventually, win or lose, become so addicted to it that he can more easily go without sleep than without gambling, as you can see from those who spend the whole night rattling the dice, preferring it to the best food and drink, even if they end up losing their shirt.

They have banned gambling several times, on pain of

corporal, even capital punishment. The generals ordered the provost-marshal and his underlings to stop it by force if necessary, but it made no difference, the gamblers just moved their games to secret corners or behind hedges and went on taking each others' money, quarrelling and breaking each others' necks over it. It was in order to prevent these killings, and because some men gambled away their muskets and horses, even their rations, that they not only allowed gambling in public again, but provided this yard for it so that the guard would be on hand if any trouble breaks out. Even then they cannot prevent the occasional man being killed here in the yard.

Since gambling is an invention of the devil and very profitable for him, he has appointed a special swarm of demons to go round the world with no other task than to encourage people to gamble. They bind various dissolute characters to them through pacts and agreements which guarantee they will win. Despite this, among ten thousand gamblers you will rarely find one who is rich. On the contrary, they are usually poor and needy since they do not value their winnings and therefore usually gamble them away again or squander them on riotous living. This is the origin of the saying that the devil never leaves a gambler but he leaves him sucked dry. He robs them of their wealth, courage and honour and does not leave them until he has robbed them (unless God in His boundless mercy prevents it) of their souls. If a gambler is of such a cheerful, light-hearted disposition that no loss or run of bad luck can bring him to melancholy, despair or any of the other sins they usually lead to, then Satan is cunning enough to let him keep on winning and ensnare him through dissipation, arrogance, gluttony, drunkenness, whoring and sodomy.'

I crossed myself at the thought that such an invention of the devil should be allowed in a Christian army, especially considering the evident material and spiritual damage it caused. My tutor, however, said what he had told me about was nothing. It would be impossible to describe all the harm caused by gambling. There was a saying that once the dice has left the hand the devil takes over. I should think of it, he went on, as if a tiny demon were running alongside the dice on the cloak or table, guiding it and making it come to rest showing the number that was to his master's advantage. And I should remember it was not for nothing that the devil took such an interest in gambling, but that he profited greatly from it.

'And just look', he added, 'at the haggling dealers and Jews hanging round the gaming-yard. They will buy up cheaply rings, clothes and jewels that have been won, or articles the players want to turn into cash so they can go on gambling. Here, too, the demons are on the alert for players who have finished, putting other thoughts in their minds, whether they have won or lost, that are harmful to their souls. For the winners he builds castles in the air; the losers, who are already distraught and therefore more open to his suggestions, he doubtless gives thoughts aimed at making them take their own lives.

I tell you, Simplicius, as soon as I am settled in my old circumstances again I intend to write a whole book on this subject. I will describe the waste of precious time spent on gambling, the violent oaths with which gamblers curse God and the abuse they hurl at each other, recounting many horrifying examples and stories which happened at, on and around the gaming tables, not forgetting the duels and murders that were caused by gambling. In my book the greed, rage, envy, falseness, deceit, cheating and thieving, in short, all the follies of those who play at dice or cards, will be described in such vivid colours that men will only have to read it once to be filled with a horror of gambling as if they had drunk sow's milk, which they give to gambling addicts, without their knowledge, to cure them of the disease. I will demonstrate to all Christian men that God is blasphemed more by a company of gamblers than by a whole army.'

I praised his intention and expressed the hope that he would have the opportunity to carry it out.

Chapter 21

*Is somewhat shorter and more entertaining
than the previous one*

The longer we were together, the fonder my tutor became of me, and I of him, though we kept our friendship a closely guarded secret. I played the fool still, but did not make dirty jokes or play vulgar pranks. My conversation and behaviour were simple enough, but tended to make people think rather than laugh.

One day the colonel, who was very keen on hunting, took me with him when he went out to catch partridges with a clap-net, an invention which impressed me very much. However, his pointer was so excitable that most of the time it went for the bird before we could snap the net shut, so that we caught very little. I advised the colonel to mate his bitch with a hawk or a golden eagle, just as they did with horses and asses when they wanted a mule, so that the puppies would have wings and thus be able to catch the partridges in the air. Since the siege of Magdeburg was going so slowly I also proposed to him that we should make a long rope as thick as a half hogshead, drag it round the city and get all the people and animals in the two camps to pull on either end and raze the city to the ground in a single day. I thought up an abundance of these silly jokes and stories every day; that was my trade and my store was never empty.

My master's secretary, who was an evil customer and a real rogue, gave me a lot of material to keep me well supplied on the road we fools take. I did not just believe the things this joker told me, I passed them on to others when the conversation turned that way. Once I asked him what kind of person the regimental chaplain was, since he dressed differently from the others. He said, 'He is Sir Dicis-et-non-facis, which in plain German means a fellow who gives wives to other men but does not take one himself; he loathes thieves because they do not talk about what they do while he talks about things he does not do; the thieves are not very fond of him either since it is usually when they are being hanged that they have most to do with that kind of person.' Later on I called the chaplain, who was a good honest priest, by that name and he was mocked while I was thought a nasty, malicious fool and given a thrashing for it.

He also persuaded me that they had torn down and burnt the brothels behind the walls in Prague and the sparks and soot had been blown all over the world, like dandelion seeds, setting it on fire; likewise that none of the brave or stout-hearted soldiers would go to heaven but the simpletons, malingerers and other such whose only military act was to draw their pay; similarly no fashionable cavaliers or gallant ladies but only spineless weaklings, henpecked husbands, tedious monks, joyless priests, pious old bigots, poverty-stricken whores and all kinds of scum who are no use to anyone, as well as young children still crapping all over the benches. He further told me that innkeepers were so called because of all men they were the ones who tried most to keep in with both God and the devil. Talking of warfare, he managed to convince me that they sometimes used gold cannonballs and the more valuable the cannonball the more damage it did. 'Yes', he said, 'you could lead a whole captured army, artillery, munitions and baggage included, by gold chains.' He also persuaded me that more than half the women wore trousers, although one could not see them, and that many, although they could not perform magic spells and were not goddesses like Diana, made bigger horns grow on their husbands' heads than Actaeon had. I was such a stupid fool that I believed everything he said.

On the other hand the conversation of my tutor when he was alone with me was of a completely different nature. He introduced me to his son who, as I mentioned earlier, was a company clerk in the Saxon army and a man of quite different qualities from the colonel's secretary. For that reason the colonel was well disposed towards him and was thinking of getting the captain to release him and making him regimental secretary, a post on which his own secretary also had his eye.

I got on so well with this company clerk who, like his father, was called Ulrich Herzbruder, that we swore eternal friendship, vowing to stand by one another through thick and thin, in joy and sorrow. The fact that this was done with his father's knowledge made us stick even more firmly to our bond. After that our chief concern was to find a way of allowing me to get rid of my fool's costume honourably so we could be on an equal footing in public. Old Herzbruder, however, whom I revered and looked up to as if he were my own father, was not in favour of this. He said that if I was in too much of a hurry to change my situation I would end up in prison and in danger of my life. He also foresaw great disgrace approaching for himself and his son which made him more cautious than ever and unwilling to get involved in the affairs of a person whose imminent danger he could see all too clearly. He was afraid that if I revealed the truth about myself he might be drawn into my misfortune because he had known my secret for a long time, had known me inside and out, so to speak, but had not revealed it to the colonel.

Shortly after this it became even clearer to me that the colonel's secretary was violently jealous of my new brother because he was afraid he might be appointed to the post of regimental secretary over his head. I saw how at times he sulked, how resentment plagued him, and I noticed that he fell into deep thought and kept on sighing whenever he saw either of the Herzbruders. I was sure he was making plans to bring about his downfall. I told my brother of my suspicions, both out of affection and because of the debt I owed him, to put him on his guard against this Judas. He, however, shrugged them off, knowing he was the secretary's superior with both pen and sword and, besides, being in the colonel's good books.

Chapter 22

A cheating way of stepping into another man's shoes

It is the custom in the army to appoint old and well-tried soldiers to the position of provost-sergeant, and we had one in our regiment. He was such an out-an-out rascal, an arch-villain, that you could well say he was much more experienced than necessary. He was a true sorcerer and black magician who knew a spell for finding out thieves and another to make not only himself as bullet-proof as steel, but others too. He could also put whole squadrons of troopers in the field and looked just as poets and painters represent Saturn, though without scythe and bill-hook. Although his constant presence added to the misery of the poor troopers who fell into his cruel hands, there were people who enjoyed the company of this killjoy, foremost among them being Oliver, the colonel's secretary. The more his envy of young Herzbruder (who was of a very cheerful disposition) grew, the thicker his intimacy with the provost-sergeant became. I had no problem calculating that the conjunction of Saturn and Mercury boded no good for honest Herzbruder.

Just at that time the colonel's wife gave birth to a son. The christening feast was almost princely and young Herzbruder was asked to wait at table. He was happy to do the colonel this favour and that gave Oliver the chance of putting into effect the scheme he had long since had in mind. When it was all over the colonel missed his silver-gilt goblet, which he thought it was unlikely he had mislaid since it had still been there after all the guests had left. The page said that he thought the last time he saw it Oliver had it, but he would not swear to it. The provost-sergeant was consulted and ordered that if he could recover the goblet by magic he should do it in such a way that the thief would be revealed to the colonel alone. Some officers from his own regiment had been present and, he said, if one of them had perhaps let himself be tempted he would not want to shame him publicly.

Since we were all sure of our innocence, we laughed and joked as we came into the colonel's great tent where the sorcerer was to perform his magic. We all looked at each other, wanting to know what was going to happen and where the lost goblet would reappear. Then the sorcerer muttered a few words and puppies started to jump out of people's pockets, sleeves, boots, flies and any other openings in their dress, one, two, three or more at a time. They were all very handsome, with different colours and markings, and it was a hilarious sight to see them scurrying here and there round the tent. The tight calfskin breeches that the Czech arquebusiers had made for me were so full of puppies that I had to take them off and since my shirt had disintegrated long ago in the forest I stood there naked. Finally one leapt out of young Herzbruder's flies. It was wearing a gold collar and it was the nimblest of them all. The tent was so full of puppies scrabbling round we couldn't move without treading on them, but the one from Herzbruder's breeches ate them all up. And when it had finished it grew smaller and smaller while its collar grew bigger and bigger until it turned into the colonel's goblet.

Then not only the colonel but everyone present was forced to the conclusion that no one other than Herzbruder had stolen the goblet. The colonel said to him, 'You ungrateful fellow! I would never have believed it of you. Is this the reward for all the kindness I have shown you? I was going to appoint you regimental secretary in the morning, now you deserve to be hanged this very evening. And I would do it, too, if it wasn't for your honest old father. Get out of my camp right away and never let me see your face again.'

Herzbruder tried to defend himself but did not get a hearing since his guilt appeared self-evident. As he left, his father collapsed unconscious and it took all our efforts to bring him round and even the colonel tried to comfort him, saying that a God-fearing father should not have to answer for the sins of his son. That was how Oliver used the devil's help to obtain the position he had long been striving for but had not been able to get by honest means.

Chapter 23

Ulrich Herzbruder sells himself for a hundred ducats

As soon as the captain heard the story he removed Ulrich Herzbruder from his post as company clerk and put him with the pikemen. From that time on he was so generally despised that any dog might piss on him and he often wished he were dead. His father was so stricken with grief over the affair that he fell seriously ill and prepared himself for death. Since he had previously prophesied that he would face danger to life and limb on the 26th of July and that day was close at hand, he obtained permission from the colonel for his son to visit him so that he could talk to him about his inheritance and give him his last will and testament.

I was also present at the meeting and both witnessed and shared their sorrow. I saw that the son did not need to justify himself to his father. He knew what kind of person his son was and how well brought up, and he was convinced of his innocence. As a man of profound understanding and insight, he had no difficulty deducing from the circumstances that it was Oliver who had conspired with the provost-sergeant to concoct the predicament his son was in. But what could he do against a sorcerer? If he attempted to avenge himself he could expect even worse. Moreover he was making himself ready for death and yet could not die happy knowing he would leave his son behind in such disgrace. His son, for his part, could not face living with the shame and wanted to die before his father. Their grief was so heart-rending I could not hold back my tears.

Eventually the two of them agreed to bear their cross patiently and put their trust in God. The son, however, ought to think of ways of quitting the regiment and seeking his fortune elsewhere, but the problem was that they had no money for him to buy himself out. It was only while they were bemoaning the way poverty kept them imprisoned in their plight, cut off from all hope of improvement, that I remembered the ducats I still had sewn up in my donkey's ears. I asked them how much they needed. 'If someone came along with a hundred thalers for us', the son replied, 'I am sure it would solve all our troubles.'

'Then cheer up, brother', I replied. 'If that is what you need I will give you a hundred ducats.'

'What is this, brother?' he said, 'Are you really a fool to make a joke out of our misery?'

'No, no', I said, 'I will supply the money.' I took off my jerkin, slipped one of the donkey's ears off my arm and made him count out a hundred ducats himself and put them in his pocket. The rest I kept, saying, 'This I will use to look after your father, if he needs it.'

They threw their arms around me and kissed me; they were so overjoyed they hardly knew what they were doing. They wanted to draw up a document making me joint heir to old Herzbruder along with his son, or a note to the effect that, if God should help them to recover their estate, they would gratefully pay me back the sum with interest. I refused both offers, trusting in their constant friendship. Then young Herzbruder wanted to swear an oath to have his revenge on Oliver or die, but his father forbade it, telling him that the man who killed Oliver would die at my hands. 'But', he said, 'I am sure that neither of you will kill the other since I foresee that neither will be killed by weapons.' After that he made us swear an oath to love each other till death and stand by each other in all adversity.

Young Herzbruder bought himself an honourable discharge from the captain with thirty ducats. With the rest, and a measure of good fortune, he made his way to Hamburg where he equipped himself with two horses and enlisted in the Swedish army as a volunteer trooper, leaving our father in my care.

Chapter 24

Two prophecies are fulfilled at the same time

There was no one among the colonel's men better suited to care for old Herzbruder than I and so, since the patient himself was also more than happy with me, the colonel's wife, who showed him much kindness, gave me the job of nursing him. Being well looked after and also relieved of his worry about his son, the old man's health improved daily so that he was almost completely recovered before the 26th of July. However, he so dreaded that day that he decided to remain on the sick list until it was past. In the meantime he was visited by all kinds of officers from both armies who wanted to know what the future held for them. As he was a good mathematician and expert at casting horoscopes as well as being an excellent palmist and physiognomist his prophecies were seldom wrong. He even predicted the date of the Battle of Wittstock because he told so many who came to him they were threatened with a violent death on that day.

He had told the colonel's wife, six weeks before she was due, that she would have her baby in the camp because Magdeburg would not fall to us before that time. He made it clear to the treacherous Oliver, who insisted on pestering him, that he would die a violent death, adding that whenever and wherever it happened, I would avenge it and kill his murderer, with the result that from then on Oliver treated me with respect. He told me the whole course of my future life in great detail, as if it were past and he had been with me all the time. I paid little attention however and later on I remembered things he had predicted after they had occurred. Above all, he warned me to beware of water because he was afraid it might bring about my end.

When the 26th arrived he warned me and an orderly the colonel had sent at his request not to let anyone into his tent. He lay in bed and spent all the time in prayer. In the afternoon, however, a lieutenant from the cavalry camp rode over asking for the colonel's equerry. He was directed to us and when we turned him away he refused to accept it and made all sorts of promises to the orderly to let him in to the equerry whom, he said, he urgently had to see before that evening. When that didn't work he started swearing and blinding. A pox on it but he had ridden over so many times to see the equerry and had never found him in; now that the old man was here, was he going to have to leave again without having had a single word with him? He dismounted and started unfastening the tent-flap. I tried to stop him and bit his hand, for which I got a good box on the ears. When he saw the old man he said, 'I do beg you to forgive me, sir, for taking the liberty of coming to have a word with you.'

'Of course', said old Herzbruder. 'What can I do for you?'

'I was hoping, sir', said the lieutenant, 'you would be so kind as to see your way to drawing up my horoscope.'

'I hope you will forgive me', replied Herzbruder, 'but I really cannot, because of my illness. That kind of work demands a lot of calculations and my head is not up to it just now. If you can come back tomorrow I hope I shall be able to oblige you then.'

'Very well', said the lieutenant, 'but would you read my hand in the meantime?'

'Sir', replied Herzbruder, 'that art is very uncertain and can be deceptive so I would ask you to excuse me for the moment. I will do everything you want tomorrow.'

But the lieutenant refused to be put off. He went right up to my father's bed, stretched out his hand and said, 'Just a few words about the way my life will end, sir. I assure you that if what you say contains bad news I will regard it as a warning from God to take better care of myself. For God's sake, do not keep the truth from me.'

The honest old man's reply was brief and to the point. 'Then, sir, you had better take care not to be hanged this very hour.'

'What, you old rascal', cried the lieutenant, who was drunk as a fiddler's bitch, 'is that how you address a gentleman?' drew his sword and stabbed my dear friend to death in his bed. The orderly and I immediately set up a cry of 'Murder' so that the whole camp ran to arms. The lieutenant did not wait but made a swift exit on his horse and would doubtless have escaped had not the Elector of Saxony arrived at that very moment with a large contingent of cavalry, some of whom he sent to catch him. When the Elector heard what had happened he said to Hatzfeld, our general, 'It says little for discipline in an Imperial camp if a man is not safe from murderers on his sick-bed.' It was a severe verdict, enough to cost the lieutenant his life, for the general had him strung up straight away by his precious neck.

Chapter 25

Simplicius is transformed into a girl and is courted by a variety of people

This true story shows that not every prophecy should be rejected out of hand, as some people do whose minds are so closed they cannot believe anything at all. It shows how well-nigh impossible it is for any man to live beyond his pre-destined end, even if he has been been forewarned of it a short or long time before. To those who ask whether it is a good idea for people to have their horoscope drawn up and their future foretold I will just say that old Herzbruder told me so many things that I often wished, and still do wish, he had said nothing at all. I have been unable to avoid any of the mis-fortunes he predicted and the sleep I lose over those which have still not happened is to no avail; whether I make prepara-tion for them or not, they are going to come about, just as the others did. And as for the pieces of good fortune that are predicted, I think they are very often a disappointment, or at least people find they do not live up to the expectations the wretched prophecies raise. What good was it to me that Herzbruder swore by all that was holy that I had been born and bred of noble parents when the only ones I knew of were my Da and my Ma and they were common peasants in the Spessart? Similarly, what good was it to Wallenstein, Duke of Friedland, that it was prophesied he would be crowned king to the sound of viols? Do we not all know the violent end he met at Eger? However, I will let others rack their brains over this question and get back to my story.

Once I had lost my two Herzbruders there was nothing left for me in the camp outside Magdeburg, which, anyway, had been so battered during previous sieges that it was no more than a collection of canvas tents and straw huts surrounded by earthworks. I was so completely fed up with my role as fool you would have thought I had been eating jokes and quips by the ladleful. I decided I would get rid of my jester's outfit, whatever the cost, and stop being an object of ridicule. However, as I will now relate, I went about it in a rather careless fashion, since no better opportunity came my way.

Oliver, the secretary, had been appointed my tutor after old Herzbruder's death, and he often allowed me to ride out foraging with the servants. One day, when we were in a village where some of the cavalry baggage was stored and everyone kept going in and out of the houses, looking for anything they could take, I slipped away to see if I could find some old peasants' clothes to put on in place of my fool's costume. However, I couldn't find what I was looking for and had to make do with a woman's dress. As soon as I was alone I put it on and dropped my calfskin outfit down the lavatory, imagining my troubles were now over. Dressed like this I set off across the street to where some officers' wives were standing, taking little mincing steps such as Achilles might have done when his mother sent him disguised as a girl to stay with Lycomedes. Hardly had I left the house, however, than some of the foragers saw me and soon had me legging it as fast as I could. 'Hey, stop!' they shouted, which only made me run all the quicker. I reached the officers' wives before they caught me, fell down on my knees and begged them, in the name of women's honour and virtue, to protect my virginity from being ravished by this lecherous crew. Not only was my request granted, the wife of a cavalry captain took me on as her maid and I stayed with her until our forces had taken Magdeburg, the ramparts at Werben, Havelberg and Perleberg.

This captain's wife, although still young, was no innocent babe. She became so infatuated with my smooth cheeks and slim figure that, after making great efforts with veiled hints and insinuations, she finally told me only too clearly how I could be of service to her. In those days, however, I was much too strait-laced and pretended I had not understood and did nothing to suggest I was anything other than a pious young virgin. The captain and his servant were both suffering from the same disease, and the former ordered his wife to find me some better clothes so that, he said, she would not be shown up by my peasant smock. She did more than that and decked me out like a French doll, which only served to add fuel to the fires all three of them were consumed with. Eventually they were all so hot with desire that the master and his servant were both begging for what I could not give them, while I also refused it, most politely, to the lady.

Finally the captain decided to set up an opportunity to take by force what it was impossible for him to have from me. His wife realised this and since she was still hoping to overcome my resistance herself, she put obstacles in his path at every turn and frustrated all his ploys so he began to think he was going out of his mind. One night, when his master and mistress were asleep, the servant appeared beside the carriage where I had to sleep, poured out his passion for me with tears running down his cheeks and solemnly begged me to have pity on his distress. But I stayed as hard as stone and gave him to understand I intended to remain chaste until I was married, at which he immediately offered a thousand times to marry me. When I told him it was impossible for me to wed him, he became desperate, or at least pretended to, drew his dagger and placed the point on his breast, the hilt against the carriage, as if

169

he were about to run himself through. Perhaps he really does intend to kill himself, I thought, so I put him off with a promise that I would give him a final decision the next morning.

That satisfied him and he went off to his bed. I, however, lay awake thinking about the strange situation I was in. It was clear that no good could come of it in the long run. The lady's caresses were becoming more and more importunate, the captain's suggestions more and more brazen and the servant's protestations of love more and more desperate. I felt I was in a labyrinth from which there was no escape. The lady often made me catch fleas in broad daylight just to let me see her alabaster breasts and touch her delicate body which, since I was only flesh and blood too, I found more and more difficult to bear, and if his wife left me in peace the captain tormented me. And at night, when the two of them left me alone and I ought to be getting some rest, the servant came pestering me.

All in all, I was much worse off in my woman's clothes than I had ever been in my fool's costume. It was at this point – far too late – that I remembered old Herzbruder's prophecy and imagined I must be in the prison he had warned me of. I was imprisoned in my women's dress and could not escape without danger to life and limb, for if the captain realised who I was and caught me catching fleas with his beautiful wife I would have been in for a terrible thrashing. What should I do? Finally I decided to tell the servant the truth when he came in the morning, thinking, 'That will soon cool his ardour and if you slip him a few ducats he'll surely get you some man's clothes and that should solve all your problems.' It would have been a well thought-out plan if luck had been with me, but it wasn't.

For Hans the next morning began immediately after midnight, and he came to get his answer, shaking the carriage just as I was falling into my deepest sleep. He called out, a bit too loudly, 'Sabina, Sabina, oh darling, get up and keep your promise', so that he woke the captain, whose tent was next to the carriage, before he woke me. As the latter was already consumed with jealousy, this sent him into a fury. However, he didn't come out and interrupt but just got up to see how things would turn out.

Eventually the servant managed to wake me with his importunate rattling and demanded I either come out and join him or let him into the carriage. I told him off for this. Did he think I was a whore? Any promise I had made yesterday was on condition of marriage and that was the only way he was going to possess me. He replied that I should get up anyway as it was already starting to get light. He would go and get water and wood and light the fire for me.

'If you're going to do that', I answered, 'then I can sleep a bit longer. You go, I'll come soon.'

However, the fool would not leave off so I got up, more to do my work than to please him, especially since the desperation he had shown the previous evening seemed to have gone. In the camp I managed to pass pretty well for a maid-servant as I had learnt to cook, bake and wash when I was with the Czech arquebusiers. The soldiers' women do not spin when they are in the field anyway, and the captain's wife was happy to overlook the other woman's work I could not do, such as brushing and braiding her hair, since she knew very well that I had not been trained.

When I climbed out of the carriage with my sleeves rolled up Hans was so aroused by the sight of my white arm that he could not stop himself kissing me. And since I did not put up any great resistance the captain, before whose very eyes it was happening, leapt out of his tent, sword drawn, to run my poor lover through who, however, ran off and forgot to come back. To me the captain said, 'I'll teach you, you damned whore.' He was in such a fury he was incapable of saying any more, but struck out at me as if he had gone out of his mind. I started to scream and he had to stop for fear of raising the alarm, since both armies, the Saxon and the Imperial, were stationed close together because the Swedes under Banér were approaching.

Chapter 26

How he was imprisoned as a traitor and sorcerer

When it was light and both armies were striking their tents, my master handed me over to the stable-boys. They were the scum of the earth, which meant the treatment I was going to have to endure would be all the more terrible. As was the custom of these fiends when a woman was handed over to them like this, they hurried off to a thicket with me, where they could more easily satisfy their bestial lusts, and a lot of other men followed to watch the fun.

Among these was my Hans, who had not let me out of his sight. When he realised what was about to happen he determined to rescue me by force, even if it meant risking his life. He said I was his promised bride-to-be and found some supporters who felt sorry for both of us and were willing to help him. That, of course, the stable-boys would not have. They thought they had a better right to me and refused to hand over such a prize, meeting force with force so that the two sides started to exchange blows. The longer the fight went on the more people joined in and the greater the tumult became until eventually it was almost like a tournament in which each was doing his best for the sake of one fair lady.

The screaming and shouting attracted the attention of the provost-marshal, who arrived just as they had torn the clothes from my body and seen that I wasn't a woman. When they saw him, everyone froze; they were more afraid of the provost-marshal than of the devil himself. All those who a moment ago had been at each others' throats quickly separated. He briefly inquired into the matter and, contrary to my hope that he would save me, in fact arrested me. That a man should be found in a military camp dressed as a woman was unusual, not to say downright suspicious. Accordingly he and his men set off with me, passing all the regiments, which were drawn up in marching order, to hand me over to the judge-advocate-general or the provost-general. As we were passing my colonel's regiment, however, he recognised me and addressed me. As a result he found me some rags to put on and I was handed over to our old provost-sergeant who clapped me in irons, hand and foot.

It was hard work marching in chains and fetters and I would also have been tortured by hunger if Oliver, the secretary, had not paid for my meals. I had managed to keep hold of my ducats, but I couldn't afford to let them be seen or I would have lost the lot and put myself in even greater danger into the bargain. That same evening Oliver told me why I was kept in such close custody and the regimental intelligence officer was ordered to question me immediately so that my statement could be sent to the judge-advocate-general as soon as possible. They not only thought I was a spy but also that I was involved in witchcraft. Shortly after I had left my colonel they had burnt a number of witches who, before they died, confessed that they had seen me when they gathered together to try and dry up the Elbe so that Magdeburg would be captured more quickly. I was required to answer the following points:

1: Had I been to university or at least learnt to read and write?
2: Why had I come to the encampment outside Magdeburg dressed as a fool, since both now and when I was in the captain's service it was obvious I was not in the least simple-minded?
3: What was the reason I had disguised myself in woman's clothing?
4: Had I attended the witches' sabbath along with the other sorcerers?
5: Where did I come from and who were my parents?
6: Where had I been before I came to the encampment outside Magdeburg?
7: Where and for what purpose had I learnt women's work such as washing, baking, cooking etc? Likewise playing the lute?

I wanted to tell them the story of my whole life so that the circumstances of my strange adventures would explain everything and reveal the true answers to these questions. However, the intelligence officer, tired and in a bad mood after all the marching, was not that interested and told me just to answer the questions as briefly as possible. I therefore answered as follows, although no one could understand what had really happened to me from it:

1: I had not attended university, but I had learnt to read and write German.
2: I came in my fool's costume because I had no other clothes.
3: Because I was fed up with my fool's outfit and couldn't get any men's clothes.
4: Yes, I had been there, but against my will; I was not a sorcerer.
5: I came from the Spessart; my parents had been farmers.
6: With the governor in Hanau and with a colonel of arquebusiers by the name of Corpus.
7: I had been forced against my will to learn to wash, bake and cook when I was with the Czech arquebusiers, but I had learnt to play the lute in Hanau because I wanted to.

When my statement had been written down, he said, 'How can you deny you have been a student? Once, at the time we still thought you were a fool, when the priest celebrating mass said, *Domine non sum dignus*, people heard you say in Latin that we all knew that already?'

'Sir', I answered, 'some other people taught me that. They told me it was a prayer to be used when the chaplain was saying mass.'

'Oh yes?' said the intelligence officer. 'I can see you're just the type whose tongue will have to be loosened by torture.'

'God help me', I thought, 'I hope they don't loosen my head too.'

The next morning the judge-advocate-general sent word to our provost-sergeant that he should keep a good eye on me for he had a mind to examine me himself once the armies halted. Doubtless that meant I would have been tortured, if God had not decided otherwise. While I was in custody I kept thinking of both the pastor in Hanau and old Herzbruder, both of whom had prophesied what would happen to me if I were to get rid of my fool's costume.

Chapter 27

What happened to the provost-sergeant in the Battle of Wittstock

Hardly had we made camp that evening than I was taken to the judge-advocate. He had my statement and writing materials on the desk in front of him and began to interrogate me more closely. I told him all my adventures, just the way they had happened, but I was not believed. The answers to his questions were so pat and the whole story so strange that the judge-advocate could not make up his mind whether he was dealing with a fool or an arch-villain. He told me to take a pen and write something, to see whether he could recognise my handwriting or make any other deductions from it. I took the pen and paper with the ease of someone who uses them every day and asked what I should write. The judge-advocate-general, being perhaps annoyed that the interrogation was going on so late into the night, said, 'Oh, write that your mother's a whore.' I wrote down the exact words he had said and when he read them it just made my situation worse, for the judge-advocate said he really did believe I was a villain now. He asked the provost-sergeant whether I had been searched and whether any papers had been found on me.

'No', answered the sergeant, 'there was no point in searching him since he was naked when the provost-marshal handed him over.'

But it was no use, the provost-sergeant was made to search

me in the presence of all the rest, and since, unfortunately, he did it thoroughly he found the two donkey's ears full of ducats round my arms. Immediately the judge-advocate said, 'What do we need any further proof? This traitor was doubtless planning some mischief. Why else would a person in his right mind dress up in a fool's outfit? A man disguise himself in woman's clothes? Why else would he have such a considerable sum of money on him unless he was planning some big operation? Did he not admit that he learnt to play the lute while he was staying with the governor of Hanau, that pastmaster of trickery. What other artful practices do you think he learnt from those rogues, gentlemen? The best way to deal with him is to have him tortured tomorrow then burnt at the stake. He deserves no better anyway, since he was in company with the sorcerers.'

Anyone can easily imagine how I felt. I knew I was innocent and I trusted in God, yet I could see the danger I was in and mourned the loss of my ducats, which the judge-advocate-general had pocketed.

However, before this harsh verdict could be carried out, Banér's forces fell upon us. For a while the two armies struggled to gain the upper hand, then the Swedes attacked and quickly captured our heavy artillery. Our provost-sergeant kept well back from the battle-line with his men and prisoners, but we were still close enough to our brigade to be able to recognise each man from behind by his clothes. And when a Swedish squadron attacked them we were as much in danger of our lives as those who were fighting. At one point there were so many bullets singing through the air above us that it looked as if the salvo had been aimed deliberately at us. The faint-hearted ducked, as if they thought they could hide inside themselves, but those with more nerve and more experience of these affairs let the bullets fly over their heads without batting an eyelid.

In the battle itself, however, each man tried to avoid death by dispatching the enemy immediately in front of him. The dreadful noise of the guns, the clatter of harnesses, the clash of pikes and the cries of both attackers and wounded combined with the trumpets, drums and fifes to produce fearful music. You could see nothing but thick smoke and dust, which seemed to be trying to hide the horror of the dead and wounded. In the middle of it all you could hear the pitiful wails of the dying and the excited cheers of those who were still full of fight. The longer the battle went on the livelier the horses seemed to get in defending their masters, so furious they were in performing the duties that were imposed on them. Some fell dead under their riders, covered in wounds which were the undeserved reward for their faithful service. Others fell on top of their riders, thus in their death having the honour of being carried by the men whom they had had to carry during their lives. Yet others, relieved of the intrepid burden which had controlled them, left the men to their mad frenzy and ran off to enjoy their old freedom in the open fields.

The earth, whose usual task it is to cover the dead, was itself strewn with corpses, all with different mutilations: there were heads that had lost the bodies they belonged to and bodies lacking heads; some had their entrails hanging out in sickening fashion, others their skull smashed and the brain spattered over the ground; you could see dead bodies emptied of blood and living ones covered in the blood of others; there were shot-off arms with the fingers still moving, as if they wanted to get back into the fighting, while some men ran away without having shed a single drop of blood; there were severed legs lying around which, even though they had been relieved of the burden of their body, had become much heavier than they were before; you could see mutilated soldiers begging to be put to death, others to be granted quarter and spared.

In a word, it was a pitiful sight. The Swedish victors drove our defeated army from the field, splitting it up and scattering it completely with their swift pursuit. At this turn of events our provost-sergeant also decided to flee with his prisoners although we would have had nothing to fear from the conquerors. The provost-sergeant was threatening to kill us if we did not go with him when young Herzbruder galloped up with five other troopers and fired his pistol at him, saying, 'So it's you, is it, you old dog. Let's see if you still have time to make a few more puppies. Take that for your pains.' But the bullet bounced off the provost-sergeant as if he had been a steel anvil.

'Oho, is that the way it is?' said Herzbruder. 'Well, I'm not doing you the favour of coming to see you for nothing. You're going to die, even if your soul is glued fast to your body.' At that he forced one of the musketeers of the provost-sergeant's guard to strike him down with an axe if he wanted to be spared himself. Thus the provost-sergeant got his just reward and I was recognised by Herzbruder, who released me from my fetters and chains, put me on a horse and got his servant to lead me to safety.

Chapter 28

Of a great battle in which the triumphant conqueror is captured through concentrating on his victory

Although my rescuer had his servant lead me out of any further danger, he himself was driven by the desire for honour and booty so far into the midst of it that he was captured. When the victors were dividing up the spoils and burying their dead after the battle, it was discovered that Herzbruder was missing so I, along with his servant and horses, became his captain's property. He employed me as a stable lad, which I had to accept, getting nothing out of it but his promise that if I did well he would mount me (that is make me a trooper) when I was a bit older, and with that I had to be content.

Immediately afterwards the captain was promoted to lieutenant-colonel. I had the office David performed for Saul: in camp I played the lute and when we were on the march I had to carry his cuirass for him, which I did by wearing it, and an onerous task it was too. Although this armour is designed to protect the wearer from the blows of the enemy, I found the opposite was the case. Protected by it, the animal life that I hatched out could attack me all the more safely. Underneath the cuirass they were free to go about their business as they pleased so that it seemed more as if I were wearing it for their protection rather than my own, especially since I could not get my hands under it to carry out a punitive raid on them.

I spent my time thinking up all kinds of stratagems by which I could destroy this army. I had neither the time nor the opportunity to exterminate them by fire (i.e. in an oven), by water or by poison, though I was well aware of what quicksilver can do, and I simply did not have the means of getting rid of them by wearing different clothes or a clean shirt. I had to put up with them and supply them with flesh and blood. And when they nibbled and gnawed at me under the cuirass I would whip out a pistol as if I were going to fire on them, but all I did was to pull out the ramrod and use it to scrape them away from their fodder. Finally I discovered how to tie a scrap of fur round it to make a delousing rod with which I fished them out by the dozen and then killed them on the spot. It didn't make much difference, though.

Once the lieutenant-colonel was ordered to take a strong detachment on an expedition through Westphalia. If he had had as many men as I had lice he would have terrified the whole world; as it was, he had to proceed with caution and make a secret camp in the Günner Mark, a wood between Hamm and Soest. At that time the problem with my lodgers was coming to head; they so tormented me with their tunnelling that I began to be worried they were going to set up house between my skin and my flesh. They are such a plague it is no surprise the Brazilians eat them out of rage and desire for revenge. There came a point where I could bear the agony no longer. Most of the troopers were either feeding their horses, sleeping or on sentry duty, so I went a little way away, under a tree, to fight it out with my enemies. I took off the cuirass, even though others put one on before going into battle, and started such a massacre that soon my two swords – my thumb-nails – were dripping with blood and covered in dead bodies. Those I could not kill I sent into exile, wandering under the tree.

Whenever I remember this engagement my skin immediately starts to itch, just as if I were still in the middle of the battle. It did occur to me that I should not wage war on my own blood, especially not on such loyal servants who would stick to me through thick and thin, even if I were executed or broken on the wheel, and who, there being so many of them, had often softened the hard earth when I slept out in the open. Nevertheless, I continued my savage butchery and was so engrossed in it that I did not even notice when a party of Imperial cavalry attacked the lieutenant-colonel's position and eventually came upon me, relieved the poor lice, and took me prisoner. They showed not the slightest fear, despite the fact that I had a thousand times more claim to valour than the seven-at-one-blow tailor. I fell to the share of a dragoon and the best booty he had from me was the lieutenant-colonel's cuirass, for which he got a fairly good price from the commandant in Soest, where they were quartered. I had to serve the dragoon, who thus became my sixth master in these wars.

Chapter 29

The pleasures a pious soldier enjoyed in Paradise before his death, and how the Huntsman filled his place after it

Our landlady soon saw that she would have to get rid of my lodgers unless she wanted them to take over both herself and the whole house. She wasted no time, but threw my rags in the oven and fumigated them. They came out clean of vermin and I felt as if I were in a garden of roses. You have no idea how marvellous it was to be freed of the torment of the last months, which had been like living in an ant-hill.

To make up for it, though, I discovered I had another cross

to bear. My master was one of the few soldiers who think they will go to heaven. He was quite content with his pay and wouldn't harm a fly. His whole fortune consisted of what he could earn from sentry duty and save out of his weekly wages which, although they were pretty meagre, he guarded more closely than some do oriental pearls. Every copper he sewed tightly into his clothing, and his poor horse and I had to scrimp and save to help add to his store. The result was that I had to break my teeth on dry pumpernickel and make do with water or, if I was lucky, with small beer, which was not to my taste, especially now my throat was raw from the hard black bread. I grew quite thin, but if I wanted better food, he said, then I would have to steal it, only he made it quite clear that he did not want to know about it.

If everybody had been like him there would have been no need for gallows or rack, torturers, executioners or surgeons, nor even for sutlers or drummers to beat lights out. Nothing was further from his thoughts than eating and drinking, gambling and fighting. If he was ordered out on a convoy, raid or other kind of sortie he would amble along like an old woman with her stick. If this good dragoon had not exhibited these heroic military virtues he would never have captured me since he would have been dashing after the lieutenant-colonel. There was no hope of getting any cast-off clothes from him as he went about in rags and patches himself, just like the old hermit; his saddle and bridle were hardly worth a few coppers and his horse so weak with hunger neither Swedes nor Hessians had anything to fear from his hot pursuit.

All this led the captain to send him on guard duty to Paradise – the name of a nearby convent – as protection for the nuns. Not that he would have been much protection for them, but the captain hoped he might get himself fattened and his uniform smartened up. The main reason he sent him in particular, however, was because the nuns had asked for a pious, conscientious and quiet soldier. So off he rode, with me walking along beside him, since unfortunately he only had one horse.

'Now there's a piece of luck, Simbrecht', he said (he never

did manage to get my name right), 'won't we fill our bellies when we get to Paradise.'

'The name is an auspicious portent', I answered, 'let's hope the place lives up to it.'

He didn't understand what I said properly and replied, 'We'll certainly live it up if we can pour ten pints of good beer down our throats every day. I'm going to get myself a fine new cloak made and if you behave yourself you can have my old one, there's still plenty of wear in it.' He was right to call it his old cloak, I imagine it could still remember the Battle of Pavia a hundred years ago. It was so weather-stained and threadbare I was hardly overjoyed at his offer.

Paradise, on the other hand, was all we had hoped it would be, and more. Instead of angels, it was full of beautiful young women who kept us so well supplied with food and drink I was soon my old plump self again. There was plenty of the strongest beer, the best Westphalian ham and sausages, tasty and tender beef, boiled in salt water and eaten cold. That was where I learnt to spread salted butter thickly on the black bread so that it slipped down nicely when I ate it with a hunk of cheese. And when I sat down to a gigot of lamb pricked with garlic and a mug of fine ale beside it, I felt I was refreshing both body and soul and forgot all the suffering I had been through. In a word, this Paradise agreed with me as well as if it had been the real one. My only complaint was that I knew it would come to an end and that I would have to leave it in such a shabby coat.

But just as misfortune, once it had started to pursue me, had attacked me on all sides, it seemed that now good fortune was trying to make up for it. My master sent me back to Soest to bring the rest of his baggage and on the way I found a pack with several yards of scarlet cloth for a coat together with red silk for the lining. I took it and exchanged it at a cloth merchant's in Soest for enough ordinary green worsted to make me a suit of clothes, plus all the other bits and pieces, on condition he made the clothes for me and included a new hat. All I needed now was a new pair of shoes and a shirt, so I gave the merchant the silver buttons and braid that went with the coat as well and he obtained them for me so that I was kitted out from head to toe in fine new clothes. When I got back to my master in Paradise he was furious I had not brought my find to him. I thought I had done a good piece of business, but he talked of giving me a good beating and even came close to stripping me and wearing the suit himself. Indeed, I think he would have if the clothes had fitted him and he had not after all been somewhat embarrassed at the idea.

After that the penny-pinching skinflint was ashamed to see his groom better dressed than he was, so he rode into Soest and fitted himself out in style with money borrowed from his captain, which he promised to pay back from the wages he got for guarding the convent, a promise he duly kept. He in fact had enough money of his own to pay for it, but he was far too crafty to dip into his savings. If he had done so, it would have been goodbye to the life of ease he intended to enjoy through the winter in Paradise, for some other indigent soldier would have been given his post. As it was however, the captain had to leave him there if he wanted to get his money back.

From then on we led the idlest life in the world; playing skittles was the hardest work we did. Once I had groomed, fed and watered my master's nag I could play the gentleman and go for walks. The convent was also under the protection of a musketeer from of our opposite numbers, the Hessians in Lippstadt. By trade he was a furrier, which meant he was not only a mastersinger but also an excellent fencer. In order to keep his skill honed he spent a long time every day practising with me in all the different arms until I was so accomplished that I was not afraid to accept his challenge whenever he wanted. My dragoon played skittles with him instead of fencing, the loser having to drink most beer at dinner; that way it was the convent that paid for the losses of both men.

The convent had its own hunting grounds and therefore employed a huntsman. Since I was also dressed in hunting green I used to go out with him, and during that autumn and winter he taught me all his skills, especially as far as catching small game was concerned. Because of this, and since the name Simplicius was unusual and difficult for ordinary people to remember, or even pronounce, everyone called me *the Wee Huntsman*. I came to know all the paths and tracks, and afterwards put the knowledge to good use. When the weather was too bad for me to wander through the fields and woods I read all kind of books that the steward of the convent lent me. However, as soon as the aristocratic ladies of the convent realised that as well as having a good voice I could also play the lute, and a little on the clavichord as well, they started to look at me more closely. Since I was also well-proportioned and good-looking they concluded that my whole manner and bearing was noble so that before I knew it I was a very popular young gentleman and they could not work out why I put up with serving such a vulgar dragoon.

At the end of this delightful winter my master was relieved of his duties in Paradise, which so vexed him that it made him ill. His condition was aggravated by a violent fever and the old wounds he had received in the wars so that he did not last long and three weeks later I had a body to bury. I wrote the following epitaph on his grave:

> Here lies Skinflint,
> He was a warrior bold
> Who never spilt a drop of blood,
> If the truth be told.

It was the customary right in such cases for the captain to inherit the dragoon's horse and arms and his sergeant all the rest. Since, however, I was a lively, well-built lad and looked as if in time I would be perfectly capable of holding my own, they offered to let me have the lot if I would join up in place of my late master. I accepted, all the more willingly because I knew that my master had sewn into his old trousers a considerable number of ducats he had managed to scrape together over the years. When I gave my name, Simplicius Simplicissimus, to the clerk who kept the roll (his name was Cyriacus), he didn't know how to spell it and said, 'There's no demon in hell has a name like that.'

'There is one called Cyriacus, then?' I riposted, to which he had no answer, even though he thought himself so clever. This amused my captain and made him well-disposed towards me right from the start.

Chapter 30

How the Wee Huntsman set about learning the soldier's trade, from which a young soldier might learn much

Since the commandant in Soest needed a lad for the stables and he thought I was ideally suited for the job, he was unhappy that I had become a dragoon. He tried to get me by claiming to my captain that I was too young and not yet a man. He sent for me too and said, 'Wee Huntsman, I want you to be my servant.' When I asked what my duties would be, he said, 'You'll help look after my horses.'

'Sir', I said, 'we're not for each other. I would rather have a master whose horses served me, but since I can't find one like that, I'll stay a soldier.'

'Your beard hasn't grown enough yet', he said.

'I guarantee to beat a man of eighty, however long his beard', I replied. 'A beard never killed a man, or goats would be highly valued as soldiers.'

'Well', he said, 'if your courage matches your lip, you'll certainly pass for a soldier.'

'That can be tried out at the earliest opportunity', I said, giving him to understand that that I refused to be employed as a stable lad. He acquiesced in this, saying the proof of the pudding would be in the eating.

After that I made straight for the dragoon's old trousers and after I had dissected them I removed from the entrails enough to buy a good mount and the best musket I could find and polished it till it shone like a mirror. I had a new suit of green clothes made, since I liked being called 'the Huntsman', and gave my old one to my groom, since it was now too small for me. I rode around like a young lord and thought no end of myself. I made so bold as to wear a huge plume in my hat, just like an officer, with the result that there were soon some who looked on me with an envious and jaundiced eye. It came to words between us and eventually to blows, but once I had shown two or three what I had learnt from the furrier in Paradise not only did everyone leave me in peace, they wanted to make friends with me as well.

At the same time I went out on raids, both on foot and on horseback, for I was a good rider and could run faster than the rest. And whenever we encountered the enemy I threw myself at them and was always in the van. Very soon I was well known to both friend and foe. Such was my fame that both sides thought highly of me since I was given the most dangerous assaults to carry out, being put in command of whole detachments for that purpose. I started to grab booty like a Czech and whenever I made a valuable catch I gave my officers such a good share that I could even plunder in places where it was forbidden, since I was backed up in whatever I did.

General Count Götz had left three enemy garrisons in Westphalia, at Dorsten, Lippstadt and Coesfeld, and I was a constant thorn in the side of all three. I was at their gates daily with small detachments, now here, now there, and snapped up many a good prize. And since I always managed to get away, people came to believe I could make myself invisible and was as bullet-proof as iron or steel. I was feared like the plague and a party of thirty of our opponents were not ashamed to flee if they knew I was in the vicinity with just fifteen. Eventually it came to a point where, whenever there was a contribution to be levied from any place, I was the man to do it, and my purse grew as much as my fame. My officers and fellow soldiers loved their Wee Huntsman, the leaders of the opposing party were terrified, and the country people I kept on my side by a combination of fear and love, since I punished those who opposed me and richly rewarded those who did me the least service. In fact I gave away almost half of my booty, or used it to pay for information. The result was that no raiding party, convoy or expedition left the enemy's camp but it was reported to me, allowing me to work out their plans and make my dispositions accordingly. And I carried them through successfully, often with a portion of good luck, so that everyone was astonished at how young I was and even many of the officers and best soldiers among our opponents were keen to make my acquaintance. I treated my prisoners well, so that they often cost me more than the booty I had taken, and if I could do a favour to any of the opposing side, especially officers, without contravening my duty or allegiance, then I did so.

My behaviour would have quickly led to me being promoted to officer rank had I not been so young. Anyone of my age who aspired to become an ensign had to be of noble birth. In addition, my captain could not promote me because there were no vacancies in his company and he refused to let me go to another, since in losing me he would lose the equivalent of several milch-cows. I was made a lance-corporal, however. This honour, albeit a small one, for which I was preferred to much older soldiers, and the praise that was daily heaped on me spurred me on to higher things. Day and night I was trying to think of deeds I could do to make myself even greater, often I could not sleep because of these foolish fantasies. And since I realised I lacked the opportunity to show my true mettle, I was annoyed that I did not have the chance of crossing swords with the enemy every day. I often wished I was back in the Trojan wars, or in a long siege, like that of Ostend; fool that I was, I forgot that the day of reckoning was bound to come. It always does when a young and reckless soldier has money, courage and good fortune. The result is overweening arrogance. In my arrogance I had two servants instead of a stable lad, and I decked them out splendidly and mounted them, attracting the envy of all the officers.

Chapter 31

*How the Devil stole the priest's bacon and
the Huntsman trapped himself*

There are one or two stories I must tell of things that happened to me before I quit the dragoons which, even though they are not particularly important, are amusing. I did not confine my activities to great deeds alone but was happy to be involved in minor affairs if I thought they would enhance my reputation.

My captain was ordered to take fifty or so men on foot to the Recklinghausen district, where we were to carry out an ambush. We thought that before the plan was put into effect we might have to spend several days hiding in the woods, so each man took a week's provisions with him. However, since the rich convoy we were lying in wait for did not appear at the expected time, we began to run short of bread. We could not steal any for fear of giving ourselves away and ruining our plan, so that we were getting extremely hungry. In that area I had no contacts, as I had in other places, who would have secretly brought us some food, so that we had to think of other means of getting supplies if we were not to return home empty-handed. My comrade, a student who had only recently run away from the university and enlisted, sighed in vain for the gruel his parents had given him and which he had often spurned and left untouched. He talked of meals he had enjoyed in the past, especially some he had been given when he was a wandering scholar on his way between his home and the university.

'Oh my friend', he said to me, 'isn't it a scandal that I haven't studied anything which would help me fill my belly now? I tell you for sure that if I could just go to the priest in that village I'd get a real feast from him.'

I thought over what he had said and assessed our situation.

Those who knew the area could not go out or they would be recognised, those who were unknown did not know where there was the chance of stealing or buying something without being noticed. I made a plan involving the student and explained it to the captain. Although there was still a danger of our presence being given away he had such confidence in me, and we were in such a bad way, that he agreed to it.

I exchanged clothes with another soldier and strolled off with the student to the above-mentioned village, taking a long detour, even though it was only half an hour away. When we got there we saw immediately that the house next to the church was where the priest lived as it had the look of a town house and was built against the wall that went round the whole of the presbytery and garden. I had told the student what to say. He was still wearing his threadbare student dress while I was pretending to be a painter's apprentice, since I imagined there would be no call for that art in the village as farmers do not often have their houses decorated. The reverend gentleman received us very civilly and when my companion made a deep bow, greeted him in Latin and told a pack of lies about how he had been attacked by soldiers and robbed of all his provisions, offered him some bread and butter with a drink of beer. I pretended we were not together, but said I would have something to eat at the inn and then call back for him so that we could go some way before nightfall.

I went to the inn, more to give me the opportunity of spying out the land to see what we could steal that night than to fill my belly. And I was in luck. On my way there I saw a farmer plastering over the door to his oven in which were large loaves of pumpernickel bread which are baked slowly for twenty-four hours. Since I already knew where there was bread to be found I did not waste any time at the inn but just bought some white loaves to take to the captain. When I got back to the presbytery to tell my comrade it was time to go he had already eaten his fill and told the priest that I was a painter and on my way to Holland to perfect my art. The priest welcomed me warmly and asked me to go to the church so he could show me some paintings that needed repairing. I had to

189

go with him to keep up my disguise. He took us through the kitchen and as he unlocked the heavy oak door leading out into the churchyard I saw a sight for sore eyes or, rather, empty bellies: hanging up in the chimney were hams, sausages and sides of bacon. They seemed to be smiling at me, so I gave them a come-hither look, wishing they would come and join my comrades in the woods, but in vain; the hard-hearted things ignored me and stayed hanging there. I tried to think of ways of getting them to join the above-mentioned oven-load of bread, but it was not that easy. There was a wall round the presbytery and garden and all the windows had iron bars; there were also two huge dogs lying in the courtyard and I was sure they would not be sleeping during the night when people would try to steal the food of which they would get a portion in reward for their faithful vigilance.

In the church we discussed the paintings and the priest was keen to hire me to restore some of them. I kept making excuses, in particular my journey to study in Holland, and eventually the sexton said, 'You look more like a runaway soldier to me, you young rascal, than a painter's apprentice.' It was a long time since anyone had spoken to me like that, but I had to grin and bear it, so I just shook my head and replied, 'Just give me a brush and some paint, you old rascal, and I'll paint you the portrait of a fool in no time at all, if you'll just keep still.' The priest made a joke of it and told us both it was not proper to argue in a sacred place like the church. It was clear he believed both me and the student. He gave us another drink and we left, but my heart stayed behind with the smoked hams and sausages.

We were back with our companions before nightfall. I told the captain what had happened, put on my own clothes and arms and selected six good men to help carry the bread home. We got to the village about midnight and took the bread out of the oven without causing any noise, since there was one amongst us who knew a spell to keep dogs from barking. As we passed the presbytery I could not bring myself to go on and leave the bacon behind. I stopped and looked carefully to see if there was any way of getting into the priest's kitchen.

The only way in was the chimney, which would have to serve as a door. We stowed the bread and our arms in the charnel house, found a ladder and rope in a barn and, since I could climb up and down chimneys as well as a sweep, having practised from my earliest days in hollow trees, I climbed up onto the roof myself. It had a double layer of hollow tiles and was ideal for my purpose. I twisted my long hair up into a bunch on top of my head and had myself lowered down on one end of the rope to my beloved bacon. There I tied the hams and sides of bacon one after another to the rope, the man on the roof pulled them up and the others carried them to the charnel house. But, pox on it, after I had tied on the last sausage and was about to climb up again, the bar I was standing on broke and poor Simplicius tumbled down to the ground. Now it was the huntsman who was caught in a trap. My comrades on the roof let the rope down, but when they tried to pull me up it broke before they had even lifted me off the floor. The noise had wakened the priest, who told his cook to light a candle. I thought to myself, 'Now, Wee Huntsman, you're the one who's going to be hunted and you could well be torn to pieces like Actaeon.'

The cook came into the kitchen in her nightgown, her dress slung over her shoulders, and stood so close to me it touched me. She picked up a glowing ember from the stove, held the wick of the candle to it and blew on it. But I blew much harder, startling the poor woman so that she dropped the ember and the candle and ran back to her master. That gave me some breathing space to think up a way of getting out of this, but nothing occurred to me. My comrades whispered down the chimney that they were going to break open the door and bring me out by force, but I forbade it. I told them to put their weapons away and leave only Tearaway on the roof to wait and see if I could get out quietly and unnoticed and not jeopardise our ambush. If, however, that were not possible, then they could do their worst.

In the meantime the priest had lit a candle himself, but the cook told him there was a dreadful ghost with two heads in the kitchen (perhaps she had seen my hair bunched up on top

191

of my head and taken it for another head). Hearing this, I rubbed ashes, soot and coal over my face so that I looked a fearful sight and quite the opposite of the angel the nuns in Paradise had called me. If the sexton had seen me he would have readily agreed I was a quick painter. Then I set up a terrible clattering in the kitchen, throwing pots and pans all over the place. My hand fell on the cauldron handle and I hung it round my neck, but the poker I kept hold of, to defend myself if necessary.

The good priest was not put off by all this, however. He entered the kitchen in procession with his cook, who was carrying two wax candles and a stoup of holy water. He himself was arrayed in surplice and stole, with a sprinkler in one hand and a book in the other from which he began to read the exorcism, asking who I was and what I was doing there. Since he took me to be the devil, it seemed perfectly reasonable for me to play the Father of Lies, so I answered, 'I am the devil and I have come to wring your neck, and your cook's too.'

He continued his exorcism, telling me I had no business either with him or his cook and bidding my by the most powerful incantation to return to the place I had come from. That, I replied in a fearsome voice, was impossible, even if I wanted to. In the meantime Tearaway, who was a wily rascal and would stop at nothing, added some special effects of his own from the roof. When he heard what was happening in the kitchen, namely that I was pretending to be the devil and the priest believed me, he hooted like an owl, barked like a dog, neighed like a horse, bleated like a billy goat and brayed like a donkey; sometimes he sounded like a whole ruck of cats on heat in February, sometimes like a hen about to lay an egg. He could imitate any animal noise; if he wanted, he could howl just like a whole pack of wolves together. The priest and his cook were frightened out of their wits but I was somewhat conscience-stricken at letting myself be exorcised as the devil. I believe the reason he took me for the Arch-fiend was that he had read or heard somewhere that the devil likes to dress in green.

In the middle of these terrors, which affected all three of us, I fortunately noticed that the door out into the churchyard was not locked, only bolted. Quickly I pushed the bolt back and slipped out into the churchyard, where I found my companions stationed with their muskets cocked, leaving the priest to continue his exorcism for as long as he liked. Tearaway jumped down from the roof with my hat and we packed the food and set off back to our camp in the woods, since there was nothing left to do in the village, except that we should have returned the ladder and rope we had borrowed.

The whole party was reinvigorated by the provisions we had stolen and such was our continued good luck that not one of us got the hiccoughs. Everyone had a good laugh at my adventures, only the student was unhappy that I had robbed the priest who had filled his belly so generously. He swore blind that he would gladly pay him for the bacon if he only had the wherewithal, though that did not stop him eating as if he had the sole rights to it. We spent another two days there waiting for the convoy for which we had been lying in ambush so long. We did not lose a single man in the attack, took thirty prisoners and as excellent booty as I have ever helped divide up. Since I had done most, I got a double share, consisting of three handsome Friesland stallions, laden with as much merchandise as they could carry, given that we had to make haste. If we had had time to look through the booty properly and bring it to a place of safety, each one of us would have been a wealthy man. We had to leave more behind than we carried off because we had to make all speed to get away, taking what we could with us. For security, we went back to Rheine, where the main body of our army lay and where we ate and shared out the booty.

While we were there I remembered the priest from whom we had stolen the bacon. You can imagine what a swaggering, conceited, honour-craving young man I was. Not satisfied with having robbed the good priest and frightened him to death, I wanted to come out of the affair with honour. I took a gold ring with a sapphire set in it that I had picked up on the expedition and sent it to the priest by a trustworthy messenger, together with the following letter:

Reverend Sir,

If, during the last few days, I had had enough food in the woods to keep me alive I would have had no cause to steal your bacon, during the course of which robbery I probably caused you great alarm. As the Lord is my witness, I had no intention of giving you that fright and hope you will therefore forgive me for it. As far as the bacon is concerned, however, it is right and proper that it should be paid for. I am therefore, in lieu of payment, sending this ring, given by those for whom your provisions were stolen, and ask your reverence to do with it as you see fit. I assure your reverence that you have an obedient and faithful servant in the one your sexton thought was no painter and who is generally known as

The Huntsman

To the peasant whose oven they had emptied, the party sent sixteen thalers from the common purse, for I had taught them that we must do this to keep the country people on our side, for then they will often help a party in difficulties, when otherwise they might well betray them and cost them their lives. From Rheine we went to Münster, from there to Hamm and then back to our quarters in Soest where, a few days later, I received a reply from the priest, which went as follows:

Most noble Huntsman,

If the man whose bacon you stole had known you would appear to him in such devilish form he would not have so often expressed the desire to see the celebrated Huntsman. The fact, however, that the borrowed meat and bread have been paid for at many times their value, makes the fright easier to forgive, especially since it was caused unintentionally by such a famous person. This pardon is coupled with the request that the Huntsman will not hesitate to return once more to visit the man who is not afraid to exorcise the devil.

Vale.

This is the way I behaved everywhere I went and I acquired a great reputation through it. The more I gave away, the more booty I took, and I thought that the ring, even though it was worth a hundred thalers, was a sound investment.

And that is the end of the Second Book.

Book III

Chapter 1

How the Huntsman strayed too far from the straight and narrow

You will have realised from the previous book how ambitious I had become in Soest, how I sought and found honour, glory and favour through actions which in others would have deserved punishment. Now I will tell you how I let my folly lead me even further astray so that I lived in constant danger to life and limb. As I have already mentioned, I was so desperate to gain honour and glory that at times it kept me awake at night, and when the mood was on me I would lie in bed thinking up new plots and ploys. The most bizarre ideas occurred to me. I invented a kind of shoe that you put on back to front, so that the heels came underneath your toes, and had some thirty pairs made at my own cost. I used to share them out among my men before we went on a raid, making it impossible to track us since we sometimes wore these, sometimes put them back in our knapsacks and wore our ordinary shoes. If someone came to the place where we had changed them, from the tracks it just looked as if two parties had met there then completely vanished. If, however, I kept my back-to-front shoes on, then it looked as if I were going to the place I had actually come from, or vice versa. Thus if we left tracks on an expedition they were more confusing than a maze, making it impossible for any pursuers to catch me. I was often right next to an enemy party that was setting off to look for me far away, and even more often miles away from the thicket they had surrounded and were searching in the hope of catching me. I did just the same when we were on horseback. It was not unusual for me to have the men dismount at junctions or crossroads and turn the horseshoes back to front. The usual tricks people employed to make a weak party appear strong from their tracks, or a strong party weak, were so common and I valued them so little that I do not think them worth recounting.

I also invented an instrument by means of which, during nights when there was no wind, I could hear a trumpet three hours' march away, a horse neighing or a dog barking at two hours' distance and people talking at one. I kept this a close secret and gained quite a reputation through it, since what I did appeared impossible. This instrument, which I usually kept in the pocket of my breeches along with my telescope, was not much use by day, unless we were in a very quiet, lonely place, since you could hear everything that made a noise, from the horses and cows to the smallest birds in the air or frogs in the water. It sounded just as if you were in a market place surrounded by people and animals, all making themselves heard, so that you could not distinguish the one from the other.

I know there are still people who do not believe this, but whether they do or not, it is the truth. Using it, at night I can recognise a person speaking normally from the sound of his voice when he is so far away that by day you would need a good telescope to recognise him from his clothes. However, I am not surprised if people do not believe what I have just written. Even those who saw me use the instrument with their own eyes refused to believe it. I would say, 'I can hear cavalry coming, the horses are shod', or 'I can hear farmers coming, the horses are unshod', or 'There are carts coming, but it's only peasants, I can tell by the way they speak', or 'There are musketeers coming, roughly so many, I can tell by the rattle of their bandoliers', or 'There's a village over here or over there, I can hear cocks crowing, dogs barking etc', or 'Here comes a herd of cattle, I can hear sheep baaing, cows mooing, pigs grunting', and so on. At first my comrades thought it was all just talk, then when they saw that I was right each time they assumed it must be magic, and that the devil had revealed to me the things I saw. That, I imagine, is what the reader will be thinking. Nevertheless it often helped me to escape the enemy when they had received information and were coming to capture me. I also think that if I had made my invention known it would have become very common as it is so useful in wartime, especially during sieges. But now back to my story.

If there was no foray for me to take part in, I would go out stealing on my own account and no horse, cow, pig or sheep was safe from me for miles around. I had boots or shoes I could put on horses and cattle until we came to a well-trodden road, so that they left no tracks to follow. There I would put the horseshoes on back to front; for cows and oxen I had specially made shoes that made them look as if they were going in the opposite direction with which I could bring them to a safe place. Fat porkers are so lazy they do not like to journey at night, but I had a masterly way of getting them to move, no matter how much they grunted and refused to stir at first. I soaked a sponge, to which I had attached a strong string, in a savoury mash of meal and water, then let the pig I was after eat the gruel-soaked sponge, keeping tight hold of the string. After that it would follow me unprotesting and give me hams and sausages for my trouble. Whenever I brought back something like this I always shared it with the officers and my comrades so that I was allowed to go off again, and if my plan had been betrayed, or I was spotted executing it, they would help me out. I thought far too much of myself to steal from poor people or to take chickens or other such trifles.

With all this gorging and guzzling I gradually started to lead a life of self-indulgence. I had forgotten what the hermit had taught me. I was still young and had no one to guide me, no one I could look up to. The officers joined in my gluttony, and those who should have been telling me off and punishing me, instead encouraged me to try out all the vices, with the result that I became so wicked and ungodly no villainy was too great for me. The consequence was that I was secretly envied on all sides: by my comrades because I was better at thieving and by the officers because I was so bold and success-ful at forays and had made a greater name for myself than they had. I am sure there were one or two among them who would have soon sacrificed me had I not been so liberal with my money and goods.

Chapter 2

The Huntsman of Soest gets rid of the Huntsman of Werl

I continued my depredations. I was having some devil's masks made and frightening costumes with cloven hooves to go with them to help me terrify the enemy and also take goods from our friends unrecognised (it was the episode with the priest's bacon that had given me the idea for this). At this point I heard there was a man in Werl who was an excellent raider, dressed himself in green and went round the country-side, though especially those areas that owed tribute to us, committing atrocities such as rape and pillage under my name. This brought serious complaints against me and would have cost me dear if I had not been able to prove I had been elsewhere at the time when he had carried out some of his attacks disguised as me. I could not let him get away with this and determined to stop him going round in my name, taking booty in my dress and bringing shame on me. With the know-ledge of the commandant in Soest I challenged him to meet me in the field with swords or pistols. He did not have the guts to turn up, so I let it be known that I intended to take my revenge on him even if, to do it, I had to beard him in the lair of the commandant of Werl himself, who did not punish him. I publicly declared that if I met him out on a foray I would treat him as an enemy.

I not only abandoned work on the masks, for which I had had great plans, I also chopped up my green suit into little pieces and burnt it publicly outside my quarters in Soest, even though my clothes were worth over a hundred ducats without the plumes and other accoutrements. I was so furious about the whole affair that I swore that the next person to call me Huntsman would have to kill me if he did not want to die at my hands, for that was what would happen, even if it cost me my life. I refused to lead forays (which I was not bound to do, since I was not an officer) until I had had my revenge on the impostor in Werl. I stopped taking part in any military activities, except for my guard duty, unless I was specifically ordered to do something, which I would then carry out in a very lethargic fashion, like any malingerer. This was soon public knowledge throughout the area and made the enemy's raiding parties so confident and bold that they daily took up position outside at the very gates of our camp. I found this unbearable, but what I found even more unbearable was the fact that the Huntsman of Werl was still pretending to be me and taking a lot of booty.

While everyone was thinking I was sitting twiddling my thumbs and was likely to do so for a long time, I was in fact spying out everything my double in Werl did. I discovered that not only did he use my name and my clothes, he also went out secretly at night to steal things, whenever there was something for the taking. At this I immediately awoke from my torpor and made my plan accordingly. I had trained my two servants so that they were as obedient as a pair of spaniels. They were so loyal they would have gone through fire for me if necessary, since with me they had plenty to eat and drink and plenty of booty. One of them I sent to my enemy in Werl. He claimed that since I, his former master, had started to live the life of a chicken-livered idler and had sworn never to go out on a foray again, he had refused to stay with me any longer and had come to offer his services to the dragoon in Werl, who had taken over my Huntsman's dress and behaved like a real soldier. He knew all the paths and tracks in the area, he said, and could give him a lot of tips to help him take good booty. The poor, simple-minded fool believed him and took him on.

At my servant's suggestion he and his comrade went with him one particular night to a sheep-farm to steal some fat sheep. I was lying in wait for them with Tearaway and my other servant. We had bribed the shepherd to tie up his dog and let the others dig their way into the sheep-fold unhindered, promising we would give them a warm welcome. Once they had made a hole in the wall the Huntsman of Werl wanted my servant to go in first but he said, 'No, there might be someone on watch inside who'll hit me over the head. I can see you don't know the first thing about the business. First of all we have to send in someone on reconnaissance.' He drew his sword, stuck his hat on the end and pushed it in through the hole several times. 'That's the way to see if there's anyone at home or not.' After that it was the Huntsman of Werl who was the first to crawl in and Tearaway immediately caught him by his sword-arm and asked if he surrendered. His companion heard this and decided to make a run for it. However, since I didn't know which of them was the Huntsman of Werl and was quicker than him, I ran after him and soon caught him. I asked, 'Which side?'

'The Emperor's', he answered.

'Which regiment?' I asked. 'I'm in the imperial army too. Only a villain would deny his lord.'

'We're from the dragoons in Soest', he replied, 'and we've come to get a few sheep. If you're with the Empire too, brother, I hope you'll let us go.'

'You're from Soest?' I said. 'Who are you then?'

'My comrade in the sheep-fold is the Huntsman', he replied.

'Villains, that's what you are', I said. 'Why are you plundering your own district? The Huntsman of Soest is not such a fool as to be caught in a sheep-fold.'

'Sorry, I meant the Huntsman of Werl', the other replied.

While this discussion was going on, my servant and Tearaway came up with the impostor. 'So there you are, you scoundrel, at last we meet. If it wasn't for the respect I have for the imperial uniform, I'd blow your brains out on the spot. Until now I have been the Huntsman of Soest and unless you take up one of these swords and face up to me like a true soldier, you are nothing but a craven blackguard.' As I was saying this my servant, who like Tearaway was dressed in a horrible devil's costume with huge goat's horns, put two similar swords I had brought from Soest on the ground at our feet and offered the Huntsman of Werl the choice. The Huntsman was so terrified at this that he did what I did when I spoilt the dance in Hanau and made such a mess of his trousers that no one could stay near him. He and his comrade were trembling like drenched dogs, fell to their knees and begged for mercy. But Tearaway boomed, as if his voice were coming from inside a hollow jug, at the Huntsman, 'You're going to fight or I'll wring your neck.'

'Oh, good sir Devil, I didn't come here to fight. If your devilship will spare me that I will do whatever you want.'

While he was gabbling away my servant put one of the swords in his hand and gave me the other but he was trembling so much he couldn't keep hold of it. The moon was bright and the farmer and his servants could see and hear everything from their hut. I called him over so that I should have a witness. When he came he pretended he could not see the two in devil's costumes and asked what I thought I was doing, quarrelling with these fellows in his sheep-fold. If I had anything to settle with them we should find another place for it. Our disputes were nothing to do with him, he went on, he paid his monthly 'conterbissions' and hoped we would leave him and his sheep-farm in peace. Then he asked the other two why they allowed me to lord it over them and did not just knock me down.

'You ungrateful idiot', I said, 'they were going to steal your sheep.'

'Then they can kiss the arses of all my sheep and mine too', he said and went off.

After that I started to press for a duel again, but the poor Huntsman of Werl was so terrified he couldn't even stand up, so that eventually I came to feel sorry for him. Then he and his comrade made such moving speeches that I ended up forgiving and forgetting everything. Tearaway was unhappy with this and forced the Huntsman to kiss the arses of three sheep (that was the number he had intended to steal) and also scratched him all over the face, so that he looked as if he had been joining the cats at their feeding bowl. I was content with this poor revenge, but the Huntsman was so ashamed he soon vanished from Werl. His comrade told everyone he met, and backed it up with violent oaths, that I had two genuine devils at my beck and call, with the result that I was more feared, but less loved, than ever.

Chapter 3

The great God Jupiter is captured and reveals the counsel of the gods

I soon became aware of this, so I gave up my former godless life and turned to virtue and piety. I did start going out on forays again, but I was so affable and courteous to friend and foe alike that everyone who came into contact with me found me different from the reports they had heard. I gave up my spendthrift ways and accumulated a hoard of beautiful jewels and ducats which from time to time I hid in hollow trees in the countryside around the town, because that was what the famous fortune-teller of Soest advised, telling me I had more enemies in the city and in my own regiment, who were after my money, than in all the enemy garrisons. The news had got round that the Huntsman had disappeared, but those who rejoiced in the fact soon found me breathing down their necks again. Scarcely had one town heard a rumour that I had wrought havoc in another than I was reminding them too that I was still a force to be reckoned with. I was like a whirlwind, here, there and everywhere, so that people had more reason than ever to say that there must be more than one Huntsman.

Once I was not far from Dorsten with twenty-five muskets, lying in wait for a convoy of carts that was supposed to be heading for the town. As usual, I was on look-out myself, since we were close to the enemy. I saw a single man come along the road, respectably dressed, talking to himself and shadow-fencing with the cane he had in his hand. All that I could hear was that he said, 'If the world won't recognise my divinity then I shall just have to punish it.' From this I deduced that it might be some powerful prince who was going round incognito to find out how his subjects lived and had decided to punish them since he was displeased with what he had found. I thought to myself, 'If this man belongs to the enemy, he'll bring a good ransom. If not, then treat him with the greatest respect so that you win his favour and you'll be well set up for the rest of your life.' I jumped out with my musket at the ready and said, 'Would you be so good as to take a walk into the trees here, sir, keeping in front of me. Otherwise I will have to assume you are an enemy and deal with you accordingly.'

He answered gravely, 'I am not accustomed to be treated like this', but I ushered him politely into the thicket saying, 'I'm sure your Honour will not regret bowing to necessity just this once.' When I had him safely with my men and had set a new lookout, I asked him who he was. He answered very haughtily that there was not much point to my question since I was already aware that he was a great god. At first I thought he was perhaps a nobleman from Soest who had recognised me and was only saying this to pull my leg, since the people of Soest are often teased about their silver statue of Christ with its long gold apron that they call the 'great God'. I quickly realised however that I had not caught a prince but a lunatic who had studied too much and been driven mad by poetry. Once he had thawed out a little he told me he was the great god Jupiter.

It was a catch I wished I had not made, but since I had the madman, I had to keep him with us until we left. As the wait was becoming rather tedious I decided to humour the fellow and make some use of him, so I said, 'Well, then, my dear Jove, how is it that your divine majesty has left his heavenly throne and come down to us on earth? Forgive me, o Jupiter, if my question seems somewhat forward, but we are related to the gods of heaven, being simple wood spirits, born of the nymphs and fauns, with whom your secret will ever remain a secret.'

'I swear by the Styx', Jupiter replied, 'that even if you were Pan's own son I would reveal nothing to you, were it not that you resemble my cup-bearer Ganymede. But for his sake I can inform you that a great outcry over the sins of the world has risen up through the clouds to me. The council of the gods discussed it and decreed that I would be justified in destroying the world by flood, as I did in the days of Lycaon, King of Arcadia. Since, however, I regard the human race with especial favour and am, moreover, always more disposed to lenience than to severity, I am going about the world to see the ways of men for myself. And although I find things worse than I imagined, I am not minded to destroy all men without distinction, but to punish those who deserve punishment and then bend the rest to my will.'

I had to laugh, but kept as straight a face as I could and said, 'Oh, Jupiter, I fear all the pains you have taken will be in vain if you do not, as you did once before, visit flood, or even fire on the world. If you send war then you will give free rein to all the wicked, villainous rogues who will torment the pious, peace-loving people; if you send famine that is playing into the hands of the profiteers by inflating the price of their corn; if you send plague then the misers and those who survive will feather their nests, for they will inherit everything. If you are going to punish us at all, then you must destroy the whole world, root and branch.'

Chapter 4

Of the German hero who will conquer the whole world and make peace among all nations

Jupiter replied, 'You are talking like an ordinary mortal, as if you did not know that we gods are well able to devise a punishment that will strike down the evil and spare the good. I intend to awaken a German hero who will bring this about through the power of his sword. He will kill all the wicked and protect the righteous and raise them up.'

'But a hero like that will need soldiers', I said, 'and where you have soldiers you have war, and where you have war the innocent suffer along with the guilty.'

'Do you earthly gods think like earthly men?' was Jupiter's response. 'You seem to understand nothing. I will send a hero who does not need soldiers and yet will reform the whole world. In the hour of his birth I will give him a well-made body, stronger than the one Hercules had, and endow him with more than enough prudence, wisdom and understanding; then Venus will give him such a beautiful face that he will outshine Narcissus, Adonis and even my Ganymede. In addition to all his virtues I will get her to bestow a particular elegance, grace and presence on him which will make him well liked by everyone he meets (with this in mind I will look on her more warmly than ever in the hour of his nativity). Mercury will grant him incomparably profound intelligence and the inconstant moon will help, not harm him by endowing him with incredible speed. Pallas will bring him up on Parnassus, and Vulcan will forge his weapons, especially a sword with which he will conquer the whole world and cut down all the ungodly without the help of a single soldier. He will not need any help. Every city will tremble at his presence and he will subdue any fortress, however impregnable, in fifteen minutes. Eventually the greatest potentates in the world will bow down before him and he will rule the land and the seas so excellently that both gods and men will rejoice in it.'

'But how', I said, 'can all the ungodly be cut down without bloodshed, how can dominion over the whole world be achieved without a strong arm and extreme force? I confess, o Jupiter, that I understand less of these things than an ordinary mortal.'

'That does not surprise me', replied Jupiter, 'since you do not know what extraordinary power my hero's sword will have. Vulcan will forge it from the same material from which he makes my thunderbolts and my hero will only need to draw it and wave it once to cut off all the heads of a great army, even if they are a whole league away on the other side of a mountain, so that the poor devils will be lying there headless before they even know what is happening to them. When he begins his campaign and comes to a town or fortress he will do as Tamburlaine did and fly a white flag as a sign that he has come in peace and to further the general good. If the people come out and accept him, well and good; if not, then he will unsheathe his sword and by its power chop off the heads of all wizards and witches in the city and raise a red flag; if they still do not come out, he will kill all murderers, thieves, usurers, rogues, adulterers, whores and catamites in the same way and show a black flag; if all those left do not then immediately come out and humbly submit he will condemn the whole city as a stiff-necked and disobedient people that is to be wiped out; however, he will execute only those who kept the others from yielding earlier.

Thus he will go from town to town and give each the land around it to govern in peace, and from each town throughout Germany he will take two of the wisest and most learned men to form a parliament and will unite the towns for ever. He will abolish serfdom as well as all tolls, taxes, interest, rents and dues in the whole of Germany and order the land so that the people can forget forced labour, guard duty, contributions, levies, warfare and other burdens and will be happier than if they were living in the Elysian fields.

Then', Jupiter went on, 'I will often come with the whole assembly of the gods to visit the Germans and take my ease under their vines and fig-trees; I will set Mount Helicon in the middle of their land and establish the Muses on it again; I will bless Germany with greater abundance than Arabia Felix, Mesopotamia and the land round Damascus; I will renounce Greek and speak German alone. In a word, I will be so thoroughly German that I will grant them dominion over the whole world, as I did to the Romans before them.'

'But, mighty Jupiter', I said, 'what will the lords and princes say if this future hero, contrary to the law, takes their land away from them and puts it under the jurisdiction of the towns? Will they not resist with force or at least make protestations to gods and men?'

'The hero will no let that worry him', replied Jupiter. 'He

will divide the great up into three: those who have lived wicked lives and set a bad example he will punish just as he will the commoners, since there is no earthly power can resist his sword; the rest he will give the choice of staying in the country or leaving. Those who love their fatherland and stay will live like all the other ordinary people, though the Germans' way of life then will be much more agreeable and joyful than the life of a king at present. The Germans will be all like Fabricius, who refused to share Pyrrhus's kingdom because he loved his country as well as honour and virtue. The third group, those who want to remain true lords and continue to rule, he will send beyond Hungary and Italy to Moldavia, Wallachia, Macedonia, Thrace and Greece, even across the Hellespont to Asia Minor. He will conquer these countries for them, make them kings and give them all the mercenaries from the whole of Germany to assist them.

Next he will take Constantinople in one day and all those Turks who refuse to obey and convert will find their heads under their backsides, after which he will reestablish the Roman Empire there. Then he will return to Germany and, together with his parliament – for which, as you will remember, he will choose two members from each German town whom he will call the leaders and fathers of his German Fatherland –, build a city in the middle of Germany which will be much bigger than Manoah in America and richer in gold than Jerusalem at the time of King Solomon. Its walls will be like the mountains of the Tyrol and its moat as broad as the sea between Spain and Africa. He will build a temple in it of diamonds, rubies, emeralds and sapphires and a treasury full of precious objects from all over the world that will be given to him by the kings of China and Persia, the great Mogul of India, the great Khan of the Tartars, Prester John from Africa and the Tsar in Moscow. The Emperor of Turkey would be even more generous if the hero had not taken his empire away from him and given it as a fief to the Roman Emperor.'

I asked this Jupiter what the Christian kings would do in all this. He replied, 'Those of England, Sweden and Denmark, being of German blood and descent, will receive their crowns, kingdoms and colonies as fiefs of the German nation, as will those of Spain, France and Portugal because the old Germans once conquered and ruled their countries. Then there will be perpetual peace between all nations of the world, as there was in the time of Augustus Caesar.'

Chapter 5

*How the hero will combine all religions together and
pour them into one mould*

Tearaway, who was listening, almost offended our Jupiter and spoilt the whole game by saying, 'Then Germany will be like the land of Cockaigne where it rains nothing but grapes and twopenny pies come up overnight like mushrooms. I'll have to eat like a horse and drink like a fish.'

'That you will if you continue to mock my divine majesty', Jupiter replied, 'for I will curse you with insatiable hunger, as Diana did to Erysichthon.' To me, however, he said, 'I thought I was among wood spirits, but I see there is a Momus or Zoilus here. Should I reveal decrees of the gods to such a carping traitor, cast fine pearls before such swine? I might as well shit on his back to make him a fine linen shirt.'

This was a strangely foul-mouthed god, I thought, mixing lofty sentiments with such squishy matter. However, I could see that he did not like being laughed at, so I contained my laughter as best I could and said, 'Most gracious Jove, you will surely not let a coarse wood-demon stop you telling your second Ganymede what is to happen next in Germany?'

'Certainly not', he answered, 'but first tell this mocker, this Theon, he better curb his sharp tongue or I will turn him into a stone, as Mercury did to Battus when he let his tongue run away with him. But come now, admit it, you are my very own

Ganymede, aren't you? Did that jealous wife of mine, Juno, banish you from Olympus in my absence?'

I promised to tell him everything that had happened after he had answered my question, so he continued, 'My dear Ganymede – don't deny it, I can see it's you – the next thing to happen in Germany is that making gold will become as straightforward and as common as making pots so that every stable-boy will carry the philosopher's stone around with him.'

'But how will Germany enjoy such long-lasting peace with such great differences in religion?' I asked. 'Will not the various priests incite their followers to start another war for their faith?'

'Definitely not!' said Jupiter. 'In his wisdom my hero will prevent this by uniting all the Christian sects in the world.'

'A miracle!', I said. 'That would be a great achievement. How will it be brought about?'

'I'll gladly tell you', said Jupiter. 'After my hero has established universal peace he will address the spiritual and temporal leaders of the Christian nations in a very moving sermon and open their eyes and hearts to the damage the divisions in matters of faith have caused. After hearing his convincing reasons and irrefutable arguments they will of themselves desire general unification and put the whole thing into his most capable hands. Then, as King Ptolemy of Egypt did with the seventy-two translators, he will bring together the most ingenious, learned and pious theologians from all places and all religions in a quiet yet cheerful place where they can ponder important matters undisturbed. Food, drink and all other necessities will be provided. They will be required first of all to resolve the differences between the religions as quickly as possible while giving each word the most careful consideration; when that is done they must come to unanimous agreement on the right, true and holy Christian religion, according to Holy Writ, ancient tradition and the established opinion of the Fathers, and set it down in writing.

While this is being done, the Lord of the Underworld will start worrying that his empire will be diminished and will be scratching his head to think up all kinds of ploys and tricks to put a spanner in the works and if not stop the whole thing, then at least put it off for ever and a day. He will remind each theologian of his self-interest, his position, his quiet life, his wife and child, his reputation and anything else that might get him to support his opinion. But my brave hero will not be idle either. As long as the council lasts he will keep the bells ringing throughout Christendom as a constant reminder to all Christian people to pray to the Supreme Deity and beg for the spirit of truth to be sent down. If, however, he should notice that one or other is being won over by Pluto, he will torment the whole assembly with hunger, as in the conclave of cardinals. And if they still refuse to speed this noble enterprise, he will preach them a sermon on hanging, or show them his miraculous sword. Thus first of all with kindness and then with severity and threats he will see that they get down to business and stop deluding the world with their obstinacy and false doctrines. Once unity has been achieved he will order a great festival of rejoicing and announce this purified religion to the whole world. Any heretic who denies it he will smear with tar and brimstone or spatter with thorns and send him to Pluto as a New Year gift.

I have answered your question, Ganymede, and now it is your turn. Tell me why you left Olympus, where you poured me so many a goblet of nectar.'

Chapter 6

What the embassy of fleas achieved with Jupiter

I thought perhaps this fellow was not such a fool as he appeared but was just giving me a taste of the medicine I had given to others in Hanau in order to be allowed to pass more easily. I decided to try and provoke him to anger, since that is the best way to tell whether a fool really is a fool, and said, 'The reason I have left heaven is that I missed you. I took Dedalus's wings and flew down to earth to look for you. But wherever I asked, I found people spoke ill of you. Zoilus and Momus have vilified you and all the gods to the whole world, describing you as so wicked, licentious and stinking that you have lost all credit with mankind. You yourself, they say, are nothing more than an adulterous, whoring pubic louse; with what justification can you punish the world for those same vices? Vulcan is a complaisant cuckold who let Mars's adultery pass without any real revenge; Venus herself is the most hated slut in the world because of her promiscuity, how can she grant grace and favour to anyone else? Mars is a robber and murderer, Apollo a shameless whoremonger, Mercury an idle gossip, thief and pimp, Priapus an obscenity, Hercules a brainsick bully, all in all the whole crew is so rotten the only suitable place for them is the Augean stables which already stink to the whole wide world.'

'Oh!' said Jupiter, 'Would it surprise anyone if I forgot my kind-heartedness and blasted this slanderous scum, these blasphemous mud-slingers with thunder and lightning? What do you think, my faithful and beloved Ganymede? Should I punish these purveyors of calumny with eternal thirst like Tantalus? Should I crucify them along with that loose-tongued Daphitas on Mount Thorax? Or crush them in a mortar with Anaxarchos? Put them in Phalaris's red-hot bull in Agrigentum? No, these plagues and punishments are all much too lenient! I will refill Pandora's box and empty it out over the heads of these rogues. Nemesis will awaken the three Furies and set them on these villains and Hercules will borrow Cerberus from Pluto and hunt them down like a pack of wolves. And when I have plagued and pursued them enough I will bind them to a pillar with Hesiod and Homer in the house of hell and hand them over to the Eumenides to be tortured mercilessly for all eternity.'

Whilst Jupiter was uttering these threats he pulled down his trousers in the presence of myself and the whole party without the slightest show of embarrassment and proceeded to hunt out the fleas which, as we could see from his speckled skin, were tormenting him terribly. I could not imagine what was going to happen next, but then he shouted, 'Off you go, you little pests! By the Styx, you shall never have what you begged me to grant you.' I asked him what he meant by this and he answered that when the fleas heard that he had come down to earth they sent their envoys to greet him. These then complained to him that, although he had assigned dogs' coats to them to live in, some (because of certain characteristics of women) had strayed into women's fur. These poor lost souls, they went on, were treated terribly by the women, who caught them and not only murdered them, but first of all crushed and tortured them between their fingers that it would make a heart of stone bleed.

'And', Jupiter continued, 'they presented their case so movingly that I felt sorry for them and agreed to help them, with the proviso that first of all I should hear the women's case as well. To that the fleas objected that if the women were allowed to reply they knew very well that they would either paralyse my goodness and kindness with their poisonous tongues and drown out the fleas, or seduce me into a wrong verdict with their sweet words and sweet looks. They hoped, the fleas said, they would be allowed to continue to enjoy the very close relationship between us, pointing out how loyal they had been, and would continue to be. Although no one knew better than they what had gone on between myself and Io, Callisto, Europa and others, they had never told tales, not even one single word to Juno, with whom they also used to stay. And they were, they emphasised, still as discreet as ever. They were not like the ravens, who informed Apollo of his lover's unfaithfulness; no human being had ever learnt anything from them, even though they had observed all my affairs from the closest proximity. If, however, I was determined to allow women to hunt, catch and slaughter the fleas they found in their own game reserves, then their request was that in future they should be given an honourable execution. They wanted to be either pole-axed like oxen or dispatched like game and not, as at present, suffer the ignominy of being broken and crushed between women's fingers. In doing this, they went on, these women were turning members with which they often touched something quite different into instruments of torture. It was, they concluded, a thing that brought dishonour to all upright men.

"You gentlemen", I said, "must torment them terribly for them to treat you so?"

"That's true", they replied, "but they're full of ill-will towards us anyway. Perhaps they are worried we see, hear and feel too much. As if they hadn't had enough assurances of our discretion! What's the problem? They won't even leave us in peace in our own territory. Some of them them give their lapdogs such a thorough going-over with brushes, combs, soaps, shampoos and other things that we have to leave our rightful homes and find somewhere else to live. They'd be better off spending the time delousing their own children."

After that I gave them permission to come and lodge in the human body I had assumed so that I could feel for myself the effects of their activities and come to an informed judgment. And what did the odious little vermin do? They immediately started tormenting me so badly that I had to get rid of them again, as you have just seen. They want a special dispensation? Well I'll dispense them one right out of my arse: any woman can crack and crush them whenever she wants. Indeed, if I catch one of the little villains myself, I'll do just the same.'

Chapter 7

The Huntsman once more gains booty and honour

We couldn't really laugh out loud, both because we had to keep quiet and because our lunatic didn't like it, and Tearaway was almost bursting. Just then the look-out we had posted high up in a tree called out that he could see something coming in the distance. I climbed up and saw through my telescope that it must be the carts we were lying in wait for. However, they were not accompanied by foot-soldiers but by an escort of some thirty-odd dragoons. From that I quickly deduced that they would not come through the wood where we were lying in wait but keep to the open where we would not have been able to take anything from them, even though there was a nasty stretch where the track ran across the plain some six hundred yards from us and about three hundred yards from the end of the wooded hill.

I was determined not to have wasted all that time lying in wait to catch nothing but a fool, so I rapidly made another plan which also seemed feasible. By our position was a water-course which ran down through a gully to the open country. It was easy to ride along and I posted twenty of my men where the stream came out of the trees, taking up my position with them but leaving Tearaway in the place where we had been lying in ambush with orders to keep well hidden. I told my musketeers each to make sure of his man; some I detailed to shoot as soon as the escort was close, some to hold their fire in reserve. A few of the old hands asked what I had in mind. Did I think the escort had taken this route, where no peasant had been seen for a hundred years, assuming they would have nothing to do? Others believed I had magic powers, for which I had a great reputation at the time, and thought I would cast a spell to make the convoy fall into our hands. But I had no need of devilish arts, only Tearaway's.

When the escort, which was keeping pretty close order, was about to pass directly in front of us, Tearaway, at my command, began to bellow like an ox and neigh like a horse so loudly that the whole wood echoed with the sound and you would have sworn there were horses and cattle there. As soon as the escort heard it, they thought there was a chance of booty, of picking up something they did not expect to find in the whole area since the countryside was almost completely deserted. They broke ranks and rode so quickly into our ambush it looked as if each wanted to get the best of the bullets, which came so thick and fast that our opening volley knocked thirteen out of the saddle and wounded a few others. Then Tearaway came dashing down the gully shouting, 'Here they are, Huntsman!' which so frightened and confused the dragoons that they were incapable of riding backwards, forwards or sideways, but dismounted and tried to escape on foot. However, I took all seventeen prisoner, including the lieutenant commanding them. Then we attended to the carts, unharnessing twenty-four horses. Apart from that we only took some silk and linen, for I could not afford the time to rob the dead, never mind go through the carts properly. The carters had got away on horseback as soon as the ambush began and might alarm the command in Dorsten which would send out a party to intercept us on our way back.

When we had finished packing Jupiter came running out of the woods shouting, 'Is Ganymede going to desert me?' to which I replied that I would if he refused to grant the fleas the dispensation they wanted.

'I would rather see them all drowned in Cocytus first', he replied. I had to laugh at this and since I still had spare horses I let him mount one. However, he rode like a turnip and I had to tie him to the horse. This led him to remark that our skirmish had reminded him of the ancient battle between the Lapithae and the Centaurs on the occasion of King Pirithous's wedding.

When it was all over and we were galloping back to Soest as if the enemy were in hot pursuit it suddenly struck the lieutenant what a dreadful error he must have made to let such a fine troop of dragoons fall into enemy hands, thirteen of them being killed into the bargain. He became desperate and wanted to reject the quarter I had granted him, trying to compel me to have him shot dead. His carelessness, he thought, would not only bring him disgrace and the accusation of irresponsibility, but would damage his prospects of promotion; at worst he might have to pay for the losses with his life. I tried to cheer him up, reminding him that many good soldiers had suffered reversals of fortune but I knew of none who had been driven to despair. His behaviour, I told him, was a sign of faint-heartedness; a brave soldier would immediately be thinking of ways to make good the loss. I made it clear he would never get me to commit such a deed, that was against all the rules and conventions governing the treatment of prisoners.

When he saw I would not do him the favour he started to insult me, thinking he could make me angry. It hadn't been an honest fight, he said. I had behaved like a rogue and a highwayman and had stolen the lives of the soldiers under his command like a thief. This made his own men whom we had captured extremely afraid. Mine, on the other hand, were so furious they would have riddled him with bullets if I had let them, and it was as much as I could do to hold them back. I didn't turn a hair at the things he said. Instead I called on everyone, friend and foe, to witness what had happened and had the lieutenant bound and guarded like a madman. I promised him that as soon as we reached our camp – assuming my officers allowed it – I would give him free choice of my own horses and weapons and prove to him in open combat with sword and pistol that deceiving the enemy was allowed in warfare. I asked him why he had not stayed with the carts he had been assigned to? Or if he wanted to see what was in the wood, why had he not first sent out a proper reconnaissance party? That would have been better than this silly performance that impressed no one. Both my own men and the captured dragoons agreed with me and said they had been out on raids with a hundred different leaders and every one would not only have shot the lieutenant dead for such an insult but have sent all the prisoners to the grave with him.

The next morning I arrived back safely at Soest with my booty and my prisoners and got more honour and glory from this foray than from any before. Everyone said, 'He'll turn out to be another young John de Werth', which tickled me greatly. However, the commandant refused to allow me to cross swords or exchange shots with the lieutenant, saying I had already defeated him twice. And of course, the more praise was heaped on me, the more envious became those who begrudged me my good fortune.

Chapter 8

How he found the devil in the trough and how Tearaway
got some fine horses

I could not get rid of my Jupiter. The commandant did not
want to have anything to do with him because there was no
money to be got out of him, so he made a present of him, as
he put it, to me. This meant I now had my very own fool,
when only a year ago I had been forced to let people treat me
as one. It just goes to show how strange fortune is and how
things can change with time. Not long ago I was being tormented by lice and now I had the god of fleas in my power;
six months ago I was groom to a useless dragoon, now I
lorded it over two servants who called me master; less than a
year had passed since the stable lads were chasing me to ravish
me and now it was the girls who were mad with love for me. I
learnt at an early age that there is nothing as certain as
uncertainty and this made me afraid that once Lady Luck
decided to make me the object of her whims once more she
would make me pay dearly for my present prosperity.

At that time Count von der Wahl, as supreme commander
of the Westphalian District, was collecting troops from all the
garrisons for an expedition through the lands of the bishopric
of Münster towards the River Vechte, the neighbourhood of
Meppen, Lingen and those places. His principal object, however, was to dislodge two companies of Hessian cavalry which
were stationed some nine or ten miles outside the city of
Paderborn and were causing our people there a lot of trouble.
I was with the dragoons that were detailed to join them from
our regiment and once a few troops had been collected at
Hamm we set off quickly and by the time the rest of our
forces arrived we had stormed the quarters of the Hessian
cavalry, which were in a small and poorly protected town.
They tried to escape, but we drove them back into the village.

We offered to let them leave without horses and weapons, but keeping whatever they could take in their belts, but they would not agree and decided to defend themselves with their carbines, like musketeers.

So it happened that I had the chance that very night to see how my luck would be in an assault, for the dragoons were to lead the attack. And my luck held so well that Tearaway and I were among the first to enter the little town, completely unhurt. We soon cleared the streets, since everyone bearing arms was simply cut down and the townsfolk had refused to join in the defence, and started to enter the houses. Tearaway said we should find a house with a large dung-heap in front for that was where the fattest cats usually live on whom they billeted the officers. So we found one like that and, each having lit the candle in his torch, Tearaway went to inspect the stable, I the house, first agreeing that each would share what he found with the other. I called out for the master of the house but received no answer since they had all hidden. I came to a room where I found nothing but an empty bed and a kneading-trough with the lid fixed down. I prised it off, hoping to find something valuable inside, but as I lifted the lid some coal-black thing rose up towards me which I took to be Lucifer himself. I swear I never had such a fright in all my life as when I saw this black fiend appear so unexpectedly before me. Despite the shock I raised the axe with which I had opened the trough, saying, 'If this doesn't kill you may the powers of hell do it for me.' However, I didn't have the heart to bring it down on his head. He fell to his knees, raised his hands and said, 'Master, spare me for the love of God.' As soon as I heard him mention God and beg for his life I knew he wasn't a devil, so I told him to get out of the trough. He did so and came with me, as naked as the day he was born. I cut off a piece of my candle and gave it to him to light my way which he did, most obediently, leading me to a small room where I found the master with all his household who stared at the spectacle and trembled as he begged for mercy. This was readily granted since he handed over to me the Hessian captain's baggage, which included a fairly well filled, locked trunk;

anyway we were not allowed to harm the townspeople. He reported that the captain and all his men, apart from one servant and the negro I had found, had gone to their posts to defend the town.

While all this was going on Tearaway had caught the above-mentioned servant in the stable with six fine horses, ready saddled. We brought these into the house, told the negro to get dressed and ordered the master of the house to serve us the food he had prepared for the Hessian captain. Unfortunately, once the gates had been opened, guards posted and our General, Count von der Wahl, entered the town he made his quarters in the house we were in so that we had to go out in the dark and look for somewhere else to sleep. We found a billet with our comrades, who had also taken part in the assault, and after Tearaway and I had divided up our booty we spent the rest of the night eating and drinking. My share was the negro and the two best horses, one of which was a Spanish stallion on which any soldier would be proud to face the enemy and on which I made a fine show later on. From the trunk I took various valuable rings and a portrait of the Prince of Orange in a gold case set with rubies and left the rest for Tearaway. If I had wanted to dispose of everything, including the horses, it would have brought me over 200 ducats. The most hard-earned part of the my booty, the negro, I presented to the General, who gave me a mere twenty-four thalers for him.

From there we rode quickly to the River Ems but found very little to do. As we then passed close to Recklinghausen I got permission to go with Tearaway to visit the priest from whom we had stolen the bacon. We had a very enjoyable time there and I told him how the negro had given me the same fright he and his cook had got from me. As a farewell gift I gave him a fine repeater on a chain that I had also taken from the Hessian captain's trunk. In that way everywhere I went I made friends of people who would otherwise have had good reason to hate me.

Chapter 9

*An unequal contest in which the weaker party is victorious
and the conqueror is arrested*

As my good fortune increased, so did my pride and it led, as was inevitable, to a fall. We were camped about half an hour's distance outside Rehnen and my comrade and I asked for and were granted permission to go there to have some repairs done to our arms. As our real intention was to have a good time together, we went straight to the best inn and ordered musicians to play as we drank our wine and beer. Things got pretty lively and anything that could be had for money, we had; I even stood rounds for men from other regiments, just like a young prince with land and subjects and lots of money to get through each year. Because of this we got better service than a party of cavalrymen who were not as wild as we were. That annoyed them and they started to pick a quarrel with us. 'How is it', one asked, 'that these footsloggers' – they thought we were musketeers; no beast is as like a musketeer as a dragoon and when a dragoon falls off his horse a musketeer gets up – 'can make such a show with their few coppers?'

'That milksop', replied another, 'must be a country squire whose mother has sent some pin money and he's using it to treat his comrades so they'll pull him out of the mud or carry him across the next ditch they come to.'

This was aimed at me since they took me for a young nobleman. The girl who was serving us told me this, but since I hadn't heard it myself I couldn't do anything about it. All I did was to have a large beer tankard filled with wine and to pass it round with a toast to all honest musketeers, making such a racket that no one could hear himself speak. That made them even more angry and they said so that everyone could hear, 'What a life these footsloggers lead!'

'And what business is it of you bootblacks?' replied Tearaway, but they let it pass; he had such a grim, threatening expression on his face none of them felt they wanted to cross him. After a while, however, another could not resist shooting off his mouth, a rather well-built fellow who said, 'I suppose if these wall-shitters can't cut a dash on their own dung-heap' – he assumed we belonged to the garrison since our clothes were not as weather-worn as those of musketeers who spend all their time in the field – 'then where can they show their faces? Everyone knows that as soon as they get onto a battle-field they fall to the cavalry just as surely as a pigeon falls to a goshawk.'

'We're the ones who have to take towns and fortresses', I replied, 'and they're given to us to guard, whereas you cavalry couldn't drive the horse out of a one-horse town. Why shouldn't we enjoy ourselves in a place that belongs to us more than to you?'

'The fortresses go with the side that is master in the field', the trooper replied, 'and that means we have to win battles. I wouldn't be afraid of three children like you, muskets and all. I'd pin two to my hat and ask the third where all the rest were. And if I was sitting next to you', he added with derision, 'I'd give your little lordship a couple round the ear on account.'

'Although I'm willing to bet I have a pair of pistols as good as yours', I answered, 'and although I'm not a cavalryman, but just a cross between you and a musketeer, this milksop is ready to meet a braggart on horseback like you, with all your weapons, in open combat, on foot and armed with just his musket.'

'I say you are a cowardly rogue', said the trooper, 'if you don't back up those words with deeds like a man of nobility and honour right away.'

At that I threw my glove to him and said, 'If I can't get this back from you in the field with my musket and on foot, then you have the right to call me publicly by the name you have just had the presumption to give me.'

So we paid the innkeeper and the trooper prepared his carbine and pistols, I my musket. And as he rode off with his comrades to the place we had agreed on, he told Tearaway he'd better start digging my grave, but Tearaway replied that it was the trooper who should be getting one of his own men to dig one for himself. To me, however, he said I had been foolish to provoke them like that and he was afraid I was about to meet my maker. I, however, just laughed. I had long since worked out how I would deal with a fully armed trooper if I should be attacked by one in the field when I was on foot and only had my musket. By the time we came to the place where the fight was to happen I had already loaded my musket with two balls, primed it and smeared the lid of the priming pan with tallow, as careful musketeers do in rainy weather to protect the touch-hole and the powder in the pan from damp.

Before the duel began, our comrades agreed that it should take place in a field surrounded by a fence, that one of us should enter from the west, the other from the east, and that we should treat each other as if we were facing an enemy soldier. They further stipulated that none of the soldiers watching the fight should try to help their comrade, either before, during or after the contest, nor attempt to avenge his death or any wound he might receive. After they had sealed this agreement with a handshake, my opponent and I shook hands and each gave the other in advance his forgiveness if he should be killed. For two supposedly rational men it was the most absurd piece of foolishness. Each hoped to demonstrate the superiority of his arm of the service, as if the entire honour and reputation of both depended on the outcome of our iniquitous affair.

I entered my side of the field with both matches burning, and as soon as I saw my opponent I made as if to shake out the old priming powder as I walked. I then pretended to replace it, but in fact I just poured some powder onto the lid of the pan, blew up my match and checked the pan with two fingers, as is the habit of musketeers, my opponent keeping a close watch on me all the time. Before I could see the whites of his eyes I took aim and burnt off the priming powder on the pan lid. My opponent, assuming my musket had misfired and the touch-hole would be blocked, charged straight at me, pistol in hand, all too eager to make me pay for my presumption.

Before he realised what was happening, I had uncovered the pans and fired again, stopping him dead in his tracks.

Then I retired to join my comrades, who all embraced me. The other troopers saw to the body, freeing it from the stirrup, and behaved decently towards us, returning my glove with great praise. But just at the moment when I thought my reputation was at its height, twenty-five musketeers came from Rehnen and arrested me and my comrades. I was shackled and sent to headquarters since all duels were forbidden on pain of death.

Chapter 10

The general spares the Huntsman's life and holds out hope of great things for him

As our general was a stickler for discipline, I was afraid I might end up minus my head. Yet I still had hopes of escaping with my life since, although still young, I had always behaved well in the face of the enemy and gained a great reputation for courage. However, my hopes were rather uncertain because this kind of thing was happening every day, so that it was becoming necessary to make an example of someone.

At that time we had just blockaded a fortified town, but the enemy, knowing we had no heavy artillery, refused to surrender. Count von der Wahl moved all his forces there and sent a trumpeter to demand they hand over the town, threatening to storm it if they did not. The only reply was the following letter:

> Most noble Count von der Wahl,
> I hereby acknowledge receipt of your Excellency's communication and the request in the name of His Imperial Majesty contained therein. However I do not need to

remind your Excellency how dishonourable and irresponsible it would be for a soldier to hand over such a place as this to the enemy without pressing need. In consideration of this, your Excellency will not, I hope, take it amiss if I presume to remain here until your Excellency has sufficient forces to take this stronghold. If, however, there is any service it is in my limited power to render your Excellency, apart from things touching my duty, be assured that I remain

Your Excellency's most obedient servant,
signed X.Y.Z.

This led to great discussion in our camp about the town. On the one hand it was hardly advisable to leave it as it was, on the other to try to storm it without a breach would cost much blood and the outcome would still be uncertain; and it would take a great deal of effort, time and expense to bring up the guns and equipment from Münster or Hamm. While everybody, from the general to the lowest private, was deliberating on this, it seemed to me it would be a good idea to use the opportunity to get myself out of prison. So I racked my brains to think up a way of fooling the enemy into thinking we had the guns, which was all we lacked. One immediately occurred to me, so I sent word to my lieutenant-colonel that I had a plan for taking the place without trouble or expense, if I would be pardoned and set at liberty.

Some of the experienced campaigners laughed at this and said, 'A hanged man will even clutch at the noose. This young lad thinks he can talk his way out of it.' But the lieutenant-colonel and others who knew me took my proposal seriously. He went to see the general himself and told him all he could about me. Since the general had already heard of the Huntsman, he had me temporarily freed from my fetters and brought to him. When I arrived, the general was at table and the lieutenant-colonel was telling him about my first spell on sentry duty at St. James's Gate in Soest the previous spring. A violent storm had suddenly broken, with thunder and lightning, sending everyone rushing from the fields and gardens into the city. In the great crush of people on foot and on horseback I had had the presence of mind to call out the guard, because that kind of throng provided an ideal opportunity to take the town. 'The last of all to come', he went on, 'was an old woman who was soaking wet. As she went past the Huntsman she said, "I've been feeling this storm in my back for the last fourteen days." The Huntsman happened to have a stick in his hand, and when he heard her say that he hit her across the back with it and said, "Why didn't you let it out earlier, you old witch, instead of waiting till I'm on sentry duty?" And when his officer told him to stop, he replied, "It serves the old crow right. She must have heard everyone crying out for rain a month ago. Why didn't she let them have it sooner? The barley and hops might have done better."' Count von der Wahl, although he was in general a rather serious-minded person, laughed out loud at this and I thought to myself, if the lieutenant is telling him that piece of tomfoolery then he'll have surely not kept quiet about all my other silly pranks. However, I was still shown in.

When the general asked me what I had to say, I replied, 'Sir, although your Excellency's warranted ban on duelling and my crime mean that my life is justly forfeit, yet the loyalty I owe my most gracious lord, His Majesty the Holy Roman Emperor, until my dying day, demands that I do anything in my power, however feeble it be, to injure the enemy and further the interests and aid the forces of His Aforesaid Majesty, the Holy Roman Emperor.' The Count interrupted me and asked, 'Are you not the man who brought me the negro recently?'

'Yes, sir', I replied.

'In that case', he said, 'perhaps your zeal and loyalty do merit a reprieve. What is your plan for getting the enemy out of this place without any significant loss of time or lives?'

'Since the town cannot resist heavy artillery, my humble opinion is that the enemy would quickly come to terms if they believed we had the guns.'

'Even a fool could have told me that', the Count replied, 'but who is going to persuade them that we do have them?'

'Their own eyes', I answered. 'I have examined their look-out post through my telescope and they can be deceived by fixing some pieces of timber shaped like water-pipes to carts and having them drawn by a strong team of horses. They will believe it is heavy artillery soon enough, especially if your Excellency has some earthworks thrown up, as if you meant to position them there.'

'But my dear young chap', said the Count, 'they're not children in there. They won't believe a piece of bluff like that, they'll want to hear the guns. And if the trick fails', he said, turning to the officers standing around, 'we'll be the laughing stock of the whole world.'

'Sir', I replied, 'I'll give them guns that will make their ears ring if I can just have a few blunderbusses and a fairly large barrel. The sound will be the only effect, of course, and if, contrary to expectation, all we get from it is mockery, then let it be directed at me and, since I am condemned to die anyway, I will take it to the grave with me.'

The Count was still not keen on the idea, but the lieutenant-colonel talked him round, saying I was blessed with such luck in this kind of thing that he had no doubt this stratagem would be successful too. The general ordered him, since he believed it was feasible, to organise the matter, adding, as a joke, that any honour from it would redound to him alone.

So three large logs were found, each hauled by twenty-four horses though two would have been sufficient and brought up in sight of the enemy towards evening. In the meantime I had also got hold of three blunderbusses and a large barrel from a castle and set them up the way I wanted them. Once it was dark they were taken up to our sham artillery. I gave the blunderbusses a double charge and fired them through the barrel, which had had the bottom knocked out, as if we were firing three trial shots. It made such a thunderous noise that anyone would have sworn blind they were great siege guns or demi-culverins.

The general had to laugh at our fake salvo and once more offered the enemy terms, with the proviso that if they did not accept them that evening they would suffer for it the next day. At that hostages were exchanged, terms agreed and one of the town gates handed over to us that same night. All this turned out very well for me. Not only did the general pardon me for having broken his ban on duelling but he ordered the lieutenant-colonel, in my presence, to give me the first ensign's post to fall vacant. This, however, did not suit the lieutenant-colonel, for he had too many cousins and in-laws waiting for a post for me to be given precedence over them.

Chapter 11

*Contains all kind of things of little importance and
great self-importance*

Nothing else of note happened to me on that expedition. When I got back to Soest I discovered that the Hessians from Lippstadt had captured the servant I had left behind with my baggage in my quarters together with a horse which he had taken out to graze. From him the enemy learnt more about the way I went about things and came to respect me even more, for until then they had accepted the general rumour that I had magic powers. He told them that he had been one of the 'devils' that had given the Huntsman of Werl such a fright at the sheep-farm. When the said Huntsman heard this he felt so humiliated that he made himself scarce again, leaving Lippstadt to join the Dutch. For me, however, the capture of my servant turned out to be a great piece of good fortune, as will become apparent from later instalments of my story.

Now I began to tone down my behaviour, since I had such great hopes of soon being made ensign. I associated more and more with the officers and with the young noblemen who were hoping to achieve what I imagined would soon be mine. That made them my worst enemies, though to my face they behaved as if they were my best friends; the lieutenant-colonel was no longer so well-disposed towards me either because he had been ordered to promote me over the heads of his relatives. My captain, an old miser, also bore me a grudge because I had much finer horses, clothes and arms than he and no longer treated him to free drink as liberally as before. He would have been happier to see my head chopped off than an ensign's post promised me, since he had hoped to inherit my splendid horses.

The lieutenant hated me for a careless word I had let slip recently. It happened during the last expedition when we were both sent to act as look-out in a particularly exposed position. When it was my turn to keep watch, which had to be done lying down, even though it was pitch dark, the lieutenant crawled up to me on his belly, like a snake, and said, 'Look-out, can you see anything?' to which I replied, 'Yes, sir.'

'What? What?' he said.

'I can see that you're afraid', I said.

From then on I was completely out of favour with him and I was always the first to be sent wherever the danger was greatest. He kept looking for any opportunity to give me a good thrashing before I was made ensign, because until then I could not resist. The sergeants were no less hostile to me either because I was preferred to them. Even the love and friendship of the ordinary soldiers was beginning to waver, since it looked as if I despised them because, as I said, I had started associating more with my betters, who liked me none the better for it.

The worst thing about all this was that no one told me how everybody was against me and I was not aware of it myself because those who would rather have seen me dead were most friendly to my face. In my blindness I felt secure and grew more and more arrogant. And even when I did know that some people were annoyed – for example nobles and officers of rank when I cut a more splendid figure than them – that still didn't stop me. After I had been made lance-corporal

I thought nothing of wearing a doublet that cost sixty thalers, fine red breeches and white satin sleeves, trimmed all over with gold and silver, which was what the highest officers wore at the time, so that I stuck out like a sore thumb. I was a young fool with my spendthrift ways. Had I behaved differently, had I used the money I threw away on this finery to grease the right palms, I would not only have soon become ensign, I would not have made so many enemies. And as if that were not enough, I decked out my best horse – the one Tearaway had taken from the Hessian captain – with such a saddle, bridle and other accoutrements that when I mounted it you would have thought me a noble knight, another St. George even.

Nothing annoyed me more than the fact that I wasn't a nobleman and so could not dress my servant and groom in my livery. I thought to myself, everything has to start somewhere, if you can get a coat of arms, that will mean you already have your own livery, and when you become ensign, you have to have a seal, even if you're not Lord So-and-so. It was not long before I acted on this idea and had an earl marshal devise a coat of arms for me. It had three red masks on a white field; the crest was the bust of a young jester in calfskin costume with two hare's ears and little bells hanging down at the front. I thought this best suited my name, Simplicius. I also wanted to have the fool to remind me, in my future greatness, of what I had been in Hanau, to stop me becoming too haughty, for I already had no small opinion of myself. Thus I became the first of my name, family and escutcheon, and if anyone had tried to make fun of me because of it, he would certainly have found me offering him the choice of swords or pistols.

Although at the time I wasn't yet interested in women, I used to accompany the nobles when they went visiting young ladies, of whom there were many in the town, in order to let myself be seen and to show off my fine hair, clothes and plumes. I have to say that as far as my looks were concerned I was preferred to all others, but at the same time I overheard the spoilt minxes compare me to a handsome, well carved wooden statue, completely lacking in spirit and sparkle, for my outward appearance was the only thing they liked about me. Apart from playing the lute, there was nothing I could do or say to please them, since I still knew nothing about love-making. However, when those who were at ease in the company of young ladies also started making fun of my wooden manner and gaucheness, just to curry favour with them and show off their own fluency, I simply said I was happy at the moment to get my pleasure out of a gleaming sword or a good musket. The ladies backed me up, which annoyed the others so much that they secretly swore to kill me, though there was not one of them had the guts to challenge me, or to give me cause to challenge him. A slap would have been enough, or a mild insult, especially since I gave them all a provocative stare. From this the ladies guessed I must be a pretty resolute young man and said out loud that my good looks and sense of hon-our were more persuasive than all the compliments Cupid ever devised, which only made the others angrier than ever.

Chapter 12

*How Lady Luck unexpectedly presented the
Huntsman with a noble gift*

I had two fine horses that were my pride and joy; every day when I had nothing else to do I exercised them in the riding-school or through the town and fields. It wasn't that the horses had anything to learn, I just wanted people to see that these beautiful beasts belonged to me. When I went cantering down a street or, rather, the horse pranced down it with me on its back, the simple folk would watch me and say to each other, 'Look, that's the Huntsman. What a fine horse! What a magnificent plume!' or, 'Lord, look at the man!' and I would prick up my ears and wallow in it, as if the Queen of Sheba had compared me to Solomon in all his glory. But, fool that I was, I didn't hear what sensible people thought or my enemies said of me. The latter doubtless hoped I would break my neck because they could not match me; others certainly thought that if everyone got their due I would not be riding round in such splendour. In a word, the wisest doubtless considered me a young show-off whose ostentation would not last long, since it was based on a poor foundation, being supported by uncertain booty alone. And to tell the truth, I must admit that this assessment was not far wrong, even though at the time I couldn't see it. All I knew was that I could make things hot for any man who had to deal with me, so that even though I was little more than a child I could still pass as a good soldier. But what made me such a great personage was the fact that nowadays the least stable-boy can shoot the greatest hero in the world dead. Had gunpowder not been invented my main food would have been humble pie.

It was my custom on these outings to ride over every path and track, every ditch, marsh, thicket, hill and stream in order to familiarise myself with them and fix them in my memory so that if it ever came to a skirmish with the enemy I could exploit any advantage a place might offer for attack or defence. With this in mind I was once riding along an old wall not far from the town where there had formerly been a house. As soon as I saw it I thought it would be an ideal spot to lie in ambush, or to retreat to, especially if we dragoons were outnumbered and pursued by cavalry. I rode into the courtyard, the walls of which were in a fairly ruinous state, to see whether one could take refuge there on horseback if necessary and how it could be defended on foot. I rode round, inspecting everything closely, but when I was about to ride past the cellar, the walls of which were still sound, I could not get my horse, which was usually never afraid of anything, to go where I wanted, despite all my coaxing and cajoling. I spurred him till I began to feel sorry for him, but it was still no use. I dismounted and led him by the bridle down the ruined steps, which was what he was shying at, to have a look at the place for future reference. He still kept backing as much as he could, but with much coaxing and stroking I eventually managed to get him down. As I patted him I realised he was sweating with fear and his eyes were fixed on one corner of the cellar where he absolutely refused to go, yet where I could not see the slightest thing to make the most skittish animal take fright.

While I stood there in amazement, watching the horse trembling with fear, I was also suddenly overcome with a feeling of dread, as if I were being pulled up by the hair and at the same time had a bucket of cold water poured over me. I still couldn't see anything, but my horse's strange behaviour made me imagine we must both be under a spell and that I would never get out of the cellar alive. So I tried to go back up the steps, but my horse would not follow, which made me even more terrified and so confused that I didn't know what I was doing. Finally, taking one of my pistols, I tied my horse to the trunk of a large elderberry that was growing there, intending to go and look for some people to help me get my horse out. While I was doing this, however, it occurred to me that perhaps there was a treasure hidden in the old masonry and that was why the place was haunted. I had a closer look round, especially at the corner where my horse refused to go, and I noticed that one part of the wall there, about the size of an ordinary window-shutter, was different from the rest in both colour and workmanship. When I started to go towards it I had the same feeling as before, as if my hair were standing on end, which strengthened my suspicion that there must be a treasure hidden there.

I would ten, no, a hundred times sooner have been exchanging shots with an enemy than be seized with such dread. Something was tormenting me but I had no idea what it could be, since there was nothing to be seen or heard. I took the other pistol from the saddle holster, intending to escape myself and leave the horse there, but I could not get up the steps, it felt as if there was a strong wind pushing me back. That really made my flesh creep. Finally it occurred to me to fire my pistols to get the farmers working in the fields nearby to come and help me and, since I could think of no other way of getting out of that eerie, bewitched place, that is what I did.

I was so angry or desperate (even now I don't know exactly what I felt) that I aimed my pistols at the spot where the cause of this uncanny experience seemed to lie. The two balls hit the aforementioned piece of masonry so hard they made a hole in it big enough to put both hands through. After the shots my horse neighed and pricked up his ears, which revived my spirits. I don't know whether that was the point at which the ghost or wraith disappeared or whether the beast was simply glad to hear the shooting, but it gave me new heart. I no longer felt afraid, nor could I feel anything trying to impede me, so I went over to the hole my pistol shots had made. As I started to pull down the wall I discovered such a large treasure of silver, gold and jewels that I could still be living in comfort on it today, if only I had managed to keep it and invest it safely. There were six dozen silver cups in the old German style, a large gold chalice, several double goblets, four silver and one gold salt cellar, an old German gold chain, various diamonds, rubies, sapphires and emeralds set in rings and other items of jewellery, a whole casket full of large pearls, though all of them were spoilt or discoloured, and then in a mouldy leather bag eighty of the oldest and finest Joachimsthalers. There were also eight hundred and ninety-three gold coins with the French coat of arms and an eagle on them which everybody refused to accept because, so they said, they could not read the inscription.

The coins, rings and jewels I stuffed into my pockets and down my boots, breeches and holsters; since I was only out riding for pleasure and had not brought my saddle-bag, I cut the blanket off my saddle (it was lined so served well as a sack), packed the rest of the silver in it, hung the gold chain round my neck, leapt back up into the saddle and set off for my quarters. As I was coming out of the courtyard I noticed two peasants who ran off the moment they saw me. Having six legs and a level field to ride over, I easily caught up with them and asked them why they were trying to get away, what was it had frightened them so much? They told me they thought I was the ghost that lived in the deserted mansion and used to give people who came too close a terrible mauling. When I asked them more about it they told me that everyone was so afraid of the spectre that for years hardly anyone had gone near the place, apart from the occasional stranger who was lost and happened to end up there. The story going round the country-side was that there was an iron chest full of money there, guarded by a black dog and a maiden with a curse on her. According to the old story, which they had heard from their grandparents, a nobleman would come, a stranger who knew neither father nor mother, release the maiden from the curse, open the chest with a fiery key and take away the hidden money. They told me lots of other silly tales like that, but they are not worth wasting ink on. Finally I asked them what they were doing there, since it was a place they avoided. They said they had heard a shot and a loud cry, so had come running to see if there was anything they could do. I told them I had fired my pistols, hoping someone would come and help me as I had been very frightened, but knew nothing about a cry. They replied, 'You could hear shots from this castle for a long time before anyone from the neighbourhood would go in. It's such an uncanny place that we wouldn't believe your lordship had been there if we hadn't seen you riding out.'

Then they bombarded me with questions: What was it like in there? Had I seen the maiden? Had I seen the black dog on the iron chest? If I had had a mind to, I could have told them all kinds of tall stories, but I said nothing, not even that I had found the treasure. I just went on my way to my quarters where I examined and gloated over my find.

Chapter 13

Simplicius's strange notions and castles in the air, and how he put his treasure into safe keeping

It is not without good reason that some people, who know the value of money, look on it as their god. If there is anyone who has experienced its impact, its almost divine powers, then that person is me. I know how someone feels who has a considerable supply of it; I have also learnt, and that more than once, what it is like not to have a penny. I think I could go so far as to say that its powers and effects are much greater than those of all precious stones. Like diamonds, it drives away melancholy; like emeralds it makes people love and enjoy their studies (which is why in general more children of rich than of poor parents become students); like rubies it takes away fear and makes people cheerful and happy; like garnets it often disturbs their sleep; on the other hand, like jacinth it also has great power to promote rest and sleep; like sapphires and amethysts it strengthens the heart and makes people glad, well-behaved, lively and mild; like chalcedony it drives away bad dreams, makes people happy, sharpens their wits and, if they are in dispute with someone, makes them win (especially if they grease the judge's palm with it); it gets rid of lustful and lecherous thoughts, especially since beautiful women can be had for money. All in all, money can do more than one can say (I have already said something on this subject in my book *Black and White*) if only you know how to use it and invest it properly.

The money I had amassed from plunder and finding this treasure had a strange effect. In the first place it made me even more arrogant than I had been, so that it irked me that I was only called Simplicius. It disturbed my sleep, like amethyst, because I spent many nights lying awake wondering how best to invest it and get even more. It improved my arithmetic, since I worked out how much the silver and gold objects might be worth and added the sum to the rest that I had hidden here and there or kept with me in bags. It came to a pretty penny even without the precious stones! My hoard also gave me a taste of money's mischievous and evil nature by using me to demonstrate the saying, 'The more you have, the more you want'. I became such a miser anyone would have hated me. It also put all sorts of foolish plans and strange notions into my head, but I didn't follow up any of the ideas I had. Once I thought of leaving the army and settling down somewhere to spend my days filling my stomach and staring out of the window, but I very quickly changed my mind when I considered what a free life I led and what hopes I had of becoming a person of consequence. I said to myself, 'Hey, Simplicius, why don't you get ennobled and use your money-bags to recruit a company of dragoons for the Emperor? You'd be the perfect young gentleman and who knows how high you might rise in time.' However, when I remembered that my greatness could be cut short by one disastrous engagement or quickly brought to an end along with the war by a peace treaty, that plan lost its appeal. Then I started wishing I had reached my majority, for if I had, I told myself, I would find a beautiful, rich, young wife, buy a noble estate somewhere and lead a quiet life. I would raise cattle, which would easily ensure me a decent income. However, I knew I was much too young and let that plan drop too.

Lots of ideas like this occurred to me, but in the end I decided to take my best things to a safe town and give them to some man of means to look after, then wait to see what fortune had in store for me. I still had my Jupiter with me, in fact I couldn't get rid of him. Sometimes the things he said were quite sharp and he could appear to be in his right mind for weeks at a time; he was also extremely fond of me because of my kindness to him. Seeing me always deep in thought, he said, 'Give away your accursed money, gold and silver, my son.'

'Why should I do that, Jove?' I said.

'In order to make friends with it', he answered, 'and to get rid of these pointless worries.'

I said I would rather get more money, to which he replied, 'Go and try to get more, then, but you'll have no peace or friends for the rest of your life. Leave meanness to the old skinflints. A fine young lad like you should be behaving like one; you should worry more about being short of good friends than of money.'

I thought about this and saw that there was a lot of sense in what Jupiter said, but parsimony had me so tightly in its grip that I couldn't bring myself to give anything away. However, eventually I did present the commander with two silver-gilt double goblets and my captain with a pair of silver salt cellars, but they were rare antiques and all I achieved was to whet their appetites for the rest. My faithful friend, Tearaway, I gave twelve imperial thalers. In return he advised me to get rid of my wealth or to expect trouble from it, for the officers didn't like it when an ordinary soldier had more money than them. He had already seen one of his comrades murdered by another for money. Until now, he said, I had been able to keep the amount of booty I had picked up a secret, since everyone believed I had spent it all on clothes, horses and arms, but I couldn't pull the wool over people's eyes any more. Everyone made the treasure I had found larger than it actually was, he went on, and since at the same time I had given up my spend-thrift habits, there was no way I could fool them into thinking I had no money to spare. He kept hearing what the men were muttering and if he were in my place, he concluded, he would let the war look after itself, settle down somewhere safe and take things as they came.

'But', I answered, 'do you expect me to abandon my hope of being made ensign just like that?'

'Don't make me laugh', said Tearaway. 'You can have my guts for garters if you're ever made ensign. All the others who are hoping for a post would see to it you broke your neck a thousand times if one were to become vacant and you were in line for it. You don't need to tell me the difference between a sprat and a mackerel, my father was a fisherman. Don't take this the wrong way, but I've been observing the way things go on here longer than you. You haven't watched any number of sergeants that deserved to have command of a company more than many who do grow old still wearing their stripes. They had justified hopes, too, you know. By rights they deserve promotion more than you, as I'm sure you'll agree.'

There was nothing I could say since Tearaway, in his honest German way, was telling me the truth instead of flattering lies, yet I was secretly grinding my teeth, for I had a very high opinion of myself at that time.

But I still gave serious consideration to what Tearaway and Jupiter had said. It was true, I thought, that I had not one single friend from birth, nor a kinsman to help me if I should fall into difficulties or to avenge my death, whether I was killed secretly or openly. I could easily see for myself the way things were, but my craving for money and honour, not to mention my hope of achieving greatness, would not let me give up soldiering and live a quiet life. I stuck to my original plan, and when an opportunity to go to Cologne presented itself – to be one of an escort of a hundred dragoons for some merchants and several cart-loads of goods from Münster – I packed up the treasure I had found and took it with me. There I put it into the care of one of the leading merchants in return for a receipted inventory: finest silver to the value of seventy-four marks, fifteen marks worth of gold objects, eighty Joachimsthalers, a sealed casket containing various rings and jewels, gold and precious stones weighing eight and a half pounds in all together with eight hundred and ninety-three antique gold coins, each weighing the equivalent of one and a half gold crowns. I took Jupiter with me. He had asked to come because he had prominent relatives there. To them he praised my kindness towards him so that they made a great fuss of me. He was still advising me to use my money to buy myself some friends, who would be more use to me than chests full of gold.

242

Chapter 14

How the Huntsman was captured by the enemy

On the way home I thought a lot about how I should behave in future to get everyone to like me, for what Tearaway had said was going round and round in my mind and he had persuaded me that everyone was jealous of me, which was the truth. And now I remembered what the famous fortune-teller in Soest had told me, which made me even more worried. These thoughts certainly sharpened my wits and that made me realise that a person who lives a life free of worries is little more than a brute beast. I thought over the reasons why this or that person might hate me and considered how I should act to get back in favour with them. At the same time I was amazed how two-faced they were to be so affable to my face when they didn't like me. I came to the conclusion that I should behave like all the rest, tell people what they wanted to hear and treat everyone with respect even though I didn't really feel it. Above all I came to see that it was my own arrogance that had made me most enemies, so I decided I must pretend to be humble, even if I wasn't. I would go round with the ordinary soldiers again, doff my hat to my superiors and reduce the finery of my dress a little until my rank changed. I had borrowed a hundred thalers from the merchant in Cologne, to be deducted with interest when he gave me back my treasure, and I thought I would use half of this to treat the escort on the way home, having realised that parsimony brings no joy.

Thus I had resolved to change and this was to be my first step on the new road, but I had counted my chickens before they were hatched. While we were passing through the duchy of Berg the enemy set an ambush for us in ideal terrain with eighty guns and fifty horse. I had been sent on ahead in a squad of five led by a corporal to reconnoitre the track. The enemy stayed quiet when we came to the ambush and let us pass, so as not to warn the convoy before it had reached the defile. They sent a cornet and eight troopers to keep us in sight until the the convoy was attacked and we turned back to protect the carts. Then they rode down on us and asked if we were going to surrender. I was well mounted, for I was riding my best horse, but I did not think of trying to make a run for it. I turned to face them on a small piece of flat ground, to see if there was any honour to be gained from fighting, but as soon as I heard the volley our convoy received I knew it was no use and tried to escape. However, the cornet had thought of that and blocked our retreat. As I was trying to hack my way through he offered me quarter again, thinking I was an officer. I decided it was better to come out with my life than trust to chance and asked for his word on it as an honest soldier, which he gave me. So I handed over my sword and surrendered. At once he asked me my rank and station, saying he assumed I was a nobleman and therefore an officer. When I replied that I was known as the Huntsman of Soest he said, 'Then you're very lucky you didn't fall into our hands four weeks ago. I couldn't have given you quarter then, since our side thought it was common knowledge you were a sorcerer.'

This cornet was a brave young cavalier and not more than two years older than me. He was delighted to have captured the celebrated Huntsman and kept the promised quarter in very honourable fashion, following the custom of the Dutch, who let their Spanish prisoners keep everything they have in their belt. He did not even have me searched and I was equally obliging in taking the money out of my pockets and handing it over to them when they were sharing out the spoils. I whispered to the cornet that he should make sure he got my horse, saddle and bridle as his share since he would find thirty ducats in the saddle and it would be hard to find an equal to the horse anywhere. After that the cornet treated me as if I were his own brother. He immediately mounted my horse and gave me his to ride. No more than six of the escort had been killed and thirteen captured, of which eight had been wounded; the rest had fled and didn't have the guts to attack the enemy when they came out into open terrain and recapture the booty, which they could easily have done since they were all mounted.

Our attackers came from different garrisons, and after sharing out the spoils and prisoners the Swedes and Hessians separated that same evening. The cornet kept me and the corporal and the three dragoons he had captured and we were taken to Lippstadt, a fortress which was less than ten miles from our own garrison. As I had in the past been a pretty irritating thorn in the side of this place, my name was well known there, though I myself was more feared than loved. When the town came in sight the cornet sent a rider on ahead to announce our arrival to the commandant, tell him the result of the engagement and who the captives were. That brought out a huge throng in the town since everyone wanted to see the Huntsman; they all had something to say about me and it looked for all the world as if some great potentate were making his entrance.

We prisoners were taken straight to the commandant, who was amazed to see how young I was. He asked me where I came from and whether I had ever served on the Swedish side. When I told him the truth he wanted to know whether I had a mind to be on their side again. I replied that I had no objection except that I had sworn an oath to the Holy Roman Emperor and felt that I ought to keep it. He first ordered us to be taken to the provost-general but then granted the cornet's request to be allowed to treat us as his guests because that was how I used to treat my prisoners, one of whom had been his brother. In the evening various officers and well-born soldiers of fortune gathered at the cornet's quarters. He sent for me and the corporal and I must admit that they treated us very courteously. I was lively, not at all as if I had just had a great loss, and I talked as freely and openly as if I were with my closest friends instead of the enemy. At the same time I behaved as modestly as I could, since I could well imagine everything I did would be reported back to the commandant, which did in fact happen, as I heard later.

The next day we prisoners were taken, one after the other,

before the regimental intelligence officer, who interrogated us. The corporal was first and I the next. As soon as I went in he expressed his amazement at how young I was, and asked, 'What have the Swedes ever done to you, child, to make you fight against them?' That annoyed me, especially since I had seen soldiers as young as me on their side, so I answered, 'The Swedish soldiers came and stole my marbles and I want to get them back.'

When they heard how I paid him back in his own coin the other officers in attendance were embarrassed and one told him in Latin that he should talk about serious matters with me as he could see he wasn't dealing with a child. While this officer spoke I noticed that he called him Eusebius. When he asked me my name and I told him, he said, 'There's no devil in hell called Simplicissimus', so I replied, 'There's one called Eusebius, then, is there?' paying him back as I had our regimental clerk, Cyriacus. However, this was taken amiss by the officers and they told me to remember that I was a prisoner and had not been brought there just for the fun of it. I didn't blush at this, nor did I apologise, but told them that since they were holding me prisoner as a soldier, and had not just let me go, as they would a child, I intended to make sure they did not make fun of me as if I were a child. I had merely replied in the same tone as I had been questioned, I said, and I hoped there was nothing wrong in that. So then they asked me where I came from, who my parents were, when I had been born and especially whether I had ever served on the Swedish side, what conditions in Soest were like, how strong the garrison was and that kind of thing. I gave quick, concise and clear answers to all this. As far as Soest and its garrison were concerned, I told them what my duty allowed, but I kept quiet about the fact that I had been a jester because I was ashamed of it.

Chapter 15

The terms on which the Huntsman was set free

In the meantime the people in Soest heard what had happened to the convoy, that I had been taken prisoner along with the corporal and the others and where we were being kept. The very next day a drummer came to collect us. The corporal and the others were handed over to him together with the following letter, that the commandant sent over to let me read first:

> Monsieur,
> I acknowledge receipt of your letter, brought by your drummer, who will convey this reply to you. In return for the ransom received I am sending with him the corporal and the three other prisoners; as far as Simplicius, the Huntsman, is concerned, however, he cannot be allowed back since he previously served on this side. If, sir, I can be of any other service to you, as far as my duty to my lord allows, I shall be happy to oblige and remain,
> your obedient servant,
> Daniel de St. Andrée

This letter did not please me at all, but I still had to thank the commandant for communicating it to me. I asked to speak to him, but was told he would send for me after he had dealt with the drummer, which he would do the next morning; until then I would have to be patient.

I waited therefore until the commandant sent for me. It so happened that he was at dinner and that was the first time I had the honour of dining with him. While we were eating he kept on toasting me repeatedly, but let out not a single word of what he intended to do with me, and I felt it was not my place to ask. When we had finished, however, and I was rather tipsy, he said, 'You will have seen from my letter the pretext under which I am keeping you here, my dear Huntsman. What I am doing is not unlawful, nor against the conventions of warfare. You confessed both to me and to the intelligence officer that you had previously served on our side with the main army so you will have to bow to the inevitable and accept service under my command. And in time, if you perform well, you will find the rewards much greater than anything you could expect from the imperial side. If you refuse, you will, I am sure, understand that I shall have to send you back to the lieutenant-colonel whose servant you were when the dragoons caught you.'

'Colonel', I replied (at that time it had not yet become the custom for soldiers of fortune to be addressed as 'your Grace', even if they were colonels), 'I have never been bound by oath to the Swedish crown, nor to her allies, much less to the lieutenant-colonel. I was just a stable-lad, and I would hope that does not commit me to taking service with the Swedes and thus breaking the oath I swore to the Emperor. I humbly beg you to withdraw your proposal, sir.'

'What?!' said the colonel. 'You spurn the Swedish service? You're my prisoner, I'll have you know, and rather than let you return to Soest to serve the enemy I will put you on trial for a serious charge, or let you rot in jail', concluding that now I knew where I stood. What he said frightened me, but I still didn't give in. I replied that I trusted in God to keep me from both perjury and such unjust treatment, and that I humbly hoped the colonel, with the fairness for which he was well known, would continue to treat me as a soldier.

'I know', he said, 'very well how I could treat you if I were to follow the law to the letter. I advise you to think it over so that I'm not forced to show you my other side.' With that I was taken back to the goal.

You will have no problem guessing that I did not sleep much that night, with all kinds of thoughts going through my mind. The next morning several officers came to see me, together with the cornet who had captured me. Ostensibly their purpose was to help me pass the time, in fact to suggest to me that the colonel had a mind to put me on trial as a sorcerer, since I would not accept his terms. They were trying to frighten me to see what I was made of. However, since my conscience was clear I took everything very coolly and did not say very much. What I realised was that the colonel's main concern was to stop me returning to Soest. He knew very well that if he let me go, I would stay there because it was there that I expected promotion and also had two fine horses and other valuables.

The next day he had me brought to him again and asked me what decision I had come to. 'My decision, colonel', I replied, 'is that I will die rather than break my oath. If, however, you were so good as to set me at liberty and not require any military duties from me, sir, I would promise faithfully not to bear arms against the Swedes or Hessians for six months.' The colonel immediately agreed to this, gave me his hand on it and exempted me from having to pay a ransom. He ordered his secretary to draw up a document in duplicate, which we would both sign, guaranteeing me freedom of movement and his full protection as long as I remained in the fortress he commanded. For my part I committed myself to the two points touched on above, namely that as long as I stayed in the fortress I would do nothing to harm either the garrison or its commander, nor would I conceal any action that was taken against them; on the contrary, I undertook to do everything in my power to support them and prevent any loss, and if the enemy should attack the town I pledged myself to help them defend it.

When that had been done he kept me with him for lunch and honoured me more than I could ever have expected from the imperial side as long as I lived. In this way he gradually won me over, so that I would not have returned to Soest, even if he had been willing to let me go and released me from my promise.

Chapter 16

How Simplicius being freed made free with his goods

If something is to be, then everything falls into place. When, sitting at the commander's table, I was told my servant had come from Soest with my two fine horses, I thought Lady Luck must be wedded to me, or at least so closely connected that the worst things that happened to me turned out for the best. At the time I did not know what I learnt at the end, namely that luck is like the Sirens, who show their greatest favours to those they wish to harm the most, and raises a man up higher so that his fall will be all the greater.

This servant, whom I had previously captured from the Swedes, was extremely loyal to me because I treated him so well. Therefore every day while the drummer, who was supposed to bring me back, was away, he saddled my horse and rode a good way out from Soest to meet him so that I would not have to walk too far; and to save me having to enter Soest naked or in rags, for he assumed I would have been stripped, he had packed my best suit of clothes. When he met the drummer and the other prisoners he saw I wasn't with them and they told him I was being kept there to take service with the enemy. At that he spurred his horse, saying 'Adieu, drummer, and to you corporal. Where my master is, that's the place for me', and galloped away from them, arriving just as the commander had given me my freedom and done me the honour of asking me to dine. He ordered my horses to be stabled at an inn until I found lodgings to my liking and said how fortunate I was to have such a loyal servant. He also expressed his amazement that an ordinary dragoon, and so young a one at that, should have such fine horses and so well equipped! When I took my leave to go to the inn, he was so fulsome in his praise of the horse that I immediately realised he would like to buy it off me. Since he was too well-mannered to make me a direct offer, I said that I would consider it an honour if he kept it. He declined, however, more because I had drunk quite a lot and he didn't want people saying he had talked a drunken man into giving him something he might regret when he was sober than because he didn't want such a thoroughbred.

That night I thought over how I was going to organise my life in future and decided to stay where I was for the six months and spend the winter, which was rapidly approaching, in peace and quiet. I knew my money would last out, even without breaking into my treasure in Cologne. And in that time, I thought to myself, you'll have grown to your full strength and can be an even better soldier in the imperial army when the campaigning starts again in the spring.

Early next morning I dissected my saddle, which was much better lined than the one the cornet had taken. Afterwards I took my best horse to the colonel's quarters and told him that, since I had decided to spend the six months, during which I could not take part in any fighting, in the town under his protection, my horses would be of no use to me. It would be a pity, I went on, to let them get out of condition so I hoped he would be good enough to find room for this soldier's hack in his own stables and have no scruples in accepting it as a token of gratitude for all he had done for me. The colonel thanked me very civilly, saying if there was anything he could do for me I had only to ask. That afternoon he sent his steward with a well fattened ox, two fat hogs, a cask of wine, four casks of beer and twelve cart-loads of firewood to the new lodgings I had just taken for six months. The steward also brought a message from the colonel that, since I had decided to set up house there, the colonel could well imagine I might initially be short of provisions so he was sending me something to drink as well as a bit of meat and the wood to cook it with as a house-warming present, adding that I was to be sure to tell him if there was anything I needed. I thanked the steward with all due courtesy and handed him two ducats, asking him to give my compliments to his master.

Seeing that my liberality put me so high in the colonel's

favour, I thought it would be worth my while to enhance my reputation with the ordinary men, so they wouldn't take me for some malingering pauper. Therefore I called my servant to me when my landlord was present and said, 'Nicholas, you have been more loyal to me than any master has a right to expect, but I don't know how to repay you for it. At the moment I have no master to serve and no battles to fight in which I might collect some booty to reward you as you deserve. Also, I intend to lead a quiet life in future and not to keep a servant so instead of your pay I hope you will accept my second horse, together with the saddle, harness and pistols, and look for service with another master. If there's anything I can do for you in future you know you only have to ask.'

He kissed my hands and could hardly speak for tears. He refused to take the horse, saying it was better I should sell it and use the money to pay for my own keep. Finally I persuaded him to accept it after I had promised to take him back if ever I needed a servant again. The landlord found this scene so touching that the tears came to his eyes as well. And just as my servant sang my praises to the soldiers, so did my landlord to the citizens of the town. The commandant thought me so staunch he would have risked his life on my word of honour. Not only had I faithfully kept the oath I had sworn to the emperor, but in order to keep the promise I had made him as strictly as possible I had given up my horse, my arms and my loyal servant.

Chapter 17

How the Huntsman planned to spend the six months;
also something about the fortune-teller

I think there is no one in the world who does not have a screw loose somewhere or other. We're all from the same stock, and

I can tell from the fruit on my own tree when others' is ripe. 'Come off it', you might say, 'just because you're a fool doesn't mean others are too.' No, that would be going too far, I agree. But what I do think is that some are better at hiding their foolish side than others. A man is not a fool just because he has some silly ideas – we've all had some when we were young – but those who don't keep them to themselves are considered fools, whereas others conceal them or only let the odd one out. Those who suppress them entirely are real sour-pusses. I think people who let their silly notions pop their heads out now and then to take a breath of fresh air, so they don't suffocate, are much more sensible.

Having so much freedom and money, I let mine have too much latitude. I took on a boy whom I dressed as a page, and in the most foolish colours, namely violet-brown and yellow, which I happened to fancy as my livery. He waited on me as if I were a baron and had not recently been an ordinary dragoon, not to say a poor stable-lad, only six months ago. That was my first piece of foolishness in that town. However, although it was fairly crass, no one noticed, much less criticised it. The world is so full of foolishness that no one takes any notice or laughs at it any more; they are so used to it they're not even surprised. So I had the reputation of a good and intelligent soldier and not of a fool who needed to grow up.

I arranged with my landlord for full board for myself and my page, giving him the food and fuel I had received from the commandant in part payment. But as far as the drink was concerned, my page had to keep the key, since I liked to give some to people who visited me. I was neither citizen nor soldier and therefore had none of my own kind to keep me company, so I consorted with both sides and had companions enough who visited me daily and whom I did not send away thirsty. Among the citizens I was on closest terms with the organist because I liked music and, without wanting to brag, had an excellent voice which I did not want to allow to get rusty. He taught me composition and how to improve my playing on the clavicembalo and also the harp; I was already a master on the lute, so I bought one of my own and enjoyed playing it every day. When I had had enough of music-making, I sent for the furrier who had taught me how to use all types of swords in the Paradise Convent and practised with him every day in order to perfect my skill. I also obtained permission from the commandant to pay one of his gunners to teach me about artillery and how to use gunpowder. Otherwise I lived a very quiet and withdrawn life. The people were surprised to see me sitting over my books all the time like a student when I had been used to pillaging and bloodshed.

My landlord was the commandant's informer and my keeper. I realised he was reporting everything I did to him, but I found it easy to accommodate myself to that. I did not give warfare one single thought and when people started talking about it I behaved as if I had never been a soldier and was only there to carry out my daily practice, which I had just remembered. Of course I said I wished my six months would soon be up, but no one could deduce on which side I would serve. Whenever I visited the colonel he kept me to dine with him and he always ended up sounding me out about my intentions. My replies were so circumspect that no one could tell what I had in mind. Once he asked me, 'How about it Huntsman, have you still not decided to turn Swedish? One of my ensigns died yesterday.'

'But colonel', I replied, 'if it is right for a woman not to remarry immediately after her husband's death, surely I can wait for six months?'

In that way I managed to avoid committing myself and yet still kept the colonel's favour, which increased as time went on so that he allowed me to walk around both inside and outside the fortress. I even had permission to hunt hares, partridge and birds, which was forbidden to his own soldiers. I also went fishing in the Lippe and had such luck that it looked as if I could pluck both fish and crayfish out of the water by magic. I had a set of rough hunting clothes made in which I used to wander round the countryside outside Soest at night – I knew every path and track – gathering together the hoards I had hidden away and taking them back to the fortress, where I behaved for all the world as if I were going to stay with the Swedes forever.

While I was out on one of these expeditions I came upon the fortune-teller of Soest who said, 'See, my son, didn't I give you some good advice when I told you to hide your money outside the town of Soest? I tell you, being kept prisoner was a great piece of luck for you. If you had come home some of the men, who had sworn to kill you because the young ladies preferred you to them, would have murdered you while you were out hunting.'

'How can anyone be jealous of me', I replied. 'I'm not interested in the ladies?'

'Let me assure you', she said, 'that if you do not stick to that the young women will drive you out of the country in disgrace. You always laughed at me when I foretold things that would happen to you. Will you refuse to believe me this time if I tell you something else? Don't you find people are better disposed towards you where you are now than in Soest? I swear to you that they have an overpowering affection for you and this affection will harm you if you do not fall in with it.'

I replied that if she knew as much as she claimed she should tell me how my parents were and whether I would ever see them again. And not in such obscure words but in good, plain German. To that she said that I should ask about my parents when I met my foster father unexpectedly leading my wet-nurse's daughter by a rope. Then she laughed out loud, adding that she had told me more of her own free will than she told others who had begged her. Then I began to make fun of her so she quickly disappeared, though not before I had given her a few thalers, as I had almost more silver on me than I could carry.

At that time I had a good sum of money as well as a lot of valuable rings and jewels. Previously when I heard of soldiers who had precious stones, or came across some on forays or elsewhere, I bought them, often for less than half their value. They seemed to keep shouting at me that they wanted to be seen in public and I was happy to oblige. Being proud I made a show of my wealth and was not afraid to let my landlord see it, and he increased its value when he told people about it. They could not think where I had got it from since it was well known that the treasure I had found had been deposited in Cologne because the cornet had read the agreement with the merchant when he captured me.

Chapter 18

How the Huntsman started to court the ladies and made a regular trade of it

My intention to perfect my skills in artillery and fencing during these six months was a good one, as I was well aware. But it was never enough to keep me completely from idleness, which is the root of much evil, especially since I had no one to guide me. I spent a lot of time reading books from which I learnt much that was useful, but I also came across others which did me as much good as grass to a dog. Sidney's incomparable *Arcadia,* which I read to learn elegance of expression, was the first to draw me from realistic tales to books of love, from true stories to heroic epics. I got hold of this kind of book wherever I could and whenever I found one I devoured it in one go, even if I had to keep reading right through the night. Instead of eloquence, these books taught me how to lure the female sex. At that time, however, this vice did not take such a strong and violent hold over me that you would have called it a 'divine frenzy' with Seneca, or described it as a 'serious illness', as Tommaso Tomai does in his *Idea del giardino del mondo.* Whenever I took a fancy to a woman I achieved my desires easily and without any great effort, so that I had no cause to bemoan my fate like other lovers who are full of fantastic notions, troubles, desires, secret sufferings, anger, jealousy, vengeance, madness, tears, moans, threats and a thousand similar foolish things and get so impatient they long for death. I had money and was willing to spend it, I had a good voice, too, and constantly practised on all kinds of instruments. I have never been fond of dancing, instead I showed off my slim body when fencing with my furrier. I also had a fine, smooth complexion and had adopted a pleasant manner so that even women I was not particularly taken with would pursue me more than I really wanted, just as Aurora pursued Clitus, Cephalus and Tithonus, Venus Anchises, Attis and Adonis, Ceres Glaucus, Ulysses and Iasion and even the chaste Diana pursued her Endymion.

Martinmas fell at about that time, when we Germans start a bout of gluttony and boozing which some continue until Shrove Tuesday. I was invited by various people, both officers and civilians, to share their Martinmas goose with them, and those were occasions when I made the acquaintance of their women. My lute-playing and singing made them all look my way and then I would accompany the love-songs I had composed myself with such charming glances and gestures that many a pretty young girl lost her head and promptly fell in love with me. And so as not to be thought a skinflint, I also gave two banquets, one for the officers and one for the leading citizens. This kept me in their favour and gained me entry to their houses, since everything I served was of the best. All this was for the sake of those dear young ladies, and even if there were one or two from whom I did not get what I wanted (there were a few who could resist), I still went to see them now and then so as not to bring suspicion on those who granted me more than a respectable girl should, but to make people believe I was visiting them just for the sake of their conversation as well. In fact I managed to persuade them all that was the case with the others, so that each thought she was the only one to enjoy my love.

There were six who loved me, and I loved them all in return, though none had my heart or me to herself. In one I liked her black eyes, in another her golden hair, in the third her sweet manner and in the rest something the others didn't have. If I still went to visit other girls apart from them it was either for the above-mentioned reason, or for the sake of novelty. In any case, I never rejected an invitation since it was not my intention to stay for ever in the one place. My page, who was a little rascal, was kept busy arranging rendezvous and carrying love-letters back and forth. He knew how to keep his mouth shut and my dissolute ways so secret that nothing came out. For his services he was loaded down with presents by the young hussies, which I eventually paid for since in return I spent a small fortune on them. As the saying goes, what you gain on the roundabouts you lose on the swings. But I managed to keep all these affairs so secret that not one in a hundred would have thought me a libertine, apart from the pastor, from whom I no longer borrowed so many books of devotion.

Chapter 19

The means by which the Huntsman made friends
and his response to a moving sermon

When Lady Luck intends to bring you down she first of all raises you to the heights, but the Lord in his goodness faithfully warns each man before his fall. That happened to me, but I ignored it. I was completely convinced that my status at that time was based on such a firm foundation that no misfortune could knock me down since everyone, especially the commandant, was so well disposed towards me. The men he thought highly of I won over with my deference, his faithful servants I brought round to my side with presents and to those who were more on my own level I pledged my everlasting friendship in large amounts of wine and beer. The common people and ordinary soldiers liked me because I had a friendly word for everyone. 'Isn't that Huntsman friendly?' they would say. 'He talks to all the children in the street and gives no one cause to to quarrel with him.'

Whenever I caught a rabbit or some partridges I would give them to the cook of people whose friendship I hoped to gain, get myself invited to lunch and have a few bottles of wine, which was dear there, sent round. I often managed to arrange it so that I bore all the costs. And when I got into conversation with anyone at these banquets I would praise everyone apart from myself and behave with such humility you would have thought I didn't know the meaning of the word pride. Since by such means everyone came to like me and think highly of me I could not imagine any misfortune would happen to me, especially as my moneybags were still pretty plump.

I often went to see the oldest pastor in the town. He lent me many books from his library and whenever I took one back he would discuss all kinds of thing with me, for we got on very well with each other. Once not only the Martinmas geese and sausage soup were over but also the Christmas festivities I gave him a bottle of Strasbourg brandy as a New Year's present which, following the Westphalian custom, he liked to sip with sugar candy. Then I paid him a visit and arrived just as he was reading my *Chaste Joseph*, which my landlord had lent him without my knowledge. I went pale when I saw such a learned man holding a work of mine in his hands, especially when you remember that a man is best known from his writings. He told me to sit down and praised my inventiveness, but criticised me for spending so much time on the love affairs of Potiphar's wife, quoting from St Matthew, '"Out of the abundance of the heart the mouth speaketh." And if you yourself didn't know how a fornicator feels', he went on, 'you wouldn't have been able to describe that woman's passions so vividly.'

I replied that what I had written was not my own invention but that I had taken it from other books simply as a literary exercise.

'Oh, I can well believe that', he said, 'but I can assure you that I know more about you than you imagine.' This gave me something of a shock and I wondered, 'Was it old Nick told you that?' When he saw me blush he went on, 'You are young and strong, handsome and at leisure, and from what I hear you have no worries, indeed you live a life of luxury. Therefore I urge you to bear the dangers of your situation in mind. Beware the beast with braided tresses if you care for your happiness and salvation. You may well think, "What business is it of the pastor's what I do or don't do? I don't take orders from him."' (Got it in one, I thought.) 'It is true my duty is to care for the soul. But you have been generous to me and I can assure you that your well-being here on earth is of as much concern to me, as a Christian, as if you were my very own son. It is a waste which you cannot justify before your heavenly Father to hide the talents he has given you, to misuse the noble mind which I can see in this book. My honest advice as a fatherly friend would be to use your youth and money, which you are wasting at the moment, on study, so that now and in the future you can be of some benefit to God, mankind and yourself. And give up warfare for which, as I hear, you have such a great liking, before you suffer such a disaster that you will demonstrate the truth of the saying, "A young soldier makes an old beggar".'

I listened to this sermon very impatiently. I wasn't used to being spoken to like that. However, I didn't let it show so as not to lose my reputation for politeness. I even thanked him heartily for his honest advice, which I promised to think over. But to myself I thought, Like shit I will! What business is it of these bible-bashers how I live my life. Just at that time I was at the height of my good fortune and was unwilling to give up the delights of love now I had tasted them. That is what happens to such warnings when young people have got the bit between their teeth and are galloping towards their own destruction.

Chapter 20

How the Huntsman gave the honest pastor other fish to fry
so that he did not need to correct his own excesses

I was neither so drowned in lust, nor so stupid that I was not determined to keep everyone's friendship for as long as I intended to stay in the fortress, that is until the winter was over. I realised what damage it could do for anyone to attract the hatred of the priests since their opinion is highly regarded in all nations, whatever their religion. So the next day I put my tail firmly between my legs, trotted off to the pastor and gave him such a splendid load of bullshit, all dressed up in long words, about how I had resolved to follow his advice that he was delighted, as I could tell from the expression on his face.

'Oh yes', I said, 'I have found in your reverence the kind of angelic counsellor I have long lacked, even back In Soest', and I asked if he would be so good as to advise me which of the universities I should consider attending once the winter was over or the weather suitable for travel.

He replied that he had studied in Leyden, but he would advise me to go to Geneva, since he could tell from my accent that I came from southern Germany. 'Jesus and Mary!' I said, 'Geneva's farther from my home than Leyden.'

'What's this I hear?' he said in alarm, 'Does that mean you're a Papist? God, how I've been deceived!'

'How do you mean, sir?' I replied. 'Do I have to be a Papist just because I don't want to go to Geneva?'

'No', he said, 'I can tell from the way you called on Mary.'

'Is it wrong for a Christian to speak the name of his Redeemer's mother?' I asked.

'I suppose not', he said, 'but I beg you in the name of the Lord our God to tell me which religion you belong to. Even though I have seen you in my church every Sunday I doubt very much whether you believe in the Gospel, since during the recent feast to celebrate the birth of Christ you did not come to the Lord's table either with us of the Reformed Church or the Lutherans.'

'As you can hear', I replied, 'I am a Christian. If I weren't I wouldn't have attended services so often. Beyond that, however, I must confess that I am neither Papist nor Protestant. I simply believe what is contained in the Twelve Articles of the Christian Faith and I refuse to commit myself to any side until one or the other can furnish convincing proof that it is the one true religion.'

'Now I really do believe you are a soldier at heart, ready to risk your life', he said, 'since you live without church or religion and with no thought for the future, recklessly putting your eternal salvation in jeopardy. How can a mortal man, who is going to be damned or saved at the end, be so rash? Were you brought up in Hanau and is that all you were taught of Christianity? Tell me, why are you not following your parents in the pure Christian religion? And why will you not acknowledge the Reformed Faith before all others when its foundations are so clear for all to see, both in nature and in Holy Writ, that neither the Papists nor the Lutherans will ever be able to overturn them?'

'But, pastor', I answered, 'that is what all the other churches say of their faith as well. Which one should I believe? Do you think it's easy for me to entrust my soul's salvation to one that the other two decry and accuse of false doctrine? You should read – but with my impartial eye! – the things Conrad Vetter and Johann Nas have to say in print against Luther, what Luther and his supporters say against the Pope and especially what Spangenberg has said against St. Francis, who for hundreds of years has been looked up to as a holy and godly man. Which one should I join when each is screaming that the others are the work of the devil? Do you think I am wrong to wait until my mind has developed sufficiently for me to be able to tell black from white? Would anyone advise me to jump straight in, like a fly into hot porridge? I hope, in all conscience, you would not, sir. What is certain is that one is right and the other two wrong. But if I were to choose without mature reflection, I could just as well end up with the wrong one and spend all eternity regretting it. I would sooner keep off the roads altogether than take the wrong one. Besides, there are more religions than just the ones we have in Europe, that of the Armenians, for example, the Abyssinians, Greeks and Georgians, and whichever one I choose I must join my fellow believers in denouncing all the others. But if you will be my Ananias and make the scales fall from my eyes I will be for ever grateful and follow the faith you yourself profess.'

To this he answered, 'You are in great error, but I pray to God that He will enlighten you and pull you out of the mire. For my part I will give you such proof of the truth of our confession from Holy Writ that all the forces of Hell could not shake it.' I replied that I would look forward to it eagerly, but to myself I thought, 'I'll be quite happy with your religion if it stops you going on about my love affairs.' You can see from this what a wicked, godless wretch I was to put the pastor to all that wasted effort simply so that he would leave me in peace as far as my life of depravity was concerned, thinking that by the time he had finished with his proofs I would be over the hills and far away.

Chapter 21

How the Huntsman unexpectedly became a married man

Opposite my lodgings lived a superannuated lieutenant-colonel with an extremely beautiful daughter who gave herself aristocratic airs. I would have very much liked to make her acquaintance and, although she did not at first seem to be the kind of girl whom I could love to the exclusion of all others and for ever, I took many a walk past her windows and gave them ever more longing looks. But she was so closely guarded that I had not once been able to speak to her. I couldn't just march straight in, since I didn't know her parents and in any case they seemed of much too high rank for one so lowly born as I felt I was. I got closest to her when we were going into or out of church; I timed my entrances and exits so well that I often managed to give a few sighs, at which I was a master even though they came from a false heart. However, she took them so coolly that I assumed she would not be as easily seduced as the daughter of an ordinary citizen, and the more unlikely it seemed I would get her, the hotter my desire for her became.

The star that shone over our first meeting was the one the students carry around at that time of the year in everlasting remembrance of the star that guided the Three Wise Men to Bethlehem, and I took it to be a good omen that it was one of them that lit my way to her lodgings when her father himself sent for me. 'Monsieur', he said, 'I have asked you to come because of your neutral position between townspeople and soldiers. I need an impartial witness for a project I have involving both sides.' I assumed he had some important matter in mind, since the table was covered with papers and writing materials, and assured him I was happy to offer my services for any lawful business and that I would consider it a great honour if I should be in the fortunate position of being able to give him any help he wanted.

All it turned out to be was the setting-up of a kingdom, as is the custom in many places at that time of year: it was Twelfth Night, the Feast of the Three Kings, and I was to see that things were done properly and the offices shared out fairly by lot, without respect of person. For this important business, at which his secretary was also present, the lieutenant-colonel had sweets and wine served, as he was very fond of his drink and in any case it was after dinner. The daughter drew the lots, I read out the names and the secretary wrote them down while the parents looked on. There is not much else to tell about our first meeting, but the parents complained about the long winter nights and gave me to understand that, if it would help me pass the time, I would be welcome to visit them in the evenings as they themselves did not go out very much. That was precisely what I had long hoped for.

After that evening, when I only indulged in a little mild flirting with the girl, I once more set my lures and played the giddy fool so that both the young lady and her parents must have thought I had swallowed the bait, though I was not even half in earnest. Just like the witches, I decked myself out in my finery as night was falling and I was going to see her, and the day I spent poring over my romances. From them I composed love-letters to the object of my affections, as if we lived five hundred miles apart or had not seen each other for years. Eventually I became a familiar visitor, since the parents put no particular obstacles in the way of my courtship; indeed, they even suggested I should teach their daughter to play the lute. Now I could go in and out whenever I liked, not just in the evening, so that I changed my usual ditty:

> Like the bat I shun the light
> And only spread my wings at night

and composed a song rejoicing in the good fortune which had brought me, after many a pleasant evening, such blissful days when I could feast my eyes on my beloved. In the same song I also bemoaned the harshness of fate that did not allow me to spend my nights, like my days, in the delights of love. Although it turned out a little free, I sang it to my beloved with adoring sighs and a charming melody. The lute also played its part joining me, as it were, in begging the girl to cooperate in making my nights as pleasurable as my days. The answer I got was rather cool. She was a very intelligent girl and knew how to put me down politely for my flights of fancy, however neatly I delivered them. I was very careful not to speak of marriage and if it ever cropped up in the conversation I made sure anything I said was very ambiguous. Her sister, who was already married, noticed this and made sure we were not left alone together as much as before. She could see that her sister was deeply in love with me and that in the long run it was likely to end in tears.

265

There is no point in my relating every trivial stage of my courtship in detail, every romance that has been printed contains more than enough of that kind of tomfoolery. All the reader needs to know is that eventually I was allowed first of all to kiss my sweetikins and then to take certain other liberties. This much desired progress I pursued with all kinds of persuasion until my beloved let me in at night and I slipped into bed with her as if we belonged together. Now, since everyone knows what usually happens in this kind of story, you're probably thinking I did something improper. Not in the least! All my hopes were dashed. I encountered more resistance than I would ever have thought possible in a woman. The only things she was interested in were her reputation and marriage, and even though I promised her the latter with the most bloodcurdling oaths she refused to grant me anything before we were pronounced man and wife. She did permit me to stay lying beside her in bed and, quite worn out with disgust, I fell into a peaceful sleep.

My awakening, however, was rude. At four in the morning the lieutenant-colonel was standing beside the bed, a pistol in one hand and a torch in the other. 'Arquebusier!' he shouted to his servant, much more loudly than necessary since he was standing beside him, sword in hand. 'Quick, fetch the priest!' This was what woke me up and I immediately realised what danger I was in. 'Oh no', I thought, 'that'll be so you can make your confession before he makes mincemeat of you.' I kept my eyes shut, hoping he would go away, but he said, 'You libertine! Bringing shame and dishonour on my house! Would I do you wrong if I broke your necks, both yours and this trollop's who has become your whore? Oh you beast, how is it that I haven't already torn the heart out of your body, chopped it up and thrown it to the dogs?' At that he ground his teeth and rolled his eyes like a deranged animal.

I didn't know what to do and my bedmate could do nothing but cry. When I had finally recovered from the shock, however, I tried to protest our innocence, but he just told me to shut up and started upbraiding me again, telling me I had repaid the great trust he had put in me with the worst betrayal possible. Then his wife arrived and launched into a fresh sermon so that I wished I was anywhere else but there, even lying in the middle of a prickly thorn bush would have been better. I do believe that if the servant had not come back with the pastor she would have still been going on two hours later.

Before they arrived I had tried to get out of bed several times, but the lieutenant-colonel's threatening gestures kept me lying there. Now I realised how a man's courage drains away when he's caught in the act and I knew how a burglar feels when he's been apprehended after having broken in but before he has stolen anything. I thought back to the time when, if I had been attacked by the lieutenant-colonel and two arquebusiers, I would have straightaway sent all three of them packing. Now I was lying there like any other coward without the courage to raise my voice, never mind my fists.

'Isn't that a fine sight!' he said to the pastor. 'And I have to call you to witness my shame!' Scarcely had he spoken these words than he started ranting and raging again so that all I could understand were bits about 'wringing his neck' and 'washing my hands in blood'. He was foaming at the mouth like a wild boar and behaving as if he were about to go out of his mind. I kept thinking, 'Now he's going to put a bullet through your head.' The pastor had to hold him back physically, to stop him, as he put it, doing something he would later regret.

'Come now, colonel', he said, 'listen to reason. Remember the phrase about making a virtue of necessity. This fine young couple – you would be hard put to it to find another like it in the whole land – is not the first, and will certainly not be the last to give in to the irresistible power of love. This misdeed, for misdeed we must call it, can easily be put right by the couple themselves. I cannot approve of this anticipation of wedlock, but that does not mean these young people deserve to be hung, drawn and quartered. No one knows about this indiscretion and there will be no stain on your reputation, colonel, if you can just keep it secret, forgive them, consent to their marriage and announce it by publishing the banns in church in the usual way.'

'What!?' he replied, 'I have to go cap in hand and see that they come out of it with honour, instead of giving them the punishment they deserve? I was going to tie them up together and drown them in the Lippe before it gets light. No, you must marry them on the spot, that's why I sent for you. Otherwise I'll wring their necks like a couple of chickens.'

I thought, 'What can you do? It's a case of needs must when the devil drives. And you certainly won't have to be ashamed of the girl. In fact, when you consider your own origins, you're scarcely good enough to do up her shoelaces.' Out loud, however, I swore by all that was holy that we had done nothing to be ashamed of, but the answer I got was that then we should have behaved in such a way that no one would suspect we had done anything to be ashamed of. As things were, the suspicion had been aroused and wouldn't go away.

At that the priest hitched us there and then, sitting up in bed as we were, after which the pair of us were forced to get up and leave the house. As we were just going, the lieutenant-colonel said that neither I nor his daughter should darken his doorway ever again. Now that I had recovered somewhat and felt my sword at my side once more, I made a joke of it. 'I can't understand why you insist on doing everything topsy-turvy fashion. When other people have just been wed, their close relatives send them off to the bedroom, while you, dear father-in-law, are turning me not only out of bed, but out of doors as well. Instead of wishing me every happiness for my marriage, you will not even allow me the happiness of staying in my father-in-law's presence and serving him. If this habit should catch on weddings would not add much to the sum total of friendship in the world.'

Chapter 22

*How the wedding breakfast went off and what he planned
for the future*

The people in my lodgings were rather surprised when I
brought this young lady home, and even more so when they
saw she made no secret of the fact that she was going to bed
with me. Although this whole farce had put me somewhat out
of humour, I saw no reason to spurn my bride. I held my
darling in my arms, but at the same time my head was full of
thoughts of what to do about the situation. At first I decided it
served me right, but then I felt I had been treated disgracefully
and could not come out of it with honour unless I had my just
revenge. However, when I remembered that it was my father-
in-law on whom I would be taking revenge, and that it would
also rebound on my innocent darling, all my plans simply
evaporated. I was so ashamed, I resolved to stay in my lodgings
and not go out at all, but then I realised that would be the
most foolish thing of all to do. Finally I decided that first and
foremost I must win back my father-in-law's friendship; for
the rest, I would behave towards others as if nothing untoward
had happened and that as far as my marriage was concerned
everything was as it should be. I told myself that was how I
must tackle it, given the rather unusual way it had all come
about. 'If people should find out you're unhappy with your
marriage and have been trapped into it, like a poor girl married off to some impotent old moneybags', I said to myself, 'all
you'll get is mockery.'

With these thoughts going through my mind, I got up
early, though I would have preferred to stay longer in bed.
First of all I sent for my brother-in-law, who was married to
my wife's sister, told him briefly how we were now related
and asked him to bring his wife round to help us prepare some
food so that I would have something to offer the guests at my

wedding breakfast. And if he would be good enough to go and intercede with our parents-in-law on my behalf, I added, I would invite some guests who would complete the reconciliation. He agreed, and I went to see the commandant, whom I regaled with an amusing account of how my father-in-law and I had created a new fashion in accelerated marriages in which engagement, wedding and bedding all took place within the hour. And since, I went on, my father-in-law had economised on a wedding breakfast, I had decided to make up for it by giving a modest supper for a number of notables, to which he, of course, was humbly invited.

The commandant laughed fit to burst at my humorous narrative, and since I could see he was in the right mood, I became even freer in my speech. I excused myself by pointing out that he could hardly expect me to be staid and sober at such a time. Other men were out of their right minds for four weeks before and after they got married. They had four weeks to get their idiocies out of their system bit by bit, allowing them keep their lack of sense more or less concealed. Since matrimony had taken me by surprise I had to unload my silliness all at once so that I could settle down to a sober married life.

The commandant asked me about the marriage contract and how many gold pieces the old skinflint, who was not short of the wherewithal, had given me for a dowry. I replied that our marriage agreement consisted of one point and one point alone, namely that he should never see his daughter and me again. Since, however, there had been neither lawyer nor witnesses present I hoped it could be rescinded, especially as in my opinion one of the purposes of marriage was to foster friendship. Unless, that is, he were trying to marry off his daughter in the same way as Pythagoras, which I found it impossible to believe, since to my knowledge I had never insulted him.

With all these quips and jokes, which people here were not used to hearing from me, I got the commandant to agree to come to my wedding supper and to persuade my father-in-law to accompany him. He immediately sent a cask of wine and a stag to my kitchen, and I had such a banquet prepared as if I were going to entertain princes. I also gathered a distinguished company together that not only had a merry time together but, more importantly, so reconciled my parents-in-law to my wife and me that they showered more blessings on us than they had curses the previous night. The rumour was spread around the town that we had deliberately gone about the wedding in this way so as to avoid having tricks played on us by ill-disposed people.

In fact, this rapid wedding suited me down to the ground. If I had been married in the normal way and the banns been read from the pulpit then I'm afraid there would have been minxes enough to cause trouble since there were a good half dozen among the daughters of respectable citizens with whom I was on all too intimate terms.

The next day my father-in-law entertained the wedding guests, but nowhere near as sumptuously as I had, for he was stingy. In the course of the festivity he started talking to me about what business I intended to follow and how I was going to organise my household. Only then did I realise I had lost my freedom and was expected to live the life of a dutiful son-in-law. I put on a show of obedience and begged my dear father-in-law, as a gentleman of great experience, to give me the benefit of his advice.

The commandant praised this reply and said, 'Given that he's a lively young soldier, it would be extremely foolish during the present wars for him to take up any profession but soldiering. It's much better to keep your horse in someone else's stable that to feed someone else's in your own. As far as I'm concerned, I'm ready to make him a lieutenant with his own troop to command, if he wants.'

My father-in-law and I both thanked him. I did not reject the idea, as I had before, but I showed him the document from the merchant in Cologne with whom I had deposited my treasure, saying, 'I'll have to go and collect this before I enter the Swedish service. If they get word that I have gone over to the enemy they will just give me the finger and keep my treasure, which is not the kind of thing you'll find just lying by the roadside.' They both approved of this plan and so it was agreed between the three of us that I should go to Cologne in a few days' time, collect my treasure and return to the fortress, where I would take command of a troop. At the same time a day was set when my father-in-law was to be given a company and the position of lieutenant-colonel in the commandant's regiment. During that winter Count Götz was encamped in Westphalia with a large contingent of imperial troops, his headquarters being in Dortmund, and the commandant, expecting a siege in the coming spring, was accordingly on the look-out for good soldiers. However, it turned out to be wasted effort since Götz, following the defeat of his fellow general, Johann de Werth, in the Breisgau, had to withdraw from Westphalia in the spring in order to go to the relief of Breisach, which was being besieged by the Duke of Weimar.

Chapter 23

Simplicius comes to a town – for the sake of argument let's call it Cologne – to collect his treasure

Things that are destined happen in many ways. For some people adversity comes gradually, bit by bit, while others are overwhelmed by it all at once. For me it started so sweetly, so pleasantly that I didn't see it as misfortune at all but as the greatest good fortune. I had scarcely spent more than a week of married bliss with my dear wife when I donned my hunter's outfit, slung my musket over my shoulder and said farewell to her and her friends.

Since I knew all the paths and tracks, I managed to slip through unobserved and without danger. Indeed, no one saw me until I came to the barrier outside Deutz, on this side of the Rhine, opposite Cologne. I, however, saw many people.

One who struck me in particular was a farmer in Berg, who reminded me of my Da in the Spessart, and his son, who was just like my simple-minded self as a boy. This peasant lad was herding the swine and as I was passing the sows sensed my presence and started to grunt, which made the lad swear at them, 'Damn and blast ye, ye poxy beasts, why don't ye all go to hell!' The dairymaid heard this and shouted to the lad that he should stop swearing or she would tell his father. To this the boy answered that she could kiss his arse and go fuck her mammy into the bargain. The farmer heard his son and came running out of the house with his stick, crying, 'Shut thy gob, thou goddam foul-mouthed lummocks! I'll teach thee to swear, God rot thee!' caught him by the collar and thrashed him like a dancing bear. With each blow he said, 'Thou little bugger! I'll teach thee to cuss! Devil take thee! I'll teach thee to kiss my arse! I'll teach thee to go fuck thy mammy! etc. etc.' This punishment naturally reminded me of me and my Da, but I had not the honest faith to thank God for bringing me out of such darkness and ignorance to the light of better knowledge and understanding. How then should I have expected the good fortune He sent me day by day to continue?

When I arrived in Cologne I went to see my Jupiter, who happened to be in his right mind just then. When I told him why I had come, he said straight away that he was afraid I was wasting my time. The merchant with whom I had deposited my goods had gone bankrupt and disappeared. The authorities had put my property under seal and summoned the merchant to appear before them, but people thought it was very doubtful whether he would return since he had taken with him the best of the things that could be easily carried. A lot of water would pass under the Rhine Bridge before the case was dealt with.

You can imagine how delighted I was at this news. The air was blue with my cursing and swearing, but that did nothing to get me my money back. I had only brought ten thalers with me for the journey and so could not afford to stay for the time the matter would take. Anyway, it was dangerous to stay that long. I was worried that, since I was now attached to an enemy garrison, I might be identified and suffer a worse fate than just losing my fortune. Still, to return to Lippstadt with nothing but a wasted journey to show for it did not seem a good idea either.

I finally decided to stay in Cologne until the case was dealt with and sent word to my wife to tell her the reason for the delay. Accordingly I went to see a lawyer, explained my position and asked for his advice and assistance, promising him a generous bonus on top of his fee if he managed to expedite matters. Since he hoped to make something out of me, he willingly took me on and also provided me with board and lodging. The next day we went together to the officials who dealt with bankruptcies, showed them the original of the merchant's receipt and submitted a certified copy. Their reply, however, was that we would have to wait for the full hearing since not all the items in the inventory were there.

So I had to resign myself to another period of idleness, and I decided to use it to see what life was like in a great city. As I said, my landlord was a lawyer, but he also had around half a dozen lodgers and always kept eight horses in his stable, which he used to hire out to travellers. He had two servants, one German, one French, who looked after the horses and could drive a carriage or accompany a rider. With this threefold, or even three-and-a-half-fold business he doubtless not only made a living, but a huge profit for, since Jews were not allowed in the city, he could lend money at an exorbitant rate.

During the time I stayed with him I closely observed his disposition and by extending this to others I learnt how to recognise all kinds of diseases, which is the most important of a doctor's skills; once a disease has been correctly identified, the patient, so people say, is half way on the road to recovery. Many whom I diagnosed as fatally ill were completely unaware of their sickness and thought to be healthy by others, even by their doctors. I found people whose ailment was anger; when they suffered an attack they contorted their faces like demons, roared like lions, scratched like cats, laid about themselves like bears, bit like dogs, indeed, they were worse than wild animals, since like madmen they threw anything they could lay their hands on. They say this disease comes from the gall, but I believe its origin lies in the arrogance of fools. If you hear an angry man raging, especially about some trifle, you can be sure he has more pride than wits. This illness causes untold misery, both to the person himself and to others; to the sufferer it eventually brings palsy, gout and an early (perhaps even eternal!) death. And although they suffer from a fatal disease, you cannot in all conscience call them patients since the thing they lack most of all is patience.

Others I saw who were sick with envy. People say of them, seeing them always so pale and wan, that they are eating their hearts out. I consider this sickness the most dangerous of all because it comes from the devil, even though its origin lies in good fortune – the good fortune of the sufferer's enemies. Anyone who cures a man of this disease can almost boast he has brought a lost sheep back to the Christian fold, since it cannot infect true Christians because they abhor vice and sin.

I also consider addiction to gambling a disease, not just because the name implies that, but because those that suffer from it are completely obsessed by it. Its origin lies in idleness, not greed as some think; if you take away idleness the illness will disappear of its own accord. Likewise I came to the conclusion that over-indulgence in food and drink is a disease and that it comes from habit, not from an excess of wealth. Poverty is a good medicine for it, though not a guaranteed cure: I have seen beggars carousing and rich misers starving themselves. This ailment generally comes with its own remedy and that is called want – if not of money, then of health, so that sufferers generally recover on their own when, either through poverty or some other disease, they can no longer stuff their bodies.

Arrogance I considered a kind of mental illness based on ignorance. If a man knows himself, knows where he comes from and where he is going, it is impossible for him to be such an arrogant fool. Whenever I see a peacock or a turkeycock strutting along, displaying its feathers and gobbling, I have to laugh at the excellent caricature of sufferers from this complaint these brute breasts provide. I have not been able to find any particular remedy for the disease, since without humility those who have it are no easier to cure than other madmen.

I also concluded that laughing is an illness. The Greek poet Philemon is said to have died from it and Democritus was infected with it to his dying day. Even now our women say they could laugh till they died. People maintain it has its origin in the liver but I believe it comes from an excess of foolishness, since to laugh a lot is not a sign of a sensible man. It is unnecessary to prescribe a remedy for it since it is not only a jolly illness, but some people find they are laughing on the other side of their faces sooner than they would like. Inquisitiveness, too, struck me as no less of a disease, and one that is well nigh congenital in the female sex. It looks like a mere trifle, but in fact it is very dangerous; we are all still paying for the curiosity of our first mother. For the moment I will say nothing of the others, such as sloth, vengefulness, jealousy, blasphemy, debauchery and other ailments and vices, but get back to what I originally intended to write about, my landlord. It is just that he was so completely possessed by greed that he started me off thinking about other similar failings.

Chapter 24

The Hunter catches a hare in the middle of the town

He had, as I mentioned above, various business activities through which he scraped together money. He fed himself from his boarders' food and not vice versa. What they provided could have furnished generous portions for himself and his household if the tightwad had only used it for that, but he held a lot back and kept us on Spartan rations. At first, since I did not have much money with me, I did not eat with the student boarders but with his children and servants. The helpings were tiny and my stomach, which had become accustomed to the hearty Westphalian diet, felt quite strange. We never saw a decent joint of meat on the table, only what the students had had a week before, which had been well gnawed and was now as old and grey as Methuselah. The landlady, who had to do all the cooking herself since he refused to pay for a maid, would make some sour black gravy to pour over it and spice it up with plenty of pepper. The bones were licked so clean you could have made chessmen out of them, but that did not mean he had no more use for them. They were kept in a special bin and when our skinflint had enough they were chopped up into small pieces and any remaining fat boiled off. Whether it was used to make soup or grease boots I couldn't say.

Fast-days, of which there were more than enough, were religiously observed, our host being very conscientious about that, and we had to nibble at stinking kippers, salt cod and other dried and decaying fish. Cheapness was his sole criterion and he was quite prepared to go to the fishmarket himself and pick up what the fishmongers intended to throw away. Our bread was usually black and stale, our drink a thin, vinegary beer that tore my guts apart and yet had to pass for best barley wine. What is more, the German servant told me it was even worse in summer: the bread was mouldy and the meat full of maggots, the best was a few radishes at lunchtime and a handful of lettuce for supper. I asked him why he stayed with the old skinflint to which he replied that he was usually away on journeys and so depended more on the tips he got from travellers than on his penny-pinching master. You would be hard put to it to find a worse miser anywhere, he said, he didn't even trust his wife and children to go down into the cellar, he begrudged them the drips from the wine-casks. What I had seen so far, he added, was nothing. If I stayed longer I would see that he would flay a donkey for a few coppers. Once he brought home six pounds of tripe or brawn and left it in the cellar. His children, overjoyed to find the window had been left open, tied a fork to a stick and fished the whole lot out, which they ate, half-cooked, as fast as they could. They claimed it was the cat had taken the tripe, but the old cheese-parer was having none of that. He caught the cat and weighed it to prove that, hair, claws and all, it wasn't as heavy as his tripe had been.

Given this situation, I asked to eat with the students, whatever the cost, and not with the household. There was certainly more on the table, but I was not much better off for it since the dishes he gave us were all only half cooked. In that way the landlord could make double savings: he used less wood and we ate less. I believe he counted each mouthful we took and tore his hair whenever we made a good meal. His wine was well watered and not at all an aid to digestion. The cheese that appeared at the end of every meal was hard as stone, the Dutch butter so salty that no one could eat more than half an ounce at any one time and the fruit had to be served up for weeks on end before it was ripe enough to eat. If any of us complained, he would give his wife such a loud telling off that we could all hear, but on the quiet he would order her to carry on as usual.

Once one of his clients gave him a hare as a present. I saw it hanging in the larder and assumed we would get some game to eat for once. However, the German servant told me it was not for us, his master's agreement with the students stated explicitly that he did not need to provide such delicacies. I should go to the Old Market that afternoon, he said, and see if it wasn't for sale there. So I cut a piece out of the hare's ear and while we were at lunch, our host being absent, I told the others the old skinflint had a hare to sell and that I intended to cheat him out of it, if any of them wanted to come along we would have some fun and get the hare into the bargain. They all agreed; they had long wanted to play a trick on him, if they could get away with it.

The servant had told me our landlord used to stand where he could see how much the stallholder who was selling his goods got for them, to make sure he didn't cheat him out of a few coppers, so that afternoon we went there and saw him talking to some of the town notables. A man I had engaged to play the part now went up to the stallholder and said, 'Look here, friend, that's my hare there, it's been stolen and I'm taking it back. Someone snatched it from out of my window last night. If you're not willing to hand it over now I'll go before any judge you like, but you risk having to pay the costs.'

The stallholder replied that he would see what had to be done, that respectable gentleman standing over there had given him the hare to sell and he certainly wouldn't have stolen it. As the two of them argued, a crowd gathered round. Our skinflint noticed this and immediately realised which way the wind was blowing. He signalled to the stallholder to let the hare go to avoid any scandal because he had so many boarders. But the man I had engaged showed the piece from the hare's ear to all those standing round and measured it up against the hole so that they all agreed the hare was his. Now I came along with the students, as if we just happened to be passing, went up to the man with the hare and started haggling with him. After the sale was completed, I handed the hare to our landlord and asked him to take it home and prepare it for our dinner. To the man I had engaged I gave the price not of the hare, but of two pints of beer. So our skinflint was forced to give us the hare after all and couldn't make any objections, which gave us all a good laugh. If I had stayed in his house much longer I would have played a lot of tricks like that on him.

Book IV

Chapter 1

How, and for what reason, the Huntsman was dispatched to France

If you're too sharp you'll cut your own finger, if you play with fire too often you'll get burnt. The prank I played on my landlord with the hare was not enough for me, I was determined to punish him for his parsimony even more. I taught the boarders to water the salty butter to draw out the excess salt and to grate the hard cheese like Parmesan then moisten it with wine, both of which cut the skinflint to the quick. My tricks during mealtimes made my companions forget the water in the wine and I made up a song in which I compared a miser to a pig which is no use to anyone until it lies dead on the butcher's slab. That was not at all why he had brought me into his house, and the consequence was that he got his own back through the following subterfuge.

Two young nobles among the students received letters of credit from their parents with which they were to go to France to learn the language. The German groom happened to be away and the landlord could not trust the French one with the horses in France, or so he said, because he did not know him well enough yet and was worried he might forget to come back and he would lose his horses. Therefore, since my case was not due to come up for four weeks, he asked me whether I would do him the great favour of accompanying the two noblemen to Paris with his horses. He assured me that if I gave him full power of attorney he would see to my business as faithfully as if I were there myself. The two young gentlemen added their voices to his request and my own fancy to see France chimed in as well, since this would give me the opportunity of doing it with all expenses paid when the alternative was to spend four weeks kicking my heels and consuming my own resources into the bargain.

So I set off for France, acting as postillion to the two young noblemen. Nothing special happened on the way, we arrived in Paris and went to see our Cologne landlord's correspondent, who honoured the letters of credit. The next morning, however, I was arrested, along with the horses. Some man arrived claiming my landlord owed him a sum of money and, with the approval of the commissioner of the district, took the horses and sold them, ignoring all my protests.

So there I was, stuck in a foreign country with no idea what to do, nor how I was going to make such a long and, in those days, extremely dangerous journey back home. The two young noblemen were very sympathetic and even more generous with their tip than they would otherwise have been. They refused to let me go before I had found either a good position or a good opportunity of getting back to Germany. They rented lodgings and I stayed with them for several days, looking after one of them who, not being used to the long journey, had fallen ill. And since I did it so well, he gave me the clothes he was not wearing any more because he had had new ones made in the latest fashion. Their advice was to stay in Paris for a few years to learn the language, the valuables I had in Cologne would not, as they put it, run away.

While I was still wondering what to do and trying to make up my mind, the doctor who came every day to treat the sick nobleman heard me playing the lute and singing a German song, which he liked so well that he offered me a good salary with board and lodging if I would come and teach his two sons. He understood my situation better than I did myself and knew that I would not reject the offer of a good position. The two noblemen did all they could to persuade me and gave me an excellent reference, so that we soon came to an agreement, though I would only commit myself from one quarter to the next.

This doctor spoke German as well as I did and Italian like a native, which made me all the more willing to take service with him. He was invited to the farewell dinner I had with the two noblemen. I was brooding over black thoughts, thinking of my newly wed wife, my promised command, my treasure in Cologne, all of which I had foolishly allowed myself to be persuaded to abandon. And when the conversation came round to our former landlord's parsimony an idea suddenly occurred to me and I said, 'Who knows, perhaps our landlord deliberately got me stuck here so he can collect my treasure in Cologne and keep it?' The doctor replied that might well be so, especially if he believed I was not from the nobility. 'No', replied one of the noblemen, 'if he was sent here with the intention he should stay then it was done because he tormented our landlord so much for his penny-pinching ways.'

'I think there's another reason', said the one who had been ill. 'Recently I was in my room and I heard the landlord and his French servant having a loud conversation, so I listened to hear what it was about. I managed to make out from the servant's mangled German that he was complaining the Huntsman had slandered him to his mistress, saying he didn't look after the horses properly. Because his servant expressed himself in such a garbled way, however, the jealous fool misunderstood and took him to be suggesting something dishonourable and assured the Frenchman he would not have long to wait before the Huntsman was gone. After that he looked at his wife with a suspicious eye and vented his anger on her much more furiously than before, as I observed myself.'

'Whatever the motive', said the doctor, 'I'm convinced it was done to keep you here. But don't worry, I'll find a way of getting you back to Germany. In the meantime, however, write and tell him he must look after your treasure well or he will be called strictly to account. I'm coming to suspect this was all a put-up job. The man who pretended to be the creditor is a good friend of your landlord and his correspondent here and I'm willing to wager it was you yourself who brought the IOU to Paris, on the basis of which he seized the horses and sold them.'

Chapter 2

Simplicius gets a better landlord than the one he had before

Seeing how concerned I was, Monsieur Canard, as my new master was called, offered to help me both in word and deed so that I shouldn't lose the money and valuables I had in Cologne. As soon as I had moved into his house he asked me to tell him how my affairs stood. The better he understood my situation, he said, the better he could advise me. I felt I would not be held in very high esteem if I revealed the truth about my background, so I said I was an impoverished German nobleman who had neither father nor mother, only a few relatives in a fortress that was garrisoned by the Swedes. All this, I said, I had kept secret from my landlord and the two young noblemen in Cologne who, being of the imperial party, might confiscate my treasure as enemy property. My idea was to write to the commandant of the above-mentioned fortress, in whose regiment I was an ensign, tell him how it was I had been tricked into coming here and ask him to collect my property and give it to my friends to look after until I had the opportunity of getting back to the regiment. Canard approved of this plan and promised to make sure my letter reached its destination, even if it were in Mexico or China. Accordingly I wrote letters to my darling wife, my father-in-law and Colonel de Saint Andrée, the commandant of Lippstadt, to whom I addressed the envelope, putting the other two letters in with the one to him. I told them I would return as soon as I managed to get the money for such a long journey and asked both my father-in-law and the commandant to try to get my property back through military channels before it was too late. I also appended a list detailing how much it consisted of in gold, silver and jewels. I made duplicate copies of the letters, just in case one should get lost; Monsieur Canard took care of one set, while I entrusted the other to the post.

This cheered me up and put me in the right mood to start instructing his two sons, who were being brought up like young princes. As Monsieur Canard was very rich, he was also very proud and liked to make a show. He had caught this disease from the members of the aristocracy with whom he had dealings almost every day and whom he aped in everything. His household was run like a duke's palace, and the only thing lacking was that he wasn't addressed as 'Your Grace'. His opinion of himself was so great that if a marquis should happen to visit him he treated him as no better than himself. He also gave poor people his remedies and did not charge the small sum due for them but let them have them free to boost his reputation.

Since I had an inquiring mind and knew that he used me to show off when I lined up with the other servants behind him during his sick calls, I got into the habit of helping him prepare his medicines in his laboratory. Through that, and because he liked to speak German, I became quite friendly with him and asked him why he did not use the name of the noble estate outside Paris he had recently bought for 20,000 crowns as a title. I also asked why he was determined his two sons should become doctors and made them study so hard. Given that he already had a title of nobility, would it not be better, I wondered, to do as other gentlemen did and buy them some office so that they would belong fully to the nobility.

'No', he replied. 'When I go to see a prince, he says, "Ah, doctor, do sit down", but to some noble he will say, "Wait on me there".'

'But don't you know', I said, 'that a doctor has three faces: the face of an angel when the patient sees him, the face of a god when he treats him, and the face of a demon when he's well again and wants to get rid of him. The respect you get only lasts as long as the wind in his belly. Once it's gone and the rumbling's stopped, your respect's gone with it. Then it's, "Doctor, there's the door." There's more honour in a nobleman's standing than in a doctor's sitting. A nobleman waits on his prince all the time and has the honour of always being at his side. Didn't you recently have to take some of a prince's excrement in your mouth to see what it tasted of? I'd rather spend ten years standing in attendance than taste someone else's shit, even if he made my life a bed of roses.'

'I didn't *have* to eat it', he replied, 'I did it so the prince would see what great pains I went to in order to diagnose his condition and increase my honorarium accordingly. Why shouldn't I eat someone's shit if they reward me with a few hundred pistoles, while I make them eat much worse filth and don't pay them a sou? You're talking like a German; if you came from another nation I'd say you were talking like a fool.'

I left it at that, since I could see he was getting angry. To get him back in a good mood, I begged him to put it down to my simplicity and turned the conversation to more pleasant matters.

Chapter 3

How Simplicius agreed to appear on stage and acquired a new name

Monsieur Canard had more game to throw away than some people with their own hunting grounds have to eat; on top of that he was made presents of more flesh and fowl than he and his household could consume. The result was that every day he had so many parasites at his table that it looked as if he were keeping open house. On one occasion the Lord Chamberlain and other eminent personages from the court came to visit him and he gave them a princely dinner, since he knew how important it was for him to keep in with those who were always in the king's presence or were in favour with him.

As a token of his esteem, and for their pleasure and delight, he asked me to do him and his distinguished guests the honour of playing them a German song on my lute. I was happy to oblige, being in the mood at the moment – we musicians are a very temperamental lot – and gave of my best. The company was so pleased with my playing and singing that the Lord Chamberlain remarked that it was a pity I could not speak French, otherwise he would recommend me strongly to the king and queen. The doctor, afraid of losing my services, quickly replied that, being of noble birth, I would hardly want to take employment as a musician and anyway I did not intend to stay long in France. At that the Lord Chamberlain said that he had never seen such a handsome figure, a clear voice and a skilled lutenist all in the one person. There was a play to be performed soon before the king in the Louvre, he went on, and if he could get me to take part he was sure it would bring great honour. Monsieur Canard put this to me and I answered that if someone were to tell me what character I was to play and what songs I was to sing, I could learn both the tunes and the songs off by heart and sing them to my lute, even if they were in French. My brain was surely at least as good as that of the schoolboys they usually employed for these parts, and they too had to learn both words and gestures by heart.

When the Lord Chamberlain saw how keen I was I had to promise to go to the Louvre the very next day for an audition to see if I was suitable. I appeared at the appointed time and played the tunes of the various songs perfectly at sight from the tablature. Then I was given the French songs to learn by heart, including the correct pronunciation; they came accompanied with a German translation to help me find the gestures to fit. I did not find it difficult at all and had everything ready sooner than they expected. In fact I did it so well that when I sang anyone would have sworn I was a born Frenchman, or so Monsieur Canard said. The part I had was Orpheus mourning for his Eurydice and the first time we came together to rehearse I did all my gestures, songs and tunes so plaintively that everyone believed I must have played the role several times before.

I have never had such a pleasant day in all my life as the one when we performed the play. Monsieur Canard gave me something to make my voice sound clearer than ever, but when he tried to improve my complexion with talcum oil and powder my shining black curly hair he decided he was just spoiling the effect. I was crowned with a laurel wreath and dressed in a sea-green robe which left my neck, the upper part of my chest, my arms up to the elbows and my legs up to the thighs bare for all to see. Around it I flung a flesh-coloured taffeta cloak, more like a banner than a cloak. In this costume I languished for Eurydice, sang a pretty song begging Venus to help me and finally carried off my love. I acted out the whole scene excellently, gazing at my love with sighs and yearning looks. After I had lost my Eurydice I put on a black costume, cut in the same fashion so that my white skin shone out like snow. As I mourned my lost wife I became so stricken with grief that in the middle of my sad arias and melodies the tears came and threatened to stop me singing. However, I managed to get through by turning it into a nice trill. Then I went down to hell, where I sang a very moving aria in which I reminded Pluto and Proserpina of their love for each other, from which they could imagine the pain Eurydice and I felt at being separated. Assuming a most reverent posture and accompanying everything on my harp, I begged them to allow her to return to me, and when they agreed I thanked them with a joyful song, so transforming my expression, gestures and voice that the audience were amazed. But when I suddenly lost her again I imagined the greatest danger a man could face and turned as pale as if I were about to faint. Since by that time I was alone on the stage and everyone in the audience was watching me, I made a special effort and was praised for having acted best of all.

Then I sat on a rock, bewailing the loss of my love with plaintive words and a sad melody and calling on all creatures to have pity on me. At that all kinds of tame and wild animals came up to me, mountains, trees and other such things, so that it looked as if it had been done by magic. I made only one mistake, and that was at the end, after I had renounced all women, been torn apart by the Bacchantes and thrown into the water. It was so arranged that only my head was visible, the rest of my body being safely hidden under the stage. The dragon was supposed to devour me, but the man who was inside the dragon operating it could not see my head and so made the creature nibble the grass beside my head. This looked so ridiculous that I could not stop a smile from flitting across my face which was noted by the ladies, who never took their eyes off me.

Beside the praise I received from many people, this play not only brought me an excellent reward but also a new name. From now on the French insisted on calling me 'Beau Alman'. As it was carnival time there were more such plays and ballets, in which I also performed, though eventually I found that I was making others jealous because I attracted all eyes, especially those of the women. I gave up appearing on stage after one particular time when I took some rather hard blows: dressed as Hercules in nothing but a lion skin, I was fighting with Achelous for Deianira, and he used rather more force than is normal in a play.

Chapter 4

Against his will, Beau Alman is lured into the Venusberg

Through this I became known to a number of highly placed personages, and it looked as if luck was about to smile on me again. I was offered a position in the king's service, a chance even some big fish never get. One day when I was working in the laboratory with Monsieur Canard – out of interest I had learnt to dissolve, resolve, sublimate, purgate, coagulate, calcinate, filtrate and all the other many alcomical processes which he used to prepare his medicines – a lackey came to see him and handed him a note. 'Monsieur Beau Alman', said the doctor, 'this letter concerns you. A gentleman of rank requests that you go and see him straight away to discuss the possibility of your instructing his son on the lute. He asks me to do all I can to persuade you to go, and promises the he will remain for ever in your debt for your trouble.'

I replied that if I could do him (Monsieur Canard, that is) a service by being of service to anyone, then I would make every effort to do so. At that he said I should put on some other clothes and accompany the lackey; while I was changing he would have something to eat prepared for me since I had quite a long way to go and was unlikely to get there before evening. So I smartened myself up and hurriedly ate a little of the food. I noticed some of the tiny sausages seemed to have a rather strong medicinal taste. Then I went with the lackey. We followed a strangely roundabout way for over an hour until, towards evening, we came to a garden gate, which he unlocked and then closed behind me. He took me into a summer-house in the corner of the garden and down a fairly long corridor where he knocked on a door which was immediately opened by an old gentlewoman. She addressed me in German, bidding me a polite welcome and asking me to enter, at which the lackey, who spoke no German, bowed low and left.

The old woman took me by the hand and led me into the room, which was hung with the most magnificent tapestries and beautifully decorated. She told me to sit down so that I could take a rest and she would tell me why I had been brought to this place. I sat on the chair she placed beside the fire, which was lit, since it was quite chilly in the room, and she sat beside me. 'Monsieur', she said, 'if you know anything of the power of love, if you know how it can overwhelm the bravest, strongest, cleverest of men, then you will not be at all surprised to hear that it can subjugate a weak woman. You have not been brought here by some gentleman for your lute-playing, that was just a pretence to persuade you and Monsieur Canard, but for the sake of your outstanding good looks by the most excellent lady in all Paris. She feels she will die if she does not soon have the pleasure of seeing your divine body and being revived by it. Since I am also German, she has commanded me to tell you this and to beg you, more urgently than Venus did Adonis, to go to her this evening and let her feast her eyes on your handsome figure. You will surely not refuse this request from a most noble lady?'

'Madam', I replied, 'I don't know what to think, far less what to say. I cannot believe I am worthy for a lady of such quality to desire me in this way. It also occurs to me that if this lady who wants to see me is of such high rank as you suggest, she could just as easily have sent for me during the daytime and not so late in the evening, nor in such a lonely place. Why did she not command me to go directly to her? What am I doing in this garden? As a fellow-countrywoman you will forgive me, being a foreigner stranded in this country, for feeling afraid I might be the object of some trick, especially since I was asked to come and meet a gentleman and now I am here I find myself in a quite different situation. I tell you, if through some treachery I were threatened with physical danger I would make good use of my sword before I was killed.'

'Calm down, calm down Monsieur Beau Alman', she replied, 'and put these thoughts out of your mind. We women are strange and cautious in our plans so that at first you find it difficult to fall in with them. If the person who has fallen so completely in love with you had wanted you to know who and what she was, she would not have had you brought to her by this route but through the front door. There is a hood', she went on, pointing to the table, 'which you must wear while you are being taken to her. She does not want you to recognise the place, never mind the person you are visiting. And I must impress on you as strongly as I can to respect the lady's high rank as much as the inexpressible love she has for you. Otherwise you will soon discover that she has the power to punish your arrogant disdain, even in a matter such as this. If, however, you show yourself to be suitably obliging towards the lady you can rest assured that the least exertion you make on her behalf will not go unrewarded.'

It gradually grew dark and I was filled with worries and fears, so that I sat there like a wooden statue. I could well imagine that I might not get out of this place as easily as I had come in. However, I eventually agreed to everything that was demanded of me and said to the old gentlewoman, 'Well then, assuming things are as you have described them, I will entrust myself to your German honesty. You would not, I hope, allow an innocent fellow-countryman to be led into a trap. Go ahead then, do with me as you have been commanded; I presume the lady you told me about isn't planning to kill me with her basilisk eyes.'

'God forbid!' she said. 'It would be a pity if a body like yours, which our whole nation can be proud of, were to die so soon. Rather than dying you will find more pleasure than you ever imagined in your whole life.'

Now that I had agreed, she called for Jean and Pierre, who immediately appeared from behind a tapestry, each wearing a cuirass and armed from head to toe, with a halberd and a pistol in their hands. I went pale with shock at the sight. Noticing this, the old woman said, 'There's no need to be so frightened when you're visiting a young lady', and ordered the two men to take off their armour, just keeping their pistols, pick up the lantern and accompany us. Then she put the black velvet hood over my head and led me by the hand, carrying my hat under her arm. It was a very circuitous route; I could tell that we went through many doors and along a paved path. After what must have been a quarter of an hour I had to go up a short flight of stone steps, at the top of which a small door was opened which took me into a corridor with stone flags, up a spiral staircase, then down several steps again. After another six paces I heard a further door open. The old gentlewoman led me in, took off the mask, and I found myself in a charmingly decorated room. The walls were covered with beautiful pictures, the sideboard with silver dishes and the curtains round the bed with gold embroidery. In the middle was a table set with magnificent glass and cutlery, and in front of the fire a bath, which was very pretty in itself but, in my opinion, rather spoilt the effect of the room as a whole.

'Welcome, Monsieur Beau Alman', said the old gentle-woman, 'would you still say you are being deceived and betrayed? You can forget all your fears and be as you were in the theatre when Pluto gave you back your Eurydice. I can assure you that you will find a more beautiful woman here than you lost there.'

Chapter 5

What happened to him in the Venusberg and how he got out again

From these words I deduced that I had not been brought here simply to be looked at but to do something quite different. Accordingly I said to the gentlewoman that it is not much use for a thirsty man if he finds he is sitting beside a forbidden well. She replied that in France they were not so mean as to begrudge a man water, especially when there was such a surfeit of it. 'Yes, Madam', I replied, 'that would be all well and good if it were not for the fact that I am a married man.'

'Poppycock!', said the old sinner. 'You won't find anyone here who will believe that, married gentlemen don't come to France very often. And even if you were, I can't believe you would be so foolish as to die of thirst rather than drink from someone else's well, especially when it's more fun and has better water than your own.'

While we were chatting a maid of honour, whose task it was to look after the fire, was taking off my shoes and stockings, which had got filthy in the dark. Paris is a very muddy city anyway. Then came the order that I was to be bathed before dinner. The maid ran to and fro, gathering all the bath things together, and soon everything smelled of musk and fragrant soaps. The linen was finest cambric, edged with genuine Brussels lace. I was embarrassed and didn't want the old gentlewoman to see me naked, but it was no use, I had to let her scrub me, though the young maid had to go out for a while. After the bath I was given a gossamer-thin shirt to wear and a sumptuous dressing gown of violet taffeta together with a pair of silk stockings of the same colour; my nightcap and slippers were embroidered with gold and pearls. The old woman dried and combed my hair for me, as if I were a prince, or a young child. Washed and dressed in my finery, I sat there looking like the King of Hearts.

In the meantime, the maid of honour had brought in the food, and when the table was laid, three sublime young ladies entered the room. Their alabaster breasts were almost completely exposed, their faces, on the other hand, almost completely masked. They all seemed extremely beautiful to me, but one even more so than the others. I gave them a low but silent bow to which they replied in kind. It looked as if it was a gathering of the deaf and dumb. All three sat down at the same time, so that I could not tell which was the highest born, much less which was the one I was there to serve. The first question was, could I speak French? No, replied the old gentlewoman, at which the other told her to ask me to sit down. When I had done so, the third ordered my interpreter to sit down as well. Again there was nothing to tell me which was the noblest of the three. I was sitting opposite them, next to the old woman, and doubtless the proximity of the old skeleton only served to emphasise my own beauty. They all three gazed at me adoringly and I could have sworn I heard a thousand sighs, though because of the masks they were wearing I could not see the sparkle in their eyes.

The old gentlewoman asked me which I thought was the most beautiful of the three. I replied that it was impossible to choose, at which she laughed, showing all the four teeth she had left in her mouth, and asked me why. Because I couldn't see them properly, I answered, though I could certainly tell that none of them was ugly. The three ladies wanted to know what this was about and the old gentlewoman translated, adding a fabrication of her own, namely that I had said each pair of lips deserved a thousand kisses, for I could see their lips below the masks, especially those of the one sitting directly opposite me. Through this piece of flattery the old woman made me think the one directly opposite me was the highest ranking and so I observed her all the more keenly. I kept up the pretence that I could not understand a single word of

French and that was the sum total of our conversation at table. Since we were so silent we finished our meal all the more quickly and the ladies wished me good night and left. I accompanied them to the door but that was all, as the old gentlewoman locked it behind them. When I saw that, I asked where I was going to sleep. She replied that I would have to stay with her and make do with the bed in that room. I said the bed would be fine if only one of the three were in it. 'I'm afraid', said the old woman, 'that you're not going to get any of them tonight.'

While we were talking, the curtain round the bed was drawn aside a little by a beautiful lady who told the old woman to stop her chatter and get to her room. At once I took the candle from her to see who was in the bed, but she put it out and said, 'Sir, if you value your life, don't do it! You can rest assured that if you try to see who this lady is against her will, you will not leave this place alive.' With that she went, locking the door behind her. The maid of honour who had been tending the fire doused it and left by a hidden door behind one of the tapestries.

'Allez, Monsieur Beau Alman', said the lady lying in the bed, 'curme to ze bed, my 'eart, curme to me.' At least the old woman had taught her some German! I went over to the bed to see what was to be done, and as soon as I got there she threw her arms round my neck and welcomed me with many kisses. So hot was her desire that she bit into my lower lip, started to unbutton my dressing gown and tore the shirt from my body, dragging me down to her and behaving as if she were more crazy with love than I can say. The only German she could say was, 'Curme to me, my 'eart', the rest she indicated by gestures. I thought of my darling back home, but what was the use? Unfortunately I was a human being and faced with such a well-proportioned creature, and a charming one at that, I would have had to be made of wood to get away with my virtue unblemished.

I spent eight days and as many nights in that place, and I think the other three must have lain with me too since they didn't all speak like the first one, nor behave in such an extravagant way. Although I spent eight full days with these four ladies I was never allowed to see their faces except through a gauze veil, or when it was dark. At the end of the eight days I was led, blindfold, down into the courtyard and put into a coach with the blinds lowered which took me back to the doctor's house and then disappeared immediately. The old gentlewoman accompanied me and took off the blindfold en route. I was given two hundred pistoles and when I asked the old woman whether I should give someone a tip she replied, 'Certainly not! The ladies would be very annoyed if you did that. They would think you imagined you had been in a whorehouse, where everyone expects a tip.'

Afterwards I had more such customers but they made such excessive demands on my services that eventually I was unable to satisfy them any longer and tired of the whole stupid business.

Chapter 6

How Simplicius left secretly and how he was robbed when he believed he had the French disease

It was frightening how many gifts, both of money and other things, I collected through these pursuits. I was no longer surprised that women enter brothels and make a trade of this bestial obscenity, since it brings such excellent rewards. I began to be concerned about what I was doing, not for reasons of religion or conscience, but because I was afraid I might be caught during one of these escapades and given the reward I really deserved. Therefore I tried to get back to Germany, all the more because the commandant of Lippstadt had written that he had captured several Cologne merchants, whom he was refusing to release until my property had been handed over to him. He added that he was keeping the promised command open for me, but hoped to see me back before the spring, otherwise he would have to fill the post with someone else. In the same envelope was a letter from my wife that was full of loving expressions of her longing to see me. Had she known the kind of life I was leading she would surely have sent a quite different message.

I could well imagine it was unlikely I would be able to leave with Monsieur Canard's consent, so I decided to go secretly as soon as an opportunity presented itself. And that was what happened, most unfortunately for me as it turned out. One day I met some officers from the Duke of Weimar's army and introduced myself to them as an ensign in Colonel Saint Andrée's regiment. I told them I had been in Paris for some time on personal business and was now determined to return to my regiment and requested they allow me to accompany them. They willingly agreed and told me when they were leaving; I bought a nag, equipped myself for the journey as secretly as possible, packed up my money (around five hundred doubloons I had earned from those depraved women) and set off without obtaining Monsieur Canard's permission. I did write to him, however, dating the letter from Maastricht to make him think I was heading for Cologne. In it I took my leave of him, saying I found it impossible to stay any longer because his piquant sausages did not agree with my stomach.

The second night out of Paris I had a rash which made me look as if I had erysipelas, and my head hurt so badly I couldn't get up. It was in a miserable little village where I could not get a doctor. Worst of all, I had no one to look after me since the other officers continued on their way early next morning, setting off for Alsace and leaving me, as being no concern of theirs, lying there more or less on my deathbed. As they left they did have the goodness to ask the innkeeper to take care of me and my horse and left a message with the mayor to treat me as an officer of the king.

I lay there for a few days, oblivious to the world and rambling like a lunatic. They brought the priest, but he couldn't make anything of what I was saying. Seeing that he could do nothing for my soul, he looked for ways of helping my body and had me bled, put in a warm bed and given an infusion to make me sweat. This was so effective that I recovered my senses that very same night and remembered where I was and how I had got there and fallen ill. The next morning the priest came back and found me in despair because not only had all my money been taken but I assumed I had the French disease – which I deserved more than the doubloons – since my whole body was covered with more spots than a leopard. I couldn't walk or stand, sit or lie down. I was completely unreasonable and although I hardly thought the money I had lost had come from God I now insisted it was the devil himself had stolen it. I fretted and raged and the poor priest had his hands full trying to comfort me since I was suffering a double torment.

'My friend', he said, 'at least behave like a rational human being, even if you can't accept your cross like a good Christian. What are you doing? You have lost your money, do you want to lose your life and, what is more important, your hope of eternal salvation as well?'

'I wouldn't care about the money', I replied, 'if only I didn't have this horrible disease, or were somewhere where it could be cured.'

'All you need is patience', said the priest. 'What do you think the poor little children do? There are more than fifty of them in this village with the same disease.'

When I heard that children had it as well I immediately cheered up, for I could not imagine they would catch this filthy infection. I picked up my bag to see what was left in it, but apart from my linen there was nothing of value except a small case containing a lady's portrait set with rubies which had been given me in Paris. I removed the picture and handed the rest to the priest, asking him to sell it in the nearest town so that I would have something to live on. The result was that I got scarcely a third of its value and since that did not last long I had to get rid of my horse too, which provided me with just enough to keep me until the pocks dried up and I was well again.

Chapter 7

How Simplicius reflected on his past life and learnt to swim when the water came up to his mouth

The cause of our sins is often the means by which we are punished. The smallpox made such a mess of my looks that from now on women left me in peace. My face was pitted like a barn floor where they've been threshing peas. I became so ugly that my lovely curly hair, which had ensnared many a woman, was ashamed of me and bid me farewell, leaving something akin to hog's bristles in its place so that I had to wear a wig. And just as my external attractions had disappeared, so had my sweet voice since I had had pocks all over my throat. My eyes, which until now had always sparkled with fire enough to kindle love in any heart, were as red and watery as those of an eighty-year-old woman with cataracts. To top it all, I was in a foreign country where I knew neither man nor beast I could trust, could not speak the language and had no money left.

This made me think back and bemoan all the excellent opportunities to improve my situation which I had squandered. I came to the conclusion that it was my extraordinary good fortune in warfare and in finding the treasure that was the cause of my misfortune; it could not have cast me down so low had it not previously looked on me with false smiles as it raised me up. I even decided that all the good things that had happened to me were in fact bad and had led me to my ruin. Where was the hermit, who only wanted what was best for me, Colonel Ramsay, who had taken me in when I was destitute, the pastor, who had given me good advice? They were all gone and there was no one left to give me a helping hand. My money had also vanished, and I was told to go too and find board and lodgings elsewhere even if, like the prodigal son, I had to share it with the swine. It was then that I remembered the advice of the priest who said I should spend my youth and money on studying, but now it was too late to clip my wings, the bird had already flown.

How rapid the change from fortune to misfortune! Only a month ago I was admired by princes, adored by women, idolised by the common people, and now I was a nobody the dogs used as a pissing-post. The innkeeper was throwing me out because I couldn't pay any more and I must have gone over the question of what to do a thousand times in my mind. I would gladly have enlisted but, given that I looked like a mangy cuckoo, no recruiting officer would take me; I was still too weak for physical labour, and anyway I had no experience. The only comfort was that summer was approaching and I could at a pinch bed down in a hedge, since no one would have me in their house. I still possessed the good clothes I had had made for the journey and a bag full of expensive linen, which no one would buy because they were afraid some disease might be included in the bargain. I slung my bag over my shoulder, took my sword in my hand and followed a track that brought me to a small town which boasted a chemist's shop. There I had a salve made up to remove the pock-marks on my face. The chemist's assistant was not as squeamish as other fools, who would not take my clothes from me, and accepted a fine shirt in place of the money I did not have. I thought getting rid of the disfiguring marks would be the first step to improving my wretched situation. I immediately felt more cheerful when the chemist assured me that in a week's time there would be little to be seen apart from the deep scars the pocks had eaten into my skin.

It happened to be market day in the town and there was a tooth-drawer who earned plenty of money by palming off rubbish on the people. 'You fool', I said to myself, 'why don't you set up a stall like that? You must be a pretty poor specimen if you didn't learn enough in all that time you spent with Monsieur Canard to gull a simple peasant and earn a decent supper.'

Chapter 8

How he became an itinerant quack

At that particular time I had an appetite like a gannet. My belly was always crying out for more and all I had left in my purse was one diamond ring worth about twenty crowns. I sold it for twelve and, since I knew that would soon be gone and I had no money coming in, I decided to set up as a doctor. I bought the four ingredients for the universal antidote to poisons and made it up; then I mixed herbs, roots, butter and different oils to make a green ointment for treating wounds (it was strong enough to cure a horse); from cadmium, gravel, crab-stones, emery and talc I prepared a powder for whitening teeth, and from lye, copper, sal ammoniac and camphor a blue tincture for scurvy, stomatitis, toothache and sore eyes. I purchased a quantity of small tins and wooden boxes, papers and jars to keep my wares in, and to make the whole thing look more impressive I had little leaflets printed in French saying what each remedy was for.

In three days I was ready and had spent no more than three crowns on medicines and equipment. I packed up and left the small town, intending to make my way from village to village, selling my wares, until I reached Alsace. Strasbourg being a neutral city, I hoped there would be an opportunity to accompany a party of merchants down the Rhine to Cologne, from where I would make my way back to my wife. The idea was good, but the execution went badly wrong.

The first time I set up my stall outside a church and offered my quack remedies for sale my takings were very poor. I was much too timid and didn't have the cheap-jack's boasting patter. I quickly realised I would have to go about it in a different way if I wanted to make money. I went with my things to the inn and while I was eating the innkeeper told me people of all kinds would gather in the afternoon beneath the lime-trees outside. I would certainly be able to sell something there, he said, if I had something good to sell. However, he went on, there were so many swindlers going round the country that people were unwilling to part with their money unless they could see with their own eyes that the antidote really worked.

Now I knew what was needed. I took a half glass full of good Strasbourg schnapps and went out and caught a toad, one of those revolting golden or reddish ones with black spots on their bellies that sit croaking in filthy puddles in the spring and summer, which I put in a glass of water beside my goods on a table under the limes. I had borrowed a pair of tongs from the innkeeper's wife and as people gathered round they assumed I was going to pull teeth, but I addressed them as follows, 'My masters and goot frents' – I still couldn't speak much French – 'I be no teeths-pull-outer, but here haf I goot vatter for ze eyes zat make all the bad vatter go avay from ze red eyes.'

'Yes', one of the bystanders said, 'we can tell from your eyes, they look like two will-o'-the-wisps.'

'Zat is verry true', I said, 'but if I had ze vatter not I vould be qvite blind. Ze vatter I sell not. Ze poison-cure and ze powder for ze vite teeths and ze wound-cream I sell, but you buy and I gif avay ze vatter for ze eyes, I no pull ze wool ovver zem. Zis poison-cure I try out and if you not like, you not buy.'

I got one of the bystanders to choose one of my boxes of antidote, took out a lump the size of a pea, dropped it in the schnapps, that the people assumed was water, crushed it, then took the toad out of the glass of water with the tongs and said, 'See my goot frents, if zis fenomous reptile can my antidote trink and die not, zen it is no goot and you not buy.'

With that I put the poor toad, which is born in water and can stand no other liquid, into the schnapps and held a paper over the glass so it couldn't jump out. It wriggled and writhed worse than if I had dropped it onto red-hot coals because the schnapps was much too strong for it, and after a short while it curled up its toes and died. This visible proof of the effectiveness of my antidote loosened the peasants' tongues and their purses, and I was kept busy wrapping up the stuff in the leaflets and taking money for it. Having seen the evidence with their own eyes, they thought it must be the best in the world. Some bought three, four, five, even six boxes so that they would have a supply of this excellent antidote against poison whenever they needed it and some bought it for their friends and relatives who lived in other places, so that even though it wasn't market day, by that evening I had taken ten crowns and still had half my wares left.

I left for another village that very same night because I was afraid some peasant with an inquiring mind might try out my antidote by putting it in a glass of water with a toad. If the experiment failed, my back would suffer for it. However, in order to prove the excellence of my antidote in another way I made 'yellow arsenic' from flour, saffron and gallic acid and a 'sublimate of mercury' from flour and vitriol. Whenever I wanted to do a demonstration I had two glasses of water on my table, one of which had a strong admixture of aqua fortis. I put my antidote in the latter and scraped a quantity of my two 'poisons' into each glass. The water in the one without my antidote – and therefore without aqua fortis – turned as black as ink, while the other, because of the acid, remained as it was. 'Oh, look', the people said, 'what an excellent antidote, and so cheap.' When I poured the two together everything went clear and the peasants pulled out their purses and bought my cure, not only satisfying my belly, but putting me on horseback again and money into my purse as well. In this way I safely reached the German border.

Let this be a lesson to you country folk not to believe itinerant quacks. It's not your health they're interested in but your wealth.

Chapter 9

How the doctor took to being a musketeer under Captain Skinflint

I ran out of goods while I was passing through Lorraine and since I was keeping clear of garrison towns I had no opportunity to make any more. I therefore had to think of something else to sell until I could make up my antidote again. I bought two pints of schnapps, coloured it with saffron, decanted it into half-ounce glasses and sold it to people as expensive goldwater which was supposed to be good for fevers. In this way the schnapps brought in thirty guilders. I began to run short of the little bottles and hearing of a glass-works on the Fleckenstein estate in the Vosges, I set off for it to replenish my stock. Although I took byways, as luck would have it I was captured by a patrol from Philippsburg which was quartered in the castle at Wegelnburg, thus losing everything I had screwed out of the peasants during the journey. The peasant who had come with me to show me the way told them I was a doctor and so, like it or not, it was as a doctor that I was taken to Philippsburg.

I was interrogated there and told them straight out who I was, but they would not believe me. They were determined to make more of me than I was or could ever be and insisted I was a doctor. I had to swear I belonged to the imperial dragoons in Soest, declare under oath everything that had happened to me between then and now and tell them what I intended to do. 'But', they countered, 'the Emperor needs soldiers in Philippsburg as much as in Soest', and said they would give me quarters with them until I found an opportunity of rejoining my regiment. However, they added, if I did not like that suggestion, I was welcome to a room in the goal, where I would be regarded as a doctor until I was freed, since it was as a doctor that I had been captured.

So I changed from horse to donkey and had to become a musketeer against my will. I had a terrible time because they were niggardly with the food. The regimental loaves were so small I could have easily eaten mine at one go and yet it had to last me the whole day. To tell the truth, a musketeer's life is a wretched one when he's stuck in a garrison with nothing but dry bread – and not enough of that – to fill his belly. He's no better than a prisoner eking out his miserable life on bread and water. In fact a prisoner is better off, since he doesn't have to go on watch, do the rounds or stand on sentry duty, but can rest on his mattress and has more hope of eventually being released than a poor garrison soldier.

There were some who supplemented their pay in several ways, though none that I liked or thought honourable. Their situation was so wretched that they took wives (whores who'd escaped from the brothel if need be) simply in order to be fed on the proceeds from their work, be it sewing, washing, spinning, hawking goods or even stealing. There was an ensign among the woman who drew her pay like an NCO; one was a midwife and earned many a good meal for herself and her husband from that; others could wash and starch and laundered the shirts, stockings, nightwear and God knows what else of the unmarried officers and soldiers. There were some who sold tobacco and provided the men with pipes when they needed them; others who sold schnapps, and had the reputation of mixing it with spirits they had distilled themselves, which did not make it any the less strong. One earned her money as a seamstress and could make up different patterns using all kinds of stitching, and there was one who got all her food from the countryside around. In the winter she dug up snails, in the spring she picked salad, in the summer she collected bird's eggs and in the autumn she got all sorts of delicious fruits. Some carried wood to sell, like donkeys, and others dealt in other things.

To feed myself in this way was not for me, since I already had a wife. Some earned their keep from gambling. They were better at it than professional card-sharps and took the money from their naive comrades with loaded dice and marked cards, but that profession disgusted me. Others worked like the devil building the ramparts, but I was too lazy for that. There were those who could practise some trade but, fool that I was, I had never learnt one. If a musician had been required I would have been well off, but that frugal place made do with fifes and drums. Some did sentry duty for others and were on watch day and night, but if I was going to let my body waste away, I would rather do it by starving. Some brought back booty from patrols, but I was not even trusted to go outside the gate. Some were better at catching mice than cats, but I hated such work like the plague. In a word, wherever I looked there was nothing I could do to fill my belly. What annoyed me most of all was that the men taunted me saying, 'You're supposed to be a doctor and all you can do is starve.' Finally I was so hungry that I was forced to persuade some fine carp in the moat to leap up onto the wall beside me, but as soon as the colonel heard of it I was made to ride the wooden horse as punishment and forbidden to catch any more fish on pain of death.

Eventually others' misfortune proved to be my good fortune. I cured some men who were suffering from jaundice and fever (they must have had great faith in me!) and was allowed to go out of the fortress on the excuse of gathering roots and herbs for my medicines. Instead of that I set snares for rabbits and was lucky enough to catch two the very first night. I took them to the colonel who gave me a thaler for them and permission to go out and catch rabbits whenever I wasn't on guard duty. Since the countryside was pretty deserted and there was no one there to hunt them, they had multiplied considerably. I was back in business once more, especially since it looked as if it was raining rabbits, or I had a magic spell to charm them into my snares. When the officers saw from this that I was to be trusted, they let me go out on patrol with the others. It was the old life I had led in Soest again, except that I did not command the patrols or lead them, as I had done in Westphalia, since first of all it was essential to get to know the paths and tracks – and the river Rhine.

Chapter 10

How Simplicius did not enjoy bathing in the Rhine

I will recount two more incidents before I tell you how I was released from my musket. One was a great physical danger, from which through God's grace I escaped, the other a spiritual danger in which I obstinately persisted. As you can see, I intend to conceal my vices no more than my virtues, not only for the sake of completeness but so that the untravelled reader can learn what strange folk there are in the world.

As I reported at the end of the last chapter, I was allowed out on patrol, a privilege which in garrisons is not granted to any Tom, Dick or Harry, but only to responsible soldiers. One day, then, nineteen of us were scouting along the Rhine above Strasbourg, looking out for a boat from Basle which was supposed to be secretly carrying officers and goods belonging to the Weimar army. Upstream from Ottenheim we got a fishing dinghy to take us across to an island in the river which was well situated for forcing approaching ships to land. The fisherman took the first ten over, but when one of the soldiers, who did know how to handle a boat, was ferrying the other nine of us across, the dinghy capsized, tipping us into the Rhine. I didn't bother about the others but just concentrated on saving myself. However, although I fought with all my strength and all the skill of a good swimmer, the river tossed me about like a ball, throwing me up to the surface, then down to the bottom again. I struggled so manfully that I often came up for breath, but if the water had been just a bit colder I would not have been able to keep going so long and come out of it alive. I kept trying to reach the bank, but the swirling current stopped me, sweeping me from one side to the other. I reached Goldscheuer very quickly, but it seemed such a long time to me that I began to despair of my life However, after I had passed the village and was already resigning myself to floating under the bridge at Strasbourg, dead or alive, I saw not far away a big tree with branches sticking up out of the water. The current was strong, but heading straight for it, so I summoned up all the strength I had left to get to it. Through my efforts and the force of the water I managed to reach the largest branch, which I had initially taken for the tree itself, and clamber up onto it. Unfortunately the waves and eddies pulled and tugged at it so much that it was constantly bobbing up and down, making my stomach churn so that I could have spewed up my lungs and liver. Everything was dancing before my eyes and I had difficulty holding on. I would almost have preferred to be back in the water except that I could not face even a hundredth part of what I had already been through. So I stayed where I was, in the uncertain hope God might send someone to rescue me, for that was the only way I could see that I would come out of it alive. But my conscience gave me little comfort, reminding me that I had thrown away the chance of His mercy through my dissolute life over the past few years. Yet I still hoped I might get better than I deserved and began to pray as fervently as if I had been brought up in a monastery. I determined to live a more God-fearing life in future and made several vows: I renounced the soldier's life and forswore plundering for ever, throwing away my cartridge pouch and knapsack; I insisted I would become a hermit again, do penance for my sins and spend the rest of my days thanking God for the rescue I hoped He would send. I sat for two or three hours on that branch, wavering between fear and hope, when the very ship came down the Rhine that we had been sent to ambush. I set up a pathetic wailing, begging them in the name of God and all that was holy to come and help me. Their course took them close to me so that everyone on the ship could see the danger and wretched situation I was in. They were moved to pity and pulled in to the shore to discuss how to go about rescuing me.

This took quite some time. The branches and roots of the tree caused so much turbulence that it was too dangerous for anyone to swim out to me, or to come close in a boat, large or small. Finally they sent two men in a dinghy upstream from the tree who let out a rope which I managed, with great difficulty, to grasp and tie round my waist. They then pulled me into the dinghy, like a hooked fish, and took me to the boat.

Having thus escaped death, it would have been right and proper for me to fall on my knees on the bank and thank God in His goodness for saving me. I ought also to have made an immediate start on mending my ways, as I had vowed and promised in my hour of need. Like hell I did! When they asked me who I was and how I had come to be in that situation, I straight away started lying like anything. If, I thought to myself, you tell then you were a member of a platoon that was going to ambush them they'll throw you straight back in the Rhine. So I pretended I was an out-of-work organist heading for Strasbourg to find work in a school or such on the other side of the Rhine. I claimed I had been captured by a patrol, robbed and thrown into the Rhine, which had carried me down to the tree. I backed up my lies with plausible detail and oaths so that they believed me and very kindly gave me food and drink to revive me, which I was certainly in need of.

Most people disembarked at the customs house in Strasbourg and I did the same. As I was thanking them warmly I noticed a young merchant among them whose face, gait and gestures seemed familiar. I was sure I had seen him before, but couldn't remember where. When he spoke, however, I realised it was the cornet who had captured me on my way back from Cologne. I could not imagine how such a brave young soldier had become a merchant, especially as he was of gentle birth. Curious to ascertain whether my eyes and ears had deceived me or not, I went up to him and said, 'It is you, Monsieur Schönstein, isn't it?' to which he replied, 'I'm no von Schönstein, I'm a merchant.'

'And I'm no Huntsman of Soest', I said, 'but an organist or, rather, a common vagrant.'

'My brother!' he replied. 'What in the devil's name are you doing wandering round like this?'

'Brother', I said, 'as Heaven seems to have appointed you to save my life – it's happened twice now – my destiny obviously requires me not to be too far away from you.'

At that we embraced, like two friends who had sworn to love one another until death. I went with him to his lodgings and told him everything that had happened to me since I had left Lippstadt to fetch my treasure from Cologne. I did not conceal the fact that I had been with a patrol that was lying in wait for their ship and what had happened to us, though I did keep quiet about my activities in Paris in case he let it out in Lippstadt and got me into trouble with my wife.

For his part he told me he had been sent by the Hessian generals to report to Duke Bernhard of Weimar on matters of great importance concerning the wars and to discuss plans for future campaigns with him. Having done this, he was now returning disguised as a merchant, as I could see. In addition, he told me that my darling had been expecting a child when he left, that both she and her parents and relatives were in good health, and that the colonel was still keeping the ensign's post open for me. He also teased me, saying the smallpox had so ruined my looks that neither my wife nor the other women in Lippstadt would recognise me as the Huntsman. After that we agreed I should stay with him and take the opportunity to get back to Lippstadt, which was what I wanted. Since my clothes were in tatters, he advanced me some money to clothe myself like a merchant's assistant.

But if something is not to be, then it is not to be. While we were going down the Rhine and the ship was searched at Rheinhausen, the soldiers from Philippsburg recognised me and took me back to Philippsburg where I had to become a musketeer again. The cornet was as dismayed as I was at our being separated once more, but could not do much to help me since he had to make sure he got through himself.

Chapter 11

*Why men of the cloth should never eat rabbits
that have been caught in a noose*

Thus I survived the great physical danger, but as far as the danger to my soul was concerned I must tell you that as a musketeer I became really wild, without the least concern for either God or God's word. No deed was too evil for me; forgotten all the goodness and loving kindness I had received from Him. I was not bothered about this world or the next, but lived from day to day like a brute beast. No one would ever have believed I had been brought up by a pious hermit. I rarely went to church and never to confession. I cared nothing for the welfare of my own soul, which made me all the more of a danger to my fellow men. If I could trick anyone, then I did so and prided myself on it, so that no one who had dealings with me came away unscathed. I often got a good beating for this and was made to ride the wooden horse even more often. I was threatened with the gallows or the strappado, but it had no effect, I continued on my iniquitous way so that it looked as if I were determined to take the fast road to hell. Although I committed no crime by which I would have deserved death, my behaviour was so infamous that it would be almost impossible to imagine a greater reprobate (apart from sorcerers and sodomites).

I came to the attention of the regimental chaplain, who was a real zealot. At Easter he sent for me and asked why I had not come to confession or communion, but I treated his well-meant admonitions as I had done those of the pastor in Lippstadt so that the poor priest got nowhere with me. Finally, coming to the conclusion that Christ and baptism were wasted on me, he exclaimed, 'Oh, you miserable wretch! I thought you sinned out of ignorance, but now I see you do it out of wickedness and are determined to continue in your sinful ways. Do you think anyone will take pity on your poor soul and try to save it from damnation? Before God and the world, I swear that it is none of my fault. I have done everything I can to ensure your salvation and would have continued to do so undaunted. I am afraid, however, that my only duty will be to make sure your body, when your soul leaves it in such an unregenerate state, is not buried in consecrated ground with other Christians, but hauled off to the carrion pit with the carcasses of dead beasts or to the place where the ungodly and those who give way to despair are disposed of.'

This solemn threat was no more effective than his previous exhortations, though the only reason was that I was ashamed to confess my sins. What a fool I was! I would often recount my villainies to a whole company and lie to make them seem worse, but now that I had to mend my ways and humbly confess my sins to a single person, as God's intermediary, in order to receive forgiveness, I stubbornly kept them locked away saying, 'I am a soldier and I serve the emperor. If I die as a soldier it will not be surprising if I have to find a grave outside the churchyard like other soldiers. We cannot always be buried in consecrated ground, but often have to make do with a pit on the battlefield, a ditch or even the bellies of wolves and carrion crows.'

With that parting shot I left the chaplain. His zealous efforts got him nothing from me but the refusal of a rabbit he begged me to let him have. I told him it had hung itself in a noose and killed itself and that it would be wrong for one who had given in to despair to be buried in consecrated ground.

Chapter 12

How Simplicius was unexpectedly relieved of his musket

So there was no improvement in my conduct; in fact, the longer things went on, the worse I got. The colonel once said to me that since I refused to behave properly he was minded to give me a dishonourable discharge. Knowing he did not mean it seriously, I replied I would be quite happy with that as long as the discharge did not come from a gun. He dropped the idea, knowing full well that if he let me go he would not be punishing me but doing me a favour. I had to remain a musketeer against my will and starve until well into the summer. But the closer Count Götz came with his army, the closer was my liberation. When he set up his headquarters in Bruchsal, Herzbruder, whom I had helped with my money in the camp outside Magdeburg, was sent by his commander on business to the fortress, where he was received with great honour. I happened to be on sentry duty outside the colonel's quarters and recognised him as soon a I saw him, despite the black velvet coat he was wearing. But I could not bring myself to address him at once. I was afraid that, given the way of the world, he would be ashamed of me or refuse to recognise me, since from his dress he had clearly reached a high rank while I was only a lowly musketeer. After I had been relieved, I checked his name and rank with his servants, just to make sure I was not confusing him with someone else before speaking to him. However, I still lacked the nerve to address him to his face so I wrote a letter which I gave his manservant to hand to him next morning:

Monsieur etc,
If it should please Your Honour to use your great influence to deliver a man – whom you have already rescued from bonds and fetters during the Battle of Wittstock –

from the most wretched state in the world, into which he has been cast by the whim of fickle fortune, it would be easily done and you would gain the eternal thanks of one who is already your faithful servant but now signs himself,

Yours despairingly,

Simplicius Simplicissimus.

As soon as he read it he sent for me and said, 'Who is the man who gave you this letter, my friend?'

'Sir', I replied, 'he is a captive in this fortress.'

'Well then', he said, 'go and tell him I will help to free him, even if the noose is already round his neck.'

'Sir', I replied, 'that will not be necessary. I am poor Simplicius myself. I have come to thank you for releasing me at Wittstock and to ask you to release me again, this time from this musket which I have been forced to bear against my will.'

He did not let me finish, but hugged me in an embrace the warmth of which showed his willingness to help me. He assured me he would do everything a true friend would do, and before he asked me how I came to be serving in the garrison, he sent his servant to the Jew to buy a horse and clothes for me. While we were waiting for him to return I told Herzbruder everything that had happened to me since the death of his father in Magdeburg. When he heard that I was the Huntsman of Soest, of whom he had heard many famous exploits, he regretted that he had not known sooner, since he could have helped me to the command of a company.

When the Jew arrived with a whole sackful of soldier's clothes he picked out the best, told me to put them on and took me to see the colonel. 'Sir', he said to him, 'in your garrison I came across this man to whom I am under such a great obligation that I cannot allow him to remain in such a base position, even if his qualities did not deserve better. I therefore ask if you would do me the favour of finding him a better place, Colonel, or of allowing me to take him with me so I can help further his career in the army, for which you perhaps lack the opportunity here.'

The colonel was so astonished to hear someone praise me

that he crossed himself. 'My dear sir', he said, 'you will forgive me if I assume this is just a test to see if I am as willing to be of use to you as you deserve. If that is the case, then ask for anything it is my power to do and you will see how willing I am. As far as this fellow is concerned however, he is not really under my command but belongs, from what he claims, to a regiment of dragoons. Added to that, he is such a tiresome pest that he has given my provost-sergeant more trouble since he has been here than a whole company. He seems to be completely incorrigible. Every time he's put down he bounces straight back up again.' The colonel finished with a laugh and wished me luck.

But that was not enough for Herzbruder. He asked the colonel to invite me to dine with them, which the latter also agreed to. His purpose in doing this was to tell the colonel, in my presence, everything he had heard in Westphalia about me from Count von der Wahl and the commandant of Soest, which he did to such good effect that all those present were forced to conclude that I was a good soldier. At the same time I kept modestly in the background so that the colonel and his officers must have thought that the change of clothes had brought a change of personality. When he had finished, the colonel then wanted to know how I had acquired the name of doctor, so I told him all about my journey from Paris to Philippsburg and how I had cheated the peasants to fill my belly, which they found very amusing. Finally I confessed that it had been my intention to vex the colonel with all kinds of mischief until he was so tired of me that he would have to expel me from the garrison just to get peace from all the complaints about me.

Then the colonel recounted some of my misdeeds since I had been in the garrison, how I had boiled up some peas, poured a layer of lard over them and sold it for pure lard; how I had sold sacks of sand as salt by filling the tops of the sacks with salt; he told them some of the hoaxes I had played on people and how I had annoyed them by circulating lampoons. They spent the whole meal talking about me and if I had not had such a highly respected friend, all my activities would have been regarded as punishable offences. I looked on it as an analogy to what happens at court when a rogue has the prince's favour.

After the meal we found that the Jew had no horse Herzbruder thought good enough for me. However, he stood in such high regard that the colonel could not risk losing his favour and presented him with a steed, complete with saddle and bridle, from his own stable. This my lord Simplicius mounted and rode joyfully out of the fortress with his Herzbruder. Some of my former comrades wished me the best of luck while others, green with envy, muttered something about fortune favouring the knave.

Chapter 13

Describes the Order of Merode's Brethren

While we were riding, Herzbruder and I agreed that I should pretend to be his cousin so that I would be treated with greater respect. He promised to buy me another horse, together with a groom, and send me to Colonel Neuneck's regiment where I could serve as a volunteer until there was an officer's post free in the army, which he would help procure for me.

In no time at all I looked like a proper soldier again, but I saw very little in the way of action that summer, apart from helping to steal a few cows here and there in the Black Forest and getting myself thoroughly acquainted with the Breisgau and Alsace. I had very little luck at all and after my horse and groom had been captured by Weimar troops at Kenzingen I made much greater demands on the one I had left and ended up riding it into the ground and joining the Order of Merode's Brethren. Herzbruder would have been willing to buy me a new mount, but since I had got through the two horses so quickly he decided to let me sweat it out for a while until I learnt to be more cautious. I was quite happy with that. I found my new companions such congenial company that I wished no better until it was time to go into winter quarters.

I will tell you a little about Merode's Brethren since there are doubtless some readers, especially those with no experience of war, who know nothing about them. I have so far not come across any writer who has included anything on their customs, habits, rights and privileges in his works, even though it would be very useful for both commanders and country folk to know what kind of a crew they are. As far as the name is concerned (and Marauder Brethren might be more apposite), I am sure it will not bring the bold gentleman from whom they got it into disrepute, otherwise I would not bandy it about in public in this way. The fact that a certain kind of boot with twisted threads instead of eyelets (to make them better for going through mud) is called a Mansfelder does not make General Mansfeld a cobbler, and it is the same with this name, which will stick as long as Germans wage war. The way it came about is as follows: General Merode once raised a regiment, but the men were as weak and decrepit as the Breton troops Richelieu sent Guébriant. They could not stand up to all the marching and rigours soldiers undergo in the field and their brigade was rapidly so reduced it was scarcely more than a company. The result was that whenever anyone came across sick or wounded men in the market place, in houses, in fields or hedges, and asked them what their regiment was, they would generally answer, 'Merode's'. Eventually all troops, whether sick or healthy, wounded or not, who straggled along out of line or for any reason did not quarter with their own regiment in the field, came to be known as 'Merode's Brethren'. They used to be known as 'honeystealers' because they are like drones in the hive that have neither stings to defend it nor work to make honey, but just eat. A trooper loses his horse, a musketeer's strength fails, a soldier's wife and child fall ill and have to stay behind: there you already have a trio of Merode's Brethren. They are best compared to gypsies. They not only wander round at will in front of, behind, beside and in the middle of the army like gypsies, but they have the same habits and customs. You see them huddled together, like partridges in winter, behind hedges, in the shade or sunshine depending on the season, or round some fire, smoking and idling, while honest soldiers who stay with their regiment have to put up with heat, thirst, hunger, cold and all kinds of misery. You will see a pack of them alongside the column, thieving and pilfering, while many a weary soldier is almost collapsing under the weight of his arms. They plunder everything they can find in front of, alongside and behind the army, and anything that is no use to them they spoil, so that when the regiment reaches its quarters or camp the men often cannot find any decent water to drink. When it is made clear that they must stay with the baggage train, that often becomes more numerous than the army itself.

When they march, quarter, camp and mess together they have no sergeant to keep them in line, no corporal to send them on guard, no drummer to remind them of lights out, patrol or sentry duty, no adjutant to give them their battle orders and no quartermaster to assign them a billet. All in all they do as they please, but whenever there's a hand-out for the men they are the first in the queue, even though they have done nothing to earn it. Their bane is the provost-marshal and the provost-general who, when they go too far, clap them in iron bracelets or even give them a hemp collar and hang them by their precious necks.

They don't stand guard, they don't dig trenches, they don't line up in battle formation, they don't storm ramparts, and they still get fed! But the harm a large number of such vermin can do their general, their comrades and the army itself is beyond description. The most bungling raw recruit who can do nothing but forage is more use to his commander than a thousand Merode's Brethren who make a profession of malingering and spend all their time sitting on the backsides doing nothing. They get captured by the enemy (in some places even the country folk give them what-for), thus weakening the army and strengthening the opposing side. And if one of these dissolute rogues (I don't mean soldiers with genuine wounds or illnesses, but troopers who have lost their mounts through not taking proper care of them and join Merode's Brethren to have an easy life) survives the summer, all that means is that the army has to go to the expense of re-equipping him during the winter so that he has something he can lose during the next campaign. They ought to be leashed together like greyhounds and sent to the garrisons to learn how to fight, or even chained to the galleys, if they refuse to do their bit with the infantry until they get a new mount. All this is without mentioning the many villages they carelessly or deliberately burn down, the soldiers from their own side they unseat, plunder, rob and even murder, and any spy can hide among them as long as he can give the name of one regiment and company in the army.

This, then, was the honourable brotherhood I now joined, and I stayed with them until the day before the Battle of Wittenweier, when our headquarters were in the monastery at Schuttern. My comrades and I went to the county of Geroldseck, to steal cows or oxen as was our wont, and were taken prisoner by Weimar troops who knew just how to deal with the likes of us. They gave us muskets and dispersed us among various regiments; I was put in Colonel Hattstein's.

Chapter 14

A duel to the death in which each party escapes with his life

That was the time when it became clear to me I was born to misfortune. About four weeks before the above-mentioned battle took place I had overheard some officers from Götz's regiment discussing the war and one of them said, 'We won't get through this summer without a battle. If we defeat the enemy, we're sure to occupy Freiburg and the four Forest Towns, and if we get beaten, we'll still end up in winter quarters.' I drew my own conclusions from this prophecy, telling myself I could look forward to drinking good Lake and Neckar wine next spring and everything else the Weimar troops would win. Unfortunately this was well wide of the mark. Now that I was a Weimar soldier myself, I was destined to take part in the siege of Breisach, which was started immediately after the Battle of Wittenweier. Like all the musketeers I had to dig trenches and stand guard day and night and all I got from it was that I learnt how to use approach trenches to undermine a town, something I had not paid much attention to at the siege of Magdeburg. Otherwise conditions were pretty wretched; we slept two or three to a tent, my purse was empty, wine, beer and meat a rarity and my greatest delicacy some apples or a half portion of bread.

I found this hard to put up with when I thought back to the fleshpots of Lippstadt with its Westphalian hams and sausages. I didn't think of my wife at all, except when I was lying in my tent half-frozen. Then I would say to myself, 'Well Simplicius, and can you complain if someone does to you what you did to others in Paris?' I was tormented by this thought like any jealous cuckold, even though I had no reason to believe my wife was anything other than faithful and virtuous. At last I became so impatient that I told my captain what my situation was and sent a letter by post to Lippstadt. Colonel Saint Andrée and my father-in-law wrote to the Duke of Weimar who ordered my captain to give me a pass and let me go.

About a week, or maybe four days before Christmas I set off from the camp with a good musket to make my way through the Breisgau and down to Strasbourg, assuming I would find the twenty thalers my father-in-law had sent waiting there for me at the Christmas fair. Then I intended to attach myself to some merchants and go down the Rhine with them, since there were many imperial garrisons en route. However, as I was passing a lonely house beyond Endingen, there was a shot which nicked the brim of my hat and a strong, burly man came dashing out of the house, shouting to me to put my gun down. 'Not on your life, mister', I said, and cocked my musket. At that he drew something that was more like an executioner's sword than a soldier's blade and came running towards me. Now that I saw he was in earnest I pulled the trigger and hit him full on the forehead so that he staggered and fell to the ground. To make the most of my advantage I ran up to him, pulled the sword out of his hand and tried to run him through. However, it didn't even pierce his skin and he suddenly jumped back on his feet and grabbed me by the hair. I dropped the sword and did the same to him. Then began a desperate struggle in which each in his fury showed what he was capable of, but neither could gain the upper hand. Now I was on top, now he, then we were both back on our feet again, but not for long since we were each determined to kill the other. My nose and mouth were bleeding, and since he was so clearly after my blood, I spat it out into his face, half blinding him. We spent an hour and a half rolling around in the snow like this until we were both so weak and weary that neither could finish off the other without the aid of a weapon. I had often practised wrestling in Lippstadt and it served me well here, otherwise I would quickly have lost, since my opponent was much stronger than I and proof against steel. When we were both almost dead from exhaustion he finally said, ' Stop, brother, I surrender.'

'You should have let me pass in the first place', I said.

'What will you get out of killing me?' he answered.

'And what would you have got out of shooting me?' I asked. 'I haven't a penny on me.'

At that he begged my forgiveness, and I gave in, allowing him to get up after he had solemnly sworn that not only would he not attack me again but he would be a loyal friend and servant to me. If I had known then all the evil deeds he had already committed, I would have neither believed nor trusted him.

When we were both back on our feet we shook hands, agreeing to forget what had happened. Each of us was surprised to have found his master in the other, and my assailant assumed that I, like him, had a magic spell to make my skin proof against all weapons. I did not disabuse him so that when

323

he got his sword back he would not bother trying to use it against me. He had a huge bruise on his forehead from my bullet and I had bled a lot, but it was our necks that were worst; we had grabbed each other so fiercely by the throat that now neither of us could hold his head up straight.

Night was beginning to fall and my adversary told me I wouldn't find a cat or a dog, never mind another human being until I came to the Kinzig. He had a decent joint of meat and a good drop of wine in an isolated cottage not far from the road, he said, so I let him persuade me to accompany him. As we made our way there he kept sighing and saying how sorry he was he had attacked me.

Chapter 15

How Oliver thinks he can justify his highway robbery

A resolute soldier who has accepted that he is risking his life and holds it cheap must be a stupid beast! You could take a thousand men and not one would dream of accepting an invitation from someone who had just tried to kill them to go and stay with them in an unknown house.

On the way I asked him which side he was on, to which he replied that at the moment he served no one, but just fought for himself. Which side was I on? I told him I had been with the Weimar army but had got my discharge and intended to go home. At that he asked me what my name was. When I answered Simplicius he turned round (for I still didn't trust him and made him walk in front of me), looked me straight in the face and asked ,'Is your surname Simplicissimus.'

'Yes', I replied, 'only a rogue would deny his own name. What are you called?'

'Why, brother', he replied, 'I'm Oliver. Surely you remember me from the camp outside Magdeburg?' Having said that, he threw his musket to the ground and went down on his knees begging my forgiveness for trying to harm me. He couldn't imagine a better friend in the world than I would be, he said, since according to old Herzbruder's prophecy I was to bravely go and avenge his death. I was amazed at this strange coincidence but he said, 'That's nothing new at all, it's only mountains and valleys that never meet. What I do find strange, though, is how much we have both changed, I from a secretary to a bandit, you from a fool to a brave soldier. I tell you, brother, if there were ten thousand like us we could relieve Breisach tomorrow and make ourselves masters of the whole world.'

Talking like this we reached a small, isolated labourer's cottage just before nightfall. I didn't like his boasting but said I agreed with him because I knew his crafty, double-dealing ways, and I went with him into the cottage even though I didn't trust him an inch. The farm labourer was just lighting the fire. 'Have you cooked anything?' Oliver asked.

'No', replied the labourer, 'I've still got the roast leg of veal I brought back from Waldkirch today.'

'Well go and get out what you have', said Oliver, 'and bring out the cask of wine too.'

When he left I said to Oliver, 'Brother' – I called him that to keep on the right side of him – 'you have a very willing landlord.'

'The devil I have!' he replied. 'I feed him, and his wife and child, and he gets a decent haul for himself into the bargain; I give him all the clothes I take, to use as he sees fit.'

I asked him where he kept his own wife and child, and he said he had found them safe quarters in Freiburg where he visited them twice a week and brought back rations as well as powder and lead. He went on to tell me he had been a bandit for some time now, he preferred it to serving some master and intended to go on until he had filled his purse fit to burst.

'Brother', I said, 'that's a dangerous trade. You know what they'll do to you if they catch you.'

'Ha!' he said, 'I see you're still the same old Simplicius. I know the risks, but nothing venture, nothing win. And let me remind you the authorities don't hang a man unless they have him.'

'Well then', I replied, 'even assuming you don't get caught – which is pretty uncertain, there's many a slip between cup and lip – this life you are living is the most dishonourable in the world. I can't believe you want to die in it?'

'What!?' he said. 'Dishonourable!? I assure you that robbery is the most noble occupation you can have nowadays. You just tell me how many kingdoms and principalities have been acquired by robbery and violence? Is there a king or prince anywhere in the world who is criticised for enjoying the revenues from his lands, which their forefathers generally conquered by force. Therefore what could be called more noble than my current activity? I can see you're about to tell me how many men have been broken on the wheel, hung or beheaded for murder, robbery and theft. I know that myself already; that's what the law prescribes. But you'll only have seen poor, petty thieves executed, and quite right too! They shouldn't have taken up this excellent profession, which is only suitable for men of courage and nerve. When did you ever see the law punish a person of rank for oppressing their country? And usurers who pursue that fine art under the cloak of Christian charity are never punished. Why should I deserve punishment when I do these same things openly, without any attempt at concealment or hypocrisy? I can see you haven't read Machiavelli, my dear Simplicius. I have my principles, I follow this way of life openly and I'm not ashamed of it. I live by the sword and I risk my life doing so, just like the heroes of old. I know that all professions are permitted where those who pursue them endanger their lives, and so it is only logical that, since I put my life in danger, my occupation is allowed.'

To this I replied, 'Leaving aside the question of whether robbing and stealing is allowed or not, I do know that it is against the law of nature, which says that one man should not do to another what he would not like done to himself. And it is against the laws of man as well, which ordain that thieves should be hung, robbers beheaded and murderers broken on the wheel. Finally, it is against the highest law of all, the law of God, which leaves no sin unpunished.'

'It is just as I said', replied Oliver. 'You're still the same old Simplicius who hasn't read his Machiavelli yet. If I could establish a kingdom by such methods, I'd like to see who would preach a sermon against them.' Our argument could have gone on for a long time, but the labourer came with the food and drink, so we sat down and concentrated on the inner man, which in my case was very necessary.

Chapter 16

How Oliver interpreted Herzbruder's prophecy to his own advantage and thus came to love his worst enemy

We had white bread and cold roast veal to eat, a good glass of wine to drink and a warm room to sit in. 'Now Simplicius', said Oliver, 'this is better than sitting in a trench before Breisach, isn't it?'

'It certainly would be', I said, 'if one could enjoy a life like this with greater security and greater honour.'

At that he laughed out loud and said, 'Are those poor devils in the trenches, worrying all the time about the next sortie, more secure than we are? I can see you've got rid of your fool's cap, Simplicius, but you've still got that foolish head of yours, still can't tell what is good from what is bad. If you weren't that same Simplicius who, according to old Herzbruder's prophecy, is going to avenge my death, I'd soon have you agreeing I lead a nobler life than any baron.'

Where's all this leading? I thought. You'd better take a different tone, Simplicius, otherwise this monster might do away with you, especially given he's got the labourer to help him. So I said, 'Who ever heard of an apprentice being better at his trade than his master? Brother, if the life you lead is as happy-go-lucky as you claim, then share it with me, I'm in dire need of a bit of luck.'

'Brother', replied Oliver, 'I love you as I love myself, of that you can be assured. The disrespect I showed you this afternoon in attacking you hurts me more than this bruise on my forehead you gave me in defending yourself like man. How can I refuse you anything? If you like, you can stay with me and you'll be looked after as well as I look after myself. But if you don't want to be with me, I'll give you a fat purse and accompany you wherever you want to go. Believe me, Simplicius, this offer comes from the bottom of my heart. You'll understand why when I tell you why I have such high regard for you. You remember how accurate old Herzbruder's prophecies were? Well, he made me a prophecy in the camp before Magdeburg which I have made sure I remembered ever since. "Oliver", he said, "whatever you think of our fool, the day will come when his boldness will put the fear of God into you. He will give you the worst drubbing you have ever had and it will be your fault for provoking him at some time in the future when neither recognises the other. But he will not only spare your life when he has you at his mercy, a while afterwards he will come to the place where you will be killed, where he will be happy to avenge your death." Because of this prophecy, Simplicius my friend, I am ready to share everything with you, even the heart in my breast. One part was fulfilled when I gave you cause to shoot me in the head, like a brave soldier, and take my sword from me, which no one has ever managed before. You also spared my life when you had me pinned to the ground, almost choking on my own blood. I have no doubt that the part dealing with my death will also come about. From your vengeance, Simplicius, I must conclude that you are my most faithful friend. If you weren't, you wouldn't take it upon yourself. And now I have revealed my heart to you, tell me what you intend to do.'

The devil might trust you, I thought, but I don't. If I take money for my journey from you, then you're quite likely to dispatch me before I set out; if, on the other hand, I stay with you I'm in danger of being hung, drawn and quartered along with you. Accordingly I decided to dupe him into thinking I was going to stay with him and then get away at the first opportunity. Therefore I told him that if he would put up with me I would stay with him a week or so and see if I got a taste for this kind of life. If I did, he would find me a good friend and accomplice, if not, we could always part friends. At that he started to ply me with drink, but I still didn't trust him and pretended to be drunk before I was to see if he would attack me when I was incapable of defending myself.

Meanwhile the fleas starting pestering me terribly. I had brought a good supply with me from Breisach and in the warmth of the room they were not content to stay in my rags but started wandering round, enjoying themselves. Oliver noticed this and asked me if I had lice as well. 'Yes', I said, 'more than I'll ever see ducats in my whole live.'

'Don't say that', said Oliver, 'if you stay with me you'll easily get more ducats than you have lice at the moment.'

'That's just as likely as getting rid of these lice', I said.

'That's right', he said, 'we'll do both', and he told his landlord to go and get me a suit of clothes that was hidden in a hollow tree not far from the house. There was a grey hat, a jerkin of elkskin, a pair of scarlet breeches and a grey coat. He would find me some socks and shoes in the morning, he said. Such generosity gave me greater confidence in his good faith and I went happily to bed.

Chapter 17

Simplicius's thoughts when engaged in robbery were more reverent that Oliver's in church

Next morning, as it was getting light, Oliver said, 'Up you get, Simplicius. For God's sake, let's be on our way and see what there is to be had out there.'

'Good God!' I said to myself, 'am I going to go out robbing for your holy name's sake? To think that at first after I left the hermit I was horrified just to hear someone say, "Come on, let's go and sink a few glasses of wine for God's sake." I thought that was a double sin, getting drunk for God's sake. O Lord, what a transformation since then! Dear Father in heaven, what will become of me if I don't change my ways? Turn me back from this road, Lord, or I will end up in hell if I do not repent.'

These were my thoughts as I followed Oliver to a village where there was not a living soul to be seen. To get a better view we went up the church tower, which was where he had hidden the stockings and shoes he had promised me the previous evening. Together with them were two loaves of bread, some pieces of dried meat and a half-full cask of wine, enough for him to survive on for a whole week. While I was putting on the things he had given me, he told me he used to lie in wait there when he was on the look-out for a good haul, which was why it was so well provisioned. He had several such hide-outs, he added, each with its store of food and drink, so that if he drew a blank in one place he could try another. I was full of admiration for his ingenuity, but made it clear I did not approve of such misuse of a holy place that was dedicated to the service of God.

'What do you mean "misuse"?' he said. 'If churches could talk they would tell you that what I am doing here is nothing compared to all the other sins committed in them. How many men and women, do you suppose, have come into this church since it was built ostensibly to serve God but in fact only to show off their new clothes, their handsome figure, their high rank and suchlike? One comes to the church dressed like a peacock and yet kneels before the altar as if he would pray the very feet off the saints; another sighs like the publican in the temple, but his sighs are directed at his beloved, and he feasts his eyes on her face, which is the only reason why he has come; a third comes to the church (he may even go in) with a bundle of papers, like someone collecting fire insurance, more to remind those who owe him rent than to pray. If he hadn't known his debtors would be at church he would have stayed at home with his ledgers. On occasions it even happens that when the authorities have something to announce to a village the crier does it on Sunday at church so that some country folk fear church more than a condemned man the judge who will pronounce sentence. Don't you agree there are many people buried in church who deserved to die on the block, gallows, fire or wheel?

Some men would never manage to get anywhere with their adulterous affairs if the church wasn't such a good place to pursue them; in places if anything is to be sold or rented a notice is put on the church door; usurers who have no time to spare during the week sit in church during service thinking up new ways of squeezing money out of their victims; people sit talking with each other during mass or the sermon as if that was what the church had been built for; matters are often arranged which they wouldn't dream of discussing in private houses; some sit there and sleep as if they had hired the place for that; others spend all their time gossiping about people, saying, 'Didn't the pastor get this or that person to a T in his sermon.' Some pay great attention to the sermon, not in order to learn from it but so that they can criticise their pastor and pull him to pieces if he makes the slightest mistake, as they see it.

I won't mention all the lecherous stories I have read where the church serves as a house of assignation. There is much more I could say on this whole subject than I can remember at the moment, but there is one more thing you should realise. People not only misuse the church for their vices during their life, but fill it with their vanity after their death. As soon as you enter a church you will see on gravestones and epitaphs the boasts of people who have long since been eaten up by worms. And if you look up you will see more shields and helmets, swords and daggers, banners, boots and spurs and the like than they have in some armories. It's not surprising that during the present wars in some places the country folk used the churches as fortresses to defend their lives and possessions.

Given all this, why should I not be allowed as a soldier to

carry on my trade in a church? You'll remember the story of the Abbot of Fulda and the Bishop of Hildesheim who, during an argument over nothing more important than precedence, caused such a bloodbath in the church that it looked more like a slaughterhouse than a holy place. I am a layman and I would happily give up using the church for my business if others used it for divine worship alone; but those two, as ecclesiastics, did not respect the majesty of the Holy Roman Emperor. Why should I be forbidden to use the church to earn my living when so many others do just that? Is it right that rich people can pay for a tomb in the church, a monument to his pride and that of his family, while a poor person, who has no money but is just as much a Christian as the other, and may indeed have been more pious, is buried in some corner outside? It all depends on your point of view. If I'd known you'd have qualms about using the church as a lookout post, I'd have thought of somewhere more suitable to take you. However, since we're here you'll have to put up with it until I can persuade you to change your mind.'

What I would most like to have said was that I thought both he and the other people who defile the church were sinners who would get their just rewards, but since I still didn't trust him and didn't want to quarrel with him again, I let it be. Then he asked me to tell him everything that had happened to me since we had been separated at Wittstock. He also wanted to know how I came to be wearing a fool's costume when I arrived at the camp outside Magdeburg. However, my throat was still so sore I didn't feel up to it, so I asked him instead to tell me the story of his life, which probably, I said, contained some amusing episodes. He agreed and started to recount his infamous life.

Chapter 18

*Oliver tells about his family and how he spent his
childhood, especially what he did in school*

'My father', said Oliver, 'was born not far from the city of
Aachen. His parents were poor so that even as a child he had
to go out to work for a rich merchant who dealt in copper.
He behaved so well that the man had him taught to read,
write and do accounts, and put him in charge of his whole
business, as Potiphar did Joseph. Both sides profited from this:
through my father's hard work and prudence the merchant
became richer and richer; my father on the other hand grew
prouder and prouder with his prosperous life and came to feel
ashamed of his parents, even to despise them, which they
often bemoaned, though to no avail.

When my father was twenty-five, the merchant died, leaving behind his old widow and their only daughter, who not
long before had committed an indiscretion and let a young
stallion father a bastard on her which, however, quickly followed his grandfather to the cemetery. Seeing that the daughter was now without father or child, but not without money,
my father did not let himself be put off by the idea of taking
spoilt goods. It was her wealth he had in mind when he began
to court her, and her mother was happy to encourage him, not
only to restore her daughter's tarnished honour but because
my father was the only one who knew about the business and
was good at driving a hard bargain. The marriage instantly
turned my father into a rich merchant and I was his son and
heir. He lavished all the tender loving care on my upbringing
that his wealth allowed; I was clothed like a gentleman, fed like
a baron and waited on like a count. All of which I had copper
and zinc to thank for rather than silver and gold.

Before I was fully seven years old I had already shown how
I was going to turn out; nettles sting even when they're young

shoots. No piece of mischief was too much for me and if I could play a prank on someone I did so, since neither my father nor my mother punished me for it. I roamed the streets with other like-minded miscreants and had the guts to fight with boys bigger than myself. If I had the worst of it, my parents would say, "What's this? A big lout like you fighting a child?" but if I came out on top (I could bite and scratch and throw stones), they would say, "Won't our little Oliver grow up to be a big, brave fellow!" That made me even bolder. I was still too young to pray, but I could swear like a trooper, to which their response was that I didn't know what I was saying. I became worse and worse until I was sent to school where I played all the tricks other naughty boys think up but daren't actually carry out. If I blotted or tore my books my mother would buy me new ones to avoid a fit of temper from my skinflint father. I gave my schoolmaster a hard time since he couldn't be too strict with me because of all the presents he received from my parents and he knew their little darling could do no wrong in their eyes. In the summer I caught crickets and hid them in the school where they entertained us with their merry chirping. In the winter I would steal some ground hellebore root and scatter it over the place where the boys were punished; whenever some obstinate young rascal struggled, my powder would fly all round the room, making everyone sneeze and me laugh. Eventually I thought myself above playing such ordinary tricks and concentrated on more ambitious things. I would often steal something and slip it into the bag of a boy I wanted to see get a thrashing. I became so crafty at this kind of thing that I was almost never caught. I don't need to tell you about the wars we fought, in which I was usually our general, or the blows I received (my face was always covered in scratches, my head in bruises). Everyone knows the kind of thing boys get up to, but from these few stories you can tell how I spent my childhood.'

Chapter 19

How he was a student in Liege und how he behaved there

'Since my father's wealth was increasing daily, he was surrounded by more and more parasites and toadies. While they all
praised my intelligence and insisted I must go to university,
they said nothing about my bad habits, or at least excused them,
knowing full well that anyone who didn't do thåt would not
get very far with my father or my mother. Consequently my
parents felt prouder of their son than a reed warbler that raises
a cuckoo. They hired a private tutor and sent me to Liege
with him, more to learn French than to study, since they
didn't want to make a theologian out of me but a merchant.
He had his orders not to be too strict with me so that I shouldn't
turn into a timorous, servile type; he was to let me join in with
the other students and encourage me to be sociable, always
remembering they didn't want me to become a monk but a
practical man of the world who knew what was what.

These instructions were completely unnecessary, however,
since my tutor himself was given to a dissolute life. How could
he forbid me what he did himself? How could he take me to
task for my minor misdemeanours when he committed much
worse? By nature he was most inclined to boozing and whoring, I to fighting and brawling, so that I was soon roving the
streets at night with him and his cronies and learnt more
lechery from him than Latin. As far as my studies were concerned, I could rely on my good memory and quick mind,
which made me even more casual in my approach to them; for
the rest I was already deep in all kinds of mischief, vice and
villainy. My conscience was already so accommodating a hay-
cart could have driven through it. I didn't care as long as I
could read stories by Aretino, Berni or Burchiello during the
sermon, and the part of the mass I looked forward to most was
ite missa est.

At the same time I thought no end of my appearance and dressed in all the latest fashions. Every day was a feast day or carnival to me, and since I behaved as a man of substance and spent both the generous allowance my father sent me and the lavish pocket-money from my mother as if the supply were inexhaustible, the young ladies began to take an interest in us, especially my tutor. From those little minxes I learnt to woo, wench and gamble; quarrelling, fighting and brawling I could do already and my tutor did not stop me boozing and guzzling either, since he liked to join in himself. This glorious life lasted for eighteen months, until it was reported to my father by his agent in Liege, with whom we had boarded at first. He received orders to get rid of the tutor and keep a closer eye and a tighter rein on both me and my money. This annoyed both of us and although my tutor was dismissed we still kept company together, day and night. Since, however, we no longer had as much money to throw around as we had before, we joined a gang that snatched people's coats from them at night, sometimes even throwing the owners into the Meuse. The money we got from these highly dangerous operations we squandered with our whores and let our studies go hang.

Then one night when, as was our habit, we were prowling round trying to filch students' coats, we were overpowered, my tutor stabbed to death and I, along with five others who were real rogues, caught and locked up. When we were questioned the next day I named my father's agent, who was a well-respected man, to vouch for me. They sent for him, asked him about me and released me on his security and on condition I stayed in his house under arrest until further notice. In the meantime my tutor was buried, the other five convicted of theft, robbery and murder and sentenced, and my father informed of my situation. He came straight to Liege, sorted out my problem with money, gave me a good talking to and told me how much worry and unhappiness I had caused him and my mother, who was close to despair at my terrible behaviour. He threatened that if I did not mend my ways he would disinherit me and send me packing. I promised to be good from now on and rode home with him. Thus ended my student days.'

Chapter 20

The ex-student returns home then says farewell,
seeking preferment in the wars

'When my father got me back home he decided I was depraved through and through. I had not become the respectable scholar he had presumably hoped for, but a squabbler and a braggart who imagined he knew everything. I had scarcely warmed my hands at the fire when he said, "Listen Oliver, I can see your asses' ears growing even as I look at them. You're no use to anyone, a dead weight, a scoundrel who's good for nothing! You're too old to learn a trade, too ill-mannered to serve a master, and completely unfit to learn my business and carry it on. What have I achieved with all the money I spent on you? I hoped you'd be my pride and joy. I wanted to make a real man of you and what is the result? I've had to pay to save you from the hangman! Oh the shame of it! The best thing would be to put you in a treadmill until you've atoned for your wicked behaviour and sweated it out of your system."

I had to listen to sermons like this almost every day until my patience ran out and I told my father it wasn't my fault, but his own and my tutor's, who had led me astray. It served him right if he had no joy of me; his parents had none of him, who left them in penury to starve. At that he grabbed a stick to pay me out for telling him the truth, swearing by all that was holy he would send me to the goal in Amsterdam. I ran off and that same night I went to the farm he had just bought, took the best stallion in the stable when no one was looking and set out for Cologne.

I sold the horse and soon found myself once more in the

company of the kind of thieves and rogues I had left behind in Liege. They recognised me at once by the way I played cards, and I them: we both knew the same tricks. I immediately joined their gang and helped them break into houses at night whenever I could. However, I lost my taste for thieving shortly afterwards when one of us was caught in the Old Market trying to snatch a plump purse from a lady, more especially when I saw him stand in the stocks with an iron collar half the day, then have one ear cut off and receive a good thrashing. At that time the colonel we served under at Magdeburg was recruiting men to strengthen his regiment, so I enlisted as a soldier. In the meantime my father had heard where I was and wrote to his agent to find out what I was doing. This happened just after I had taken the emperor's shilling, which the agent reported to my father, who told him to buy me out, whatever the cost. Hearing of this, I was afraid he was going to send me to prison and didn't want to be bought out. However when the colonel heard I was the son of a rich merchant, he set such a high price on my freedom that my father left me where I was with the idea of letting me cool my heels in the army for a while to see if I might mend my ways.

It wasn't long afterwards that the colonel's clerk died and he appointed me in his place, as you know. Then I began to have hopes of rising step by step, even, perhaps of ending up as a general. I learnt from the secretary what kind of behaviour was expected and my ambition led me to assume a decent and respectable manner instead of getting up to my old tricks. However, I still made no progress, but then the secretary died and I told myself I must make sure I got his post. I was as free with my money as possible; when my mother heard I had turned over a new leaf she started sending me money again. But young Herzbruder was the colonel's favourite. He was preferred to me and being convinced the colonel was going to give him the secretary's post I decided to get rid of him. In my impatience to ensure my promotion I got the provost-sergeant to make me proof against all weapons, intending to challenge Herzbruder to a duel and settle matters with the sword. However, I never managed to find the right opportunity and the provost-sergeant also advised against it, saying, "Even if you do dispose of him, it'll do you more harm than good because you'll have murdered the colonel's favourite." He suggested it would be better if I stole something when Herzbruder was also present and passed it on to him – the provost-sergeant – and he would see to it that Herzbruder lost the colonel's favour. I fell in with this and took the silver-gilt goblet at the colonel's christening party and gave it to the provost-sergeant, who used it to get young Herzbruder out of the way when, as you'll doubtless remember, he filled your clothes with little puppies by magic.'

Chapter 21

How Simplicius fulfilled Herzbruder's prophecy to
Oliver when neither recognised the other

When I heard Oliver tell me with his own lips what he had done to my dearest friend I saw red, yet could not take revenge; on the contrary, I had to suppress my reaction so that he wouldn't notice how I felt, so I asked him to tell me what had happened to him after the battle of Wittstock.

'In that encounter', he said, 'I didn't behave like a pen-pusher who looks no further than his inkwell, but like a true soldier. I had a good mount, I was sword- and bullet-proof and I wasn't assigned to any particular squadron, so I gave a demonstration of my valour, like a man who is determined to rise in the world through his sword or die. I rushed hither and thither round our brigade, looking to involve myself and show that I was more use for fighting than writing. It was no good, however, luck was with the Swedes and I had to share our general misfortune and accept the quarter I had been refusing not long before.

With other prisoners I was put into an infantry regiment

which was sent to Pomerania to get back up to strength. Since there were many new recruits and I had given proof of outstanding bravery, I was made corporal. However, I had no intention of spending longer sitting on my backside there than was necessary. I was determined to rejoin the imperial army, since that was where I felt I belonged, even though I would doubtless have had better chances of promotion with the Swedes. My escape I arranged as follows. I was sent with seven musketeers to bring in the arrears of war-levies from an out-of-the-way part of the district where we were quartered. When I had collected more than 800 guilders I showed the money to my men till their eyes glittered greedily and we agreed to share it and decamp together. When we had done that, I persuaded three of them to help me shoot the other four. We then redistributed their share so that we had two hundred guilders each and set off for Westphalia. On the way I persuaded one of the three to help me shoot the other two and, when we started dividing up the spoils, I strangled him and thus had the eight hundred guilders when I reached Werl, where I enlisted and had a good time with all the money.

At the time when this was running out, though not my taste for high living, I heard a lot about a young soldier in Soest who had taken a large amount of booty, making a great name for himself into the bargain, and I was encouraged to emulate him. Because of his green dress people called him the Huntsman, so I had a similar outfit made and proceeded to steal under his name in the territories of both our regiments, going to such extremes that they threatened to ban both of us from foraging. At that he stayed in his quarters, but I continued my pilfering as much as I could under his name so that the Huntsman issued a challenge to me. Let the devil fight him, not me! In fact, I was told he had the devil behind him, so he would have made short work of my bullet-proof skin!

However, he was too clever for me in the end. With the help of his servant he inveigled me into a sheep-fold along with my comrade and tried to force me to fight with him there and then, in the moonlight and in the presence of two demons he had brought as seconds. When I refused, he forced me to do the most humiliating thing in the world, which my comrade told people about. I was so ashamed I ran away to Lippstadt and took service with the Hessians. However, they didn't trust me so I didn't stay there for long but trotted off to join the Dutch. There I found I was paid more punctually, but life in their army was too boring for my liking. Discipline was as strict as in a monastery and we were expected to live as chastely as nuns.

Now I didn't dare show my face among the imperial, Swedish or Hessian forces, having deserted from all three, and it was about time for me to leave the Dutch as well since I had raped a girl and it looked as if the fruit of my act was soon to see the light of day. I decided to take refuge with the Spanish army, hoping I could get home from there to see what my parents were doing. But when I tried to put my plan into effect my compass went haywire and I ended up with the Bavarians and joined the troop of Merode's Brethren following them. I marched with them from Westphalia to the Breisgau and kept myself by gambling and stealing. When I had money I spent my days in the gaming yard, my nights in the wine-booths, and when I had nothing I stole whatever I could find. I often stole two or three horses in one day, both from the pasture and the stables, sold them and gambled away the proceeds. At night I would sneak into people's tents and take their most valuable possessions from under their very heads. When we were on the march and going through a narrow pass I would keep a sharp eye on the knapsacks the women carried and cut them off. In this way I managed to keep body and soul together until after the Battle of Wittenweier, where I was captured and once more put into an infantry regiment, this time as a Weimar soldier. However, I didn't like the camp before Breisach so I quickly deserted and set up as a soldier on my own account, as you can see. And since then I've dispatched many a proud fellow and earned a deal of money, I can tell you. I don't intend to stop until the supply dries up. And now it's your turn to tell me what you've been doing.'

Chapter 22

What happened to Oliver when he let the cat out of the bag

When Oliver had finished I couldn't get over my astonishment at the workings of Divine Providence. I came to see how the Lord in His fatherly goodness had not only protected me from this monster when I was in Westphalia but had contrived that he should go in fear of me. Only then did I realise what a trick I had played on him, which old Herzbruder had prophesied but which Oliver, as I reported in Chapter 16, had interpreted differently, and to my great advantage. If this fiend had known that I was the Huntsman of Soest, he would certainly have paid me back for what I did to him in the sheepfold. I also thought how wise Herzbruder had been to couch his predictions in such obscure form, and yet, although his prophesies generally came true, it was difficult to see how, except by some bizarre twist of fate, I was going to avenge the death of a man who deserved the gallows and the wheel. I also realised how fortunate it was that I had not told my story first. If I had, I would have revealed to him how I had humiliated him. While these thoughts were going through my mind I noticed some marks on his face which had not been there in the camp outside Magdeburg and I assumed the scars were a memento of Tearaway, who, disguised as a demon, had scratched him all over the face. So I asked him where they came from, adding that although he was telling me his life story, he must be keeping quiet about the best part since he hadn't told me who had marked him like that.

'Oh, Simplicius', he replied, 'if I were to tell you all of my doings we would both soon weary of it. However, to show you that I'm keeping nothing back I'll tell you the truth about these scars, even though it makes me look a fool. I think I must have been destined from birth to have a face covered in scars. Even as a child I was scratched by my schoolmates whenever I wrestled with them. One of the demons attending the Huntsman of Soest gave me such a going-over you could see the marks of his claws on my face for six weeks afterwards. However, they healed up and left no traces; the weals you can see came from somewhere else. When I was quartered with the Swedes in Pomerania I had a beautiful mistress and made my landlord give up his bed to us. His cat had got used to sleeping there and, unlike its master and mistress, was unwilling to give up its comfortable bed tamely, and used to come and pester us every night. This annoyed my mistress so much (she couldn't stand cats anyway) that she swore she wouldn't make love to me again until I got rid of the cat. I naturally wanted to continue to enjoy her favours and decided to carry out her wishes in such a way that I would get my own back on the cat and enjoy myself into the bargain. I put it in a sack and went with it to a big open field together with my landlord's two powerful watch-dogs, which didn't care for cats at all but had taken to me. I chose the field because I thought that with no tree in sight for the cat to climb up the dogs would chase it all over the place like a hare, which would amuse me no end. But damn me if that cat didn't have other ideas. When I let it out of the sack and it saw nothing but an open field with its two worst enemies and nothing to climb up it didn't just sit there and wait to be torn to pieces, it shot up onto my head, that being the highest place it could see. I knocked my hat off attempting to stop it and the more I tried to dislodge it, the deeper it stuck its claws in to hold on. The dogs naturally joined in, baring their teeth and jumping up all round me to get at the cat, which refused to get down and clung on as best it could, with its claws fixed into my face and other parts of my head. It kept lunging at the dogs with its needle-sharp claws. Most of the time it missed them, but never me. Since it did occasionally catch the dogs on the nose, they tried to knock it off with their paws, giving me even more slashes across the face. And when I tried to get hold of the cat with both hands to pull it off, it bit and scratched with all its might. I was so badly scratched, mauled and savaged by both the dogs and the cat that I was unrecognisable and, worst of all, I was in

343

danger of having my nose or ears bitten off completely when the dogs snapped at the cat. My collar and jerkin were as covered in blood as the stalls used to restrain horses when they bleed them on St. Stephen's Day. The only way I could think of to stop my head being used as a battle-ground was to fall down onto the ground so the dogs could get at the cat. Eventually the dogs did kill the cat, but instead of the fun I had expected all I got were derisive remarks and the face you now see before you. I was so furious I later shot the two dogs and beat my mistress, since she had put me up to it, black and blue so that she ran away from me. Doubtless she couldn't have loved such a repulsive face any longer anyway.

Chapter 23

A brief story as an example of the trade in which Oliver
was a master and Simplicius an apprentice

I was tempted to laugh at Oliver's tale but had to put on a show of sympathy. Then, just as I was starting to tell him my own story, we saw a coach with two outriders approaching, so we went down from the church tower and took up position in a house on the street from which it was easy to waylay them as they passed. I kept my loaded musket in reserve while Oliver shot down one of the riders before they knew we were there. The other galloped off and I, with my gun cocked, forced the coachman to stop and get down, at which Oliver leapt on him and split open his head from skull to teeth with his broadsword. He would have gone on to butcher the women and children in the coach – they already looked pale as corpses – but I refused to allow it, telling him he would have to deal with me first.

'Oh you fool, Simplicius', he said, 'I would never have thought you would get cold feet like this.'

'What have you got against these poor innocent children,

brother?' I replied. 'If they were men and could defend themselves it would be different.'

'Fry the eggs and you get rid of the brood', he replied. 'I know these young bloodsuckers well. Their father, the major, is a real slave-driver, the biggest bully in the whole army.' With that, he was all for killing them again, but I managed to restrain him until eventually he relented. It was a major's wife, her maid and three pretty children, for whom I felt heartily sorry. We locked them up in a cellar so they wouldn't raise the alarm too soon. All they had to eat there, until someone came to free them, was fruit and some turnips. After that we stripped the coach of everything of value and rode off with seven fine horses into the densest part of the forest.

Once we had tethered them, I looked around and saw a man standing stock-still beside a tree not far from us. I pointed him out to Oliver, saying we had better be careful, but he just laughed. 'It's only a Jew I tied up there, you fool. The blackguard froze to death ages ago.' He went up to him, gave him a pat under the chin and said, 'But you gave me lots of lovely ducats, didn't you, you cur!' As he shook the dead Jew's chin a few doubloons fell out which the poor soul had managed to keep hidden even after his death. Oliver felt in his mouth and collected twelve doubloons and a precious ruby. 'I have you to thank for this, Simplicius', he said and gave me the ruby, keeping the money for himself. Then he went to fetch the labourer and told me to stay with the horses, but to be careful the dead Jew didn't bite me, by which he meant to suggest that I lacked his bravery.

Once he had gone, I started reflecting on the dangers of the situation I was in. I thought of mounting one of the horses and riding off, but I was worried that Oliver might catch me in the act and shoot me, since I suspected he was just testing my loyalty and hiding somewhere nearby to see what I did. Then I contemplated slipping away on foot, but I was afraid that even if I avoided Oliver I was unlikely to escape the Black Forest peasants, who had the reputation of knocking any soldiers they caught on the head. On the other hand, I told myself, if you take all the horses, so that Oliver has no means of pursuing you, and are caught by Weimar troops you'll be condemned as a murderer and broken on the wheel. All in all, there seemed to be no safe means of getting away, especially as I was in a trackless forest I was completely unfamiliar with.

At the same time I was having qualms of conscience for stopping the coach and allowing the poor coachman to be butchered and the two women and the innocent children locked in a cellar, where they might perhaps languish and die like the Jew over there. I tried to comfort myself that I was innocent, having been compelled to take part against my will, but my conscience countered that with all the other evil deeds I had recently committed I deserved to fall into the hands of justice in the company of that arch-murderer. Any punishment I received would be my just desserts; perhaps the Lord of Righteousness had even ordained I should be brought to book in this manner. Finally I became more optimistic and asked the Lord in His great goodness to rescue me from this predicament. Having worked myself into a more pious mood, I told myself, 'What a fool you are! You're not tied up or imprisoned, the whole wide world is open to you. Haven't you got enough horses to escape on? Or if you don't want to go on horseback, aren't your legs fast enough to get you away?'

While I was tormenting myself with these thoughts and not coming to any decision, Oliver returned with the farm labourer, who led us to a farm where we ate and each slept in turn for a few hours. After midnight we rode on and came about noon to the Swiss frontier, where Oliver was well known. We ordered a splendid meal and sat down to have a good time while the landlord sent for two Jews, who bought the horses from us at half price. It all went so smoothly there was no need for much discussion at all. The main thing the Jews wanted to know was whether the horses had come from the Swedish or the imperial army. When we told them they were from the Weimar forces they said, 'In that case we can't take them to Basle. We'll have to ride them to Swabia to sell them to the Bavarians.' I was astonished at their wide acquaintance and familiarity with the different armies.

We enjoyed a princely banquet and I tucked into the tasty

Black Forest trout and delicious crayfish. We left towards evening, having loaded the labourer down with roast meat and other provisions like a pack-horse, and reached an isolated farmhouse the next day where we were given a friendly welcome. As the weather was bad we stayed there for a few days then continued along byways through the forest back to the cottage to which Oliver had originally taken me.

Chapter 24

Oliver comes to a sticky end and takes six men with him

While we were sitting there resting and recuperating Oliver sent the labourer out to buy food and some powder and shot. When the latter had gone, he took off his coat and said, 'Brother, I'm tired of carrying all this damn money round with me.' Then he untied a couple of rolls he wore next to his bare skin, threw them down on the table and said, 'You'll have to look after these until we've both got enough and I call it a day, the blasted money's giving me blisters!'

'Brother', I replied, 'if you had as little as I have it wouldn't chafe.'

Oliver interrupted me. 'What do you mean? What's mine is yours and anything we get together will be shared out equally.'

I picked up the two rolls. They were extremely heavy, since they contained nothing but gold coins. I pointed out that it was an uncomfortable way to pack them and offered to sew the coins into our clothes, making them less awkward to carry. He agreed and took me to a hollow tree where he kept scissors, needles and thread. Using a pair of trousers, I made us both a kind of singlet, not unlike a monk's scapular, into which I sewed the gold pieces. When we put them on under our shirts it was as if we had golden armour over our chests and backs. I was suddenly struck by a thought and asked him why he had no silver coins, to which he replied that he had a hoard of more than a thousand thalers hidden in a tree. He let the labourer take the housekeeping money from it and never asked for an account; it wasn't worth it for sheep-shit like that, he said.

When we had finished stowing the money we went back to our quarters, where we spent the night cooking and warming ourselves at the stove. An hour after daybreak, when we were least expecting it, a corporal and six musketeers entered the cottage with guns at the ready, burst open the door of the room and shouted to us to surrender. But we always kept our cocked muskets to hand, Oliver his sharp sword as well; the table was between him and the soldiers and I was behind the door, by the stove. Oliver replied with two bullets, which sent two of them tumbling to the ground, I dispatched a third and wounded another with similar shots. Then Oliver unsheathed his fearsome blade, which was so keen it could split hairs and could best be compared to King Arthur's Excalibur, and sliced open the fifth from the shoulder to the belly so that all his innards spewed out and he collapsed to the floor beside them. At the same time I hit the sixth on the head with the butt of my musket, killing him on the spot. Oliver received a similar blow from the seventh which was so powerful it spattered his brains over the wall, but I gave the man a crack that sent him to join his comrades in the regiment in the sky. When the soldier I had wounded saw this mayhem and realised I was going to set about him with the butt-end of my musket next, he threw away his gun and ran off as if the devil himself were at his heels. The whole fight lasted no longer than it takes to say the Lord's Prayer and seven brave soldiers went to meet their Maker.

Now that I was left sole master of the field I went to look at Oliver, to see if perhaps he was still alive, but finding him dead as a doornail I decided it would be pointless to leave so much gold on a corpse that had no use for it, so I took off the money-jerkin I had made the previous day and slipped it over my head to join the other. Since I had broken my own musket, I took Oliver's, along with his sword, and thus prepared for all emergencies I left the cottage. I followed the path by which I knew the farm labourer would come back and sat down, a little way off the track, to wait for him and to think over what I should do next.

Chapter 25

Simplicius comes out of it very rich; Herzbruder, on the other hand, appears in a wretched state

I had scarcely been sitting there, wrapped in thought, for half an hour when our landlord appeared, wheezing like a bear. He was running as fast as he could and didn't see me until I grabbed him. 'Why so fast?' I said. 'Has something happened?'

'You must get away as quick as you can', he replied. 'There's a corporal coming with six musketeers to arrest you and Oliver and to take you to Liechteneck, dead or alive. They caught me to make me lead them to you, but I managed to escape and I've run all the way here to warn you.'

'You blackguard', I thought, 'you betrayed us to get your hands on the silver Oliver stored in the tree.' I kept this to myself, however, because I wanted to use him as a guide. When I told him that both Oliver and those who had come to capture him were dead he refused to believe it, so I did him the pleasure of taking him to see the gruesome sight of the seven bodies. 'I let the seventh man go', I said, 'and I would to God I could bring the others back to life.'

The labourer was terrified. 'What are we going to do now?'

'That I have already decided', I said. 'You have three choices: either you lead me by a safe route through the forest to Villingen, or you show me the tree where Oliver hid his money, or you join the corpses on the floor here. If you take me to Villingen you can keep the money for yourself, if you show me where it's hidden we'll share it; if you do neither I'll shoot you dead and go on my way.'

He wanted to run away, but he was afraid of my musket, so he fell to his knees and offered to lead me through the forest. We set off quickly and walked all that day and the following night – fortunately the moon was very bright – without eating, drinking or resting until we came into sight of Villingen about daybreak, when I sent the labourer back. It was fear that had kept him going, but I was driven by the desire to save my skin and my money. It almost made me think that gold must give a man great strength, for although it was very heavy I didn't feel especially tired.

I looked on it as a favourable omen that the gate was just being opened when I reached the town. The officer of the watch questioned me. I told him I was a volunteer trooper, from the regiment in which Herzbruder had put me when he released me from the infantry in Philippsburg, who had been captured by the Weimar troops at Wittenweier and forced to serve in their army. Now I was trying to get back to my regiment in the Bavarian army. When he heard this the officer told a musketeer to take me to the commandant. He was still sleeping, having been up half the night on business, so that I had to spend an hour and a half waiting outside his quarters. It was the time of early mass and a crowd of townspeople and soldiers soon gathered round me, all wanting to know how things stood at Breisach. Eventually the noise woke the commandant, who had me brought to him.

He questioned me again and I repeated the statement I had given at the gate. After that he asked for details about the siege and what I had done since, so I told him the truth, namely that I had spent a couple of weeks with another escaped soldier and that we had attacked and robbed a coach carrying the family of a Weimar officer, intending to get enough to buy mounts so that we could return to our regiments properly equipped. But, I went on, the previous day we had been attacked by a corporal and six musketeers who had been sent out to arrest us. My comrade and six of them had been killed; I and the seventh had run off, each to rejoin his own side.

I didn't say a word about the fact that I was trying to get to my wife in Lippstadt or about my well-lined vests, and I had no qualms about it. What business was it of his after all? Anyway, he didn't ask. Instead he expressed his astonishment that Oliver and I had accounted for six men and put the seventh to flight. He found it hard to believe, even though my comrade had paid for it with his life. At this I started telling him all about Oliver's sword, which I was wearing. He liked it so much that I felt obliged, especially if I wanted to get a pass, to give it to him in exchange for one he gave me in return. It was a truly excellent sword, fine and strong, with a perpetual calendar etched on the blade. I believe it must have been forged *in hora Martis* by Vulcan himself and so treated that, like the one described in the *Treasury of Heroes*, it could shatter all other blades and send the most intrepid, lion-hearted enemy running for cover like a timorous mouse. When he dismissed me, having ordered a pass to be written out, I went straight to the inn but I couldn't make up my mind which to do first, sleep or eat. I had great need of both but I eventually decided to satisfy the demands of my belly first and ordered something to eat and drink. I wondered what I was going to do to get myself and my money safely to my wife in Lippstadt for I no more intended to rejoin my regiment than to chop off my own head.

While I was thus pondering, a man hobbled into the room, supporting himself with a stick. He had a bandage round his head, his arm in a sling and was dressed in such rags I wouldn't have given a farthing for them. As soon as the servant saw him he tried to throw him out because the beggar gave off a foul stench and was crawling with lice. He begged to be allowed to warm himself a little but got nowhere until I took pity and spoke up for him, at which he was grudgingly allowed to sit by the stove. I could feel his eyes fixed on me, watching me greedily as I tucked in and sighing. When the servant went to fetch my roast he came over to my table, holding out a cheap earthenware cup. It was obvious why he had approached me so I took my jug and filled his cup before he asked. 'Oh friend', he said, 'for your Herzbruder's sake give me something to eat as well.' When he said that it cut me to the heart, for I could see now that it was Herzbruder himself. I almost

351

fainted to see him in such a wretched state, but I kept a hold on myself, embraced him and made him sit next to me, at which we both burst into tears, I out of pity, he for joy.

Chapter 26

Is the last in this fourth book because there are none to follow

This unexpected meeting meant that we scarcely ate or drank anything as each asked the other what had happened since the last time we were together. However, because the landlord and servant kept bustling to and fro, we could not discuss private matters. The landlord was surprised I let such a lice-ridden fellow join me, but I told him that was the way any decent soldier would treat a comrade in wartime. When I learnt that Herzbruder had been in the hospice until now, living on alms, and saw how badly his wounds had been dressed, I hired a room for him from the landlord and sent for the best surgeon I could find, as well as a tailor and seamstress to clothe him and clear him of lice. I had the doubloons Oliver had taken from the dead Jew's mouth in a little bag and I emptied it out on the table and said, in the landlord's hearing, 'Look, brother, that's my money and we're going to spend it together', as a result of which the landlord looked after us very well. I showed the ruby, which had also come from the above-mentioned Jew and was worth about twenty thalers, to the barber-surgeon and told him that I had to keep what money I had for our board and lodging and clothes for my comrade but that I would give him the ring if he would cure my friend quickly and completely. He was happy with the arrangement and did his best for Herzbruder.

I looked after him as if he were my other self and had a suit of plain grey clothes made for him. First of all, however, I went to see the commandant about my pass. I told him I had come across a comrade who had been badly wounded and that I wanted to wait until he was completely healed since I owed it to my regiment not to leave him behind in such a state. The commandant praised me for this and gave me permission to stay as long as I wanted, also promising that when my comrade was fit enough to go he would provide both of us with the appropriate passes.

That having been done, I went back to Herzbruder, sat down beside his bed and, as we were now alone, asked him to tell me, openly and frankly, how he came to be in such a miserable state. I thought he might perhaps have been removed from his lofty position, stripped of his rank and plunged into his present wretched state because of some grave error or piece of negligence, but he said, 'As you know, I was Count Götz's aide-de-camp and intimate personal friend. You will also know how badly this last campaign, in which he had overall command, went for us. We not only lost the Battle of Wittenweier but were unable to lift the siege of Breisach. Because of all the unjust rumours that are flying about and because the Count has been summoned to Vienna to answer his critics, I have deliberately adopted this low condition out of both shame and fear. I often wish I could either die in it or at least remain hidden until Count Götz has proved his innocence, for as far as I know he has always been loyal to the Emperor. The fact that he had no luck at all last summer has, in my opinion, more to do with divine providence, which grants victory as it sees fit, than to the Count's negligence.

While we were trying to relieve Breisach and I saw how sluggishly things were going on our side, I armed myself and joined in the attack on the pontoon bridge, charging as if I intended to lift the siege on my own. This was neither my business nor my duty; I did it to set an example and because we had achieved so little during the whole summer. As luck, or rather bad luck would have it, I was among the first that came face to face with the enemy on the bridge, where things got pretty hot. Being the first in the attack meant I was last in the retreat when the furious onslaught of the French forced us back, and so the first to fall into the hands of the enemy. I received a shot in my right arm and another in my thigh so that I could neither run nor use my sword. Since space was too cramped and the fighting too fierce for much negotiation about quarter I got a crack over the head which sent me tumbling to the ground, and as I was dressed in fine clothes I was rapidly stripped naked and thrown for dead into the Rhine.

In this plight I cried out to God, putting all my reliance on Him, and as I made various vows I felt Him come to my aid: the Rhine washed me up on shore, where I plugged my wounds with moss, and although nearly freezing to death, I felt a particular strength within me, sufficient to crawl away. With God's assistance I came, badly wounded as I was, to a band of Merode's Brethren and soldier's wives who all took pity on me, even though they did not know me. They told me it was very doubtful the siege would be lifted, which hurt me more than my wounds. They took me to their fire, where they revived me and gave me some clothes, and even before I had got round to bandaging up my wounds I saw that our side was giving up the attack for lost and preparing for an ignominious retreat. I was so upset by this that I decided not to tell anyone who I was, in order to avoid any mockery. I joined a group of wounded from our army who had their own surgeon and gave him a gold cross I still had round my neck, for which he treated my wounds until we got here.

In this wretched state I have survived so far, Simplicius, and I intend to keep my identity secret until I see what happens to Count Götz. Your kindness and loyal friendship are a great comfort to me and a token that God has not abandoned me. When I came out of early mass this morning and saw you standing outside the commandant's quarters it seemed to me God had sent you instead of one of his angels to help me in my time of need.'

I comforted Herzbruder as well as I could. I told him I had more money than the doubloons he had seen and that it was all at his disposal. I also told him about Oliver's death and the way I had avenged it. This news cheered him up, which also improved his physical state, so that his wounds began to heal visibly with every day.

Book V

Chapter 1

How Simplicius became a pilgrim and went on a pilgrimage with Herzbruder

When Herzbruder had recovered his strength and his wounds healed he told me that in his hour of need he had vowed to make a pilgrimage to Einsiedeln and since he was now so close to Switzerland he was determined to go ahead with it, even if it meant begging his way there. I was attracted by this idea and offered him money and my company, indeed, I was all for going straight out to buy two horses for the journey. It wasn't piety that made me want to go, but my desire to see the Swiss Confederation, that being the only country where peace could still be found. I loved Herzbruder almost more than myself and was delighted at the thought of being able to help him on his journey. However he rejected both my assistance and my company, saying he had to do the journey on foot, and with dried peas in his shoes. If I were to accompany him I would not only distract him from his devotions but would find his slow, laborious pace very tedious.

His real reason for trying to get rid of me, however, was because he had qualms about using money that had been gained by robbery and murder for such a sacred journey. On top of that he did not want to put me to too great an expense and told me candidly that I had already done more than I owed or that he thought he could ever repay. That set off a charmingly friendly argument, the like of which I have never heard before. Each of us maintained he had not done as much for the other as a friend should, that he had not even had the chance to make up for the good turns he had received from the other. All this did nothing to persuade him to accept me as a travelling companion until I realised it was both Oliver's money and my ungodliness that disgusted him. So I had recourse to lies and convinced him it was my desire to mend my ways that made me want to go to Einsiedeln, arguing that if he prevented me from carrying out this good intention and I were then to die, he would bear a heavy responsibility. This persuaded him to allow me to visit the holy place with him, especially as I made a great show of regret for my wicked life (although it was all a lie) and convinced him I too had resolved to do penance by walking to Einsiedeln with my boots full of dried peas.

This squabble was scarcely finished than another broke out. Herzbruder was far too conscientious. He wouldn't have it that I should accept a pass from the commandant which stated I was going to rejoin my regiment. 'But we're going to Einsiedeln', he said, ' with the intention of leading better lives, aren't we? And you want to start out with deceit, throwing dust in people's eyes? Did not Christ say, "He that denieth me before men shall be denied before the angels of God." What a pair of faint hearts we are. If all those who professed the faith or were martyred in Christ's name had behaved in the same way, how few saints there would be in heaven! Let us entrust ourselves to God's protection and in His name follow our devout purpose and desires. If we leave everything to Him, He will lead us where our souls will find peace.' I objected that one should not presume upon God's will but accept the world as it was and use any means that were necessary. Going on pilgrimage was rather unusual among soldiers, and if we revealed our plan we were more likely to be arrested as deserters. I also pointed out that the Apostle Paul, with whom we could not begin to compare ourselves, had adapted to the customs of his times, and eventually he agreed I should take a pass stating I was going to join my regiment. Using this, we left the town just as the gates were being shut, taking a man we could trust to guide us. We set off in the direction of Rottweil, but soon turned off on by-ways, crossed the Swiss frontier during the night and came to a village the following morning where we kitted ourselves out with long black robes, pilgrim's staffs and rosaries and paid off the guide.

Compared with other parts of Germany the country seemed as strange as if I had been in Brazil or China. I saw people living and working in peace, the byres were full of cattle, the farmyards swarming with chickens, geese and ducks, the roads safe for travellers and the inns crowded with people enjoying themselves. No one went in fear of enemy attack, of being plundered, of losing goods or chattels, life or limb; everyone lived secure under his own vine or fig tree. In comparison with other German states they lived lives of such pleasure and delight that, even though it seemed fairly rough, the country struck me as an earthly paradise, so that I was forever staring about me. Herzbruder, on the other hand, was saying his rosary and kept telling me off. He thought I should be praying all the time like him, but I just couldn't get myself into the habit.

In Zurich he found out that I was cheating and told me what he thought of me in no uncertain terms. We had spent the previous night in Schaffhausen, and my feet were hurting so much from the peas that I couldn't bear the thought of walking on them again the next day. So I had them cooked before I put them back in my boots and did the stage to Zurich without any difficulty, while he was in a terrible state. 'Brother', he said, 'you must have found great favour with God if you can get on like this despite the peas in your boots.'

'I have to confess, Herzbruder', I said, 'that I cooked them, otherwise I wouldn't have been able to walk so far.'

'Lord preserve us', he replied. 'what have you done? It would have been better if you had left them out of your boots altogether if all you can do is make a mockery of the penance. I fear God might punish both of us for this. Simplicius, you are like a brother to me, and I hope you won't take it amiss if I tell you in plain German what I feel. I am very much afraid that if you do not change your attitude towards God you will put your immortal soul in great danger. There's no one I love more, I assure you, but I must confess that if you do not mend your ways my conscience will not allow that love to continue.' The shock of this threat struck me dumb, and it was some time before I could speak again. Then I openly confessed that I had not put the peas in my boots out of piety but simply to persuade him to let me accompany him.

'Oh Simplicius', he said, 'peas or no peas, I can see you have strayed far from the path of salvation. May God lead you into better ways, otherwise our friendship is at an end.'

From then on I followed sadly in his wake, like a man being led to the gallows. My conscience began to torment me and as various thoughts went through my mind I saw all the misdeeds I had committed. I bewailed the loss of the innocence I had when I first came out of the forest and which I had so squandered in the world. And what made me even more wretched was the fact that Herzbruder hardly talked to me any more but just looked at me and sighed, as if he knew I was already among the damned and was lamenting my fate.

Chapter 2

Simplicius mends his ways after he has been given a fright by the devil

Still in the same frame of mind, we reached Einsiedeln and went straight to the church where a priest was exorcising a man possessed by an evil spirit. This being something unusual I had never seen before, I let Herzbruder kneel down and pray as long as he liked while I went to enjoy the spectacle. Hardly had I approached, however, than the spirit inside the poor man cried out, 'Oho, an ill wind's blown you here, has it? I expected to see you with Oliver when I got back to our home in hell. And now you turn up here, you adulterous, murderous whoremonger. You don't imagine you're going to escape us, do you? Hey, you priests, have nothing to do with him. He's a hypocrite and a worse liar than me. He's just laughing at you and making fun of God and religion.'

The exorcist commanded the spirit to be silent since, being an arch-liar, no one believed him anyway. 'Well', it answered, 'you just ask this runaway monk's companion. He'll tell you this atheist had no compunction about boiling the peas he'd vowed to walk on all the way here.'

Hearing all this and seeing everyone staring at me, I didn't know whether I was on my head or my heels. The priest rebuked the spirit and compelled it to be silent, but he could not drive it out that day. When Herzbruder came over I was so terrified I looked more like a corpse than a living man and so torn between hope and fear I didn't know which way to turn. He gave me what comfort he could and assured the bystanders, especially the priests, that I had never been a monk at any time in my life. I had been a soldier, he said, and as such might well have done more evil than good, but the devil was a liar and had made out the matter of the peas to be much worse than it actually was. I, however, was so bewildered I felt I was suffering the torments of hell already and the good fathers had their hands full reassuring me. They exhorted me to go to confession and take communion, but once again the spirit inside the possessed man started shouting and saying, 'Oh yes, a fine confession you'll get out of him. He doesn't even know what confession is! What are you going to do with him? He's one of those heretics, he belongs to us. His parents were more Anabaptists than Lutherans', and more in the same vein.

Once again the exorcist commanded the spirit to be silent, saying, 'In that case it will annoy you all the more if the poor lost sheep is snatched from your jaws and gathered into the Christian fold.' At that the spirit set up such a dreadful roaring it was terrible to hear, but I actually found comfort in its ghastly howl. The fiend would not have reacted in that way if I was excluded from God's grace.

I was not at all prepared for confession, in fact it had never once occurred to me to confess my sins, I had always shrunk back from it, like the devil from the Cross, but in that moment I felt such remorse at my sins and such a strong desire to do penance and lead a better life that I asked to see a confessor straight away. Herzbruder was delighted at this sudden conversion and amendment since from his own observation he was well aware that up to that point I had not belonged to any religion. Accordingly I publicly professed myself a Catholic, went to confession and, having received absolution, took communion, at which I felt so light at heart it is beyond description. The strangest thing of all was that from then on the evil spirit inside the man left me in peace, even though before my confession and absolution it had accused me of various misdeeds I had committed, as if its sole purpose had been to record my sins. However, those who heard it did not believe it. They assumed it was lying, especially since my pilgrim's outfit suggested I was quite different.

We spent two whole weeks in that abode of grace and I praised God for my conversion and contemplated the miracles that had occurred there. All this made me fairly pious and devout, but the transformation did not last as long as it might have. Since I had converted not out of love of God but from fear of damnation, as I gradually forgot the terror the Evil One had inspired in me, I became lukewarm and lethargic. After we had spent enough time viewing the relics of the saints, the vestments and other treasures of the monastery, we went to Baden in the Aargau, where we intended to spend the winter.

Chapter 3

How the two friends spent the winter

There I rented a pleasant sitting-room and bedroom for us which were generally used by the summer visitors who came to take the waters. (Actually, these were mostly rich Swiss who came more to enjoy themselves and show off their wealth than to take the waters for some ailment.) I agreed terms for full board, and when Herzbruder saw the magnificent arrangements I made he cautioned me to be thrifty, reminding me of the long, hard winter we had to face, not believing my money would last all that time. I would need my hoard in the spring, he said, when we set out again. Money was soon spent if you kept taking and never adding to it, he warned, it would vanish like smoke into thin air, never to return, and so on and so forth. After this well-meant admonition I could no longer conceal from him how brimful my moneybags were. And I meant us to have a good time with it, I said. It had been acquired from such an unholy source I could not think of buying a farm with it, the land would be cursed. Even if I hadn't been determined to use it to support my dearest friend, it was right and proper that he, Herzbruder, should be compensated from Oliver's money to make up for the disgrace Oliver had caused him at Magdeburg, I argued. Now that I knew I was safe, I removed my two gold-filled vests, cut out the doubloons and pistoles and told Herzbruder the money was at his disposal, to invest or spend as he thought would be in our best interest.

Seeing how much I trusted him and realising that without him I could have used the large sum of money to set myself up as a gentleman, he said, 'Brother, since I have known you, you have done nothing but give me proofs of your love and constancy. Tell me, how do you think I am ever going to repay you. It's not just the money – that I might be able to pay back in time – but your love and constancy and above all the great trust you show me, which is beyond all price. In a word, brother, your nobility of soul makes me your slave and I can only marvel at what you have done for me, not hope to repay it. O honest Simplicius it never occurs to you, even in these godless times when the world is full of deceit, that poor, penniless Herzbruder might run off with such a substantial sum of money and leave you destitute! I tell you, my brother, this demonstration of true friendship binds me to you more than if a rich man had given me thousands. But I have just one request: remain master of your own money, keep it and spend it as you see fit. For me it is enough that you are my friend.'

'What kind of talk is this, sir?' I replied. 'You assure me you are under an obligation to me and yet you refuse to take steps to see to it that I do not throw our money away, which would be to both our detriment.'

We went on talking in this rather fatuous manner for some time, since we were both drunk on the other's affection, and the ultimate outcome was that Herzbruder became my steward and my treasurer, my servant and my master. We had time to spare for each other, which we had not had before, and he told me his experiences and how he had come to the notice of Count Götz and been promoted, and I told him everything that had happened to me since his father's death. When he heard I had a young wife in Lippstadt he reproached me for having accompanied him to Switzerland instead of going back to her, as both decency and duty demanded. I excused myself by saying I had not had the heart to leave my dearest friend in misery, at which he persuaded me to write to her to let her know my situation, promising I would join her at the earliest possible opportunity. In my letter I said how sorry I was that I had been away from her for so long. My fervent desire to be with her, I wrote, had been thwarted by all kinds of adverse circumstances.

In the meantime my companion had learnt that things were looking up for Count Götz. Report had it that he would vindicate himself in his trial before the Emperor, be released and even put back in command of the army. Herzbruder therefore sent word to him in Vienna to tell him of his own situation. He also wrote to the Bavarian army about his effects, which were still there, and started to feel more optimistic about the future. We agreed therefore to separate when spring came, he going to join the Count, I returning to my wife in Lippstadt. So that we did not spend the winter in complete idleness, we had an engineer teach us how to design more fortifications than the kings of France and Spain put together could build. I also came into contact with several alchemists who, sniffing my money, offered to show me how to make gold, if I would only finance them. I believe they might even have persuaded me if Herzbruder had not sent them packing, telling them that anyone who had really mastered the art would not have to go round begging others for money.

Although Herzbruder received a cordial and encouraging reply from the Count in Vienna, not a single word came to me from Lippstadt, even though I had sent copies by separate post. That annoyed me, and when spring came I did not set off for Westphalia but got Herzbruder to agree to take me with him to Vienna, to share in the good fortune he hoped to find there. So with my money we kitted ourselves out with clothing, horses, servants and arms like two gentlemen and went via Constance to Ulm, where we took a boat on the Danube and reached Vienna in a week. All the way I had eyes for nothing but the women who answered the calls from the boats with literal rather than verbal bare-arsed cheek.

Chapter 4

How Simplicius and Herzbruder were once more engaged in hostilities and how they came out of it

It is strange how everything is constantly changing in this world. People say, *If you knew everything you'd soon be rich*, but I say if you knew how to seize the opportunity you'd soon be great and powerful. There's many a skinflint who would soon get rich because he'd use the advantage of foreknowledge to fleece his fellow men and bleed them white, but that wouldn't make him great. In fact he would stand lower in people's estimation than when he was poor. A man, however, who can make himself great and powerful will find that riches come to him automatically. After we had been in Vienna for a week or so Lady Luck, who hands out wealth and power, gave me ample opportunity to rise in the world, but I didn't take it. Why? I believe the simple reason was that my destiny had decided otherwise, namely that I should follow the road along which my stupidity took me. Count von der Wahl, under whose command I had made my reputation in Westphalia, also happened to be in Vienna when we arrived there. During a banquet, at which various members of the Imperial War Council were present along with Count Götz, the conversation came round to famous soldiers and their deeds, at which Count von der Wahl remembered the Huntsman of Soest and recounted a few of his exploits. He spoke so well of him that some expressed their surprise at how young he was, while others regretted that the crafty Hessian colonel, Saint Andrée, had hobbled him with an agreement either to lay down his arms or join the Swedish army, for von der Wahl had received news of the way the colonel had dealt with me in Lippstadt.

Herzbruder was standing nearby and, hoping to do something for me, asked permission to speak. He said he knew the Huntsman of Soest better than anyone else in the world. He was, he said, not only a good soldier who was not afraid of the smell of gunpowder, but also an accomplished horseman, a perfect swordsman, an excellent musketeer and artillery-man, and the equal of any engineer into the bargain. He had left not only his wife, by whom he had been shamefully betrayed, behind in Lippstadt, but everything he owned there, and now wanted to rejoin the imperial army. During the last campaign, Herzbruder continued, he had served under Count Götz and been captured by the Weimar forces. While trying to get back to the imperial side, he and his comrade had dispatched six musketeers and a corporal, who had been sent to bring them back, and taken a considerable amount of booty. The Huntsman had accompanied him – Herzbruder – to Vienna with the intention of offering his services once more to His Imperial Majesty, on condition he was given a position worthy of him, for he did not want to fight as a common soldier again.

By this time the distinguished gathering was so merry they insisted on satisfying their curiosity and seeing the Huntsman in person and Herzbruder was sent off in a carriage to fetch me. On the way he instructed me how to behave towards such eminent people, since my future career depended on it. Accordingly I gave pithy, laconic replies to all their questions, which impressed them since everything I said made sound sense. Everyone found my manner agreeable and they already had Count von der Wahl's word that I was a good soldier. I also managed to get drunk and I can well believe I showed how little experience of court society I had, but the end result was that an infantry colonel offered me a company in his regiment. I didn't say no, I can assure you! 'Being a captain'll be child's play', I thought to myself. The next day, however, Herzbruder told me I had acted precipitately. If I had held out a little longer, he said, I would have ended up much higher.

So I was made captain in charge of a company which, even though with me it had a full complement of officers, boasted no more than seven privates, and my non-commissioned officers were such decrepit old sweats I didn't know what to do with them. It was not surprising, then, that very soon afterwards we received a drubbing in a fierce engagement where Count Götz lost his life and Herzbruder had his testicles shot off. I was wounded in the thigh, but it was just a scratch. We returned to Vienna to have our wounds treated, which was where we had our money and belongings in any case. Despite the fact that the wounds soon healed, Herzbruder fell into a dangerous condition, which the doctors did not recognise immediately. He was paralysed in all four limbs, like a choleric person with an excess of yellow bile, even though he was not of that humour. Nevertheless, he was recommended to take the waters and Griesbach in the Black Forest was suggested.

Thus fortune can change in an instant. Shortly before, Herzbruder had expressed the intention of getting himself made a baron in order to marry a young lady of rank; at the same time he would have had me made a knight. Now, however, he had to think again. Since he had lost the wherewithal to propagate a new line and, moreover, his paralysis threatened to prove a lengthy illness during which he would stand in need of good friends, he made his will, in which he appointed me sole heir to his whole estate. He did this especially because he saw how I had thrown away my good fortune, resigning my captaincy so that I could accompany him when he went to

take the waters at Griesbach and look after him until he was
well again.

Chapter 5

*Simplicius becomes a messenger and, taken for Mercury, hears
from Jove what his intentions are regarding war and peace*

By the time Herzbruder could ride once more it was May
and pleasant weather for travelling. We sent all our spare cash
(for now we shared the same purse) by banker's draft to
Basle, equipped ourselves with horses and servants, and set off
up the Danube to Ulm and then to the spa. There we took
lodgings, after which I rode on to Strasbourg. We had had
our money sent on there from Basle and I was going to
collect some of it, but I also wanted to look for experienced
doctors to prescribe medicines and a regime for Herzbruder
while he was taking the waters. They came with me and
established that Herzbruder had been poisoned. The poison
had not been strong enough to kill him outright, but had
affected his limbs and would need to be purged with drugs,
antidotes and sweat-baths; the treatment should take eight
weeks or so, they said. As soon as he heard this, Herzbruder
knew straight away when he had been poisoned and by
whom, namely some officers who would have liked to have
his position in the army. When the doctors also told him that
the mineral waters were not necessary for his treatment, he
concluded that the army medical officers had been bribed by
his rivals to get him sent so far away. However, he decided to
stay in Griesbach to complete his treatment since not only
was the air healthy, but there was pleasant company among
the other visitors.

I was unwilling to waste all that time, since I felt a yearning
to see my wife again, and as Herzbruder no longer particularly

needed my help, I told him this. He approved and encouraged me to go to her. He also gave me some valuable jewels for her, to ask her forgiveness for being the reason why I had not returned to her sooner. So I rode off to Strasbourg, where I not only stocked up with money but also made enquiries as to what would be the best way to travel to make sure I got through safely. Going alone on horseback was impossible, I discovered. The route passed between many garrisons of the two warring sides and the foraging parties made it very unsafe. I therefore had a pass made out for a Strasbourg messenger and wrote some letters to my wife, her sister and parents, as if I were going to send him to Lippstadt with them. Then I pretended I had changed my mind, recovered the pass from him by a subterfuge, sent my servant back with the horse, dressed myself up in red and white livery and took a boat as far as Cologne, which at that time was a neutral city.

First of all I went to see my Jove, who had previously appointed me his Ganymede, to find out what the situation was regarding the goods I had left there. Unfortunately I found him in one of his deranged phrases and angry at the human race. 'O Mercury', he said when he saw me, 'what news do you bring from Münster? Do men think they can make peace without my agreement? Never! They had their peace, why did they not keep it? Was not every vice in fashion when they provoked me to send war to them? And what have they done since to deserve peace? Have they mended their ways? Have they not become worse, running off to war as if they were going to the fair? Have they turned over a new leaf because of the famine I sent in which so many starved to death? Has the terrible death toll of so many millions frightened them into improvement? No, no, Mercury, those who are left, and who have witnessed all the misery with their own eyes, have not only not repented, they have become worse than ever! If they do not reform when faced with such dreadful calamities, but continue in their godless ways amid all these trials and tribulations, what will they do when I send them the pleasurable golden days of peace again? I would be afraid they would try to storm heaven, as the Giants once did. But I will nip any such mischief in the bud and leave them stuck in their wars.'

Since I knew now how to get on the right side of this god, I said, 'Oh great Jupiter, the whole world is sighing for peace and promising repentance, how can you refuse them any longer?'

'Oh they sigh', replied Jupiter, 'but for their own sake, not mine. They do not want to sit under their vines and fig-trees and praise God, but simply to enjoy the luscious fruits in peace. Not long ago I asked a mangy tailor whether I should grant peace, but he replied that it made no difference to him, he had to ply his needle in peace as well as in war. I got a similar reply from a brass-founder who said that even if he didn't have the bells to cast he had in peacetime, in wartime he had plenty of work with cannon and mortars. Likewise a blacksmith said, "If I've no ploughs to make or cartwheels to shoe during wartime, I've still got enough horses and army waggons coming to the forge. What do I need of peace?" So you see, my dear Mercury, why should I grant them peace? It's true there are some who want it, but only, as I said, for the sake of their own bellies and their own enjoyment. On the other hand there are those who want the war to continue, not because it is my will, but because they profit by it. Although the carpenters and masons would like to see peace so they can earn money rebuilding the burnt-down houses, there are others who are not confident they could support themselves by honest labour in peacetime and want war to continue so they can continue to steal.'

Hearing my Jupiter go on about these matters, I realised he was too confused to give me any news of my affairs and didn't reveal my identity to him. Keeping my head down, I made my way to Lippstadt along the by-paths I knew so well. There, maintaining the disguise of a messenger from outside, I enquired after my father-in-law and learnt that both he and his wife had died six months ago and that my darling had also died immediately after giving birth to a young son, who was being looked after by her sister. On hearing this I delivered to my brother-in-law the letters I had written to my father-in-law, my wife and to him. He offered to put me up so that he could ask me about Simplicius's situation and what I was doing. The result was that I had a long conversation with my sister-in-law about myself in which I praised myself to the skies. The pock-marks had so spoilt my looks and changed me that no one recognised me apart from Herr von Schönstein who, being a good friend, kept his mouth shut.

After I had gone on for a long time about all the fine horses and servants Herr Simplicius had and how he went round in a black velvet coat covered in gold lace, she said, 'Yes, I always imagined he came from a much better family than he pretended. The commandant here forecast a great future for him and persuaded my late parents they had done well to saddle him with my poor sister, who was a devout young girl, though I myself never thought it would turn out well in the long run. Nevertheless he did the right thing and decided to enter the Swedish, or rather Hessian service in this garrison. With that in mind, he went to Cologne to bring back the goods and money he had there, but the business dragged on and by a trick he was dispatched to France, leaving behind my sister, who had been married to him less than a month, and another half dozen respectable young girls, all pregnant by him and all of whom gave birth one after the other – my sister was the last – to boys. Since by that time my father and mother were dead and since my husband and I cannot have children, we have made my sister's son heir to our whole estate, and with the help of the commandant we have collected the property his father had in Cologne. It amounts to about three thousand guilders so that when he comes of age he will scarcely be called poor. My husband and I love the little boy so much that we would not hand him over to his father, even if he came himself to fetch him. He's the prettiest of his step-brothers and the very mirror image of his father. I'm certain that if my brother-in-law knew what a handsome son he has here he would not be able to resist coming to see the little darling, even if he would prefer to avoid his other bastards.'

From the way she spoke I could easily tell how much my sister-in-law loved my child, who was running round in his first pair of breeches, a sight that melted my heart. I took out the jewels Herzbruder had given me as a present for my wife, telling her that Herr Simplicius had sent them as a token to his darling, but seeing that she was dead I thought it right and proper they should be passed on to his child. My brother-in-law and his wife were delighted to accept them and concluded that I was not only not short of money but also quite a different kind of person than they had hitherto imagined. Then I requested their permission to leave and when they agreed I asked to be allowed to give young Simplicius a kiss in his father's name, which I would then report back to Herr Simplicius. My sister-in-law approved of the idea, and when it was done both the child and I started to bleed from the nose, at which I thought my heart would break. But I kept my feelings hidden, and to give them no time to reflect on the significance of this sympathetic reaction I left right away. After two weeks of difficulty and danger I was back in at the spa, dressed as a beggar, for I had been robbed of everything on the way.

Chapter 6

Concerns a trick Simplicius played in the spa

As soon as I got back I saw that Herzbruder was worse rather than better, even though the good doctors and apothecaries had fleeced him worse than a fat lamb. There was something of a child about him and he could only walk with great difficulty. I encouraged him as best I could, but things looked bad. He himself must have realised from his loss of strength that he was not going to last long. His greatest comfort was that I should be with him when he breathed his last.

I, on the other hand, was determined to enjoy myself and took my pleasure where I could find it, as long as it did not interfere with my care for Herzbruder. Since I now knew I was a widower, my young blood and the fine weather drew me to the pleasures of love, which I pursued vigorously. The fright I had received at Einsiedeln was by now completely forgotten. At the spa there was a beautiful lady who claimed to have blue blood, though in my opinion she was more nubile than noble. Since this man-trap appeared to be rather sleek and shapely, I laid siege to her and very quickly obtained entry both to her salon and to any other pleasures I could desire. However, her easy virtue soon disgusted me and I looked for a way I could decently get rid of her since I suspected she was more interested in getting her hands into my purse than in marrying me. Moreover she insisted on giving me passionate glances and other tokens of her ardent affection wherever I might be, which made me blush for both of us.

At the spa there was also a rich Swiss gentleman who had not only all his money stolen but also his wife's jewellery, consisting of gold, silver, pearls and precious stones. Since it is as hard to lose such things as it is to acquire them, the said Swiss was willing to use any means to recover them. He sent for the celebrated necromancer who lived at the sign of the Goatskin and whose familiar spirit so plagued the thief that he returned the stolen goods to their rightful owner, for which the sorcerer was paid ten rix-dollars.

I would very much liked to have met this sorcerer and talked with him, but couldn't do so without damage to my reputation, or so I imagined, for at that time I thought no end of myself. So I told my servant to go and drink with him that evening, since I had heard he was very fond of his wine, to see if I might get to know him in that way, for I had heard strange stories about him which I could not believe unless I heard them from his own lips. I disguised myself as a peddler selling ointments and sat down at his table to see if he could guess, or a demon would tell him, who I was. But I did not get the least sign that he did, he just kept drinking all the time and took me for the person my clothes suggested; he did drink several toasts to me, but he showed more respect for my servant than for me. He told him in confidence that if the thief had thrown even the smallest part of what he had stolen from the Swiss gentleman into running water, thus giving the devil his share, it would have been impossible either to name the thief or to recover the goods.

I listened to this nonsense and was astonished that the arch-deceiver would get the poor man in his claws for such a trifle. I guessed that this was part of the pact he had made with the devil and I could well imagine that this kind of trick would not help the thief if a different necromancer, who did not have that clause in his pact, were brought in to clear up the theft. I therefore told my servant, who could pick a pocket better than any Slav fingersmith, to get him blind drunk, then steal his ten rix-dollars and throw a few coppers from it into the Rench, which the man did. Next morning the necromancer, when he discovered his money was missing, went to some bushes on the banks of the Rench, doubtless to confer with his familiar about it, but was so maltreated that he came back with his face all back and blue and covered in scratches. When I saw this I felt so sorry for the poor soul that I sent his money back to him with a message to say that now he saw what an evil, double-dealing type the devil was he would presumably quit his service and turn back to God. But little good did this friendly exhortation do me. From that time on nothing went right. Soon afterwards my two fine horses fell sick and died through witchcraft. But what else could I expect? I lived a life of hedonistic pleasure and never commended my goods to God's care. What was there to stop this sorcerer taking his revenge on me?

Chapter 7

Herzbruder dies and Simplicius goes back to his amorous ways

The longer I stayed at the spa the better I liked it. Not only did the number of visitors increase daily, but I found both the place itself and the way of life very pleasant. I associated with the liveliest of those staying there and started to learn the art of polite conversation and courteous address, which I had not much bothered with until then. As my servants called me Captain, it was assumed I belonged to the nobility, since a mere soldier of fortune would be unlikely to achieve such a rank at such an early age. So the rich fops became not only acquaintances but close friends and I was kept busy with all kinds of amusement, gambling, eating and drinking, which devoured many a bright ducat without me noticing, or even caring since my moneybags were still heavy with what I had inherited from Oliver.

Herzbruder's condition, however, gradually deteriorated until the doctors gave him up (though not before they had bled him white, both literally and financially) and he paid his debt to nature. He confirmed his last will and testament, making me heir to whatever he was due to receive from his late father's estate. In return I gave him a magnificent funeral and sent his servants on their way with some money and their mourning clothes.

His death grieved me very much, especially as he had been poisoned. I could do nothing to change it, but it changed me. I shunned company and sought out solitude to pursue my melancholy thoughts. I would find somewhere in the bushes to hide and reflect not only on the friend I had lost, but on the fact that I would never find another like him as long as I lived. At the same time I made all sorts of plans about how I would organise my life in future, but came to no firm conclusion.

Hardly had I decided I wanted to go back to the wars than I was telling myself the least peasant in that district was better off than a colonel, for no foraging parties came to that mountainous area. Nor could I imagine what business an army would have to go there to ruin the countryside. All the farmhouses were as well kept as in peacetime and all the stalls full of cattle, even though down in the plains there was not a cat or dog left in the villages.

I was listening to the most delightful birdsong and thinking that the nightingale with its charming strains must compel all other birds to stay silent and listen, either out of shame or in order to steal some of its beautiful notes, when a quite different kind of beauty approached the bank on the other side of the river. She was only wearing the dress of a peasant girl, but her loveliness moved me more than any lady in all her splendour. She took a basket off her head in which she was carrying some fresh butter wrapped in muslin to sell at the spa. She put the butter into the water to cool so that it would not melt in the great heat and while she was waiting she sat down on the grass, threw off her veil and hat and wiped the sweat from her brow, giving me plenty of time to observe her and feast my prying eyes on her. It seemed to me I had never seen a more beautiful person in my life. Her body was perfectly proportioned and without blemish, her hands and arms white as snow, her complexion fresh and charming, her black eyes full of fire and passionate looks. As she was putting the butter back in her basket I shouted over, 'Pretty maid! You've cooled your butter in the water with your fair hands but your bright eyes have set my heart on fire.' The moment she heard and saw me she ran off without a word, as if she had a pack of hounds at her heels, leaving me behind with all the foolish thoughts that plague an over-imaginative lover.

But my desire to bask in the warm rays of that sun again would not leave me in peace in my chosen solitude. All of a sudden the song of the nightingale meant no more to me than the howling of wolves. So off I trotted back to the spa, sending my boy on ahead to intercept the butter-seller and haggle with her until I arrived. He did his bit, and so did I, but I met with a stony, chilly reception such as I would never thought to have found in a peasant girl. The sole effect of this was to make me even more smitten, though having been through the same school myself, I knew very well that she would not let herself be so easily won over.

What I needed was either a sworn enemy or a good friend: an enemy to take my mind off these foolish thoughts of love or a friend to advise me and persuade me to forget this nonsense. Unfortunately all I had was my money, which dazzled me, my blind desires, which led me astray because I gave them free rein, and my recklessness, which ruined me and brought disaster. Fool that I was, I should have seen that the clothes we were both wearing were an omen that no good could come of the affair. Since I had just lost Herzbruder and the girl her parents, the first time we saw each other we were both dressed in mourning; what joy could come from the love between us? However, I was as blind and irrational as young Cupid and determined to make a fool of myself and, since it was the only way I could satisfy my animal lusts, I decided to marry her. 'You're only a farmer's son', I told myself, 'and you'll never own a castle as long as you live. This corner of the country is a fine place and compared with other areas has managed to remain flourishing and prosperous throughout these dreadful wars. Moreover, you've enough money to buy the best farm in the district. You're going to marry this honest country girl and acquire a peaceful estate among the country folk. Where could you find a livelier residence than close to the spa, where the departures and arrivals mean you see a new world every six weeks and can visualise how the earth changes from one age to the next.'

These were a few of the thousand thoughts that went through my mind until I finally asked the object of my desires to marry me and got her, not without difficulty, to say yes.

Chapter 8

*Simplicius enters on his second marriage, meets
his Da and finds out who his parents were*

I was in seventh heaven and made splendid preparations for
my wedding. I not only bought up the farm where my bride
had been born, but started a fine new building there, as if I
intended to keep court rather than house. Even before the
ceremony had taken place I had bought over thirty head of
cattle, because that was the number that could be fed on the
farm all year round. In short, everything was of the best, even
the expensive furnishings my folly persuaded me to get. However, I was soon laughing on the other side of my face. I
thought I was sailing for the Virgin Isles and found myself
entering the harbour of Mangalore, at which I realised, far
too late, the reason why my bride was so unwilling to take
me. What made it hardest of all to bear was that I could not
complain about it to anyone without making myself a
laughing-stock. I could see that there was a certain justice
about it, but that did not make me any more willing to put up
with it, nor to mend my ways. Since I had been deceived, I
decided to deceive the deceiver and went grazing wherever
I could find pasture, the result being that I spent more time in
good company at the spa than at home. I left my household
duties to take care of themselves and for her part my wife was
just as slovenly. I had an ox slaughtered for home use and she
salted it in several baskets; when she was to prepare a sucking-
pig for me she tried to pluck it like a fowl; she roasted crayfish
on a griddle and trout on the spit. From these few examples
you can easily tell how she looked after me in general. She was
fond of a bottle of wine, too, and enjoyed having company to
share it, all of which was a portent of disaster to come.

Once I was walking with some of the fashionable crowd
down the valley to attend a gathering at the lower baths when

we met an old peasant leading a goat, which he was taking to sell. I felt I had seen him somewhere before, so I asked him where he was coming from with his goat. He doffed his cap and said, 'I really can't tell ye, yer honour sir.'

'You haven't stolen it?' I said.

'Nay', replied the peasant, 'I'm bringing it from the wee town down the valley, but I can't tell yer honour its name in case the goat hears.'

This made the rest of my companions laugh, since the name of the town farther down the river meant 'Goat-town'. I went pale, which they all presumed was because I was annoyed or embarrassed at the neat way the peasant had sidestepped my question, but it was something quite different I had on my mind. The large wart coming out of the middle of his forehead, like a unicorn's horn, made me quite sure it was my Da from the Spessart. However, I decided to play the mind-reader a little before I made myself known to him and gave him the pleasure of seeing what a splendid son he had, as he could tell from my fine clothes. 'You come from the Spessart, don't you?' I said to him.

'Aye, sir', the peasant replied, at which I said, 'Weren't your house and farm plundered and burnt down by troopers about eighteen years ago?'

'Yes, God help me, so they were', answered the peasant, 'but it wasn't so long ago.'

'And didn't you have two children', I went on, 'a grown-up daughter and a young boy who looked after your sheep?'

'The girl was my child, yer honour sir', my Da replied, 'but not the boy, though I was bringing him up as my own son.'

That made it clear to me that I wasn't the son of this crude bumpkin. On the one hand I was pleased to hear it, on the other I was dismayed because it meant I was probably a bastard or foundling, so I asked my Da where he had found the boy and what reason he had to bring him up as his own. 'Alas', he said, ''twas a strange business with him. The war gave him to me and the war took him away again.'

At this point I began to be afraid he might say something about my birth which would reflect dishonourably on me, so

I turned the conversation back to the goat, asking him if he had sold it to the innkeeper's wife for cooking, which I would have found odd as the spa visitors were not in the habit of eating old goat's flesh. 'Oh no, yer honour', he replied, 'the innkeeper's wife has enough goats of her own and wouldn't pay for one. It's for that countess what's taking the waters. Doctor Knowall has prescribed some herbs for her, but the goat has to eat them first, then he takes the milk and makes a medicine out of it that the countess has to drink to get well again. People say the countess has nae innards and if this goat can help her it'll be more than yon doctor and his farm-assister can do atween 'em.'

While he was telling us all this, I thought of a way of speaking to the peasant again and offered to pay one thaler more for the goat than the doctor or countess had offered. The prospect of the smallest profit soon makes people change their minds, and he immediately agreed, but only on condition that he could tell the countess first that I had offered him one thaler more than she had. If she was willing to pay the extra, she would get her goat, if not, he would let me have it. Either way, he would come to see me that evening to tell how things stood.

So off went my Da on his way, and we on ours. However, the gathering had lost its attraction for me, so I slipped away from my companions and went back to find my Da. He still had the goat because the others refused to pay that much for it, which I found surprising in such rich people. It certainly didn't make me want to imitate them, so I took him to the farm I had recently bought and paid him for the goat. Then I got him half tipsy and asked him where the boy we had been talking about had come from. 'Well you see, sir', he said, 'Mansfeld's campaigns brought him to me and the Battle of Nördlingen took him way again.'

'That must be an interesting story', I said, and asked him to tell it to me to help pass the time, which he did:

'When Christian of Brunswick was defeated at Höchst while trying to join up with Count Mansfeld, his forces, not knowing where they should retreat to, were dispersed all over the countryside. Many came to the Spessart, since they were looking for wooded country where they could hide. But they often escaped death down on the plain only to find it up in our hills, and since both sides were quite happy to continue plundering and killing each other on our lands, we country folk joined in too. Much of the time it was too dangerous to stay at home with our hoes and ploughs, and it was rare for a farmer to go off into the woods without his musket. During these turbulent times I was once in a wild part of the forest not far from my farm when I heard some shots close by and immediately after came across a beautiful young noblewoman on a splendid horse. At first I took her for a man from the way she rode, but when I saw her raise her hands and eyes to heaven and heard her call on God in French and in a pitiful voice, I lowered my musket, which I was about to fire at her, and uncocked it, since both her cries and her gestures told me it was a woman in distress. I went up to her, and when she saw me she said, "If you are a true Christian, I beg you for the love of God and remembering the Day of Judgment, when we must all account for our deeds and misdeeds, to take me to some honest women who with God's assistance will help me bring the child I am carrying into the world." This earnest exhortation, together with the sweetness of the woman's tones and her beauty and grace, which shone through despite her distress, aroused my compassion and I led her horse by the bridle through thorn and thicket to the densest part of the woods, where I had found refuge for my wife, child, servants and cattle. And it was there, not thirty minutes later, that she gave birth to the boy we have been talking about.'

With that my Da concluded his story and went back to his wine, of which I had put out a liberal amount. When he had emptied his glass, I asked, 'And what happened to the woman afterwards?'

'Once she had been delivered of the child', he said, 'she begged me to be its godfather and to see it was baptised as quickly as possible. She told me her name and her husband's, so they could be recorded in the register, then opened up her satchel, in which she had many valuables, and gave me, my wife and child, the maid and another woman more than enough to reward us for our pains. But while she was doing this, and telling us about her husband, she suddenly died, first of all commending the child to our care.

Because of all the unrest, which meant people did not stay in their homes, we had great difficulty finding a pastor to bury the mother and baptise the child. Once that had been done, however, the burgomaster told me to look after the boy until he was grown up and keep the woman's property to cover our costs, apart from some rosaries, precious stones and jewelry, which I should keep for the child. My wife fed the lad on goat's milk and we were happy to have him and thought of marrying him to our daughter when he grew up. However, after the battle of Nördlingen I lost both, the girl and the boy, together with everything we owned.'

'You have told me a fascinating story', I said to my Da, 'but you've forgotten the best bit. You have not said what the woman, or her husband or the child were called.'

'I didn't realise you would want to know, sir', he replied. 'The lady was called Susanna Ramsi and her husband Captain Sternfels von Fuchshaim, and since my name is Melchior, I had the lad christened Melchior Sternfels von Fuchshaim. That is what was recorded in the register.'

And that was how I learnt, though much too late, both my parents now being dead, that I was the son of the hermit and Governor Ramsay's sister. All I could learn of my uncle Ramsay was that the people of Hanau had driven him out, together with his Swedish garrison, at which he was so furious that he went quite mad.

I drowned my godfather in wine and had his wife sent for the next day. When I revealed who I was they refused to believe me until I showed them a black hairy birthmark I had on my chest.

Chapter 9

*How he suffered the pains of childbirth and
how he became a widower once more*

Not long afterwards I rode down to the Spessart with my
godfather in order to obtain a certificate attesting my descent
and legitimacy which, with my godfather's testimony, I easily
obtained from the registrar of births. I also went to visit the
pastor who had been in Hanau and looked after me. He gave
me a written statement as to where my father had died and
that I had been with him until his death and then for a while
under the name of Simplicius with Colonel Ramsay, the
governor of Hanau. In fact I had a lawyer draw up a document based on the statements of eye-witnesses recounting my
whole story for, as I told myself, you never know when you
might need it. In all the journey cost me four hundred thalers
because on our way home we were caught and robbed by a
party of troopers. My Da or, rather, my godfather and I only
just escaped with our lives and arrived back on foot, stripped
of everything we had.

At home everything was going from bad to worse. As soon
as my wife heard that her husband was a nobleman, she not
only played the *grande dame* but completely neglected the
housekeeping, which I suffered in silence, since she was pregnant. I also had some bad luck with my cattle and most of
them died, including the best of them.

All this I could have put up with, but by Christ! it never
rains but it pours. At the same time as my wife had her baby,
her maid also gave birth and while the latter's child resembled
me, my wife's was the spitting image of the servant. Moreover
that very same night the lady I had jilted at the spa had a baby
left on my doorstep with a letter saying I was the father. Having thus become the father of three children at once, I felt that
any moment more were likely to creep out of every corner,

which caused me not a few grey hairs. But that is what happens if you lead such a godless, dissolute life as I did and give way to your animal lusts.

But it was no use complaining. I had to have them christened and pay the hefty fine imposed by the authorities. The fact that at that point the region was under Swedish rule and I had served in the emperor's army only served to increase the amount I was made to fork out, all of which turned out to be merely the prelude to my complete ruination. Although I was despondent at all these disasters, my good wife took them lightly, teasing me day and night about the fine son that had been laid at my door and about the huge fine I had to pay. If, however, she had known what had happened between her maid and me she would have tormented me even worse. Fortunately the whore was obliging enough to allow herself to be persuaded (by as much money as I would have had to pay in fines on her account) to put the blame on one of the dandies who had visited me now and then the previous year and had been at my wedding, but with whom she had actually had no other dealings. I still had to get her to leave, however. My wife suspected I knew about her relationship with the servant, but I could not do anything about it, being unwilling to point out that I could not be in her bed and the maid's at the same time. And all the while I was irked by the idea of not only having to bring up a servant's bastard while I could not make my own offspring my heirs but having to hold my tongue and just be glad no one else knew about it into the bargain.

I spent the days tormenting myself with these thoughts while my wife did not let an hour pass without enjoying a glass or more of wine. Since our marriage she had grown so attached to the bottle that it was seldom far from her lips and she was always pretty inebriated by the time she went to bed. Her drunkenness quickly sucked the life out of her child and so inflamed her own innards that soon after they dropped out and made me a widower for the second time, at which I almost died laughing.

Chapter 10

What some country folk said about
the enchanted Mummelsee

Thus I found myself free once more, but my purse rather
empty and my household overburdened with servants and
cattle. I took Melchior, my godfather, as my real father, his
wife as my mother and the bastard Simplicius, who had been
left on my doorstep, as my son and heir. I handed over the
house and farm to the two old people, together with all my
money, apart from a few gold pieces and jewels, which I kept
back for dire emergencies. My experiences with women had
left me with such a disgust for their company that I resolved
never to marry again. The old couple, whose knowledge of
farming was unsurpassed, immediately remodelled my household, getting rid of those servants and beasts that served no
useful purpose and taking on others that would bring a profit.
My old Da and Ma told me not to worry, promising that if I
left them to run things they would make sure there was always
a good horse in the stable and enough money over to allow me
to take a drink with any honest man. It very quickly became
clear to me what kind of people I had put in charge of my
estate. My godfather went out with the labourers to cultivate
the fields and haggled worse than any Jew over cattle, wood
and resin. My godmother concentrated on breeding cattle and
was better at making – and keeping – money from the dairy
than ten women like my late wife. In a short time my farm had
all the necessary equipment, animals and poultry and was soon
recognised as the best in the whole area. I, however, spent my
time going for walks and philosophising since, seeing as my
godmother made more out of the bees with wax and honey
than my wife had from cattle, pigs and all the rest combined, I
could rest assured that nothing would be overlooked.

One day my walks took me to the spa, though more to get

a drink of fresh water than to revert to my old habit of associating with the fashionable crowd there. My godparents' thrift was beginning to rub off on me, and they advised me it was not worth spending time with people who wasted their own and their parents' property. Nevertheless, I ended up joining a group (of respectable citizens, not the spendthrift dandies) because they were talking about something unusual, namely the Mummelsee, a supposedly bottomless lake on one of the highest mountains in the neighbourhood. They had sent for various old country folk to tell them what they had heard about this mysterious lake and I enjoyed listening to what they had to say, though I assumed it was all fabrication since it sounded as spurious as some of Pliny's tales.

One said that if you tied up an odd number of anything – peas, pebbles or whatever you like – in a handkerchief and dipped it in you would find an even number when you took it out, and vice versa. Another claimed, and most of them quoted examples to confirm it, that if you threw one or more stones in, a terrible storm would immediately get up with torrential rain, hail and high winds, no matter how clear the sky had previously been. From that they got onto all sorts of bizarre things that had happened there and all the fantastic spirits such as brownies and water sprites, that had been seen and had even talked to people. One told us that when some men were herding their animals by the lake a brown bull had emerged from it and joined the other cattle but a little mannikin had appeared and tried to drive it back under the water. The bull, however, had refused to comply until the mannikin wished all the ills of mankind on it if it did not return, at which they both disappeared into the lake.

Another said that once, when the lake was frozen over, a farmer crossed it safely with his ox and several tree-trunks that were to be cut up into planks, but that when his dog followed him the ice broke and the dog fell in, never to be seen again. Yet another told us what he claimed was the true story of a huntsman who, following the track of some game past the lake, had seen a water sprite sitting on the water, playing with a pile of gold coins in its lap. When he aimed his rifle at it the sprite ducked under the water and a voice could be heard saying, 'If you had asked me to relieve your poverty I would have made you and yours rich for life.'

I listened to these and other similar stories, all of which sounded like fairy tales you tell to amuse children, laughed at them and didn't even believe there could be an unfathomed lake so high up a mountain. But other country folk came, old men you could trust, who told us that in both their own and their fathers' time royalty had gone to see the lake. A Duke of Württemberg, for example, had a raft made and went out on it to measure the depth of the lake. However, after they had let down a lead weight on nine bobbin-lengths of twine (a measure the Black Forest peasant women will know more about than I or any other mathematician) and still not reached the bottom, for no apparent reason the raft, despite being made of sound wood, started to sink so that they had to give up and return to the shore. The raft could still be seen by the side of the lake, he said, and in memory of the event the coat of arms of the dukes of Württemberg and other things had been carved on a rock there. Others had witnesses to the fact that an Austrian archduke had even proposed to drain the lake, but that many people had advised against it and the plan had been abandoned after a petition by the locals, who were afraid all the surrounding countryside would be flooded. Some of the above-mentioned princes had also had several barrelloads of trout emptied into the lake, but in less than an hour they had all died before their eyes and floated away down the outlet stream. And this despite the fact that the river below the mountain (the valley it flows through takes its name from the lake) is fed by the outlet stream from the lake and is full of these same fish.

Chapter 11

*The unheard-of thanksgiving of a patient arouses
almost sacred thoughts in Simplicius*

The result of the testimony of these last speakers was that I
now almost completely believed the previous ones and was
determined to see this lake of marvels for myself. It was clear
from the various contradictory views expressed that opinion
among the others who had heard the stories was divided. I
said that the name *Mummelsee* obviously came from the
German word *mummeln*, to wrap up, to disguise, which suggested there was something hidden about it and that not
everyone could fathom either its nature or its depth, which
was still unknown, even though persons of such high rank had
attempted to discover it. With that I took myself off to the
spot where, not much more than a year ago, I had first set eyes
on my late wife and drunk the sweet poison of love.

There I lay down in the shade on the green grass. Now,
however, I ignored the twittering of the nightingales and
pondered on the changes that I had been through since then.
It had all started in this very place when I had been transformed from a free man into a slave of love; then I had been
changed from an officer into a farmer, from a rich farmer into
a poor nobleman, from a Simplicius into a Melchior, from a
widower into a married man, from a husband into a cuckold
and from a cuckold back into a widower. Also I had gone
from being a peasant's son to the son of a distinguished soldier
and back to being my Da's son again. I also reflected on how
my fate had robbed me of Herzbruder and replaced him with
an old married couple. I thought of my father's God-fearing
life and death, my mother's piteous demise, and all the vicissi-
tudes I had been through in my short life, and I could not hold
back my tears.

I was going over how much money I had possessed and

squandered, and starting to bemoan the fact when two devotees of Bacchus, who had been lamed by the gout and therefore needed to bathe and take the waters, sat down close to where I was, as it was a pleasant spot. Thinking they were alone, each told the other his troubles. One said, 'My doctor sent me here either because he despaired of my health or, along with other patients, to repay the innkeeper for the keg of butter he sent him recently. I wish either that I had never seen him or that he had prescribed the spa straight away; in the one case I would have more money, in the other I would be in better health than now, for the waters are doing me good.'

'Oh', the other replied, 'I thank God that He did not give me more money than I have. My doctor would certainly not have advised the spa if he had thought I had more. I would have had to share it with him and his apothecaries, who grease his palm every year, even if it was the death of me. Those money-grubbers never advise people like us to come to such a health-giving place as this unless they think we are beyond help or that there's nothing more to be squeezed out of us. To tell the truth, any man of means who gets involved with them is just paying them to keep him ill.'

These two had a lot more abuse to pour on doctors, but I think I had better not repeat it in case the medical profession take it amiss and at some future point give me a laxative that will purge the soul out of my body. I simply record it because I derived such comfort from the way the second man thanked God for not giving him more money that I immediately dismissed all the bleak thoughts I had about money from my mind. I made a resolution not to seek honour or money or anything else the world loves, but to give myself up to contemplation and lead a God-fearing life. In particular I determined to repent my lack of contrition and try to emulate my father in ascending the ladder of virtue.

Chapter 12

*How Simplicius journeyed with the
sylphs to the centre of the earth*

My fancy to see the Mummelsee grew stronger when my
godfather told me he had been there himself and knew the
way. But when he heard I wanted to go there as well he said,
'And what will you gain from it when you've got there? All
you'll see is a pond like other ponds, my son, in the middle of
a large forest. Once you've scratched this itch all you'll be left
with is regret, weary legs (you can hardly get there on horseback) and a long journey back. No one would have got me to
go there if I hadn't had to flee when Doctor Daniel (he meant
the Duc d'Enghien) and his troops were marching through
the country to Philippsburg.' However his attempt at dissua-
sion did nothing to dampen my curiosity and I hired a man to
guide me. Seeing I was serious, and given that, the oats having
been sown, there was no hoeing or reaping to be done on the
farm, he said he would come with me and show me the way.
He was so fond of me he was unwilling to let me out of his
sight, and because the local people thought I was his real son
he liked to show off with me, treating me just as a poor,
ordinary man would treat a son who had become a person of
substance without any help or support from his father.

So we walked together up hill and down dale, and reached
the Mummelsee in less than six hours, for my godfather was
still as strong a walker as a young man. When we got there,
hungry and thirsty from the long journey and the climb up
the mountain to the lake, we first of all ate the food and drink
we had brought with us. Once we had refreshed ourselves, I
looked round the lake and immediately found some rough-
hewn tree-trunks, which my Da and I assumed were the
remains of the Duke of Württemberg's raft. As it was rather
difficult to walk round the lake to measure it in paces and feet,

I worked out its dimensions by means of geometry and drew a scale map of it in my notebook. Once I had done that, and seeing the sky was clear, the air mild and still, I decided to see if there was any truth in the story that a storm would arise if someone threw a stone into the lake. The claim that trout could not survive there I confirmed from the mineral taste of the water.

In order to carry out my experiment I went along the lake to the left, to the spot where the water, otherwise as clear as crystal, seems to be pitch black on account of its awesome depth and looks so horrifying the sight alone makes your flesh creep. There I started throwing in the biggest stones I could pick up. My godfather not only refused to help me, but warned me and begged me to stop. I, however, went on busily with my experiment, rolling any stones that were too big or heavy for me to lift, until I had about thirty in the lake. Then dark clouds started to cover the sky and terrible thunder came from them. My godfather, who was by the outlet on the other side of the lake tearing his hair at what I was doing, shouted to me to get away before we were caught in the rain and the dreadful storm or something worse happened. 'I'm going to stay here until the end, father', I replied, 'even if it rains halberds.'

'Oh', replied my godfather, 'you're just like all those daredevil lads who don't care if they bring the whole world down about their ears.'

All the time I was listening to his scolding I did not take my eyes off the depths of the lake, expecting to see bubbles rise from the bottom, as happens when you throw stones into other deep water, stagnant or running. Nothing like that happened, but I saw some creatures, the shape of which reminded me of frogs, flitting around in the deepest part, shooting here and there the way stars from a rocket do in the air. They were approaching me, and the closer they came, the bigger they seemed to grow and more like human beings. My first response was amazement but then, when they were very near, I was seized with terror. 'Oh', I exclaimed in a combination of wonder and dread, 'how great are the wondrous works of the Creator, even in the bowels of the earth or the watery depths!'

I was talking to myself, but I said it so loud my Da could hear me on the other side of the lake. Hardly had I finished than one of the sylphs appeared on the surface and said, 'You say that even before you have seen anything of it. What would you say if you were in the centre of the earth and could see our dwelling-place, which has been disturbed by your idle curiosity?'

Meanwhile more of these water sprites had surfaced like diving ducks and were staring at me while they brought back the stones I had thrown in, which astounded me. The foremost among them, whose clothes glistened like silver and gold, threw me a shining stone, the size of a pigeon's egg and as green and transparent as an emerald, with these words, 'Take this jewel so that you will be able to tell people something of us and of the lake.' Hardly had I picked it up and put it in my pocket than I felt I was being suffocated or drowned so that I couldn't stand upright any more but rolled about like a ball of thread and eventually fell into the lake. As soon as I was in the water, however, I recovered, and the power of the stone allowed me to breathe water instead of air. I also found I could move round in the lake with little effort, just like the water sprites, and I went down into the depths with them. It reminded me of nothing so much as a flock of birds sweeping down to earth from the upper air.

My Da, seeing only part of this miracle, namely what happened above the surface of the water, including my sudden giddiness, scampered off home as if his hair was on fire. There he told everyone what had happened, especially how, in the middle of a thunderstorm, the water sprites had brought up the stones I had thrown into the lake, put them back where I had found them and then taken me back down with them. Some believed him, but most assumed it was a fabrication. Others imagined I had drowned myself in the lake (like Empedocles who threw himself into Mount Etna so that, not finding his body, people would assume he had been taken up to heaven) and told my father to spread these tales about me to immortalise my name. For some time, they said, it had been obvious from my melancholy mood I was getting pretty close to despair. Others would have liked to believe, if they hadn't known how strong I was, that my adoptive father had murdered me himself. They saw him as a miserly old man who would like to get rid of me to have the farm for himself. In the spa and the surrounding countryside all the conversation and speculation turned round the Mummelsee, me, my journey there and my godfather.

Chapter 13

The Prince of the Mummelsee tells Simplicius about the nature and origin of the Syplhs

At the end of the second book of his *Natural History*, Pliny writes of the mathematician Dionysiodorus that his friends found a letter in his grave saying that he had gone from his grave to the dead centre of the earth and had measured the distance at 42,000 stadia. The Prince of the Mummelsee, however, who accompanied me down from the surface, assured me that from the centre of the earth to the air was 4,150 miles, whether you went up to Germany or down to the Antipodes. These journeys, he told me, had to be done through lakes such as this one. There were as many as there were days in the year dotted around the world and they all came together at their king's residence. This huge distance took us less than an hour so that we travelled at little less than the speed of the moon, if at all, and yet it was no effort so that not only did I not feel tired but could converse with the Prince as we glided gently down.

Once I had realised his intentions were friendly, I asked him why they were taking me on this long journey, which was both dangerous and unusual for any human being. It wasn't far, he replied modestly, just an hour's stroll, nor was it dangerous as long as I had the stone and stayed with him and his fellow sylphs. That I found it unusual was not surprising, however. He had brought me, he said, not only on the order of his king, who had something he wanted to talk to me about, but also so that I could observe the strange wonders of nature beneath the earth and in the deeps at which I had already marvelled on the surface where what I had seen was a mere shadow of the true riches of nature. I next asked him why the Creator in His goodness had made all these remarkable lakes, since as far as I could see they were no use to mankind, indeed were more likely to harm them.

'You are quite right to ask about things you do not know or understand', he replied. 'There are three reasons for the creation of these lakes: firstly it is through them that all the seas, and especially the great ocean, are fixed to the earth, as if with nails; secondly we use these lakes – by means of something similar to your human science of hydraulics, with its pipes, tubes and cylinders – to send water from the depths of the oceans to all the springs on the earth's surface (that is our task), so that they do not dry up, but feed the small and large streams, moisten the soil, water the plants and provide drink for humans and animals; and thirdly they exist so that we, creatures God has endowed with reason, can live here, go about our business and praise the Creator in His wondrous works. That is why we and these lakes were created and will endure until the day of judgment. If, however, as those last days approach we should for any reason neglect our task then the world will be destroyed by fire. However, this probably cannot happen before that time unless you lose the moon ('as long as the moon endureth', Psalm 72,7), Venus or Mars, the morning and evening stars, for all generations of fruits and animals must first pass away and all waters vanish before the earth ignites from the heat of the sun, is burnt to ashes and regenerates. But these are things reserved to God and not for us to know, though we may conjecture and your chemists burble on in their scientific fashion.'

Hearing him speak like this and quote the Bible, I asked him whether they were mortal creatures with hope of a future life after this world, or whether they were spirits who carried out their appointed tasks as long as the world endured. 'We are not spirits', he answered, 'but mortals, endowed with rational souls which, however, die and vanish with our bodies. God is so wonderful in all His works that no created being can express them, but I will tell you about our kind in simple terms so that you can understand how we differ from God's other creatures. The holy angels are spirits, fit to be the image of God, wise, free, chaste, bright, fair, clear, swift and immortal, created to praise, laud, honour and glorify Him in eternal joy; in this temporal world, however, their task is to serve the church of God on earth and carry out His holy ordinances, for which reason they are sometimes called nuncios. As many hundred thousand times a thousand million angels were created as divine wisdom saw fit, but after an unimaginably large number fell, due to pride in their own nobility, your first parents were created by God, endowed with reason and an immortal soul, and given bodies from which they can multiply until their number reaches that of the fallen angels. It was then that the world was created, along with all the other creatures, so that earthly man could live there until the human race was numerous enough to replace the fallen angels, praising God and using all other created things, over which God made him lord, to the glory of God and to satisfy the needs of his body. At that point the difference between man and the holy angels was that he was burdened with an earthly body and did not know good and evil, and therefore could not be as strong or as swift as the angels. On the other hand, he had nothing in common with the brute beasts. However after the Fall in the Garden of Eden made his body subject to death we see him as an intermediate between the holy angels and brute beasts. Just as, when freed from its body, the soul of an earthly man whose mind is fixed on heaven has all the good qualities of a holy angel, so his body, when the soul has left it, putrefies like that of any brute beast. Ourselves we see as an intermediate stage between you and all other creatures. Although we are endowed with a rational soul, this dies along with our bodies, just as the living spirits of the brute beasts vanish when they die. We have heard that the eternal Son of God, through whom we too were created, has set the human race aloft by taking on human form, satisfying the demands of divine justice, calming God's anger and regaining salvation for you, which raises you far above us. But here am I talking about eternity, of which I know nothing because we are not capable of enjoying it. All I know about is this transient world where the Lord in His goodness has showered sufficient gifts on us, for example sound reason, enough understanding of God's holy will as we need, healthy bodies, long life, knowledge, skill and understanding of all things in nature. And most important of all is that we are not subject to sin, therefore not to punishment or His anger, nor even to the least disease. I have gone into all this in such detail, bringing in the angels, humans and brute beasts, so that you can better understand me.'

I replied that there were a few things I could not understand. If they committed no misdeeds and therefore needed no punishment, why did they have to have a king? Similarly, how could they claim to enjoy freedom if they were subject to a king? Also, how could they be born and die if they never suffered pain or illness?

My little prince replied that the king did not administer justice, nor did they serve him. His function, like that of the queen in a beehive, was to order their affairs. Their women, he went on, felt no pleasure in coitus and no pain in giving birth. It might help me understand this, he said, to think of cats, which conceived in pain and gave birth with pleasure. Nor did they die in pain or from illness or old age; their bodies simply vanished along with their souls, like a light going out when its time has come. As far as the freedom he had boasted about was concerned, the freedom of the greatest monarch among us humans was as nothing compared to it. They could not be killed by us or other creatures, nor could they be forced to do anything they didn't want to, much less imprisoned since they could pass through fire, water, air and earth without the least difficulty or tiredness, in fact that was something they never experienced.

'If that is the way you are', I replied, 'then your race has

396

been raised far higher and given greater gifts by the Creator than ours.'

'Oh no', replied the prince, 'it would be sinful to say that, for you would be accusing God in His goodness of something which is not the case. You have been given far greater gifts than we have. You have been created to achieve eternal bliss and look on the face of the Lord for ever and ever, and in that blissful state one of you will feel more joy and delight in one single moment than our whole race has from the beginning of creation to the day of judgment.'

'And what do the damned get out of it?' I asked and he replied with a counter-question, saying, 'What can God in His goodness do if one of you forgets his true nature, abandons himself to the creatures of this world and their shameful lusts, and gives free rein to his animal desires, thus putting himself on a level with the brute beasts and becoming, in his disobedience to God, closer to the fiendish rather than the blessed spirits? The eternal misery of the damned, which they have fallen into through their own fault, does not detract at all from the lofty nobility of your race since they, like everyone else, had the chance of achieving eternal bliss during their life on earth, if they had only chosen the path that leads to it.'

Chapter 14

Further conversation between Simplicius and the prince and the strange and fantastic things he heard

I had more opportunity than I needed to hear about this kind of subject up on the surface, so I asked my little prince to tell me the reason why there was sometimes a violent storm when a stone was thrown into the lake. I remembered having heard the same about Lake Pilatus in Switzerland and read

397

something similar about Lake Camarina in Sicily, which gave rise to the phrase *Camarinam movere*.

'Any heavy object that is thrown into water', he replied, 'will continue to fall towards the centre of the earth until it reaches the bottom. Since, however, all these lakes are bottomless, stones that are thrown into them naturally fall on the place where we live and would stay there if we didn't bring them back up again. This we do with a certain amount of violence, to deter those who insist on throwing them in; that is one of our most important tasks. If we removed the stones without the violent thunderstorms then we would spend all our time at the beck and call of those nuisances who amuse themselves by despatching stones to us every day from all parts of the world. From this one single activity you can see how necessary we are. If we didn't remove the stones, so many come from the various lakes round the world to the centre of the earth where we live that the structure which attaches the seas to the earth would be destroyed and the passages, which take the spring waters from the depths to the surface of the earth, would all be blocked up. The resulting damage and chaos could lead to the destruction of the whole world.'

I thanked him for this information and went on, 'I see now how you use these lakes to supply all the springs and rivers on the surface of the globe. Can you tell me then why the water is not the same everywhere, but differs as to smell, taste, effect and so on since, as I understand from what you say, they all have their origin in the abyss of the great ocean to which all waters eventually return? Some springs are pleasant mineral waters and good for the health whilst others, though also mineral waters, are unpleasant and harmful to drink; some are even deadly poisonous, like the spring in Arcadia with which Jolla is said to have poisoned Alexander the Great. Some springs are warm, some boiling hot and others ice-cold; some, like the one in the county of Spis in Slovakia, can eat through iron like aqua fortis; some, on the other hand, can heal all wounds (there is said to be one like that in Thessaly); some waters turn into stone, others to salt and yet others to vitriol. The lake near Zirknitz in Carinthia only has water in winter and is dry in summer; the spring at Aengstlen south of Berne only flows in the summer, and that only at certain hours when the cattle are being watered; the Schändlebach by Obernäheim in Alsace only runs when the country is about to be visited by some disaster; and the Fluvius Sabbaticus in Palestine dries up every seventh day. I have often puzzled over all this and could never find the reason.'

To this the prince replied that all these phenomena had natural causes, most of which had been guessed at or deduced by human scientists from the different tastes, smells, powers and effects of the water, categorised and published in our surface world. If water on its way from their home to its outflow, which we call a spring, runs through nothing but stone, then it will remain cool and sweet. If, however, it passes through metals (the interior of the earth, he pointed out, is not the same everywhere), for example gold, silver, copper, tin, lead, iron, mercury etc, or through semi-metals, that is sulphur, salt (in all its forms: natural salt, crystal salt, uric salt, root salt, saltpetre, sal ammoniac, rock salt etc), white, red yellow and green colours, green vitriol, gold, silver, lead or iron bismuth, lapis lazuli, alum, arsenic, antimony, yellow arsenic, amber, borax, sublimate of mercury etc, then it will absorb their taste, smell, nature, power and effect and thus be either health-ful or harmful to human beings. That was also the reason there were so many different salts, some good for us, others bad. In Cervia and Comacchio the water is fairly black, he informed me, reddish in Memphis, snow-white in Sicily; that from Centuripe is purplish in colour, that from Cappadocia yellowish.

'The hot springs', he continued, 'draw their heat from the fires burning within the earth which, like the waters, have vents and chimneys here and there, as for example the famous Mount Etna in Sicily, Hekla in Iceland, Gumung Api in the Moluccas and others. As far as the lake by Zirknitz is concerned, its waters appear at the Carinthian antipodes during the summer; likewise the Aengstlen spring can be seen at other places on the earth's surface at different times of the day and year, doing exactly what it does in Switzerland, and the same is true of the Schändlebach. All these springs are regulated by our people according to the will of God to increase His praise among you. Regarding the Fluvius Sabbaticus, however, we celebrate the seventh day by reposing in its source and channel, that being the most pleasant spot of our whole region. Consequently the river cannot flow at all while we are celebrating our day of rest in it in honour of the Creator.'

Next I asked the prince if it would be possible for him to take me back up to the surface by another lake. 'Of course', he replied. 'Why not, if it is God's will. That was how our forebears in the olden days took some Canaanites, who had escaped Joshua's sword and in desperation thrown themselves into one of these lakes, to America. Even today their descendants can show you the lake their ancestors came from.'

I could tell that he was amazed at my amazement, as if there were nothing amazing at all about what he had told me, so I asked him if they were ever amazed at the strange and unusual things we humans did. 'The only thing that amazes us about you humans', he answered, 'is that, being created for eternal life and the everlasting joys of heaven, you let yourselves be so seduced by the transient pleasures of the world, which can no more be had without pain and distress than roses without thorns, that you lose your right to heaven and the joy of beholding the most holy countenance of God and are cast into eternal darkness with the fallen angels. If only we were in your place! Every single one of us would make sure that he stood the test of your brief and transient time on earth better than you. The life you have is not your true life; life or death is given you after you leave the temporal world. What you call life is but a moment, a little while granted to you to see God and come near to Him so that He can take you unto Himself. We look on the world as God's touchstone for testing out humans, as a rich man tests silver and gold. Once He has found out their worth by the colour of the streak, or they have been assayed by fire, he adds the pure, fine gold and silver to his heavenly treasure, but throws the false and impure into the eternal fires. Your Saviour and our Creator made this clear enough with His parable of the tares and the wheat.'

Chapter 15

What the king said to Simplicius and Simplicius to the king

That was the end of our discussion, as we were approaching the residence of the king, before whom I was brought without time-wasting ceremony. I had good cause to be astonished at His Majesty, for I saw neither a well-appointed court, nor pomp and circumstance, no chancellor or privy councillors, no spokesmen or bodyguards, not even a jester, nor a cook, cellarer, page or any favourites or flatterers. Instead there hovered round him all the princes of all the lakes in the whole world, each dressed in the costume of the country where the lake he was in charge of was situated. I saw sylphs looking like Chinese and Africans, troglodytes and men from Novaya Zemlya, Tartars and Mexicans, Samoyeds and Moluccans. I even saw some resembling men from the arctic and antarctic, which was a strange sight to see. The two who supervised the Wildsee and the Schwarzsee, their lakes being close to the Mummelsee, were dressed like the one who had guided me; the prince of Lake Pilatus had a broad, dignified beard and a pair of baggy knee-breeches like any respectable Swiss, and the one that looked after Lake Camarina was so like a Sicilian in both clothes and features one would have sworn he had never left Sicily and couldn't speak a word of German. It was like looking through a book of national costumes, there were sylphs dressed like Persians, Japanese, Muscovites, Finns, Lapps and all other nations in the world.

I had no need of elaborate compliments, for the king immediately started to speak, in good German, by asking me why I had wantonly sent them such a pile of stones. My answer was brief: 'Because in our world anyone is allowed to knock at a closed door.'

'And what if you received your just desserts for your importunity?' he asked.

'The worst punishment I could be given', I replied, 'would be death. However, since throwing the stones I have have had the good fortune to see marvels unknown to millions of humans, so that dying would be a trifle, my death hardly count as punishment at all.'

'Oh what blindness!' exclaimed the king, raising his eyes to heaven in a look of amazement. 'You humans die only once and you Christians should only be confident of overcoming death if your faith and your love of God give you a certain hope your souls will see the face of the Most High the moment the mortal body breathes its last.

However', he went on, 'it is something else I have brought you here to talk about. It has been reported to me that the human race, especially you Christians, expect the Day of Judgment very soon because not only have all prophecies, including the words of the Sybils, been fulfilled, but everyone on earth is so given over to vice that the Almighty will not wait any longer to bring the world to its end. Since our race is to perish with the world and be consumed by fire, even though we are creatures of water, we were not a little horrified to think such a terrible time was approaching. This was why I had you brought here, to find out if we should live in hope or fear. We ourselves cannot see any indications announcing the approach of such a change, either in the constellations, or in the earth itself, so we need information from those with whom your Saviour left signs to recognise His second coming. We beg you, therefore, to tell us whether that faith, which the Son of Man will have difficulty finding when He comes, still exists on earth or not.'

I replied that he had asked me things which were beyond me. Future events, and especially the coming of the Lord, were known only to God. To this the king said, 'Well then, tell me how the different professions behave so that I can deduce from that whether the world is about to end, and our race along with it, or whether I will continue to rule my people in happiness for a long time. If you tell me the truth, I will let you see what few others have seen and send you back with a gift that will delight you for the rest of your days.' When I said nothing in reply, as I was gathering my thoughts, the king added, 'Come on, come on, start with the highest and finish with the lowest. You have to do this if you ever want to return to the surface.'

'If I have to begin with the highest, then the right thing is to make a start with the clergy. In general they are all, whatever their religion, as Eusebius of Caeseria described them in a sermon: disdaining rest, avoiding sensual delights, eager to labour in their profession, patient in scorn, impatient for respect, poor in goods and wealth, rich in conscience, humble as regards their merits, proud in their dealings with vice. Their ambition is to serve God alone and to lead men to the kingdom of God more through their example than through their words, just as the sole aim of the worldly authorities is justice, which they dispense evenly to rich and poor alike, without regard to person. Our theologians are all Jeromes and venerable Bedes, our cardinals Charles Borromeos, our bishops Augustines, our abbots new Hilarions and Pachomiuses, and all the other clerics like the congregation of hermits in the Theban wilderness!

Our merchants are not motivated by greed or lust for profit but solely by their desire to serve their fellow men by bringing them goods from distant lands. Our innkeepers do not run their inns in order to become rich, but to provide refreshment for hungry and thirsty travellers and hospitality for the tired and weary as a work of charity. The goal of the doctors, as of the apothecaries, is not their own advantage but their patients' health. Our craftsmen know nothing of tricks, lies and deceit, but do their best to provide honest, lasting workmanship for their customers. Our tailors would never dream of misappropriating part of their client's cloth and our weavers are so honest they haven't even a spare ball of yarn to throw at a mouse. Usury is unknown, the wealthy help the needy unasked, simply out of Christian charity, and if a poor man can only pay by leaving himself with no money to buy food, a rich man will cancel the debt of his own accord.

We never meet with arrogance, since everyone is aware of their own mortality; we never come across envy, since each man sees the other as the image of God, beloved of his Creator; no man gets angry with another because he knows that Christ suffered and died for all; we never hear of lasciviousness and unlawful fleshly lusts, it is all done out of love of and desire for children; there are no drunken sots, if one man buys another a drink then they never get more than respectably mellow. There is no unwillingness to attend church, since every man is keen to serve God as best he can (that is the reason there are such fierce wars on earth at the moment, each side believes the other does not worship God properly). There are no misers any more, only thrifty folk; no wastrels, only generous philanthropists; no mercenaries, who rob and kill people, but soldiers defending their country; no idle beggars, but men who despise riches and choose poverty of their own free will; no profiteers who buy up wine and corn to drive up the prices, but prudent citizens saving the surplus for the people for the lean years to come.'

Chapter 16

Some unknown facts from the depths of the bottomless Mare del Zur, also known as the Pacific Ocean

I paused for a while, wondering what else I could say, but the king told me he had already heard enough and if I wanted, his men would take me straight back up to the place they had brought me down from. However, he went on, as I was clearly of an enquiring mind, if I wanted to see some things in his kingdom rarely seen by a human he would arrange for me to be accompanied safely to any part of his realm I wanted; after that he would send me on my way home with a gift that would certainly be to my satisfaction. Since I could not make up my mind what to reply, he turned to some who were just setting off for depths of the Pacific to bring back food, both from the equivalent of a garden and what we would call a hunt, and said, 'Take him with you, but bring him back in time for him to return to the surface today.' To me he said that in the meantime I could be thinking of something it was in his power to give me to take back with me as a reward.

So I slipped off with the sylphs down a tunnel a few hundred miles long that took us to the bottom of the Pacific. There we found corals the size of oak-trees and they took pieces that had not yet hardened or become coloured for food; they eat them just as we eat new antlers. There were snails as tall as a fair-sized bastion and as broad as a barn door, pearls as big as your fist, which they ate instead of eggs, and too many other strange marvels of the deep for me to tell. The floor of the sea was strewn everywhere with emeralds, turquoise, rubies, diamonds, sapphires and other similar precious stones, most of them the size of the boulders we sometimes find in streams. Here and there we saw cliffs rising up for several miles and sticking out of the water with jolly little islands on top on them; all round they were decorated with quaint and bizarre sea-weed and inhabited by all kinds of strange erect, creeping, trotting creatures, just as the surface of the earth is with men and animals. The fish however, of which we saw huge numbers – large and small and of countless species – cruising through the water above us, reminded me of nothing so much as all the birds soaring through the air in the spring and autumn. And since there was a full moon and a clear sky (the sun was shining in our hemisphere so that it was night when I was in the Antipodes, daytime in Europe) I could see the moon and stars through the water, and the South Pole as well, at which I expressed my surprise. The sylph who had been told to look after me assured me however that if I had been there by day as well as by night I would have found it even more amazing, for you could see far-off mountains and valleys in the depths of the ocean as well as on land, and it looked more beautiful than the most beautiful landscape on the surface of the earth. When he noticed that I was surprised to find that he and all his companions, despite the fact that they were dressed as Peruvians, Brazilians, Mexicans or inhabitants of the Marianas, could still speak excellent German, he told me they only spoke one language, but that all peoples heard it as their own, and vice versa. The reason was that they had had nothing to do with the foolishness of the Tower of Babel.

Once the convoy had collected sufficient provisions, we returned to the centre of the earth via a different tunnel. En route I told some of them I had always thought of the centre of the earth as a kind of hollow cylinder, like the drive-wheel of a crane, with little pygmies running round inside to keep the earth moving, so that all parts would get their share of the sun which, according to Aristarchus and Copernicus stood motionless in the sky. They laughed out loud at my naïvety and told me to forget the idea, and the opinion of those two learned gentlemen, as the idle fancy it was. Instead I should be thinking, they said, of what I should ask their king to give me so that I didn't go back up to the surface empty-handed. I told them my mind was so full of all the wonders I had seen I could not think of anything and I asked them to advise me. One idea I had was to ask him, since he controlled all the springs in the world, for a mineral spring on my farm, like the one that had recently appeared in Germany, though that just had ordinary water. The regent of the Pacific Ocean and its caverns told me that was not in the king's power, and even if it were, such a spring would not last long. I asked him the reason and he replied, 'Here and there in the earth there are empty spaces which gradually fill up with all kinds of metals, which are generated by a damp, thick, viscous exhalation. Sometimes, while this process is taking place, water from the centre filters in through the cracks in the ores and remains with the metals for many hundreds of years, absorbing their healthful qualities. If, with the passage of time, the pressure from the centre increases and the water finds an outlet through the ground, then it is the water that has been all that time with the metals that is forced out first and has those marvellous effects on the human body that you see in new medicinal springs. Once the water that has spent so long among the metals has all flowed out, ordinary water follows. It goes through the same passages but runs so fast it cannot absorb the properties of the metals and so does not have the same healing power.'

If I was so concerned about my health, he went on, I should ask the king to recommend me to the king of the fire-spirits, with whom he was in close contact. He could treat a human body with a precious stone so that it would not burn in fire, like that special kind of linen we had on earth which we cleansed by putting it in fire when it was dirty. A person who had been treated in this way could be placed in the middle of a fire, like a stinking, goo-encrusted old pipe, and all the bad humours and harmful vapours would be burnt off so that the patient emerged from it as young, fresh, healthy and reinvigorated as if he had taken Paracelsus's elixir. I didn't know whether the fellow was joking or meant it seriously so I thanked him for his suggestion but said that being of a choleric nature I was afraid such a cure might be too hot for me. What I would like best, I went on, would be to take a rare, health-giving spring back up to the surface which would benefit my fellow humans, bring honour to the king and make my name go down in history. The prince replied that he would put in a good word for me, although as far as the king was concerned, honour and dishonour on earth were all the same to him. In the meantime we had arrived back at the middle of the earth again just as the king and his princes were about to dine. It was a cold collation with neither wine nor spirits, like the Greek nephalia. Instead, they drank the contents of pearls which had not yet hardened, like raw or soft-boiled eggs, and this fortified them immensely.

While I was there I observed how the sun shone on each lake in turn and sent its rays down to these awesome depths, making it as bright in this abyss as on the surface and even casting shadows. The lakes were like windows for the Sylphs through which they received both light and warmth. Even if they didn't always come directly, because the sides of some lakes were twisted, they were transmitted by reflection because nature had set whole slabs of crystal, diamonds and rubies where necessary in the angles of the cliffs.

Chapter 17

How Simplicius returned from the centre of the earth, indulged in strange fancies, built castles in the air, made plans and counted his chickens before they were hatched

Now the time had come for me to go back home, and the king commanded me to tell him what favour I thought he might do me. I said the greatest service he could render me would be to make a genuine medicinal spring appear on my farm. 'Is that all?' said the king. 'I would have thought you would have picked up some large emeralds from the bottom of the Atlantic and asked to be allowed to take them up to the surface with you. Now I see that greed is not a vice of you Christians.' With that he handed me a stone with strange, iridescent colours and said, 'Take this. Wherever you place it on the ground it will seek to return to the centre of the earth, passing through the most suitable minerals until it reaches us. Then we will send a magnificent mineral spring back to you which will do you the good and bring you the profit you deserve for revealing the truth to us.' Then the prince of the Mummelsee accompanied me back up by the way we had come.

The journey back seemed much longer than the way there, so that I estimated it at a good sixteen thousand miles, but the reason was probably that time seemed to drag because I did not talk to my escort this time, except for them to tell me they lived for three, four or five hundred years and were never ill at all. My mind was so full of my mineral spring that all my thoughts were occupied with working out where to site it and how to exploit it. I was already planning the fine buildings I would have to erect, so that the people who came to take the waters would have comfortable lodgings and I a handsome profit. I worked out what bribes to give the doctors to per-suade them to recommend my new miracle spa above all others, even Schwalbach, and send me crowds of rich patients. In my mind I was already levelling whole mountains, so that arriving and departing guests would not complain the journey was too wearying, hiring crafty servants, miserly cooks, cautious chambermaids, vigilant stable-boys, clean supervisors for the baths and spring. I selected a spot in the wild hills close to my farm which I would level and turn into a beautiful garden with all kinds of rare plants where my guests could walk, invalids take the air and healthy visitors amuse and refresh themselves with all kinds games and pastimes. I would get some doctors, for a fee of course, to write a brochure, which I would have printed with a fine engraving showing my farm in ground plan and elevation, so praising my spring and its excellent properties that it would fill any sick person with hope and bring him half way back to health just to read it. I would have my children brought from Lippstadt and get them to learn all kinds of skills that would be useful for my new spa. None of them, however, would train as a barber-surgeon; I only intended to bleed my patients financially, not medically.

Full of these speculations and imaginary projects, I came back to the surface, and the prince even set me on land with dry clothes. But I had to return the jewel he had given me at the start immediately, otherwise I would have drowned in the air or had to put my head under water in order to breathe. Once that had been done we bade each other farewell as people who would never meet again. He submerged and went back down into the depths with his companions, while I set off for home clutching the stone the king had given me, as happy as if I were bearing the Golden Fleece from Colchis.

But, oh dear, my happiness, which looked as if it promised to have a permanent basis, did not last long at all. Hardly had I left the miraculous lake than I got lost in the immense forest, for I had not paid attention to the route my Da had taken. I had gone quite some way before I became aware of this, as I was still preoccupied with my scheme to set up and develop the spring on my land as a profitable investment. The longer I walked, the farther away I went, without realising it, from the place I most wanted to be. Worst of all, by the time I realised what was happening, the sun was already setting and there was nothing I could do about it. There I was, stuck in the middle of nowhere without food or gun, both of which I really needed to see me through the night. But I comforted myself with the thought of the stone I had brought up from the bowels of the earth. 'Patience, patience', I said to myself, 'this will make up for any hardship you have to suffer. All in good time, Rome wasn't built in a day, otherwise if he wanted any fool could get a fine mineral spring such as you have in your pocket without even having to break sweat.'

Encouraging myself thus seemed to give me new resolve and new strength so that I stepped out much more boldly than before, even though I was overtaken by darkness. The full moon was shining brightly, but the tall pines did not let as much light through to me as the depths of the sea had done earlier that day. However, I still made progress and around midnight saw a fire in the distance. I headed straight towards it and when I was still some way off I saw that there were some woodmen who had been gathering resin sitting round it. Although these folk are not always to be trusted, necessity and my own courage prompted me to speak to them. I crept up quietly and said, 'Good night or good day, good morning or good evening gentlemen. Tell me what time it is so that I can greet you properly.' At this all six stood or sat still, trembling with fright, and didn't know what to say. I am pretty tall and this, with the black mourning clothes I was wearing because of my wife's death, and the huge cudgel I was leaning on like a wild man of the woods made me a frightening figure to them. 'What?' I said. 'Will no one answer?' Their astonished silence continued for a while until one recovered and said, 'Hoo be ye, zurr?' From his dialect I could tell he was a Swabian, who are generally, though wrongly, considered to be simple-minded. I told them I was a wandering scholar who had just come from the Venusberg where I had learnt a whole heap of weird and wonderful skills. 'Oho!" answered the oldest of them, 'now I really do believe peace is coming, thank God, if the wandering scholars be on their travels again.'

Chapter 18

*Simplicius wastes his mineral spring by
putting it in the wrong place*

We started talking and they were kind enough to invite me to join them at the fire and share their black bread and curd cheese, both of which I accepted. Eventually we got on so well that they asked me, as a wandering scholar, to tell their fortunes. Since I knew something of physiognomy and palmistry, I started telling them, one after the other, things I thought they would like to hear in order to keep on the right side of them, for I still did not feel entirely at my ease with these wild wood-folk. They wanted me to teach them all kinds of clever tricks, but I fobbed them off with promises that I would do so in the morning because I needed to sleep a while now. Having thus played the gypsy for them, I went and lay down a little way off, more in order to eavesdrop and see what they intended to do than to sleep, not that I wouldn't have dropped off straight away if I had had the chance. The more I snored, the more wide-awake they became and started arguing about who I might be. They didn't take me for a soldier because of the black clothes I was wearing, but they didn't think a respectable citizen would be wandering through the depths of the forest at this strange hour either. Finally they decided I must be an incompetent apprentice who had lost his way or, since I was so good at telling fortunes, the wandering scholar I had claimed to be. 'But', another one said, 'he didn't know everything, for all that. He could well be a soldier who's disguised himself to spy out our cattle and the tracks through the forest. If we were sure of that we'd send him to such a sleep he'd never wake up from.' Immediately another butted in who thought I was something quite different. All the while I lay there, listening with both ears. If these bumpkins set on me, I thought to myself, I'm going to take three or four with me before they finish me off.

411

While they were talking among themselves and I was worrying about what they might do, I suddenly felt as if someone were lying beside me who had peed the bed, for I was completely soaked. Oh dear! Now I could kiss all my plans goodbye, for I knew at once from the smell that it was my mineral spring. I was so furious that I almost started a fight with the six woodmen. I jumped up with my huge cudgel and shouted, 'You miserable sinners, this mineral spring welling up from where I was lying should tell you who I am. I would be quite justified in punishing you so severely, because of the evil thoughts you have in mind, that the devil himself would come to take away the remains.' At the same time I made such threatening gestures that they all cowered in fear. However I very quickly came to my senses and realised how stupid I was being. Better lose the spring, I thought, than your life, which you might easily do if you start mixing it with these louts. So I changed my tone, before they started getting other ideas, and said, 'Come and try this delicious spring that I have put here in this wilderness for you and all other resin-collecters to enjoy.' They didn't quite know what to make of all this and gawped at each other until they saw me calmly take a drink out of my hat. Then they each got up from their places round the fire and tried the water, but instead of thanking me they started to complain, saying they wished I'd put my spring somewhere else because if the lord of the manor should hear of it the whole district of Dornstetten would be forced to labour to make a road to it, which would be a great hardship for them.

'But then', I said, 'you'll all profit from it by finding a ready market for your chickens, eggs, butter, cattle etc.'

'No, no', they said, 'the lord of the manor will put in an innkeeper and he'll be the only one to make money out of it. We'll be the fools who maintain all the roads and paths for him and don't even get thanked for it.' It ended in a disagreement. Two wanted to keep the spring and four told me to get rid of it which, had it been in my power, I would certainly have done whether they wanted me to or not.

By now it was light again and I had no reason to stay,

indeed I was afraid that if I remained there much longer we would end up coming to blows. I told them that if they didn't want all the cows in the valley of Baiersbronn to give red milk for as long as my spring continued to flow they should show me the way to Seebach. They were happy to do so, and two of them accompanied me, one alone being too frightened.

So I left that place and although it was poor land with nothing more than pine trees growing I would have liked to put a curse on it to make it even more barren, since all my hopes were buried there. However, I walked on in silence with my two guides until we came to the top of the ridge, from which I could recognise the lie of the land, where I turned to them and said, 'You two can make something out of this new spring if you go and report it to the authorities. There'll surely be a reward in it for you, because the prince will want to develop it for the good and profit of the whole country and advertise it abroad to promote his own interests.'

'Oh yes', they replied, 'we're stupid enough to make a stick to beat our own backsides. We wish the devil would come and take you and your mineral spring too! You've heard why we don't want it.'

'You hopeless clods!' I said. 'Or perhaps I should call you treacherous rogues since you depart from the pious ways of your forefathers, who were so loyal that their prince used to boast he could lay his head in the lap of any of his subjects and sleep safely. But you wretches, you're so worried about a little bit of work, for which you'll eventually be paid and your children and grandchildren will reap the benefit, you refuse to make this healing spring known, even though it would bring great benefit to your prince and health and well-being to many who are ill! What's a few days forced labour compared to that?'

'If you go on like this', they said, 'we'll be forced to belabour you to death to keep your mineral spring secret.'

'There'd have to be more of you to do that!' I replied, brandished my cudgel and chased them away, after which I kept going downhill and to the south and west, reaching my farm towards evening after much toil and trouble. My Da had spoken the truth when he said all I would get from the journey was weary legs and a long journey back.

Chapter 19

A little about the Hungarian Anabaptists and their way of life

Once I was home again I lived a very retired life. My greatest pleasure was my books, of which I acquired a great number on all sorts of subjects, especially ones that made me think deeply. I had soon had enough of academic knowledge and just as quickly tired of arithmetic. Nor was it long before I came to hate music like the plague and smashed my lute to smithereens. Mathematics and geometry still had some appeal for me, but I soon dropped them for astronomy and astrology, which I studied with great enjoyment for a while before they too began to strike me as false and uncertain and not worth wasting more time on. I tried Ramon Lull's *Ars Magna* but found it was much ado about nothing, just so much empty air, so I abandoned it and turned to the *Cabala* of the Hebrews and the hieroglyphics of the Egyptians.

Eventually, however, I came to the conclusion that there was no better subject than theology if you make use of it to love and serve God. Following its guidelines I worked out a way of life which could bring men closer to the angels: if, namely, you brought together a group of men and women, both married and single, who, under the direction of a wise leader, were willing like the Anabaptists to produce everything they needed by the work of their own hands and spend the rest of their time praising God and seeking salvation. I had previously seen people living this kind of life on the Anabaptist farms in Hungary, and if these good people had not been committed to other false and heretical doctrines abhorrent to the Christian church I would willingly have

414

joined them, or at least praised their way of life as the most pleasing to God in the whole world.

They reminded me very much of the way Josephus describes the Jewish sect of the Essenes. They had great riches and a surplus of food, but they did not squander them; there was no swearing, muttering or impatience, not a single non-essential word was heard. I saw their craftsmen busy in the workshops as if their lives depended on it, their schoolmaster was teaching the young people as if they were his own children, and nowhere were the sexes mixed, men and women had their own places and their own tasks to perform. I found rooms kept for women in confinement who were cared for by other women without any help from their husbands, and there were other separate rooms that contained nothing but cradles with babies that were looked after by women whose job it was to clean and feed them so that all their mothers had to do was come at three set times a day to breast-feed them. The business of looking after the women in confinement and the babies was reserved to the widows; other women I saw doing nothing but spinning in a room with a over hundred spindles. Of the rest, each had her own responsibility: one washed clothes, another made the beds, a third kept the cattle, a fourth washed pots, a fifth waited at table, a sixth looked after the linen and so on. It was the same for the men, each had his own appointed occupation. If anyone should fall ill they had a male or female nurse to look after them, both of whom were were trained in general medicine and pharmacy. In fact, however, their diet was so healthy and their lives so well-ordered that I saw many more who were still hale and hearty at a ripe old age than you find elsewhere.

They had set times for eating and sleeping, but not a single minute for playing or going for walks, apart from the young people, who went out for an hour after lunch with their tutor for the sake of their health, but had to pray and sing hymns while they were doing so. Anger, envy, revenge, jealousy, enmity were unknown, there was no concern for worldly goods, no pride and no remorse! In short, it was a world of content and harmony, the sole purpose of which seemed to be to contribute honourably to the increase of the human race and the kingdom of God. The only time a husband saw his wife was at the set time when they were in their bedroom, which contained nothing but a bed and bedclothes, a chamber pot, a jug of water and a white towel so they could go to bed and to work in the morning with clean hands. They all called each other brother and sister and lived together in such virtuous companionship it never led to unchastity.

I would have dearly loved to be able to achieve such a blessed life as these Anabaptist heretics; to me it even seemed superior to a monastic existence. 'If you could manage to lead such an honest, Christian life under your church', I said to myself, 'you would be another St. Dominic or St. Francis, and if you could only convert the Anabaptists so they would teach your own people their way of life, what bliss that would be! Or, failing that, if you could persuade your fellow Christians to lead such honest, Christian lives as these Anabaptists, would that not be a great achievement?' Then I thought, 'You fool, what concern of yours are other people? You might as well become a Capuchin friar, since you can't stand women any more.' But I soon changed my mind again and told myself, 'You might feel differently tomorrow. Who knows what paths you might tread in future to follow Christ's teaching? Today your inclination is toward chastity, tomorrow you could well be burning with desire.'

I spent a long time musing over such thoughts. I would gladly have devoted my farm and my whole wealth to a united Christian community, but my Da told me straight out that I would never succeed in getting such a group together.

Chapter 20

Concerns an amusing little trip to Moscow

That autumn French, Swedish and Hessian troops approached, to recover their strength and at the same time blockade the nearby imperial city of Offenburg, reputedly founded by and named after an ancient English king. Everyone fled to the high woods, taking their cattle and most valuable possessions with them; I did the same as my neighbours and left the house fairly empty. A Swedish colonel on half pay was quartered in it and found some books still in the cupboard, as I had not had time to take them all with me. Among them were a few mathematical and geometrical treatises and some on fortifications which were mainly used by engineers. The colonel concluded from this that his lodgings did not belong to an ordinary farmer and so began to make enquiries about me and tried to contact me. Through a mixture of polite invitations and threats he got me to go to my farm to see him. He was very civil towards me, ordering his servants not to break or damage anything unnecessarily, and this persuaded me to tell him about myself, especially my family background. At this he expressed his surprise that I should prefer to live among peasants while there was a war going on and watch someone else tie his horse up in my stable when I could be stabling my own in another's and enjoying a more honourable position at the same time. I should buckle on my sword again, he said, and use the talents God had given me instead of letting them waste away by the fireside or behind the plough. He was certain that if I were to enter the Swedish service my talents and knowledge of warfare would soon take me to high rank.

My response to all this was cool. Promotion, I said, was a distant prospect if one had no friend at court to put in a word for one. To this he replied that my abilities would soon bring me both friends and promotion. In addition he had no doubt I would find relatives in the main Swedish main army who counted for something, for there were many Scottish noblemen there. He himself, he went on, had been promised a regiment by Torstenson and if the promise was kept, which he had no reason to doubt, he would make me his lieutenant-colonel. I allowed myself to be tempted by these fine words. Since peace looked very unlikely, I was faced with the prospect of further billeting and complete ruin, so I resolved to take up arms again and promised the colonel I would join him if he kept his promise about the position of lieutenant-colonel in his regiment.

And so the die was cast. I sent for my Da, or foster-father, who was with my cattle in Baiersbronn, and made over my farm to him and his wife, with the proviso that after his death my bastard, Simplicius, who had been left on my door-step, would inherit it, there being no legitimate heirs. By the time I had given instructions for the upbringing and education of my bastard son, gathered together what money and jewels I had and saddled my horse, the blockade had been unexpectedly lifted, so that before we knew it we were marching to rejoin the main army. I acted as steward to the colonel, keeping his whole household supplied by robbing and stealing – what the military call foraging.

Torstenson's promises, of which he had made so much on my farm, were nothing like so firm as he had pretended; indeed, I had the impression he was rather looked down on. 'Damn!', he said to me, 'some wretch must have been running me down to the general, I can see I won't be staying here for long.' Since he suspected I would not sit around waiting for ever, he forged letters suggesting he had been charged with recruiting a new regiment in Livonia, where he came from, and used them to persuade me to embark with him at Wismar and sail to Livonia. Things were just as bad there. He not only had no regiment to recruit, he was a penniless nobleman and everything he had came from his wife.

Although I had been deceived twice and taken so far from home, I went along with him for a third time. He showed me letters he had received from Moscow in which (he claimed) he had been offered a senior position in the army. At least that was how he translated them and went on and on about how excellent the pay would be. Since he was setting off with his wife and children, I assumed he wouldn't be going without good reason, and went with him, full of optimism. Anyway, I could see no means of getting back to Germany. However, as soon as we had crossed the Russian frontier and met various discharged German soldiers, especially officers, I started to get worried and said to the colonel, 'What the hell are we doing? We've left the place where there's a war going on to go to a country that's at peace, where soldiers have no value and are being discharged.' However, he continued to reassure me, saying I should leave everything to him, he knew his way around much better than these fellows who were not up to much at all.

After we arrived safely in Moscow I immediately realised it was hopeless. It was true the colonel conferred daily with dignitaries, but more with bishops than with boyars. I didn't like this hobnobbing with priests, but it didn't arouse my suspicions, though I did spend a long time thinking about it, without being able to work out what he was up to. Finally he informed me there were no prospects in war and that his conscience was urging him to embrace the Greek Orthodox religion. Since he could not help me as he had promised, his honest advice was to do the same. His Majesty the Czar had already had good reports of my character and abilities, and if I showed willing, he would graciously confer upon me, as a gentleman of rank, a fine estate with many serfs. It was an offer I could hardly afford to refuse, he went on, since any man would be better advised to have such a great monarch as a bounteous lord than as an ill-disposed prince.

I was dismayed at this and didn't know what to say. If we had been anywhere else, the colonel would have felt my answer rather than heard it. In the circumstances, however, given that I was virtually a prisoner in that place, I had to change my tune. I remained silent for a long time before deciding on my answer. I had come, I finally told him, imagining I would serve His Majesty the Czar as a soldier and he, the colonel, was the one who had persuaded me to do so. Since the czar had no need of my services, there was nothing I could do about it, nor could I blame him for having made such a long journey in vain as he had not summoned me here. That he condescended to show me such royal favour was an honour I could boast about but not, with all due respect, accept, since I could not at the moment bring myself to change my religion. I only wished I was back home on my farm in the Black Forest and not having to rely on others or cause them inconvenience.'

'You must do as you think best, sir', he replied. 'However, I would have thought that if God and fortune smiled on you, you would have had the grace to appreciate it. But if you don't want to be helped, nor to live like a prince, I hope you will at least recognise that I have spared no pains to do my best for you.' With that he made a low bow and walked out, leaving me sitting there, and not even giving me time to accompany him to the door.

While I was still sitting there perplexed and reviewing my situation, I heard two Russian carriages pull up outside our lodgings. I went to the window and saw my good colonel and his sons get into one, his wife and daughters into the other. The carriages bore the Czar's livery and contained several priests, who received the couple with expressions of obsequious good will.

Chapter 21

Simplicius's further adventures in Moscow

From that time on, although I didn't realise it, I was secretly kept under observation by members of the Czar's bodyguard. I didn't see the colonel or his family again, so that I had no idea what had become of them. During that time, as you can well imagine, not a few grey hairs appeared on my head, and not a few strange ideas inside it, either. I sought out the German craftsmen and merchants who resided in Moscow and told them of my plight and how I had been duped. At first they were sympathetic and made suggestions about how best to get back to Germany, but the moment they got wind of the fact that the czar was determined to keep me in Russia, by force if necessary, they all clammed up. They didn't want to know me, and I was even finding it difficult to get a roof over my head, for I had already sold my horse, saddle and bridle and spent the proceeds, and every day I was taking out another of the ducats I had so wisely sewn into my clothes. Finally I started selling my rings and jewels, hoping to keep myself going until I found an opportunity of getting back to Germany. In this way three months passed since the colonel and all his household had turned Greek Orthodox and been rewarded with an extensive noble estate and many serfs.

At that time a decree was published, that applied both to Russians and foreigners, announcing heavy penalties for idlers, since they took the bread out of the mouths of honest working people. Any foreigners who were unwilling to work had to leave the country within a month and the city within twenty-four hours. Fifty of us assembled, therefore, planning to make our way together through Poland to Germany. We had not been two hours out of the city, however, when we were overtaken and stopped by a troop of Russian cavalry under the pretence that the czar was mightily displeased we had had the audacity to gather in such large numbers and march through his country without a passport or even so much as a by-your-leave. For this, they added, His Majesty would be well within his rights to send us to Siberia.

As we made our way back I learnt what my situation was. The officer in command of the troop told me plainly that the czar would not let me leave the country. His advice was to submit to His Majesty's will, convert to their religion as the colonel had done and not turn my nose up at a fine estate, assuring me that if I declined I would be forced to stay there as a servant. One could not blame His Majesty, he said, for refusing to let such an experienced man as the colonel had said I was leave his country. At this I spoke slightingly of myself, pointing out that the colonel must have credited me with more skills, ability and knowledge than I actually possessed. It was true that I had come to their country to serve His Majesty the Czar and the admirable Russian nation by risking my life to fight their enemies, but I could not agree to change my religion. If, however, there was any way at all I could serve the czar without going against my conscience, there would be no lack of effort on my part.

I was separated from the others and given lodgings with a merchant where on the one hand I was openly kept under surveillance, on the other fed with delicious food and fine wines from the court kitchens. People came to visit me every day and invited me out to dine with them now and then. There was one in particular, a crafty old fox who had doubtless been told to work on me. He came round to chat with me every day, for by now I could speak Russian fairly well. He discussed all kinds of technical matters with me, siege engines and other types of machinery, fortifications, artillery etc. Finally, after he had several times sounded me out to see if I was willing to do as the czar wished and found no sign at all of my changing my mind, he asked whether, if I would not become Russian, I would not at least reveal some of my knowledge to them. His Majesty, he assured me, would esteem it an honour and reward my cooperation with royal favours. I replied that it had all along been my humble desire to serve His Majesty. That was the reason why I had come to his country in the first place, and I was still of a mind to do so, even though I was kept more or less a prisoner. 'Oh, not at all, sir', he said, 'you are not being kept prisoner. It is just that His Majesty loves you so much he cannot bear to lose you.'

'Why then', I asked, 'am I being kept under surveillance?'

'Because His Majesty is concerned lest you come to some harm', he replied.

Now that he was clear about my willingness to serve the czar he told me that His Majesty was considering extracting saltpetre in his own territories and manufacturing gunpowder. Since, however, there was no one there who was familiar with the process, I would be doing His Majesty a great service if I would undertake the task; they would see to it that I had sufficient funds and manpower. He added his own personal request that I should not reject His Majesty's proposition, since they had already been reliably informed that I was familiar with these matters.

'Sir', I replied, 'I can only repeat what I said before: if I can serve the czar in any way, apart from changing my religion, then I will do so to the best of my ability.' At this the Russian, who was one of their great magnates, got very merry and kept drinking my health, even more than a German would have.

The next day two boyars came with an interpreter to make the final arrangements and to give me a splendid Russian coat, a present from the czar. A few days after that I started searching for soil containing saltpetre and teaching the Russians who had been assigned to me how to separate it from the soil and purify it. At the same time I drew up designs for a powder mill and taught others to make charcoal, so that we were very soon producing both fine powder for muskets and coarse powder for cannons in great quantities. I had enough men under my command as well as my own special servants to look after or, rather, keep an eye on me.

After I had made such a good start, the Livonian colonel came to see me, in Russian costume and with a splendid retinue of servants, doubtless hoping to persuade me by this show of magnificence to become Russian Orthodox. However, I was well aware that the clothes came from the czar's wardrobe and had only been lent to him in order to bait the hook for me, this being very common practice at the Russian court.

To help the reader understand how things were done there, I will give an example from my own experience. Once, when I was busy at the powder mill I had had built beside the river outside Moscow, telling the men their tasks for that day and the next, the alarm was suddenly given because the Tartars were less than twenty miles away, 100,000 strong, still advancing and plundering as they went. My men and I had to go to the Kremlin immediately, where we were equipped and mounted from the czar's armoury and stables. Instead of a cuirass, I was fitted out with a padded silk jerkin which would stop any arrow, but would not keep out a bullet. To that was added boots, spurs and a princely helmet with a heron plume together with a sabre sharp enough to split hairs, mounted in pure gold and studded with precious stones; from the czar's stables I was put on a horse the like of which I have never before seen, never mind ridden. I, my saddle and bridle were all aglitter with gold, silver, precious stones and pearls, and at my side I had a steel mace that shone like a mirror and was so well made and balanced that anyone I hit with it was a dead man. The czar himself could not have been better accoutred than I was.

I was followed by a white flag with a double eagle and people poured out to join it from all quarters, so that in less than two hours we were forty thousand horse strong, sixty thousand after four hours, and with these we proceeded to advance against the Tartars. Every fifteen minutes I received new orders from the czar, all of which boiled down to the same thing: I had claimed to be a soldier and this was my chance to show His Majesty that I really was one. All the time our numbers were augmented by both individuals and small contingents and such was the confusion I could not tell who was supposed to command the whole horde or set them in battle order.

I will not say much about this encounter, which is not really central to my story. We suddenly came upon the Tartars, their horses tired and laden with booty, in a valley or deep dip in the ground, when they least expected it, and charged them from all sides with such fury that we scattered them straight away. As soon as we attacked I called out in Russian to those following me, 'Off we go, and let everyone do as I do!' They all shouted this to each other and I gave my horse free rein and charged the enemy, splitting the skull of the first I encountered, a young prince, so that my mace was spattered with his brains. The Russians followed my heroic example, so that the Tartars could not withstand the attack and turned in general flight. I fought like a man possessed, or like someone

424

who is desperately seeking death and cannot find it, striking down everyone, Tartar or Russian, who came into my path. At the same time those Russians whom the czar had assigned to keep me under surveillance followed me so closely that my back was always covered. The air was full of arrows, as if a hive of bees had swarmed, and one struck me in the arm because I had rolled up my sleeves to deal out slaughter with my mace and sabre unhampered. Before I was wounded by the arrow I was revelling in the bloodshed, but when I saw my own blood flowing my laughter quickly turned to an insane fury.

Once this fierce enemy had been forced to flee, some boyars commanded me, in the name of the czar, to report to the Emperor and tell him how the Tartars had been defeated. I therefore turned back and, with about a hundred riders following me, rode through the city to the czar's palace and was greeted by all the people with triumph and grateful rejoicing. However, as soon as I had reported the course of the battle (despite the fact that the czar had already been informed of all the details) I had to take off my princely costume, which was returned to the czar's wardrobe, even though it and the harness were so smeared and spattered with blood they were almost ruined. I had assumed it and the horse at least would be presented to me in recognition of my gallant conduct during the encounter. From that incident I could deduce where the colonel's magnificent Russian clothes came from: they were all borrowed goods which, like everything else in the whole of Russia, belonged to the czar alone.

Chapter 22

On the short and diverting road by which he came home to his Da

As long as my wound was healing, I was looked after right royally. Although my injury was neither life-threatening nor even dangerous, I went everywhere in a dressing gown of cloth of gold lined with sable and I have never in my whole life eaten so well. But that was all the reward I had for my labours, apart from the praise the czar lavished on me, which was spoilt for me by the envy of certain boyars.

When I was completely recovered, I was sent on a ship down the Volga to Astrakhan to set up a powder mill as it was impossible to keep the border fortresses there supplied with fresh powder because of the dangers of the long river journey. I was happy to do this because I had been promised that when it was done the czar would send me back to Holland with a sum of money commensurate with both my services and his imperial munificence. But alas, it is when we are most sure of our hopes and plans that a storm suddenly comes and in a twinkling blows all the foolish designs, on which we have been working for so long, to the four winds.

The governor of Astrakhan treated me as if I were the czar himself and I very quickly had everything running smoothly. The powder he had in store was rotten and mildewed and no good at all, so I reprocessed it, like a tinker using the tin from an old spoon to cast a new one. This had never been seen in Russia before and because of it, and other skills I had, some thought I was a sorcerer, others some new saint or prophet and yet others a second Empedocles or Gorgias of Leontini.

However, one night when I was hard at work in one of the powder mills outside the fortress, I was was captured along with some others by a band of Tartars and carried off so deep into their territory that I not only saw borametz, the legendary sheep-shaped melon, growing, I ate it. My captors exchanged me for some Chinese goods with the Niu-chi Tartars and they presented me as a special gift to the King of Korea, with whom they had just made a truce. There I was held in respect because there was no one could match me with the cutlass and because I taught the king how to hit the bull's-eye with his musket over his shoulder and his back to the target. Consequently he granted my humble request to give me my freedom and sent me via Japan to the Portuguese in Macao. They ignored me, and I wandered round their city like a sheep that has lost its herd until, as if by a miracle, I was captured by some Turkish pirates and sold by them, after they had carted me round with them for what must have been a whole year among various strange peoples that live in the East Indies, to some merchants of Alexandria in Egypt. They took me with their wares to Constantinople, and as the Turkish emperor happened to be fitting out several galleys to fight the Venetians and there was a shortage of rowers, many Turkish merchants had to hand over their Christian slaves, though they were paid for them. Being young and strong, I was one of them and had to learn to row, but that hard labour lasted no more than two months, for our galley was taken by the Venetians in the Levant and I and my companions were freed from Turkish bondage. When our galley reached Venice, with rich booty and some noble Turkish prisoners, I was released, since I wanted to make a pilgrimage to Rome and Loreto in order to see those places and thank God for my deliverance. I had no problems getting a passport and a number of decent people, notably some Germans, helped me with money, so that I set off on my journey in a long pilgrim's coat.

I took the shortest road to Rome, which city agreed with me very well because everybody, both great and small, was generous with alms. I spent about six weeks in that city before making my way to Loreto with other pilgrims, including some Germans and, in particular, some Swiss who were heading for home. From there I crossed the St. Gotthard, then headed back through Switzerland to the Black Forest and my Da, who had looked after my farm, bringing nothing special home with me apart from a beard which I had grown in foreign parts.

I had been away for three years and several months. During that time I had crossed various seas and seen all manner of peoples, who in general had done me more harm than good, to write about which would fill a large book. While I had been away peace had been concluded in Germany so that I could live safely and undisturbed with my Da. I left him to look after the house and farm and took up my books again, which were both my work and my delight.

Chapter 23

Is a nice short chapter and concerns Simplicius alone

I read once what the oracle at Delphi told the Roman envoys when they asked what they must do so that their subjects would accept their rule peacefully: *nosce teipsum,* meaning each man should know himself. This, given that I had plenty of leisure, made me think back and draw up a balance sheet of my life. I told myself, 'Your life has not been a life, but a death. Your days have been a dark shadow, your years a dark dream, your pleasures dark sins, your youth an illusion and your well-being an alchemist's treasure which will fly away up the chimney before you know it. You followed the wars through many dangers and met with great fortune and misfortune: now up, now down; now great, now small; now rich, now poor; now happy, now sad; now loved, now hated; now honoured, now despised. But, my poor soul, what have you got from the whole journey? This: I am poor in worldly goods, my heart is weighed down with cares, I am too lazy, slothful and corrupted to do good and, what is worst of all, my conscience is timid and heavy laden while you, my soul, are covered in sins and hideously defiled! My body is weary, my mind confused, my innocence gone, the best days of my youth spent, precious time wasted, nothing gives me pleasure and, to crown it all, I loathe myself.

When I went out into the world after my father's death I was simple and pure, upright and honest, truthful, humble, unassuming, moderate, chaste, bashful, pious and God-fearing, but I quickly became malicious, false, deceitful, arrogant, restless and, above all, completely ungodly, and all without needing anyone to teach me. I was careful of my honour not for its own sake, but in order to rise in the world. I observed the hour, not to employ it for my soul's salvation but for my body's satisfaction. I have often put my life in danger, but have never made an effort to amend it so that I could die in peace and sure of heaven. I always had an eye to the present and my immediate advantage, never thinking of the future, much less that a time will come when I will see God face to face and have to account for myself.' I was tormenting myself daily with thoughts like these when I came across the writings of Antonio de Guevara which I found so powerful in turning me away from the world that I must set down an extract from them here:

Chapter 24

Is the final chapter and shows how and in what manner Simplicius left the world again

'Farewell, world, there is no trust nor hope in you. In your abode the past has already disappeared, the present is slipping away from us and the future will never be; what is most stead-fast will fall, what is strongest will break, what is most lasting will come to an end, for you are more dead than the dead and in a hundred years do not let us live for one single hour.

Farewell, world, for you take us prisoner and do not set us free again, you bind us and do not unshackle us; you sadden and do not make glad, you take away and do not give back, you accuse us without due cause, you condemn us without hearing our plea, consequently you kill us without a verdict and bury us without our dying. None of your joys is without sorrow, no peace without discord, no love without suspicion, no rest without fear, no abundance without want, no honour without blemish, no property without a bad conscience, no rank without complaint, no friendship without malice.

Farewell, world, for in your palace promises are made without the willingness to give, service goes unpaid, caresses are used to kill, people are raised up to be cast down, help is a means of harming, honour a way of bringing disgrace, borrowing is without intention to return, punishment is without forgiveness.

God be with you, world, for in your abode the great and their minions are toppled, the unworthy preferred, traitors regarded with favour, the faithful overlooked, the evil left in freedom and the innocent condemned. The wise and experienced are dismissed, the inept well rewarded, the devious are believed, the upright and honest doubted, everyone does what they want, no one what they ought.

Farewell, world, for in you no one is called by his true name: the reckless are called bold, the timid cautious, the impatient enterprising, the lethargic peaceable; a wastrel is called liberal, a miser careful, a malicious gossip eloquent, a quiet person a fool or a dreamer; an adulterer and seducer of young girls is called a beau, a mud-slinger a courtier, a vengeful person eager, a meek one a dreamer. All in all, you present the useless as useful and the useful as useless.

Farewell, world, for you seduce everyone. You promise the ambitious honours, the restless change, the arrogant their prince's favour, the lazy a post, the miser much wealth, the greedy and lascivious joy and pleasure, enemies revenge, thieves secrecy, the young a long life and minions favour from their rulers.

Farewell, world, for in your palace there is room for neither truth nor loyalty. Anyone who talks to you is put to shame, anyone who trusts you is betrayed, anyone who follows you is led astray, those who fear you are treated worst of all, those who love you are ill rewarded, those who rely on you most are most disappointed. It is no use giving you presents, doing you favours, singing your praises, keeping faith with you, offering you friendship, still you deceive, ruin, disgrace, besmirch, threaten, consume and forget everyone. In consequence everyone weeps, sighs, moans, complains and declines, and everyone passes away. With you people see and learn nothing but hatred which turns into murder, speech which turns into lying, love which turns into despair, deeds which turn into theft, requests which turn into deception, sin which leads to death.

God be with you, world, for while we are with you, time is consumed in oblivion: our youth with running, rushing, leaping from pillar to post, along highways and byways, up hill and down dale, through wood and wilderness, over land and sea, in rain and snow, in heat and cold, in wind and weather; our manhood is consumed with mining and smelting ore, quarrying and cutting stone, sawing and chopping, digging and planting, with imagining and aspiring, with devising, ordering, worrying and bemoaning, with buying and selling, squabbling, wrangling, fighting, deceiving and being deceived; our old age is consumed in anguish and misery, our minds begin to go, our breath turns sour, our faces wrinkled, our bodies crooked, our eyes weak, our limbs tremble, our noses run, our heads go bald, our ears grow deaf, we can smell nothing, taste nothing, we sigh and groan, are weak and feeble and have, in short, nothing but toil and trouble until we die.

Farewell, world, there is no piety in you, every day murderers are executed, traitors quartered, thieves, robbers and bandits hung, killers beheaded, sorcerers burnt, perjurers punished and rebels exiled.

God be with you, world, for those who serve you have no other pastime, be it work or play, than idling, annoying and maligning others, courting young girls, running after beautiful women and flirting with them, gambling with dice and cards, dealing with pimps, feuding with the neighbours, recounting gossip, thinking up new lies, lending at exorbitant interest, devising new fashions, working out new ruses and introducing new vices.

Farewell, world, for no one is content or satisfied with you: if they are poor, they want to get money, if they are rich, they want to be looked up to, if they are despised they want to rise in the world, if they have been insulted, they want to avenge themselves, if they are in favour, they want to have power, if they are given to vice, they just want to enjoy themselves.

Farewell, world, for in you nothing lasts: tall towers are struck by lightning, mills swept away by flood, wood is eaten up by worms, corn by mice, fruit by caterpillars, clothes by moths, cattle suffer from old age, humans from illness: one has the mange, another cancer, the third lupus, the fourth the pox, the fifth gout, the sixth rheumatism, the seventh dropsy, the eighth gallstones, the ninth kidney stones, the tenth consumption, the eleventh fever, the twelfth leprosy, the thirteenth epilepsy and the fourteenth folly! And no one does what the other does: if one is crying, then the other is laughing, if one is sighing, the other is happy; one fasts while the other feasts, one gorges while the other starves, one rides while the other walks, one talks while the other is silent, one plays while the other works, and whenever one is born, another dies. Likewise no one lives in the same way as the other: one rules, the other serves, one governs people, the other herds swine, one follows the court, the other the plough, one journeys across the sea, the other travels round the country to the fairs and markets, one works at the soil the other at the fire, one catches fish in the water, the other birds in the air, one works hard, the other robs and steals.

God be with you, world, for in your abode men neither lead a saintly life nor die the same death: the one dies in the cradle, the other in childhood, the third by the noose, the fourth by the sword, the fifth on the wheel, the sixth at the stake, the seventh drowns in water, the eighth in wine, the ninth dies from gluttony, the tenth from poison, the eleventh dies suddenly, the twelfth in battle, the thirteenth through a magic spell and the fourteenth drowns his poor soul in the inkwell.

God be with you, world, I abhor your conversation: the life you give us is a miserable pilgrimage, an inconstant, uncertain, hard, rough, transient and impure voyage full of poverty and error, more rightly to be called a death than a life, in which we die every moment through all the ills of inconstancy and the many and various ways of death. Not content with the bitterness, with which you are surrounded and seasoned, you also deceive most with your flattery, encouragement and false promises; the wine from the golden chalice in your hand is bitter and false, making men blind, deaf, mad, drunk and senseless. Oh, how happy are they who avoid your company, despise your brief, fleeting, momentary pleasures, reject your society and do not perish with such a sly, false-hearted deceiver. For you turn us into a dark abyss, a wretched clod of earth, a child of anger, a stinking corpse, a filthy vessel on the dung-heap, a vessel of putrefaction full of stench and vileness; after you have toyed with us, dragging us hither and thither and tormenting us with flattery, caresses, threats, blows, trials and tribulations, anguish and torture, you consign our wasted bodies to the grave, leaving the soul to an uncertain fate. For although nothing is more certain than death, we do not know how, when and where we will die, nor (and this is the pity of it) where our soul will go and what will happen to it. But woe to the poor soul that has served you, o world, that has obeyed you and sought out your lustful and lascivious pleasures, for once such a sinful and unregenerate soul has, in a sudden moment of terror, departed from the body it is no longer surrounded, like the body in life, with servants and friends, but is led by a host of its most fearful enemies before the Judgment Seat of the Lord. Therefore farewell, o world, for I know there will come a time when you will abandon me, not only when my poor soul appears before the implacable judge, but also when the dreadful judgment *Go, o damned souls, to the eternal flames* is spoken.

Farewell, o world, o base, vile world, o stinking, miserable flesh! It is because of you, for following, serving and obeying you, that the unrepentant sinner is sentenced to eternal damnation where nothing awaits him for all eternity but suffering without respite instead of past delights, thirst without assuaging instead of carousing, hunger without repletion instead of gluttony, darkness without light instead of splendour and magnificence, pain without relief instead of pleasure, wailing, crying and moaning instead of power and triumph, heat without cooling, fire without quenching, cold without measure and misery without end.

God be with you, o world, for then, instead of your promised pleasures and delights, evil spirits will seize the condemned soul and drag it down to hell in the twinkling of an eye where all it will see and hear will be the terrible figures of the devils and the damned, nothing but darkness and smoke, fire without brightness, screaming, wailing, gnashing of teeth and blasphemy. All hope of grace and mitigation will be gone, rank and position will count for nothing, the higher a person has risen and the greater his sins, the lower he will be cast down, the harsher the torment he will suffer. From those to whom much has been given, much will be demanded; the more splendour a person has received from you, o base, vile world, the more suffering and torture he will be given here, for that is what divine justice requires.

God be with you, o world, for although the body remains with you for a while, lying in the earth and rotting, it will rise again on the Day of Judgment and after the final sentence will burn in hell for all eternity with the soul. Then the poor soul will say, "Curses on you, world! You made me forget God and myself and follow you in dissipation, evil, sin and shame all the days of my life. Cursed be the hour when God created me! Cursed be the day when I came into the base vile world! O mountains, hills, rocks, come and fall on me and hide me from the terrible wrath of the Lamb, hide me from the face of Him who sits in the Seat of Judgment. Alas, woe is me, for all eternity alas!"

Therefore, o world, o unclean world, I beg you, I beseech you, I implore you, I admonish you, I protest that you shall have no part of me; and I for my part want no part of you, will not place my hopes in you, for you know what I have resolved, namely *Posui finem curis, spes et fortuna valete* – I have put an end to cares, hope and fortune, farewell!'

I pondered deep and long on all these words and was so moved by them that I abandoned the world and became a hermit once more. I would have liked to live beside my mineral spring in the depths of the forest, but the local country folk would not allow it, even though it was the right kind of wilderness for me. They were still afraid I would reveal the existence of the spring and their ruler would force them to build roads and paths to it, now that peace was well established. Therefore I went to another wilderness and once more lived the life I had in the Spessart, though whether I will persevere in it, like my father, I cannot say. God grant us His grace so that we all come to that which we most desire, namely a blessed

END.